SHELTER ME

CATHERINE MANN

BERKLEY SENSATION, NEW YORK

THE BERKLEY PUBLISHING GROUP
Published by the Penguin Group
Penguin Group (USA) LLC
375 Hudson Street, New York, New York 10014

USA • Canada • UK • Ireland • Australia • New Zealand • India • South Africa • China

penguin.com

A Penguin Random House Company

SHELTER ME

A Berkley Sensation Book / published by arrangement with the author

Berkley Sensation Books are published by The Berkley Publishing Group.

BERKLEY SENSATION® is a registered trademark of Penguin Group (USA) LLC.
The "B" design is a trademark of Penguin Group (USA) LLC.

For information, address: The Berkley Publishing Group,
a division of Penguin Group (USA) LLC,
375 Hudson Street, New York, New York 10014.

ISBN: 978-0-425-26988-6

PUBLISHING HISTORY
Berkley Sensation mass-market edition / August 2014

PRINTED IN THE UNITED STATES OF AMERICA

10 9 8 7 6 5 4 3 2 1

Cover illustration by Anna Kmet.
Cover design by Diana Kolsky.
Interior text design by Kelly Lipovich.

To Rob—my hero, my friend, my love. Always.

Acknowledgments

People have asked me if I write about my own life. I am, after all, married to a military man who served over twenty years in the Air Force. However, this story is not autobiographical, although it was most certainly born in my heart—and in my fears as my imagination flew down a path that every military spouse has traveled at some point thinking: "What if the worst happened?" My husband eventually retired and thank heaven we never had to face that heart rending, ultimate sacrifice made by others who've lost a loved one in uniform. This book, born in my heart and fears, is in honor of every one of those fallen service members and their families.

I owe many people bucket loads of gratitude for helping me pour out this story onto the keyboard. There aren't words enough to thank Wendy McCurdy for her unconditional trust that I could pull this off even when I doubted myself. Bless her, she didn't even wince when I said I wanted to toss in a semi-feral dog's point of view. Thank you as well to Katherine Pelz and the entire Berkley team for all their hard work on behalf of my stories. I am also incredibly lucky to have the support of my stellar agent, Barbara Collins Rosenberg, a savvy voice of wisdom and direction.

And how do I thank the most brilliant critique partner and awesome friend on the planet? Joanne Rock is *the* best, hands down. Much appreciation goes to both of my amazing beta readers, too. My super-talented daughter Haley Frank, an Army wife, made sure I remembered those nuance-ey differences between Air Force lingo and Army lingo (any mistakes are purely my own—ooh-rah/hoo-uh!). And my dear friend and fellow animal rescuer Zo Carlson shared her fantastic eye for proofreading, while also understanding what my crazy-dog-lady side wanted to convey.

Speaking of kindred spirits in the animal rescue world, I am so very grateful to Executive Director Dee Thompson, her staff, and the volunteers at the Panhandle Animal Welfare Society (PAWS). Their endless capacity for compassion for abandoned and abused animals humbles me. Everyone at PAWS has taught me so much as we travel this rescue journey.

What great book-lover camaraderie I've found via the Internet. I owe Dr. Linda Hankins, DVM, a deep debt of gratitude for answering all my veterinarian questions, even patiently responding when I Facebook messaged her at midnight. (Again let me stress, any mistakes are totally my own.) And my treasured Facebook crew—Stephanie, Anne, Ann, Vickie, Linda (again), Debra, Judy, Sue, Paula, Kay, Elaine, Jan, Peggy, Pamela, Eileen, Sylvia, Dakota, Debby, Barb, Gail, Marcia—I am so lucky, lucky, lucky to have them cheering me on and helping spread the word about my books. Although I must say, as much as I enjoy visiting on the Internet, I look forward to our next gathering in person.

As always, all my love goes out to my family that continues to grow larger by the year—my husband, our four children, our two new in-law children who I love every bit as much as my blood-related kids. And of course more love than I ever even knew existed goes out to my precious, perfect granddaughter. Last, thank you to my four-legged, furry family who teaches me about unconditional love every day: Sadie, Sam, Faith, Toby, Cooper, and the one who started it all . . . Trooper.

Prologue

I WAS BORN IN the land of Babylon.

Thousands of years ago people spoke the same language there, before the Big Master scattered them. Maybe that's why I understand what humans mean even when they can't understand each other. Or possibly that's why they can't understand me, because they left.

But then perhaps they can't understand me because I'm a dog.

No. Really. I'm not putting myself down. I'm seriously a D-O-G. Yep, I can spell, too, but I can't tell people that, either, because . . . Come on, you know the reason. Say it with me. Because I'm a . . .

Dog.

And while I was born in Babylon—a.k.a. Iraq—my life changed forever the day I left that home with Sergeant Mike Kowalski. The morning I went away was tricky, because the Sergeant had to sneak me out of the forward operating base on one of those monster-big cargo planes they call a C-17. I was going for the ride to end all rides.

Back then they didn't have very many of those cool puppy rescue organizations to bring dogs back from a war zone. In my day, the Department of Defense law stood more often than not. No pets on military installations. And bringing them home? Huge negative on that.

So rules were bent, twisted and broken to rescue me, but it was a must-do operation to complete my mission. To understand my mission fully, you need to know how I ended up with Sergeant Kowalski.

Back when I ran in a pack with my cousins, we scavenged for scraps. Best place to look? U.S. military installations. The guys in uniforms, the ones from across the ocean, fed us. Good stuff, too. So we howled out the locale of new troops setting up camp so our pack buddies would know.

I hit the mother lode with those guys.

"No MREs for you, Trooper. You get steak," said a colonel with silver hair, dusty camos and creaky knees.

The first time I ate steak, I almost peed myself. Of course I peed myself for a lot of reasons in those days because I was still a puppy. Six months old then. Twelve months old when I left that place. Eleven years old now.

During my puppy days, the rest of my pack didn't want to stay at that particular camp because it was busy and big, and they were ancient and wary. But I was the youngest, the only one of my litter to survive, and gut-deep hungry from only scraps of leftovers. I was way below being the alpha dog. Not even really a beta dog. More like a zeta. Or would that be omega?

Anyhow, after we ate our fill for a week, it was a tough choice sticking around by myself, because yeah, I would lose my pack, but hunger won out. Six months later when the time came to leave on that plane? I didn't hesitate for a second. Sure I would miss this place where they tossed a tennis ball and seemed to think I was a rock star because I figured out fast they wanted me to bring it back. Like that was hard after tracking rats in the desert for dinner?

But I knew it was time to leave Babylon. Iraq. Home.

I had a mission. That was what the Sergeant told me. I was *needed*. Magic words to a dog. We live for a job, a purpose. It's what we were created for by the Big Master.

My mission: to heal a family, the family that had lost their person. I was supposed to be their link to him because he was the one who found me. The silver-haired Army colonel who fed me steak.

I'm ashamed to admit that the first time I saw him, I tried to bite him. I bared my teeth and all the fur rose up on my spine. That's dog talk for "back the hell away because I'm thinking about taking your face off."

Except he didn't back away. Colonel McDaniel dropped the slab of meat on the sand, and the smell hit my nose like a drug. Drool pooled in my mouth, and before I could think, I lunged. I ate the whole thing in three bites, along with rocks and sand scraping over my tongue into my starving belly. The silver-haired man nodded and left.

The next day, he did the same thing.

And the next.

Until my fur didn't rise anymore and I nipped the edge of the steak, tugging it from his hand.

One day, the Colonel touched the top of my head and said, "Good boy, Trooper. Good boy."

I didn't know what a human hand felt like until then. His fingers smelled like grease from the steak and salt from his sweat, tempting me to lick them. But I was afraid I might slip and bite him. So I held the steak between my teeth and stayed still while his hand brushed between my ears just once.

I was scared. Pee-myself scared. But that first quick touch? I wanted that again as much as I wanted another steak.

Maybe more.

So yes, I stayed even when my pack left. I let him scratch

my ears for a lot of days and a lot of meals. Even when he brought along a military doctor to jab me with a bunch of needles. And people wondered why I didn't like the doc. Really?

After a while, Colonel McDaniel sat in the dirt and talked while he fed me chopped-up chunks from his hand. He told me about his family, his childhood dog also named Trooper and other stuff. Secrets between him and me that made tears leak out of his eyes. I just listened because it was all I could offer in return for the food and the scratches.

Then one day he didn't come. The Sergeant did, though. Other buddies, too. They told me that before the Colonel had died, they'd promised him they would look out for me.

I didn't know what "died" meant then. So I waited for the silver-haired man to return. While I waited, I learned to play fetch, and since they kept on feeding me, I didn't go off searching for Colonel McDaniel. I would catch that ball all day long and bark when anybody came up to their camp.

That didn't always go well for me, but we'll save that tale for another time. Like the story about why the steak man didn't make it back home. Some things are hard to think about, even for a dog. We have to figure it out in smaller nibbles rather than gobbling it up. Because if we try to take everything in at once, the next thing you know, we might chew up somebody's pillow or pee on their boots. Which meant I was lucky to get a rubbery hot dog.

So to keep your pillow and boots safe since we've just met, I'll think about a happier time, that special day when I was twelve months old. The day I left home. It was all about the airplane. The family. My mission.

The day I flew to the United Steaks of America.

PART 1

Whoever invented crate training should have to spend eighteen hours in a wooden box strapped inside a cargo hold. Baby, I was born to run.   —TROOPER, OVER THE ATLANTIC

One

SIERRA MCDANIEL HAD ordered a drug test for a whacked-out Pomeranian, then milked a nanny goat to bottle-feed a litter of motherless pit bull pups. And it wasn't even noon yet.

The Tennessee summer sun baked her hair faster than the professional highlights she couldn't afford anyway. She checked the latches of each kennel run attached to her mom's converted barn/animal rescue, complete with doggie doors and an air conditioner. Someone had tampered with the locks and let all the dogs out last week, torquing off their cranky neighbors even more.

But then who wanted an animal rescue next door? Even if next door was an acre away on either side.

She double-checked the detoxing Pomeranian sprawled on a puppy bed, looking loopy. The fur ball had bitten a teenager, and the cops had soon deduced the dog discovered a hidden bag of pot, started chowing down on the weed and objected when the outraged teen tried to recover his stash. Animal Control had called her mom's rescue for the pup that Sierra now called Doobie even though his real name was Lucky.

God, what she wouldn't give to be a *regular* English Lit grad student at Vanderbilt, living in a crappy apartment with flea-market furniture. Rather than going to the local college and living in her childhood bedroom of pink ruffles and faded boy-band posters. What she wouldn't give to have her dad come home today with his unit.

But he wasn't, and no amount of wishing could change that.

She could, however, honor his memory by doing what he would want. So she spent every spare moment between summer classes and her grad assistantship duties pitching in at her mother's Second Chance Ranch Animal Rescue. Not that her mom would ask for help with the rescue or her own job teaching online classes year-round. Even though Sierra saw the pain and struggle in her mother's eyes, to the rest of the world Lacey was the ultimate independent military wife, giving all for her man. Holding down the home front. Raising Sierra and Nathan to be the perfect military brats.

Oh, hey, and caring for Grandpa McDaniel while Alzheimer's sucked him deeper into the quicksand of dementia.

As if that wasn't enough, Mom decided to save homeless and abused animals in all her free time, starting up a non-profit rescue organization that didn't pay a dime. The nanny goat—freshly milked—bleated in agreement from across the yard, bell clanking around her neck before she went back to chomping grass.

Seriously, weren't goats supposed to be gifts for third-world villages?

Huffing her sweaty bangs off her brow, Sierra yanked open the door to the mudroom on their rambling white farmhouse and quickly slammed it closed behind her, muffling the din of barking to a dull roar. Checkered curtains on the door fluttered. Through the window, Tennessee fields stretched out as far as she could see, dotted with other homesteads. Her family only owned a couple of acres total, fenced in, but even still, half the neighbors complained.

Some more vocally than others, threatening to file an injunction to shut the whole operation down at a county council meeting scheduled for next month. Another problem for another day.

She scuffed the poop off her gym shoes once, twice, then gave up and ditched her sneakers in the sink. They landed on top of the black galoshes Lacey used for kennel work, sending their old calico kitty soaring away. Sierra eyed her own purple monkey rain boots with a stab of regret that she hadn't tugged them on this morning.

She padded into the kitchen to wash her hands and grab another cup of coffee before they had to leave for Fort Campbell. Not that an IV dose of straight caffeine would help her face what waited for them at the Army post when that planeload of returning troops landed. When *Mike Kowalski* landed with a living, breathing reminder of the father that hadn't returned.

Her chest went tight and she mentally recited William Butler Yeats to soothe herself. *I will arise and go now, and go to Innisfree, And a small cabin build there, of clay and wattles made—*

Footsteps thundered down the stairs, followed by the reverberation of General Gramps's Army cadence marching across her ears seconds ahead of him entering the kitchen, overpowering her literary ramble.

"They say that in the Army the coffee's mighty fine . . ." Her silver-haired grandfather wore a smile and his old uniform, high-stepping his way to the gurgling java maker.

He didn't so much as shoot a look her way, but she knew the drill. Yeats was done for now. Gramps had his own "poems." At least it was a clean one today.

She repeated his chant like a good soldier. "They say that in the Army the coffee's mighty fine."

They'd played this game for decades. Her life had been military issue from the cradle.

"Looks like muddy water and tastes like turpentine." He snagged a chipped mug from a mismatched set of crockery as he continued chanting his current Jody of choice.

"Looks like muddy water and tastes like turpentine."

"They say that in the Army the chow is mighty fine."

"They say that in the Army the chow is mighty fine," she echoed, childhood memories curling through her like the scent of Kona blend wafting from the pot as he poured.

He lifted his mug in toast. "A chicken jumped off the table and started marking time."

"A chicken jumped off the table and started marking time."

"Hoo-ah!" her grandpa grunted.

"Hoo-ah." Happy times with Gramps were few and far between lately. Even if this moment ached as it reminded her of her dad, she could hang tough and enjoy a ritual of semi normalcy in the crazy house. "We need to leave in about fifteen minutes. I have to shower fast and change."

Preferably into something that didn't smell of dog poop and goat's milk. She washed her hands, double-pumping the antibacterial soap.

Gramps opened a Tupperware container and scowled, the light mood fading fast. "Croissants? What is this? A fancy-ass French bakery or a real kitchen? I need a soldier's breakfast."

So much for normalcy. He'd eaten breakfast three hours ago. Eggs, bacon *and* pancakes, with their family Labrador snoozing on his feet. Except reminding Gramps of that wouldn't accomplish anything. Her grandfather, Joshua McDaniel, a two-star general and veteran of three wars, remembered less and less every day.

"How about a muffin on the run, Gramps?" She patted the pan of apple nut muffins still warm from the oven. "We have to get to Fort Campbell."

He glanced down at his open uniform jacket her mom had aired out for him. Probably at about four in the morning since her supermom insisted she never needed anything so mundane as sleep. But Sierra could see her mother fraying around the edges, the little weakness slipping through, such as lost files and forgotten errands.

And God, that thought sounded petty to nitpick, but this was a crummy day, going to pick up a dog her father had found overseas—as if there weren't already enough animals here at her mother's rescue. As if there weren't already enough reminders of her dead dad. She blinked back tears. Was it so wrong to want some part of her life that wasn't military issued and full of good-byes?

Sierra pushed aside dreams of Innisfree and patted her grandfather's shoulder, right over the two shiny stars. "General, you *are* looking mighty fine today."

"A good soldier never forgets how to polish his shoes or shine his brass." He grimaced at the rare second's understanding at how much of himself he'd lost.

"Mighty fine shiny shoes and brass they are, General."

"I taught your dad, too." He looked up at her quickly with eyes as blue as her own. "Maybe he can show you when he gets back today. It's not too late for you to get a commission, you know. They let women in the Army now."

"Sure, Gramps." She didn't even wince anymore at references to her dad coming home. Alzheimer's had its perks for some. Like not knowing your son got blown up by a roadside bomb.

Gramps straightened the uniform tie, shirt buttons perfect even though he couldn't zip his own jeans anymore. General Joshua McDaniel had drawers full of track suits and T-shirts he wore with his American Legion ball cap. All easy to tug on. Yet, his fingers worked the buttons of his uniform jacket now with a muscle memory of long-ago tasks, a mystery of Alzheimer's that she'd learned not to question.

At least her mom would be happy about the uniform, and Lacey could use some happiness in her life. If getting this dog made her smile, then so be it. Sierra would suck it up and pretend seeing the mutt didn't make her want to stand in a Tennessee cornfield and scream Emily Dickinson dirge poems at the top of her lungs.

Knowing who brought the dog made it tougher. If things had been different . . . well . . . Hell. She still wouldn't have been here waiting for Mike Kowalski.

But she would have thought about him returning home today, would have lifted up a prayer of relief that he'd made it back safely, then moved on with her life. Instead, she could only think about her father. His funeral. The twenty-one gun salute still echoed in her ears louder than the pack of barking dogs outside.

Sierra willed away tears with a couple of lines from a bawdy Shakespearean sonnet and grabbed a muffin for herself. The family just needed her to hang on here a little while longer until she could move out in a guilt-free way only her multitasking mother could have devised.

Lacey had used some of the insurance money to renovate the barn loft into a studio apartment. Noisy. But with total solitude for Sierra. She could live there while she finished graduate school next year. She would have some independence, and Mom would still have an emergency backup for when General Gramps wandered off to get eggs, milk and Diet Cokes for his wife who'd been dead for ten years.

Or called out for a son who'd been blown up in Iraq.

Ever the soldier, General Joshua McDaniel marched one foot, then two, then started up again with his coffee on the way out of the kitchen. "They say that in the Army the training's mighty fine . . . Last night there were ten of us, now there's only nine . . ."

Her stomach knotted with the realization.

Gramps knew on some level that his son was gone.

She had about three seconds to grieve over that before

she also realized—damn—Grandpa was tugging the car keys off the hook by the door. What had her mom been thinking leaving them there? They couldn't do that anymore.

"Uhm, General, the motor pool is sending over a car," she improvised.

He looked back, blue eyes confused, keys dangling.

She plucked the chain from his hand and passed him the muffin while hiding the keys in her jeans pocket. "Don't forget to eat."

"I'm not hungry," he grumbled, "and I don't forget jack shit."

"Of course not."

"Where are my keys?"

"Haven't seen them." Easier to lie sometimes. Safer, too. Gramps may have muscle memory for uniforms, but not so much when it came to driving a car.

"Allen must have taken the Chevy to go out on a date with that girl Lacey. Now Millie"—he stared straight into Sierra's eyes and called her by his dead wife's name—"make sure that freeloading son of ours doesn't leave the car with an empty tank."

"Sure . . ." She patted him on his stars, something tangible left of the indomitable man she remembered.

Pivoting away, she raced up the back stairs, leaving her grandfather in the kitchen where he was stuck somewhere in the twentieth century. She wouldn't have minded escaping back a decade or two herself. Or maybe more.

But Innisfree was clearly out of reach today.

STAFF SERGEANT MIKE Kowalski never had anyone waiting for him when he returned from overseas deployments. And yeah, both times, he'd wondered what it would feel like to be the focus of one of those star-spangled reunions with family all around.

But not this way.

He just wanted to hand over the dog to the McDaniel family. Keep his cool around Sierra. Then dive into bed for a decent night's sleep on clean sheets.

Well, after he dived into a six-pack of cold beers.

He hitched his hand around Trooper's leash. Thank God, the short-haired tan and brown mutt looked enough like a Belgian Malinois that most folks assumed Trooper was a military working dog. Shit would hit the fan eventually over how he'd circumvented official channels, but he would deal with that later. He'd spent his life getting out of trouble. Even joining the Army had been a part of a plea bargain with a high school mentor.

Bluffing and bravado came easy to him. After all, he'd learned from the best growing up with a con artist grandmother who'd scammed Social Security checks in the name of three dead relatives.

A hand clapped him on the back just as his battle buddy Calvin "Pinstripe" Franklin hefted his rucksack over his shoulder. "Sergeant Major's gonna chew your ass over bringing this dog back."

"Won't be the first or last time that happens." Mike adjusted his hold on the leash and his duffel, his guitar case slung over his back. He'd come by the nickname "Tazz" honestly. Wherever he went, a whirlwind of trouble followed.

"For what it's worth, Tazz, I think what you're doing for the Colonel's memory is cool." Their boots clanged against the cargo hold's metal floor one step at a time as they filed toward the open load ramp. A marching band played patriotic tunes with a brassy gusto. A John Philip Sousa marching song segued into "The Star-Spangled Banner."

"A lecture and a write-up aren't all that intimidating after what we've seen." Most folks had flashbacks of sounds, gunfire, explosions. For him? It was the smells that sent him reeling. The acrid stench of explosives. Jet fuel. Singed hair.

Blood.

Focus on the scent of clean sheets, damn it. "Quit sweating, Pinstripe. You'll draw attention to us."

"You must not have been chewed out by the Sergeant Major lately, or you wouldn't be so chill," Calvin said, trudging ahead along the metal grating. *Clang. Clang.* "Just keep your head low. It'll go a lot easier for you if you don't make a big deal out of things now. Low-key. Walk down the ramp. Hand over the dog to his new family. Come party with us. There's a keg with your name written on it. A babe, too, if you play it right, a military groupie ready to give a soldier a warm, lap dance welcome home."

He winced. Hand over the dog then party as if this was no big deal? Except it was more than that. Facing the family of his fallen commander. Facing the Colonel's daughter. Sierra.

Low-key.

Keep it low-key.

His hand slid down to scratch Trooper's head, bristly fur clean and flea-free thanks to the under-the-table care from the veterinarian at their forward operating base—FOB. Mike flipped Trooper's ear back in place, then patted. He wasn't sure who it calmed more, him or the dog.

Mutt at his side, he stepped from the belly of the plane and into the blinding afternoon sunlight. U.S. of A. soil. Fort Campbell. The Army post sprawled along the border of Tennessee and Kentucky. The scent of fresh-mown hay rode the breeze, blanketing the smell of jet fuel just enough that Mike could shove thoughts of war to the back of his brain.

He'd made it home alive. Adrenaline evaporated from him like water steaming off the hot tarmac. His arms dropped to his side. His duffel slid from his fingers as he breathed in the scent of wheat and barley so thick it was damn near an intoxicating brewery of aromatherapy.

Soldiers jostled by, bumping his shoulders, but his boots stayed rooted, his body weighted by an exhaustion a year in the making. Then the world tilted. His arms jerked.

Trooper yanked free.

Crap.

His guitar strap slipped. Mike regained his footing, but too late. Trooper shot forward toward the roped off area of bystanders. Toward families. The band. Official post personnel.

Media.

Trooper's full-grown size, powered by puppy energy and a lack of sense, turned the mutt into a speeding, barking missile. Mike jockeyed from foot to foot, gauging which way to go. Was the dog headed for the big grill puffing burger-scented smoke into the wind? Trooper's nose definitely lifted to catch a whiff of something as he plowed forward.

The overgrown pup knocked over a tuba stand. Uniformed band members skittered to the side just as the massive brass instrument toppled and "The Star-Spangled Banner" warbled to a premature end.

Calvin jogged alongside him mumbling, "Sergeant Major's gonna be pissed."

Screw it. Low-key was clearly out of the question now. Mike hitched up his bag, which conveniently knocked his guitar in place again, and charged forward. He shouldered sideways past the orderly line of soldiers.

"Trooper, come," Mike ordered.

And the dog ignored the command.

Of course.

Trooper could sniff out an intruder in the dead of night. The mutt could dodge land mines to fetch a ball. But at heart, he was still a puppy accustomed to free roam of his world.

Mike picked up speed, boots pounding as he raced toward the loping mutt. He didn't think Trooper would hurt anyone. The dog hadn't shown feral tendencies since those first few weeks at the camp. But one false move from this dog—already on shaky ground with his entry to the U.S.—and it would be all over. His promise to the Colonel would be broken in the worst way possible.

Where the hell was Trooper going? Mike scanned the crowd of faces. Women with babies on their hips and in strollers. Men, too. Families as well as some hoochied-up girlfriends. A sea of waving flags and signs.

Welcome Home.

Love My Soldier.

People and signs parted like the Red Sea as fifty-five pounds of dog dodged and wove. Mike could only follow until the masses veed open to reveal . . .

The very family he'd been sent to meet. The McDaniel clan. Except his eyes homed in on the one that had drawn him from the first time he'd seen her at a platoon baseball game cheering in the stands.

Sierra. The daughter of his mentor. Off-limits. Untouchable. And total Kryptonite to a man who'd spent twelve long months dreaming of her citrusy scent to escape the pungent stench of war.

Mike had all of three seconds to soak up the sight of her blond hair shining so brightly in the sun he could almost smell lemons. Three seconds before . . .

Trooper leapt into the air and knocked Sierra flat on her back.

TWO

FLAT ON HER back, Sierra McDaniel squinted into the sun, grateful for her rhinestone-studded sunglasses hiding her tears from the crowd. Although she could probably write off any crying to her scraped elbows and bruised butt, thanks to the dog that had trampled over her to get to Gramps.

General McDaniel squatted down on one knee, scratching the dog behind the ears while the pup licked his chin. "Calm, Trooper. Calm." He spoke with an authority no one could ignore. "Good boy. We'll find a treat for you soon. Nathan, get a hot dog from that stand, pronto."

Nathan snatched a twenty-dollar bill from his mother's outstretched hand and pivoted away, baggy clothes rippling as he dragged his feet toward the concession stand.

As Sierra angled up to sit, she wondered if her grandfather knew which Trooper he was talking to, the new one or the one from her dad's childhood. Probably the right one, since he'd called Nathan by name. Regardless, this Trooper seemed to accept him, settling, rather than mowing down the homecoming crowd again.

Homecoming. So damn bittersweet today.

She knew the routine after life as an Army brat. The sun baked the tarmac. Homemade signs flapped in the breeze. Kids waved flags. Wives sported fresh manicures and new outfits. Husbands gathered, too, waiting for their military spouses. Excitement crackled in the air like all those people were dancing on Bubble Wrap.

For her, a bigger bubble had burst. All the joy around her felt more like electric snaps stinging her skin. Facing so many people welcoming home loved ones only reminded her of a very different homecoming. Her dad had returned in a flag-draped coffin four months ago.

This part of her life should be over. Yet it had come back to haunt her again. Her dad's unit was convinced her family needed this dog.

The *dog*?

The McDaniel family needed the *man*—the husband, dad, father, son. However, since that wasn't possible, they really needed to move forward with their lives. But because her mother was canine crazy, here they were, enduring this ceremony that was one great big patriotic poke in the eye. Sierra wanted to melt right into the tarmac.

A manly, calloused hand slid into sight, a familiar hand making her realize she was still sitting sprawled out on the ground like an idiot. Her eyes traveled up along the hard muscled arm, broad shoulders and a smile that could charm the panties off a woman.

A smile that had, in fact, charmed her undies off more than once.

"Hello, Mike. Welcome home." She clasped his palm and let him tug her to her feet. But that was all he could have. Her panties and her heart would stay firmly glued in place when she was around him from now on.

Still, her hand tingled from the contact.

Sierra regained her balance and dusted off her denim capris, wishing she could brush away the feel of him as easily.

She'd given up being able to will away the physical attraction to this man. Everything about his looks drew her, from his buzzed short hair to his square jaw peppered with a five o'clock shadow that pushed to midnight. His golden brown tiger eyes held her with a bad-boy gleam he lived up to.

And therein was the reason the attraction could only be physical. She had no intention of falling for Sergeant Tall, Dark and Rowdy.

A shoulder bumped hers as a couple flung their arms around each other, reunion in full emotional swing. Reminding her what it felt like to have Mike's mouth against her ear, singing husky soft love songs as his lips roamed over her, luring her . . .

Hold it together.

She prepared what to say to him next, some polite cluster of words. She would be poised and in control of her words. Except even poetry escaped her, leaving her with little more than "Humpty Dumpty."

Then Mike turned away before she could talk and spoke to her mother. "Mrs. McDaniel, he wanted . . ." His voice cracked even as his hulking shoulders stayed braced, guitar slung over his back. "The Colonel wanted you to have his dog. He talked of you often, and I . . . I wish I could say something other than I am so sorry he's gone. Everyone liked and respected him. He is missed, very much."

Lacey smiled with that forgiving and understanding way of hers that Sierra hadn't come close to mastering. Her mom's tangled light brown curls were tossed in the wind as messy as this whole crazy reunion, but Lacey kept her cool. How could someone be so emotional and so poised at the same time?

"Mike, thank you. You don't need to say anything more. Your being here is enough. Allen would be happy that Trooper is home with us." Lacey hugged Mike once, hard, holding for a second before taking in a shaky breath. "Let's meet this special fella."

Kneeling, she offered her hand for the dog to sniff before stroking his head. Her eyes glazed with unshed tears, but her ease with the strange dog was unmistakable. Her mom had a Dr. Dolittle gift.

"Nathan," Lacey called up to her son, waving him closer as he returned with a plain hot dog in hand. "Come say hello to Trooper."

"Sure. Whatever." Her brother dragged his feet, new deck shoes scuffing and showing bony, sockless ankles. His pants and shirt hung on his body like they'd been draped haphazardly over a coat hanger too small to hold them.

Nathan was a walking, sulking poster kid for "got bullied, went psycho."

Cameras clicked all around them. Nathan scowled. Mike winced at each flash. But the media kept right on recording. Her mom's smile was front page worthy with just the right amount of shimmering tears and a nostalgic smile.

The press would write their feel-good piece about a rescued Iraqi dog and a fallen veteran. Everybody would pat themselves on the back for empathizing. The story would probably go viral in some social network.

But no one would stick around to get Nathan from school early when he landed in the middle of another fight or search the neighborhood when Gramps wandered off.

"Sierra?" Her mother glanced up, wind tearing at her light brown spiral curls. "Are you okay?"

"Of course. Let's give him his treat before he takes off someone's hand." She plucked the hot dog from her brother and really looked at the mutt for the first time. She'd seen photos but somehow she'd expected something . . . bigger. Scarier maybe? Or a magnificent beast.

Instead, a medium-sized tan and brown dog with short hair and a black nose soaked up more ear scratches from her grandfather. With his long, lanky puppy legs, the mutt looked like some kind of smaller version of a Lab/shepherd mix. Mostly, he just looked like . . . a regular dog.

The stab of disappointment surprised her. She didn't see her father's phantom presence or feel his touch on her shoulder in some other-earthly way. Until this moment she hadn't realized how much she'd hoped to find a mystical connection to her dad.

Kneeling, she pinched off pieces of the hot dog and passed them to the dog one at a time while he stared back at her with those dark brown eyes that seemed to look right through her. Her throat squeezed tight. She just wanted to finish this and go home. Even milking the goat would be preferable to being at an Army post with her tall father's silvery blond head and big smile nowhere in sight.

The cameras went on hyper speed and the questions rolled out, all tangled together as she fed Trooper the last bite.

"Your grandfather was a General . . ."

"How is your family holding up?"

"What's the dog's name?"

"General McDaniel, how do you feel about your son's brave service to his country?"

The reporter jammed a microphone in her grandfather's face so fast his eyes went wild with that freaked-out PTSD look. Sierra searched for an escape route, or at the very least a distraction. This would be an opportune time for the dog to go berserk again.

Please, Lord, don't let Grandpa go Clint Eastwood on them. He did that a lot these days, compensating for confusion with a make-my-day rage. The explosive anger cost them a flat-screen TV last week.

Standing, she shot Mike a pleading look. "We should take care of the paperwork or something."

Mike's smile went tight. "Right. General? If you'll lead the way, sir, I can in-process."

"Roger that, Sergeant." Gramps started humming, his feet picking up marching pace a second before he started bellowing. "I was born in the back woods, raised by a bear . . . Gotta double bone jaw and four coats of hair . . . Got cast iron balls and a big steel rod . . . I'm a mighty paratrooper. I'm Airborne by God."

BY GOD, MIKE just wanted this day to be over.

He felt the Sergeant Major's eyes boring into his back as Mike helped walk Trooper to the dusty SUV covered in paw magnets. At least the Sergeant Major could be trusted to hold off—for now—since going ballistic in front of the press wouldn't look good.

No question, the media was eating this up from behind the ropes, snapping photos even as Lacey tried to hustle the General into the vehicle before he shouted something else censor worthy. Mike kept Trooper reined in tighter now, close to his leg while Nathan jogged ahead to open the back hatch, exposing the crate. Head low, the teenager ducked into the vehicle without a word.

Mike picked up the pace. He would have to in-process soon—should be doing that now. But since he was already up to his ass in trouble, might as well dive the rest of the way.

A familiar place for him.

"Sierra, I emailed your mom about Trooper's habits and stuff that should make his transition into a new home easier—"

"Oh," Sierra interrupted with an over-wide smile, "you noticed I'm here."

She was pissed? Interesting.

He'd been so focused on delivering the dog and trying not to drool all over her he'd missed her mood. "You expected more from me back there? Surely not a reunion kiss."

"Don't play games with me, not today." She was short, but her legs ate up the ground fast. Sierra had a Tinker Bell look to her, not that she liked it much when he'd made the comparison.

"I'd hoped passing over Trooper could be more low-key for everyone's sake."

She glanced up sharply, concern in her sky blue eyes. "Will you get in trouble for this?"

"I'm not the first to bring back a dog from overseas. I won't be the last." He paused and slid his duffel from his shoulder. He unzipped it and pulled out an envelope of papers. "For Trooper. His records. They've been scanned and sent to your mother, but these are the originals. He has his vaccinations, although he still needs to be neutered. Everything's in order for him to be in the country."

She tugged the envelope from him without touching. Too precisely to be anything but deliberate avoidance. "You didn't answer my question."

He closed his hand over hers. "I've dodged trouble my whole life. I learned from the best thanks to my grandma." He squeezed her hand and wanted more. No surprise. "I'll weather any storm. And you? How are you holding up?"

She tugged her hand away. "I'm fine."

Fine? Such a lame word. Sierra was smoking hot as always, but clearly exhausted, grieving. And angry at him. Nothing new there. Regardless, his part in this was done. He'd handed over the dog. His last connection to the Colonel—to Sierra—was severed.

As Mike leaned in, he caught a whiff of her citrus scent. Such an enticing air mixed with memories. Except a roar of an engine brought the memories rolling back of other scents, ones from his last moments with the Colonel.

His gut twisted. How the hell did memories have smells? Because right now the scent of explosives and dirt gave him vertigo. He needed to get out of here. Fast. Preferably on his own two feet.

He started to turn away and slammed into his friend.

Calvin high-fived him. "Tazz, party at my place after we finish up here? Sierra, are you coming, too?"

Her face closed in a snap. "I'm not in a partying mood. Thanks for the invitation all the same."

Mike gripped the straps on his bag and guitar. "Count me out. I'm not good for anything more than crashing for the night in a queen-sized motel bed."

Calvin backed away. "Wuss. We'll miss your guitar. I'll drink your share, though." He shot them both a wave. "Later, Tazz. Lookin' gooooood as always, Sierra."

Sierra's hand landed on Mike's elbow. "You said you're going to a motel. What happened to your apartment?"

He shrugged. "I gave it up. No need to pay rent on a place I wouldn't be living in for a year."

"That makes sense."

Rhinestone sunglasses tucked in her hair, she shuffled from foot to foot, toenails painted purple with glitter. "I guess this is it then. Thank you for bringing Dad's dog home."

"You always were adept at saying the total opposite of what your eyes are telling me. You're not happy about Trooper. I can tell."

Her lips went tight for a second before she burst out, "I appreciate what you've done and I mean that. Regardless of what you say, I know you risked getting into trouble bringing him to us."

"Don't worry. There's too much good press connected to his story now for me to get into any major trouble. The media coverage is a blessing in disguise."

"But . . ."

"I told you already." He rested a hand on her shoulder and left it there this time. Bad move. God, she was soft and felt like home. "I'm going to be okay."

"Liar."

"Does it really matter to you?"

"You've done something special for my mom. I appreciate that." Her eyes held his for four heavy heartbeats before they heard her mom chanting soothing comments to the

General. Sierra shook her head as if clearing a haze and slid her sunglasses into place. She opened the crate and patted the bedding. "Trooper? Come on. Inside, pup."

Trooper glanced back at Mike, dropping to sit, reluctant. The dog might not be huge, but he was stubborn. When he didn't want to move, he could turn that doggie muscle into more like a ton of bricks.

Lacey slid from the vehicle into view. "No worries. I've got this."

Sierra's mom wrapped her arms around the dog, lifting with practiced ease and the same soothing tones she'd used on the disoriented General. She tucked Trooper into the crate and reached into a satchel for a treat, before turning all smiles again. "Easy peasy. We're good to go. Thanks again, Mike, for everything."

It was really done. Delivery complete. Mission over. Wide brown puppy eyes stared at him from the crate.

An ache started in Mike's chest. Damn it, he didn't need a dog. It wasn't his dog. He'd done the right thing.

So why did he feel like an ass, like one of those people who abandoned their pets, even though he knew better? Still, Trooper's eyes seemed to speak to him, which was impossible because dogs didn't talk.

But if they did, he knew Trooper was saying, *Dude, you're screwing up again.*

LACEY FELT GUILTY about feeding the puppies while drunk. But then she deserved a glass of wine—or four—after a day like this.

Cradling the light brindle–colored pit puppy in her hand, she angled the tiny bottle of goat's milk into just the right position until the bulldog latched on. The gentle tug assured her the orphaned pup had a good suck going. Relaxing back against the screened window, she sat cross-legged in the middle of a fat dog bed on her enclosed back porch.

Lacey took comfort from the warm puppy belly against her palm. Four other satiated two-week-old babies were lined up in the padded box, warming lamp overhead. She'd named them after fairy-tale characters in hopes that adopters would see them as loving living creatures rather than judge them by their breed.

Cinderella, Aladdin, Pinocchio, Rapunzel and the little runt in her hand, Thumbelina, all twitched in their sleep, a sign of health. Did they already dream of running through fields they couldn't yet see? Or were they racing through the world looking for their mother?

Their orphaned status tugged at her more than ever with her own two children still struggling with the loss of their father.

She needed more wine. Now.

Balancing the baby bottle against a rolled-up towel, she freed a hand and reached for her glass. Cut crystal Waterford and the last one left of her wedding set. The others had been broken in a transfer from Fort Bragg in North Carolina. She'd railed at the moving company, the Army, her husband and anyone else who would listen. She'd cried for a month.

Such a silly rant now that she looked back with the perspective of worse things the Army could break.

She swirled the chardonnay in the glass once, taking in an oaky scent before tasting. Her mother had sent her to cotillion and etiquette classes with the richest teens in New England. Her parents had high hopes for their oldest daughter.

Lacey had once entertained hopes, too. Of toeing the line with her parents until she was free to leave for college. Except in her last year of high school, she'd fallen for a new senior in a Junior ROTC uniform, gotten knocked up that summer and finished her teaching degree later on when her two kids started school. Her parents had pretended for their friends that they were thrilled. The quickie wedding had been elaborate and pricey.

Only later had she learned her parents couldn't afford that lavish wedding any more than they'd been able to afford their three-house lifestyle of summers in the Hamptons and winter ski chalet jaunts.

Now her folks pretended they were happily retired in a Tampa condo they'd managed to purchase after selling off Mom's jewelry. She still wore really good fakes.

Faking it. Something Lacey had inherited from her mother even as she turned her back on their values. She stroked her bare toes along the chocolate Lab sleeping at her feet.

Life should have meaning. Allen's had. He'd saved five soldiers by throwing himself on the roadside bomb. He'd left behind a stack of medals, a folded flag and a family hanging on by a thread. The insurance money had paid off most of their debt, and she was teaching high school chemistry online to make ends meet, still running her rescue and taking care of her father-in-law. She had fourteen animals on-site, but over fifty were in foster homes. With more money, she could expand. With more time. More help.

Less stress.

She sipped again. And again. Until the alcohol hummed along her frayed nerves, soothing her like the whir of the lawn mower firing to life outside.

Her father-in-law mowed the lawn at night, as close to driving a car as they could trust. The headlight strobed across the two-acre lot. The task gave Joshua a sense of purpose, one of the few chores he could still perform without fear of hurting himself or others. Yard work was somehow ingrained in his DNA like buttoning his uniform. Thank heavens. Last time she'd mowed the two acres, she'd cut crop circles into the yard.

Might have had something to do with the wine.

There were days she wondered if maybe she had a drinking problem. Then life kicked into high gear with another crisis and she didn't have time to think about herself.

She glanced down at the puppy sleeping in her hand, Thumbelina's mouth slack with sleep. Lacey tugged a wet wipe and cleaned the little one's waste before lining her up alongside her brothers and sisters, a mix of brown, tan and brindle babies.

The mother dog had been hit by a car when her litter was three days old. The family who owned the dog had tried to care for the puppies for forty-eight hours before losing three then taking the remaining five straight to the local animal shelter. Since the shelter was overflowing, they'd called Lacey.

Five little lives.

She'd been rescuing for over ten years for other groups before starting her own. But these days, preserving life had taken on a frenetic edge. She tried and tried, yet each success left her feeling emptier. Two friends who volunteered with the rescue told her she wasn't dealing with her grief.

Like there was a way to get over losing her husband in a war.

She only knew one way to cope. Keep moving forward so quickly she didn't have time to think. She couldn't afford to dwell on the past or the present, and most especially she couldn't think overlong about that new dog asleep in a crate in the family room. Trooper was the final tie to an honorable man more committed to others than his family or even himself. If she gave in to those raging thoughts, she would surrender to the temptation to hurl the last piece of wedding crystal at the wall.

She soaked in the familiarity around her, needing something steady to hold on to in her shredded world. Trooper seemed to be settling in well—other than barking his head off at the cuckoo clock. He hadn't even protested over being crated in the family room, growling a couple more times at the clock before settling to sleep. He seemed to take comfort in all the animals around rather than feeling overwhelmed.

A novelty.

Some said she should give up rescue work, that it was too draining. They just didn't understand that saving these abandoned and abused animals hauled her grieving body out of bed each morning.

Her eyes were beyond gritty as she checked each little body in the line of puppies snoozing away in a milk coma. She wasn't far behind. Exhaustion tugged at her. Her head lolled against the screened wall, and she didn't have the energy to move from the plaid dog bed. Each breath of barley-scented air drew her deeper into the intoxicating allure of sleep. Just leaving her insane life behind for a few blissful hours. Peace, she craved it all the way to her tipsy toes. Might as well sleep here rather than in her bed with a conspicuously empty space beside her . . .

"Mom?" Her daughter's voice pierced her sleepy fog. "Mom, wake up."

Startled, Lacey jolted awake. Sunlight streamed through the screens onto her Lab Clementine sleeping at her feet. Morning? But she'd only closed her eyes for a minute. Or maybe not.

Her daughter stood beside her, wearing a tank top and blue running shorts. Sierra used to wear nightshirts and cute little PJs, but she slept in clothes these days, always ready to face the world.

Lacey looked fast at the puppies, and they all breathed and slept and twitched. Her neck screamed with a crick from sleeping sitting up. She rubbed the kink. "Sierra? What time is it?"

"Six, but Mom, we have a problem."

Lacey looked out at the freshly mowed lawn, over to the lawnmower abandoned in the middle of the driveway. Panic fired hard and fast. "Has Grandpa wandered off again?"

Sierra shook her head. "Not this time. He's asleep in his room. But Trooper's missing."

Three

SIERRA STIFLED A yawn and scratched her toe along the back of her leg, her brain still foggy even as her heart raced with anxiety over the missing dog. Her days of sleeping until noon were long gone. Life started early around here, *Little House on the Freakin' Manic Prairie* style. Of course she might not feel like a zombie if she hadn't spent half the night tossing and turning with dreams of Mike. Naughty, dangerous, distracting dreams . . .

She didn't have time for this. Not now.

"Mom," Sierra repeated, taking in her mother's tangled hair and the empty wineglass. She would think about that later. They had more pressing problems now, like Dad's legacy going MIA. "Trooper is missing."

"Missing? Are you sleepwalking again?" Her mother stood, then staggered. Drunk or were her feet asleep from sitting cross-legged so long in a dog bed? Lacey reached out with steady hands and patted her daughter's face. "Sierra, honey, wake up."

"I'm fine." Sierra batted away her mother's hands as their

three-legged Labrador went out through the doggie door. "Listen to me. *Trooper. Is. Gone.* He must have gone out through the doggie door, and then from there, who knows. But I can't find him."

Her mother frowned and looked past into the kitchen at the cuckoo clock they'd bought while stationed in Germany. "You must be mistaken. Trooper's in a crate in the family room. What are you doing up at six in the morning? You hate mornings."

A flash of irritation pierced her fear. Her mother apparently hadn't noticed she'd been waking before eight to help with the animals for months now. But her mom didn't need anyone sniping at her.

And they had more pressing concerns.

"I heard barking. Okay, barking's normal, but this was worse. The crazy, pissed-off kind of barking. I was afraid the dogs had gotten loose . . . again." It had happened too many times lately to be accidental. "When I came down-stairs, I saw Trooper's crate was open. He must have gone outside, which upset the other dogs. Except he's nowhere inside the fence. Nowhere. And I've looked inside and out. Under every bed and bush. Trooper is missing."

Lacey turned to look through the screen, palms flat on the mesh, fully alert now. "The gate outside is closed. Secured. I don't understand how this keeps happening. Heaven knows if he'd gone next door to Valerie Hammond's house we would have heard already."

And not in a good way. Mrs. Hammond already had a complaint filed with the county council to shut down the res-cue, and they couldn't afford to relocate the rescue setup—her mom's dream. Lacey had lost too much. Resolve swept away any remaining grogginess.

"Maybe Trooper jumped over the fence on the other side and headed toward the wooded area? He wouldn't be the first." Although he was smaller than the ones that had man-aged that move before. Please, Lord, let him just be hiding somewhere enjoying a good nap and doggie laugh at their expense.

"Or maybe your grandfather let him out." Tiny lines fanned from Lacey's eyes. Caregiver's stress.

Not that Lacey didn't complain or lose her cool. She ran full tilt all day, cried sometimes, misplaced her reading glasses, left her day planner in the house, ran back inside to get it and dropped her keys. Yet somehow she still managed to cram twenty-eight hours' worth of living into every day. The glass of wine probably didn't mean anything other than unwinding on a particularly bad evening.

"If Gramps did it, good luck asking him for details." There were days Sierra missed her grandfather as much as her dad. Gramps was just leaving them in a different way.

"Trooper can't have gotten far." Lacey scraped her tangled hair back and dragged a rubber band off her wrist, clearing the mess into a sloppy ponytail that somehow managed to look cool. "I'll start driving around the neighborhood. Will you get Nathan to watch your grandfather before you help me look?"

"Sure, don't forget your cell phone," Sierra called after her mom, remembering the last time she'd been unable to cancel a search for an hour.

"Right. Thanks." Lacey backtracked and swiped her phone off the iron patio table before she ran out the screen door, shouting, "Trooper! Trooooper . . ."

Sierra shot a quick look at the five puppies squirming and squawking in their box. The other dogs would have to wait for breakfast. The puppies needed feeding now. She bypassed the mudroom and pushed open the sliding door into the family room.

Nathan sat in his boxers on the sofa with his feet on the coffee table, watching the History Channel and eating cereal. He must have been in the kitchen when she found the crate—but sure enough it was still open at the end of the couch. Why was he even up this early?

"Why aren't you still asleep?"

"Why aren't you?" he retorted, then shrugged. "Noise woke me up. Started thinking about Dad . . ."

Their father had watched the History Channel with them so many times. She swallowed hard, wanting to comfort her baby brother but knowing he wouldn't let her.

Two tabby cats slept along the back of the sofa like bookends around Nathan. He cradled a bowl against his scrawny chest and shoveled Lucky Charms into his mouth, his favorite breakfast since he'd been a kid. Except it had to be doused in goat's milk because he had a serious cow's milk allergy.

And the goat's milk made her remember . . . Oh God, Mom's puppies. She didn't have time to milk the goat again, much less feed the pups and other dogs.

Sierra ran past the island and into the kitchen. She checked the fridge and saw the container still had at least a cup left. Enough. Good. She reached into a cabinet under the sink and pulled out a box of rubber gloves.

"Nathan, the animals need to eat. All of them. But the puppies on the porch need you first and since you're awake you can help. You can feed five at a time if you put goat's milk in the fingers—not cow's milk. Poke a small hole in the end of each finger of the gloves. They don't have teeth yet. Just be careful they don't suck in the latex. Keep the fingers full." She dropped the box on the coffee table next to his feet and a basket of gnawed-up tennis balls. "If you drink the last of the goat's milk, have fun milking Sookie. Okay?"

"Five puppies? Really?" He started shaking his head.

Sierra clapped his face in her hands and guided his no into a yes. "Really. Or you can feed them one at a time if you'd rather. Or go chase down Dad's dog."

"Fine. Whatever." He shrugged free, then tipped the bowl up to his mouth to slurp the leftover milk. He smacked his lips, burped, then said, "Dog hopped the fence and ran for the woods."

She froze in her tracks, halfway to the door. Anger fumed inside her that her brother could care so little for something that meant so much to their mother. Fighting with him wouldn't find the dog, though. Heaven help them all if her brother decided not to talk because he felt she was unjustly picking on him. "How do you know which way Trooper went? And how long have you been keeping that to yourself?"

"Saw him go over about a half hour ago."

"You didn't think it was worth telling anyone before now?" Sometimes she wondered if her brother wasn't just a sad nerd, but some psycho after all. "Did you happen to see exactly which part of the woods he ran into?"

"Yep."

Little shit. "Care to share?"

"He was running around the yard for a while—"

"How did he get in the yard?" If Nathan let him out unsupervised while the dog was still new, skittish and unfamiliar with regions, heaven help her she would—

"Gramps let him out late last night after he mowed the lawn." Nathan shoved off the sofa and started for the kitchen, the cuckoo chirping quarter after. "Trooper climbed the fence, jumped over and hauled ass past the picnic table there, along the path that leads out to the main road. He's probably halfway back to Iraq now."

"That's so helpful to know."

"You asked." Nathan tossed his bowl in the sink so hard the old pottery piece must have broken. "Guess I better feed the rats."

"They're puppies." What made her even bother arguing with her brother? "And you need to watch Gramps so he doesn't wander off while we're out. Truly watch him very closely and call me if he gives you trouble or if he tries to leave."

"I think we should just let Gramps go where he wants. Maybe he's just looking for Dad like the dog is."

His words knocked the wind right out of her. For all of

five seconds. She didn't have time to flip out. Sierra swatted her brother on the back of the head. "Thanks for being a jackass."

He shrugged. "Truth sucks whether you say it out loud or not."

MIKE SLOUCHED AGAINST the flimsy motel headboard, guitar on his knee. His internal clock was suffering from a kick-ass case of jet lag that left him wide awake at ten in the morning when he'd hoped to sleep the day away. The thin motel walls barely muffled the couple going at it in the room next door.

Some soldier was getting one helluva welcome home. Sounded like a professional welcome. The dude's fourth so far.

The other wall leeched the occasional sound of a baby crying. Mike plucked the strings on his guitar to create a sound barrier against the world. He picked through familiar riffs and ones he'd written himself. He wasn't good with the words, just the tunes. His beat-up old acoustic had helped him pass a lot of hours overseas.

His grandmother had encouraged him to play. One of the more honest skills she'd endorsed—definitely more appropriate than using poker to tutor him in math. Although he had to confess, she'd been a formidable gambler. He'd been tossed out of two casinos on suspicion of card counting.

She'd also taught him to be thrifty, which had worked in her favor when she drained his savings account not long after he'd deployed. She'd said she needed to pay off her car, but when she'd died there wasn't a car. And he hadn't even had a chance to say good-bye to the only person who'd taken time to parent him.

He had no place to go. He'd given up his apartment and put his belongings in storage—not much, some clothes and a wide-screen television. Why accumulate things when he

would only have to move them or have them taken away by
a relative who needed them more while he was gone?

A motel suited him fine for now. He preferred his digs
to come already furnished. Less mess. Fewer entanglements
like roommates or relationships to deal with while he got
his head on straight after a long deployment overseas and
readied himself for the next. Because there was always a
next deployment.

Hanging out here by himself, he didn't have to pretend
to be nice. Or normal. He was jumpy and empty. Every
sound had him resisting the urge to hit the deck or punch a
wall. Some called it battle stress. He didn't care about nam-
ing it, just getting through it.

After he'd locked himself in the room, he'd emptied his
weapon and stowed his ammo to be sure he didn't accidentally draw on a pizza delivery guy who honked his horn or
a family on vacation in a car that backfired. God forbid
anyone set off fireworks. He'd be flipping a table on its side
to make a barricade before anyone could shout, "Happy
Flag Day."

Mike set his guitar aside and leaned forward to tear off
another piece of pizza—topped with loads of meat. He
popped open a lukewarm soda. He'd emptied a couple of
longnecks last night for his own welcome home party with
some late show that made pop culture references he'd lost
track of while overseas.

A *scratch, scratch, scratch* echoed outside.

He stopped chewing. Probably just something brushing
against the door. Chill. Out. He bit off more pizza and forced
himself to chew extra times so he wouldn't choke due to the
panic constricting his throat.

The *scratch, scratch, scratch* continued, definitely
against the door. What the hell? He tossed the pizza crust
back in the box. He reached for his 9mm—

Shit.

It took every ounce of restraint to move his hand away

and walk to the door like a normal guy, in a normal motel room. Granted, it was a normal, *cheap* motel room. He peered through the nice normal peephole and saw . . . nothing.

Scratch. Scratch.

Okay, alarms were seriously buzzing in his war-fogged brain. He pushed back the curtain on the window next to the door and—

Thud!

He screamed like a damn five-year-old, leaping back before he realized a dog skidded down the glass, then jumped up again. Recognition hit him like a blow to the chest. Trooper. The stunned feeling eased, replaced by something else entirely. Was Sierra outside?

Mike slid the chain, flipped the bolt and flung the door wide. No Sierra. No people period. His gaze slid down. Sure as hell, Trooper sat in front of his door with a battered tennis ball in his mouth and tail wagging, brown eyes doing that talking thing again.

Wanna play?

SIERRA CURSED THAT damn missing mutt as she sagged against the porch post. Exhausted. Defeated.

She scraped her wrist under her eyes, then her nose, crying like a baby over a dog she didn't even really like. Of course she hadn't gotten a chance to know the ornery beast beyond feeling jealous Trooper got to spend time with her dad during his last days on earth.

Hiccupping, she stared at the empty gravel road leading out to the highway. Woods sprawled to the left. On the right, their distant, cranky neighbors lived in a brick ranch house. They hadn't seen Trooper, either, and if they had, they damn straight would have called Animal Control first rather than let Lacey know.

Sierra had helped her mom search the neighborhood and

woods for five hours with no luck. To make matters worse, Trooper had ditched his collar before he'd left their property. They'd found the bright red collar with tags lying in the dirt. The dog was scheduled to be neutered and microchipped tomorrow, which didn't help them today. They'd finally agreed to take a break and regroup at home.

Her mom was calling every shelter in a hundred-mile radius. Lacey had them all on speed dial since she worked rescues with all of them. If Trooper landed anywhere else, she would be notified.

If.

Of course, thanks to her mom's rescue work Sierra knew the thousand other "ifs" that could have happened to Trooper. If he hadn't been hit by a car. If he wasn't starving on the streets. If he hadn't eaten mushrooms or a zillion other toxic things that lurked in the woods.

And then there were all the horrible people in the world who did terrible things to stray animals. She'd seen the fallout from those neglect and cruelty cases every time her mother drove home from the shelters with her latest residents joining the Second Chance Rescue. These dogs, cats—not to mention a miniature pony, snake, goat and other critters— came with sad-sack histories that even a shelter couldn't rehab and rehome.

How could Trooper have survived life as a feral pup in Iraq and a trip across the ocean, only to run away on his first day with a real family? Somehow, she felt like this was her fault, that she'd let her dad down on the very last thing he'd needed from her. Her breath hitched on a hysterical sob, one far beyond plain old tears, a gut-deep sobbing session she hadn't allowed herself in four months. She clenched her teeth together to hold it back.

She would not, could not lose control.

Longfellow. She needed some one-on-one time with Henry Wadsworth Longfellow right now, something like "The Day is Done." She sucked in deep breaths of barley-scented air, grateful for the post behind her. *Come, read to me some poem, Some simple and heartfelt lay, That shall soothe this restless feeling, And banish the thoughts of day . . .*

The final lines were drowned out by Grandpa turning on his cassette player. "Amazing Grace" on the bagpipes rattled through the windows. He couldn't work the CD player anymore, but he still knew how to operate a cassette player to make use of his collection, which remained in pristine condition along with his collection of John Wayne movies for the old VCR. He cranked the volume until the dogs howled in time with the bagpipes.

Her legs folded and she stumbled back into a rocking chair.

She was living in a freakin' sitcom. Or a docudrama. Reality show? She wasn't sure. Right now she just wanted her dad to materialize in the rocking chair beside her. He would say something like, "Sierra girl, I've loved your mom since we were seniors in high school and I saw her climbing a tree trying to put a baby bird back in a nest with the mama. You just need to roll with it. Lacey has a way of making all the craziness come together into something magnificent— like our family."

Her dad had a gift for putting the mayhem into perspective, bringing a Longfellow type of calm, flavored with a splash of Ogden Nash–esque humor.

She missed her father so much. She pressed the heels of her hand to her eyes to hold back the tears that accomplished absolutely zip. Crying didn't change anything. Did Gramps even remember bagpipes had played at her dad's funeral?

The sound of an approaching car and their chocolate Lab barking her head off cut through the third verse. She tugged the neck of her T-shirt up to her eyes and wiped away tears, then smoothed the hem back in place.

Blinking fast, she cleared her sight and . . . oh crap. She recognized the old red truck rattling up the driveway. Mike's truck. But why was he coming here? Her heart did that crazy flutter thing.

She squinted and realized he wasn't alone. Someone sat in the passenger seat. She stepped up to the porch post and held on. Just in case her knees turned traitorously wobbly. Except it wasn't a person in the front seat.

A dog stuck its head out the window, tongue lolling. And not just any dog. Trooper barked hello as if he'd just been out for a spin with his pal. She tried to wrap her brain around the fact that somehow, someway Trooper had jumped the fence and located Mike. Or Mike had found him, which didn't make sense because he didn't even know to look for the dog. Maybe they should have called him in the first place.

The twelve-year-old Ford stopped in front of her house, and she kept her eyes off the back where she'd lain on a quilt under the stars, tangled up with Mike and a crazy infatuation.

He stepped out, one long leg at a time, looking too hot in faded jeans and a rumpled brown T-shirt. "Did you lose something?"

She hooked her arm around the post and tried to appear casual. "I may have." Lost her heart, once upon a time, to this guy in fact. "Cute dog you have there. He seems vaguely familiar."

Trooper spun a quick circle on the seat before leaping out and onto the ground, sniffing Clementine in greeting once before galloping past the three-legged Lab over to Mike. Relief made her grip the post harder.

The screen door swung open and slammed against the side of the house. Lacey ran out, flip-flops slapping the wood porch all the way down the step as she chanted, "Ohmigod," again and again.

She fell to her knees and wrapped her arms around Trooper's neck. "You silly, naughty dog. What were you thinking running away like that?" She ran her hands over his fur as if checking for damage inflicted by the harsh, cold world. Never mind he'd survived in the desert on his own before sucking up to her dad. "Did someone tell you about your visit to the vet tomorrow? I promise to get you good drugs to sleep it off . . ."

Lacey paused long enough to gasp and bury her face in the dog's scruff and extend an arm to include Clementine in the hug. Sierra stared at Mike over her mother huddled around the two dogs. Pain glinted in his eyes, something mighty like an echo of what radiated off her mom and what Sierra herself felt every day. Somehow she'd lost sight of how much Mike looked up to her father. So much so, Mike had walked away from her, from what they'd shared.

Her mother glanced up, her lopsided ponytail shifting. "I don't know how to thank you enough, Mike. How did you find him? Or know to search? Did Sierra call you?"

Mike walked past the front of the truck, stopping beside her. "He showed up at my place."

Standing, Lacey hugged Mike hard. "Well, thank you for bringing him home."

He patted her shoulder awkwardly before backing away. "I was going to call, but my cell phone wasn't charged and I tried once from the motel but your home phone went straight to voice mail, so I decided to just drive over."

"I must have been talking to Animal Control when you phoned." Lacey exhaled hard. "I'm just glad Trooper's okay. I need to let all my shelter and rescue contacts know so they can cancel the alert . . ." She continued rambling her list of to-dos all the way into the house.

Leaving Sierra alone with Mike.

Awkward.

She rested her head against the porch post, eyeing Trooper on one side of Mike. Clementine ambled back up to the porch and flopped down in front of the door. Sure, the Lab only had three legs, but she was the alpha boss of the house and the other dogs knew it. "Mom's rescue network is large. She'll be on the phone for a long while."

"Monster large, or so I hear."

She winced. "That's an understatement."

"You're not cool with her officially opening her own rescue?"

"That's not what I meant." Well, okay, it sorta was, but she felt guilty for not supporting her mom's dream when her mother had always been there for her kids, often alone. But helping the local shelter was one thing. Making their home the point of contact for a full-fledged rescue took things to another level. "I'm not expressing myself well. I was just so worried. Trooper was gone. It's not like he knows the neighborhood. What if he'd been hit by a car? Does he even understand regular traffic? My dad trusted us."

Mike walked up the steps, long, loping strides bringing him closer to her. "Sierra, it's okay now." He rested a broad hand on her shoulder, squeezing once. "Trooper's home. He's safe. Your dad knew what he was doing when he sent him here."

"Can we not talk about my father after all?" She was too close to losing it. Totally. Even the comforting touch threatened to send her flying into his arms. She held herself rigidly in control.

He seemed to get the message and backed up a step, slumping back against the opposite post. Trooper stayed plastered by his side, ears back. "The dog's not a comfort, is he?"

"It's not that." She studied the wide brown puppy eyes staring back up at her, and she could swear she saw her father's reflection in them. "He's just a reminder."

"Like I am."

She looked up sharply. "I didn't say that."

"You didn't have to."

Guilt and a little shame churned around inside her.

"Thank you for bringing him here. We've been freaking out since we noticed he was missing early this morning."

"He traveled a lot of ground to find me." He crossed his feet at the ankles, wearing boat shoes with no socks. He pulled off casual so very well. "He must have been on the move the whole time."

"Were you at a party?" The words fell out of her mouth before she could call them back. At least she didn't ask if he was with a date.

"At my motel room"—he half smiled as if he could read her mind—"alone."

She almost managed to hold in her sigh of relief. Almost. Her face heated with a blush. "How did Trooper track you?"

Mike's eyes swept her face for a flash that said loud and clear he hadn't missed her embarrassment or interest. "You would have to ask him," he said, playing along with not openly acknowledging the attraction crackling between them, "except Trooper can't talk."

"If only he could, the things he might tell us."

What a time to realize that as they stood face-to-face, leaning against the posts, their feet were almost touching. It was just feet, for crying out loud. They weren't naked. She wore sandals so broken in she'd taped the toe thong, and his boat shoes had a frayed shoelace retied together. But somehow being this close still felt . . . intimate. She could stretch her leg just an inch and run her toes along his bared ankle.

A year ago, she would have. Then he would have extended an arm. She would have linked hands with him and he would have tugged her against his chest for a kiss so long and sweet she'd see stars. The steam they'd generated had left her breathless every time they got close.

An effect she was still feeling even now . . . long after that breakup.

There'd been so much good between them, a chemistry and something else, something worth pursuing. Until he'd decided they couldn't be together because he wasn't good enough for her and it would be disloyal to her father.

His excuses sounded thin to her then and now. There had to be more. Or Mike simply didn't want to be with her any longer and thought too much of her dad to simply dump her. So he'd given her a made-up excuse.

Now wasn't that a sobering thought? She cleared her throat and straightened, which took her feet away from temptation. "Thank you again for bringing Trooper. I'm hungry and need a shower . . . So . . ."

"Right." He nodded, shoving away and starting down the steps backward. "I should go now that I've delivered your dog—twice."

She knew his leaving was inevitable and it was silly to expect anything different. Must be exhaustion making her weak. She spun away and—slammed straight into her grandfather standing in the open doorway. How long had he been there and how had she not noticed?

Gramps clapped her on the back once before stepping around toward Mike.

"Hello, boy." Joshua's avoidance of using a name was always clue number one he didn't know the person even though he should. "Stay for lunch."

At least he knew what time it was. She shot an apologetic smile at Mike.

"Thanks, sir. That's a generous offer." He paused half in, half out of his truck. "But you don't need to feed me. I'm done returning your dog, so I'll just be on my way."

"There's plenty of chili, and I know that because I made it myself while the women were gone."

The women? Apparently Gramps was in his un-PC mode right now.

The General continued, "They don't like for me to cook—afraid I'll burn the house down. So we compromise and I use the Crock-Pot."

There were child locks all over the kitchen and stove, as well as notes. Gramps could still read. For now.

"I do love good chili, General." Mike stepped around the front of the truck, nearly giving her a heart attack with the notion he might stick around. "But I'll have to take a rain check."

The gleam in Mike's eyes shouted loud and clear he knew exactly how his words were affecting her. She ground her teeth. So he wanted to play games, did he? "By all means, stay for lunch, Mike, if that's what you would like."

"Thanks, but—"

"Boy." Gramps yanked the door open further and pointed inside. "Come on. I know full well home-cooked food is a treat after being overseas."

Or maybe her grandfather was having a good day. Sometimes she wondered if he liked to mess with their minds by pretending it was a bad day. Ornery old cuss. She almost grinned. Almost.

Time for everyone to stop playing games.

"Gramps, Mike probably has things to do. We've already take enough of his time with him coming all the way out here to return Trooper."

Gramps snorted. "Doesn't look like Trooper plans to stay with us."

What the hell?

She looked around her and the dog was gone again. She started to panic, then—there was Trooper—sitting in the front seat of the truck.

Gramps threw his shoulders back and barked, "Stay for lunch. We're eating out back at the picnic table. That's an order."

Mike looked at her, back at his truck, then surrendered. "Yes, sir. Thank you."

What the hell? He'd actually agreed? Was this some kind of ploy on Mike's part to get close to her, see if she would be open to a "welcome home" quickie after chili? If so, he was in for a rude awakening when dessert was nothing more than a scoop of ice cream on his way out the door.

SITTING AROUND THE McDaniel patio table again was supremely surreal.

Mike had come to their house for meals before, during the brief time that he and Sierra had told everyone about their relationship. Very brief time. Shortly after that, they'd broken up, just before his deployment.

He'd seen the way it was tearing her up, saying good-bye to him *and* her father. He'd figured out fast that being a military brat was hard enough for her to handle. Being a military spouse was out of the question. And without the military, he was nothing more than the screwed-up kid of a criminal grandma and a father who couldn't handle raising a boy who was a constant reminder of the woman who'd died bringing him into the world. Mike was through being a reminder of dead people.

So why was he sitting here on the McDaniel family's patio like this was a regular family get-together? The umbrella flapped overhead and dogs barked in the background while a cat slept on his foot.

He wasn't sure why he'd stayed other than it had felt easier to accept than getting in his truck and leaving her again. Maybe by the end of the lunch, he would have his answer and some closure.

But God, he had to admit he'd missed being around this quirky, awesome family. The mom with her galoshes, shorts and a pit bull T-shirt. Nathan with a large snake—Bo—draped over his shoulders, and no one thought that was strange. Not even the memory-challenged General in his sweatpants and an Army T-shirt commented on the four-foot-long reptile.

And Sierra. Lord help him every time he looked at her he was damn near mesmerized by her, with her easygoing

style that made a side ponytail and tank top look classy—
and all the while he knew underneath she had a short Shakespearean quote tattooed on her hip bone.

"Crackers?" Lacey thrust a basket full of saltines Mike's way.

"Sure, thank you, ma'am." He took a handful and crushed
them on top of his bowl of chili, which actually didn't taste
half bad. The General had definitely lost more of his memory in the past year, but not his ability to cook. "This beats
what I would have microwaved at my motel. Thank you."

One thing Mike missed with his vagabond lifestyle—
being able to cook whenever he felt like it.

The General shook Tabasco sauce into his deep pottery
bowl. "What kind of motel are you staying at, soldier? You
have to be careful of the hookers. They'll steal your wallet
and give you gonorrhea."

Sierra spluttered on her iced tea. "Gramps—"

Nathan crushed crackers in his chili. "Do you know
about that from experience, Gramps?"

Lacey gasped.

Mike interjected quickly, "I'll be careful to steer clear of
trouble."

"Damn straight." The General plunked the hot sauce
down so hard the ice rattled in the glasses. "And if you're
just saying that to pacify me, at least remember to wrap your
rascal when you're with a hooker."

"Sir." Best to rechannel this conversation away from
"rascals," wrapped or otherwise. "Let's talk about this
another time. There are ladies present."

"By God, you're right. Sorry, my dears." He looked to
the side sharply. "Lacey, could you pass the hot sauce?"

"Dad, you've already—" Lacey started only to be interrupted by Nathan.

"Here, Gramps."

Sierra swatted her brother's wrist. "Gramps, how about
you taste it first. It's really awesome."

The General shook his head. "Lacey never puts enough spices in the food."

Sierra glanced at Mike apologetically. The old guy had already forgotten cooking the meal. As if this family didn't have enough grief on their plate. Guilt tugged at him, over being here, over being alive when the man they needed so badly wasn't. He wanted to help them, but at the same time being around Sierra was torture—for both of them.

Birds chirped along with the barking dogs as Mike just shoveled another bite into his mouth. Joshua dumped more hot sauce on his chili and still seemed to like the meal fine. Distant traffic rumbled, everything but voices filling the awkward silence.

Nathan looked up from his lunch, the snake's head rising in sync with him. "Mike, you should move into our new studio apartment in the barn loft. It's clean. And there's no risk of hookers or gonorrhea."

Four

SIERRA COULDN'T DECIDE who she wanted to kick first—her brother for making the absurd offer or Mike for looking so horrified at the notion of living in her family's studio apartment. Fine. He didn't want to be around her anymore. He didn't have to be so overt about it.

To be frank, she wasn't turning cartwheels over the notion of having him in her face—and in her apartment. That loft studio was her only chance at a little privacy and independence. At twenty-three years old, she was ready for a place of her own. She loved her job as a graduate assistant teaching 101-level college courses, and she could have afforded a one-room studio on her own, but the cost to her mom to replace Sierra's help would be expensive. Not to mention stressful. She had to stay. She understood and accepted this was the right thing to do.

But back to Mike and his ill-hidden horror over living near her. She ground her teeth and tried to find some kind of Zen centering in the soothing sound of rustling branches overhead.

He nudged his chili bowl away and placed his wadded paper napkin carefully beside it. "Thanks for the offer, kid. But I'm fine where I am."

Nathan curled the boa constrictor around his arm, guiding its face toward Sierra. "You may be okay. But we're not."

Gasping, Lacey grasped her son's wrist. "Nathan, stop talking and quit taunting your sister—"

Mike frowned, looking around the table, then pinned Sierra with his golden-brown eyes. "What does he mean about your family not being okay?"

"Nothing," Sierra snapped, glaring at Nathan. What happened to her sweet little brother who'd shared his Teddy Grahams and once gave her his favorite G.I. Joe because he'd seen her crying about their father leaving. "We're handling things. Right, Mom?"

"We've got it under control." Standing, her mother started stacking mismatched pottery bowls, signaling an end to the lunch picnic with a tight smile on her face.

Nathan snorted. "Of course, Lacey McDaniel always manages everything."

Gramps barked, "Nathan, don't sass your mother."

Bo hissed.

"Really, Gramps?" Nathan rolled his eyes. "You pick now of all times to remember my name? Great. Maybe while you're clicking on all cylinders, you could let Sergeant Rambo know how Mom's struggling to pretend everything's normal when it isn't. Or tell him how I almost broke my hand trying to fix the stuck window."

Sierra sunk deeper in her chair while her brother kept right on listing all their recent failures.

"And remember when the pipes burst in the bathroom? Gross. I'm trying to help but I'm still just fifteen freaking years old. There's only so much I can do with duct tape and a staple gun." Nathan leaned forward, all hundred and twelve pounds of scrawny teenage manliness clearly zeroing in for the kill. "Dad wasn't around long enough to teach me much—"

Lacey slammed the eclectic mix of pottery bowls on the table hard enough to halt him midsentence. "Maybe you could stop talking and realize we're not Mike Kowalski's responsibility. Nathan? I mean it. Enough."

"Fine. Whatever. I'll shut up." Nathan scraped back his patio chair and tossed his napkin in the middle of his half-eaten chili. He picked up a king-sized pillowcase and unwrapped his snake from around his neck. He tucked the curled reptile into the pillowcase and knotted the top. "Mom, could you take Bo back inside? I'm going for a walk."

Without waiting for an answer, Nathan dropped the writhing pillowcase in the middle of the table, knocking over his glass of tea and sending ice tumbling out. He popped in his earbuds and sulked toward the woods behind the house, attitude radiating from every slouchy step.

At what age did it stop being okay to walk away from things a person didn't want to deal with?

A hefty breeze whipped at the dog blankets and towels hanging on the clothesline, the *snap, snap, snap* of the fabric echoing like some kind of comic locker-room prank.

The General scratched his temple, his forehead furrowed with confusion and agitation. "I need more hot sauce."

He shot from his seat and fast stepped up the stairs onto the screened porch and into the house.

Lacey abandoned the pile of bowls and started toward her father-in-law. "I should follow Dad. He's confused and he senses the tension. That's never a good combination."

She hurried after her father-in-law, so flustered she even forgot to take the snake. Which left Sierra alone, again, with hot Mike and a bunch of unresolved feelings. Suddenly, the absurdity of her life just hit her like a ton of bricks. Why bother fighting or pretending? Might as well just dive right in.

Sierra picked up the king-sized pillowcase and tightened

the knot on top. "Want a new pet?" She thrust the wriggling bag his way. "We have plenty."

A CHUCKLE STARTED somewhere in the middle of Mike's chest. He'd forgotten about Sierra's great sense of humor. Somehow over time he'd only remembered their arguments—and the sex.

But as he looked at her now with her pillow-cased snake in her fist and a grin crinkling her nose, he recalled so much more. The fun times they'd had on dates, everything from Nashville concerts to partying with friends at the river. She had her father's knack for easing the most awkward moments and bringing out the best in people, putting others' needs first. Just like her dad. Even as the Colonel had died in Mike's arms, Allen had managed to slide a moment of dry humor into his final words.

His good mood deflated.

The scent of explosives and blood overwhelmed him so hard and fast he swallowed down rising bile. He pushed the memories back, but he knew from experience once the lid lifted on those recalled moments they wouldn't stay pushed down for long. He had to get out of here fast.

"Thanks for lunch. You didn't have to include me, but it was good." He stood, fishing in his pocket for his truck keys. "I should head back to the motel and catch a nap. My internal clock's all screwed up from the time change."

"Oh, of course." She inched away. "I appreciate your returning Trooper. His disappearance really scared my mom and me. We spent a lot of time looking so I should probably get moving on the morning chores we never got to. Thank goodness it's Sunday and I don't have classes to attend or teach."

Mike stopped short. "Is there something I can help with?"

"I wasn't hinting. I swear," she said quickly.

"I know. You and your mom are both fiercely independent. I totally get that." Mike scratched the back of his neck, looking around the farmhouse and seeing it with new eyes, especially after what Nathan had just said.

The porch needed a coat of paint. A shutter hung loose. And the weeds in the garden . . . Holy crap, how did weeds get so tall yet the lawn was perfectly mowed? A strange dichotomy he couldn't wrap his brain around.

The Colonel had always talked about how well things were going at home. How strong his wife was. How proud he was of his daughter's grad school grades and graduate assistantship. "Your father didn't know how bad things had gotten around here with repairs . . . and with your grandfather's Alzheimer's, did he?"

"What good would it have done to tell him? Worry can be distracting, and we didn't want to do anything that put him in even greater danger."

Not that it had mattered in the end. "I'm surprised he didn't notice changes with your grandfather when you Skyped."

"We just told him Grandpa hated Skype, which kept their interactions brief. We managed."

He wanted her life to be about more than just managing. She could have moved out with the money from her assistantship, yet she chose to stay here and help with her grandfather. That kind of selflessness was rare.

Mike snagged a strand of her hair that had escaped her ponytail and tucked it behind her ear. Her silken skin tempted his fingers to linger against her. "I mean it when I say call me if you need help with anything around here."

"Of course I will." She never did lie well.

He started to confront her on that when her brother stepped out of the woods and shouted, "She won't ask for help, you know. Not ever."

Sierra scowled and extended her arm with the pillowcase still in her fist. "Nathan, don't forget your snake."

"What?" He stuffed his earbuds back in again. "Can't

hear you." He walked past her without looking as he jogged into the house.

If Mike had thrown around that much bad attitude, his dad would have chewed his ass, not that his dad had been home often. And Allen sure as hell wouldn't have tolerated so much lip from his son, although the Colonel had a quieter way of relaying his displeasure. Silent disappointment. But then would Nathan be this defiant, lashing out at everyone if his father hadn't died?

Mike turned back to Sierra. "Is he okay?"

"Honestly? Who knows with him anymore." Her blue eyes darkened with a mix of sadness and frustration as she set the makeshift serpent sack on the table. "He was difficult before, and he's even tougher to gauge now. Every time I read about one of those teens going postal, I wonder if we should be doing more. Mom has spoken to his teachers and the school counselor. Everyone thinks he just needs time to process his grief."

"With counseling?"

"Maybe."

"You're seriously worried."

"He's a fifteen-year-old boy who just lost his father." She dropped back into the patio chair with a weary sigh. "Hell yes, I'm worried."

"Yet you keep insisting you're okay." He leaned back on the table so he could see her beautiful eyes better. "Why is it all right for him to be hurting but not you?"

"Of course we're all hurting, but I'm an adult." She gripped the arms of the chair. "And this conversation is now moving past my comfort zone."

"Guess I've given up the right to pry," he said with more than a hint of regret. "But I can't stop feeling like I can be of help here."

She shook her head. "My brother was just going for shock value in offering you the studio apartment in the barn."

"Clearly."

"You'll need to find a place of your own now that you're back."

"Actually, there's kind of a problem with that since so many places want long-term leases." He thought about the future, something he tried to avoid when he could. Living in the moment was tough enough when transitioning from over there to back home. "I'll be moving in a couple of months, so I'll probably just stay in the motel."

She bit her lip, and he could see her trying to hold back the urge to ask. And he shouldn't care that she was still conflicted about them, but he did. Even though he'd let her go and knew that was the right decision, he couldn't deny there was still chemistry left between them.

Major understatement.

Truth was, he struggled not to touch her every second they were together. He knew exactly how to kiss her the way she liked best, the when and the where, too. The memories of other times together clouded his brain every time he got near her.

"Moving?" She tipped her head to the side, ponytail trailing over her shoulder. "Where are you going?"

And wasn't that a wake-up call to get his head on straight?

"Fort Bragg. Looks like I'm going to get a Special Forces slot."

Her eyes widened. "Congratulations. You'll be a Green Beret? That's awesome. You deserve to be proud."

Unless the Sergeant Major busted his chops over bringing the dog home and used it as an excuse to take away the slot. He and his boss had never quite seen eye to eye on a lot of things. The fact that he nabbed the opportunity still stunned him. He would have thought for sure the Sergeant Major would have found a way to block it.

Regardless, soon he would be gone, away from Fort Campbell, away from the memories . . . away from Sierra. Would he still think of her every time he caught a whiff of citrus scent?

Unable to stop himself, he tucked her hair behind her ear again even though she must know darn well it wasn't loose this time. He savored the silken feel between his fingers.

"I really should go now." He jammed his hand in his pocket so he didn't keep touching her. "Good-bye, Sierra. Take care of yourself."

His eyes ate her up even if his hands weren't on her.

"You, too. Stay safe." Clouds chased through her sky blue eyes.

Regret for all they'd lost kicked him. Hard.

Angling down, he kissed her forehead and held, her bangs whispery and sweet smelling. Fire burned through him, urging him to haul her up and into his arms. To say to hell with it all and let them enjoy whatever time he had left here. Forget about the past or the future and just immerse themselves in the present.

His kiss ended, but he stayed close, his cheek against her temple. Each breath ruffled her hair. What was wrong with both of them that they couldn't just let each other go, damn it?

The pillowcase on the table started writhing again, bump, bump, bumping along until the bag fell to the ground. Mike jumped back, startled, not sure whether to be grateful or not for the wake-up call from Bo.

Sierra sat rooted and still in that chair for so long he thought she might do something—like pull him back for a real kiss. Or say something—like ask him to stay.

But she didn't.

So finally he backed away, two, three, four steps, then turned toward his truck. He kept his eyes on the ground, focusing on putting one foot in front of the other, boots stirring up dust on the rutted driveway. He hauled himself into the front seat and cranked the key, engine roaring to life. Throwing it into drive, he couldn't tear out of here fast enough. The mile-long driveway felt like it ran twice as long. His shock absorbers took a beating, reminding him of something else the family needed help with—filling potholes.

Sierra loved college life before, living in the dorms, dreaming of getting her own apartment. She'd been saving her money working part-time on campus in the library. And she'd clearly given that up to help her family when her dad's deployment came around. Mike had respected her for that sacrifice. Except now her year of living at home had been extended. For how long?

There were so many things he wanted to say to her, to ask her. But their relationship had been complicated enough when her father was alive. Now that he was gone, the barriers between them felt higher. He wasn't the right man for her. He knew that and it didn't stop him from wanting to finish that kiss they'd barely started. Unable to resist, he took one last look in the rearview mirror—

And saw Trooper in the back of his truck, ears and tongue lolling in the wind.

SIERRA SLAMMED THE front door and sagged back against it, her heart hammering in her ears. Only because she'd run like hell inside rather than watch Mike drive away from her.

Again.

Full nakedness! All joys are due to thee . . . Words of wisdom from a John Donne poem that trotted through her head whenever Mike Kowalski was around. Except that his kiss had made her think of more than full nakedness. It had made her heart hurt with memories of what would never be.

Easing the pillowcase to the floor, she slid down the door to sit on the braided scatter rug. She was tired of saying good-bye to people who never returned. She was through with putting her heart on the line. Her emotions had taken more than their fair share of hits for the year.

For the decade, actually.

The cuckoo clock blared through the house. Her head ached. She willed her heart to slow and her thoughts to gather into a coherent flow. With each even breath in and out, she began to realize something wasn't right. The house was too quiet, other than that damn clock that kept reminding her of a military life with a patchwork of pieces collected from around the world. Every time they moved, her mother had reminded them saying good-bye to friends was a part of the lifestyle. Family mattered most.

She'd gone along like a good little soldier for her whole life, and still, her family had been shattered.

Sierra searched the length of the hall, looking into the empty dining room with a towering birdcage in one corner, then over to the living room with the cats sleeping on the sofa. The television wasn't even on in the family room. She pushed to her feet and headed to the kitchen with Bo. Her brother sat quietly at the table with another bowl of chili, dished up in a *Game of Thrones* trencher she'd given him as a gag gift for Christmas.

She put the snake down in front of Nathan as she looked past her brother into the empty family room. "Where are Mom and Gramps?"

"I thought I was supposed to shut my mouth." He ate a heaping spoonful of chili.

"Quit being a pain in the ass, just for a little while, please. Where are Mom and Gramps?"

"Gramps is taking a nap and Mom is feeding the animals." He chugged half a glass of iced tea.

"Okay, then. Please take Bo and put him back in your room for a while. If Mom comes in, let her know I need a quick shower before I help her feed all the critters." She could catch up on homework before supper.

"Not all of them."

Her brother's calmly spoken words sent premonition dashing up her spine like crawling spiders. "What do you mean?"

Nathan smiled, such a rare event it launched a fresh scuttle of spidery tingles. "Trooper jumped in the back of Mike's truck."

Shit. Shit. Shit!

She didn't even have the luxury of time to be pissed at her brother. She tugged her cell phone out of her pocket just as the doorbell rang. Sierra sprinted out of the kitchen and into the hall, refusing to acknowledge that her heart was thumping faster over the thought that her good-bye to Mike had been delayed a few minutes longer.

She jerked open the front door, and sure enough, there stood Mike with Trooper.

MIKE KNEW THAT before he left this house again, he would have to kiss Sierra.

Maybe that wasn't honorable or smart. But facts were facts. The flush along her cheeks and the sparkle in her eyes as she'd opened the door were real. She'd been glad to see him. For just one instant, someone on this godforsaken planet was happy to have him back home safely. Majorly intoxicating to a man who'd been on a dry spell of anybody caring whether he woke up each morning.

She held up her cell phone. "I was about to call you. Nathan just told me he saw Trooper jump in the back of your truck."

"Sorry I didn't notice right away." The tan and brown mutt leaned against Mike's leg. Mike scratched the top of his head. "He's playing Velcro dog."

"Let's take him to the backyard to play so he'll have more time to get used to the scent of here." She tugged her tank top down, her toes crinkling in her worn sandals, all those awareness twitches that stoked his resolve. "He can play with Clementine."

"Lead the way."

"Sure, just hold a second while I switch into more substantial shoes."

Kneeling by the shoe rack, she ditched her sandals and tugged on red cowboy boots. She stood and angled past, just close enough that the scent of citrus and perspiration hit him

like a drug with reminders of warm, sexy nights of them
tangled up together in the back of his truck or in his bed in
the small apartment he'd rented.

Mike cleared his throat, determined to bide his time.
Anticipation made the payoff all the sweeter. "Did you ever
figure out how he escaped last night? Trooper's quite a
Houdini. He found ways in and out of the FOB not even our
top security knew about."

"Gramps let him out of his crate and Trooper managed
the rest of the escape on his own. Clearly, he's still attached
to you. That's understandable with so much change in life.
It's a lot for any dog to process."

"Maybe if I stick around for a couple of hours, he will
settle in. I could put the time to good use and fix anything
that's broken."

She glanced over her shoulder, her blond ponytail swishing.
"In spite of what my brother says, we've got it under control."

"Of course you do," he said, not bothering to point out
she was walking past a loose shutter that smacked the side
of the house. "Surely there's something I could help out with
to pass the time while Trooper gets his bearings."

Her eyes narrowed suspiciously. "What's really going on
with you?"

"I don't have anything else to do." Except fantasize about
getting her naked again. Although watching her walk in
shorts and cowboy boots was definitely sweet. "I'm at loose
ends for the next few weeks. Mandatory leave after battle
to get my head on straight again before going back to work,
and not even working that much since I'll be moving soon."

"Surely you would rather party with your friends than
fix broken kennel latches here."

"You have broken kennel latches?"

"Damn." She winced. "You tricked me."

He spread his hands wide. "I couldn't have tricked you
if you didn't keep secrets. What else is broken? Throw the
whole list at me. I can take it."

"What's broken? Everything." She half laughed as she opened a gate to a fenced area within their larger property enclosure. "Seriously, just the regular sorts of stuff that you tend to let slide when you're busy and Dad's away. To-do list kinds of items. We've been focused on expanding the rescue. We'll get around to catching up on the other stuff in time."

Serious remodeling had gone on in the past year, especially with the barn, things he hadn't seen when eating in the family's patio area. Some of the horse stalls had been converted into a line of five long kennels that were half inside, half out. The barn doors were open today, and he could see a bigger play area with dog beds and toys.

Outside of the barn, a large part of the yard had been sectioned off into a doggie haven. Fat oak trees sprawled, providing shade for a couple of napping pooches. Plush grass stretched like carpet from edge to edge of the fence, some kind of minor miracle given how many animals must tromp through.

There was a sheltered area over a concrete slab with a baby pool full of fresh water. Trooper took off like a bolt of lightning and charged straight in. Clementine looked up from under the tree then went back to sleep. A couple of older beagle puppies raced over to meet and sniff the new guy on the block.

Sierra watched with perceptive eyes. She had her mother's gift with animals even if she'd chosen a different path for her life.

He looked around at the other changes made to the place. When they'd deployed, Lacey had only just started her animal rescue, fostering a few animals in her house along with the help of three other foster families. The Colonel had shared her plans for expanding. He'd been proud and a little bemused. Allen McDaniel had said that at first it seemed his wife was empty nesting over their kids growing up, but he'd soon realized she was passionate about her rescue work.

And well organized.

It appeared to Mike that only about three animals were in the kenneled areas. He'd seen some younger pups on the porch. The whole place was controlled chaos. He was more than a little surprised. This all had to come with so much work and expense for something he knew from talks with the Colonel didn't bring any income to the family. Lacey managed the Second Chance Ranch Animal Rescue in a purely volunteer capacity. The organization ran off donations.

Sierra blocked his hand before he could reach his fingers into a kennel with a Pomeranian curled up asleep on a pink bed. "Be careful. He bites."

His skin still hummed where she'd touched him.

"Why is he here then?"

"He's detoxing. We won't know what he's really like until his system's clean."

He scrubbed a hand over his beard-stubbled face. "You're going to have to explain that one."

"The family he lived with had a teenage drug user." She leaned back against the barn, one booted foot up. "The dog got hold of a bag of pot and ate a significant portion. The teenager tried to take it back and got bitten in the tug of war. Apparently the teen and his friends had given the dog drugs in the past. They thought it was funny to let the dog get high with them."

"Seriously?"

"Hand to God, it happened. They called Animal Control." The humor left her eyes. "Once a dog has bitten, the shelter's hands are tied when it comes to adopting that animal out. Since this didn't appear to be the dog's fault, the shelter called my mom to see if Second Chance Ranch could take in Lucky . . . That's his official name, even though I think of him as Doobie."

"Doobie." He chuckled. "Cute."

"Yeah, but Mom says Lucky's a more 'marketable' name."

"What happens if Lucky's still a biter afterward?"

Her cheeks expanded with a puff. "We've got a foster

home that rehabs abused dogs, but sometimes the animal is too far gone to ever be safe around people . . . But we're thinking positive for Lucky right now. Okay?"

"Positive thoughts. Got it." He realized in a flash that this place wasn't just a second chance for some animals. It was a last chance. "So all of these animals came from the local shelter?"

"Different shelters in all the surrounding counties. Others came from people who contacted Mom directly. And there are more in foster homes." Her voice was filled with pride . . . and an exhaustion most wouldn't have seen but he couldn't miss. "My mother's role as head of the rescue isn't a paid position. She pours every cent of donations back into the rescue."

"How have you paid your bills since your father died?" He didn't remember the Colonel talking about that aspect, but then they wouldn't have discussed money. "Sorry, that's none of my business."

"It's okay. I have my graduate assistantship. Gramps has his retirement. My mother still teaches through a virtual school online, high school classes year-round, and she's able to work from the house. My living at home and helping with Gramps saves us money, too. We're fine, better off than plenty of people."

Still, all the renovations converting the barn to a rescue facility could have bought a lot of repairs around this place. Did Sierra resent the money that went to animals rather than her education? "You used to dream of moving, getting an efficiency with thrift store refurbished furniture." They'd talked about how she would be able to leave after her father finished this deployment and could help with the General. "You wanted to rent a writer's garret, like that Virginia Woolf, *A Room of One's Own*."

He'd loved listening to her dream out loud. She had a way of painting pictures with words that let him see things differently. She'd once described her ideal space to him, in detail, while he'd messed around on the guitar after love-making. It had been one of the most perfect times they'd ever spent together.

"You remember all of that?" She toyed with her ponytail, her fingers plaiting it into a loose braid.

The glide of her fingers hypnotized him. "I read the book, actually." Along with other novels she'd talked about, as if that somehow kept her close even though he'd been the one to push her away. "I had a lot of time to think when I was deployed. And you are a memorable woman."

Besides, he'd been better served remembering their talks and her words than reliving the other ways they'd spent their time together.

"Thank you," she said simply, avoiding his eyes, and she slipped the band from her ponytail down and twisted it at the end of the braid.

What he wouldn't give to comb a finger down the braid and undo it all again. To sketch a touch along the back of her scalp and angle her for his kiss.

Instead, he grazed his knuckles along her jaw, guiding her face back to look at him. "I didn't mean for anyone to get hurt."

"Nobody ever does." She smiled bittersweetly but didn't pull away from his touch.

Her skin felt every bit as soft as he remembered. The need to be with her fired as hot as ever through him, surging heat south. He wasn't any better at resisting her now than he was a year ago. So he gave her the chance to push him away. "I'm going to kiss you now, Sierra."

"No. You're not."

Disappointment burned. "Why not?"

She slid her hand up to his shoulder. "Because I'm going to kiss you first."

Five

S IERRA ARCHED UP on the tips of her boots and pressed her lips to Mike's.

Pure sensation washed through her in a tingling shower. She wasn't sure why this urge had consumed her since the minute he'd returned. But as she'd raced to that door when Mike came back, then walked with him out here, she realized how little he'd returned to. No family. No welcome home committee. Not even parties with friends. Since he'd stepped off that plane he'd carried around the weight of an incomplete homecoming. She thought of all those homecomings past, of the homecoming he should have had . . . the homecoming they could have had if things had been different between them.

Now, she was no longer able to resist the overwhelming urge to give him a welcome home kiss to end all kisses.

His hands slid from her shoulders up to cradle her face. A sigh melted through her. She leaned into him, her lips parting. She'd ached for this during long nights thinking of him, worrying for him, accepting she'd given up any right to know what happened to him.

She gripped the warm cotton of his T-shirt in tight fists and wished the moment could be held as firmly. The taste of sweet tea and Mike intoxicated her, and she was so glad she'd taken this moment. To hell with worrying about afterward. Right here and now, they both needed this for . . .

Closure?

She cringed at the word and just lost herself in sensation instead. Rational thoughts would have to come later; for now she ached to enjoy this kiss for herself as well.

Her touch confirmed what her eyes had already admired. Mike had worked out while overseas. The muscles of his chest rippled under her fingers. She explored the hardened planes of him, such a mix of familiar and new. The attraction between them had been instantaneous. Combustible. And that certainly hadn't changed.

Sighing, she skimmed her hands up and over his close-shorn hair. Her leg hooked around his with the practiced ease of so many kisses they'd shared in the past. No wonder she hadn't been drawn to anyone else since their breakup. She'd told herself she was too busy. But right now with the taste and scent of him filling her senses, she couldn't escape the truth. No one came close to setting her on fire the way this man did.

She rocked closer, her hips sealed to his in a way that let her know exactly how much he wanted her. The feel of him, right *there*, made her knees go weak. She would have lost her balance if not for Mike's hands anchoring her, his finger splayed over one thigh as he kept her wrapped around him like she was one of Nathan's serpentine pets.

The thought would have made her giggle if she hadn't been so dazed with lust that she was already calculating the distance to the closest bed . . .

Until the sense of being watched startled her, reminding her where they were.

Her hands eased from Mike's shoulders to his bulging arms and she glanced down. Trooper sat at their feet, looking up, his tail swishing back and forth through the dirt. The dog stared up at her with strangely knowing eyes as he really looked at her rather than toward Mike for the first time.

She swallowed hard. Tried to pull herself together as she lowered her foot to the ground and found her balance. Still, the knowledge of how fast things could get out of hand with Mike rattled her.

He eased back, his hand trailing down her arm before he stepped away. "Well, that was unexpected."

No kidding.

She glanced at him quickly, struggling to get her head around what had just happened. "I, uh, wanted to say welcome home."

"I liked it," he said simply, the rough catch of his voice sending a fresh wave of longing through her while her heartbeat still danced like mad.

"Maybe I should have thought that through, but it seemed the right thing to do." She held up her hands. "Not that I expect it to go further. It was a salute to what we had. You deserved more of a homecoming than delivering a dog to this strange family of mine. You deserve to be celebrating."

"I'm exactly where I want to be." He stared straight back at her, intensely.

A shiver tingled through her, tightening her breasts with awareness and yearning. And more than a little regret for what might have been.

"I don't understand what you're saying. You broke things off, and I came to understand the wisdom of that." Kind of. Mostly it just hurt like hell. "You're right that I'm not cut out for a military life. God, that's truer now than it was then—"

Her eyes stung and she blinked fast. Too many emotions were tangling up before she could process them.

His hand fell to rest on her shoulder. "Stop. You don't need to say anything more."

"I'm just emotional, I guess. And confused." And totally wanting to lean her head against his chest. "I can't be with you but I missed you. Every time we packaged up a box of treats and cookies for my dad I thought about the times I sent those same care packages to you whenever you went away for training."

They'd been friends before they'd been lovers. Really, really good friends. She missed him on so many levels.

He smiled. "You do make amazing brownies."

"I wish we could be still friends, but this"—she stroked along his chest—"just isn't a friendship kind of feeling."

The answering pounding of his heart beneath her palm seemed to make a reply all its own.

"And having me around is a painful reminder for your whole family."

She hated the pain that brought to his eyes. She knew he missed her father as well. "My mother never said that, but I worry about her. Taking care of Gramps was tough enough before."

"Have you considered . . . alternative arrangements?"

"You mean putting him in a nursing home?"

"Or assisted living facility or even one of those adult day cares, just to give your family a break."

"I honestly don't know if we can afford it," she admitted reluctantly, "and something in his eyes is still too 'here' for that to feel right."

"There can be a difference between your conscience and what he needs."

"Sounds good in theory." While she knew he had a point, she just couldn't wrap her brain around it. "Mom and I have talked about it. And yes, I've wondered if we're truly doing this for Gramps, to make sure we don't miss a single lucid moment left, or if we're doing this to keep the connection to my father longer. Honest to God, I wish I knew the answer, but I don't. So I just keep putting one foot in front of the other."

The crunch of approaching steps echoed, and she sidled away with a guilty flush. Her brother came around the corner of the barn and she chewed her lip. Damn it, she shouldn't feel self-conscious over talking to Mike, and it wasn't as if she had a sign across her chest that said *We Just Kissed and It Was Amaaaaazing.*

Her brother jogged closer, his oversized clothes rippling with each hop. "Are you two a couple again or just sex buddies?"

Apparently she didn't need to wear a sign.

Mike stepped forward and cut short the need for her to answer. "Did you lose the snake?"

"Nah, just thought I would play with the dog. Ya know, toss the ball and maybe he will want to stick around." Nathan shrugged as if it was no big deal that the nicest words he'd spoken in a year had just fallen out of his mouth. "Dad said in his letters that Trooper likes to play fetch."

Mike nodded. "That's right. Trooper had a whole unit of guys who couldn't wait to get out there to toss around the ball with him. It was a major stress reliever for us."

"Makes sense." Nathan pointed to the covered area. "Mom keeps the dog toys and treats in bins on that table over there."

"Cool, mind if I join you?"

Nathan shrugged again. "Doesn't make any difference to me one way or another."

Sierra rolled her eyes behind her brother's back. Mike winked at her, then jogged toward the covered area. Trooper loped alongside him and Nathan followed more slowly. Clementine stood from her nap under the tree and stretched with interest. Nathan hadn't played with her for a while, and yet her eyes lit with excitement and forgiveness as if Nathan hadn't ignored her for the past year and a half. The beauty of that love made her choke up and want to shake her brother as the old three-legged Labrador galloped across the lawn with a tennis ball in her mouth.

She watched Mike and Nathan pitch balls back and forth to the dogs, the young and old pups leaping in the air as if all was right with the world in this simple moment. As if her life hadn't been turned upside down all over again by a dog.

And a broad-shouldered man who still made her want to forget the reasons he was wrong for her and the fact that he'd rejected her completely and totally.

LACEY SAT IN her small barn office with all her rescue records and cabinets full of supplies, a part in the curtains giving her a narrow but clear view of the dogs' play yard. At first she'd been trapped by not wanting to interrupt her daughter making out with Mike—a surprise. But she'd given up trying to understand her daughter's on-again, off-again relationship with that particular soldier. And quite frankly, watching anything romantic felt like alcohol being poured over a thousand paper cuts.

Was she just being selfish? She wanted her daughter to be happy—God, Sierra had already given up so much to help out here. Still, the thought of life once her daughter left felt so very lonely and overwhelming.

Lacey stroked the cat in her lap, a gorgeous Persian that had been abandoned by a family who didn't feel up to taking their pet with them when they retired to Florida. Thinking of that self-centered couple enjoying their golden years of happily ever after in Miami made her want to scream.

She was a forty-two-year-old widow, who'd spent half her married life alone while her husband traveled the world—saving the world. The future stretched out before her, a barren, sexless wasteland of just her and her vibrator. How pathetic was that?

Biting back the urge to scream out her grief over all she'd lost, she drew in a breath, willing acceptance to fill her. This was just the way life had played out for her. She had to accept who she was and the hand fate had dealt her. Because she sure as hell wasn't planning on trying to go back in time to re-create some magical new happily ever after. Marriage had brought her two precious children. She'd had her shot at love, and her time had been cut short. Her nights were filled with bottle-feeding puppies these days.

The thought of dating again made her nauseated. She still felt married. Even if she didn't, she couldn't envision how she would even go about meeting men. She wasn't into face-lifts, boob jobs or tummy tucks.

It wasn't like the pool to pick from was all that huge, either. Most guys in their forties were married. A man who had never been married and lived alone for a couple of decades would most likely run shrieking in horror from her zoo. Sure, some of the divorced guys might be great fellas, but others were divorced for a reason. And the baggage? Good God, she understood all about baggage.

Her cell phone chimed on the small desk. She checked the screen to make sure it wasn't one of the "Shut Down the Ranch" brigade ready to harass her again.

She recognized the number of a shelter in the next county over and thumbed the answer button just as the ringing stopped. Damn. She was off her game this week, so sluggish she could have been walking through peanut butter.

The sound of voices and laughter and barking outside were all too energetic for her right now. She needed a few more minutes to level out.

She had a full life and she needed to get to it. She had animals to save and people counting on her. Since she wasn't ready to face whatever romance was happening between Sierra and Mike—or any couple for that matter—Lacey punched in her voice mail code.

The shelter's kennel supervisor's voice came through, loud barking in the background. "Lacey, we just got a litter of three shih tzu puppies, nine weeks old, from a backyard breeder. We just don't have the room . . . and they have parvo. Please say you have a foster home that can take them.

We'll help with the meds . . . Call me before the end of the day. We can't keep them in isolation any longer than that."

A parvovirus through a shelter would be beyond horrible, costing so many lives. Too many shelters didn't have any choice but to euthanize in that situation . . . Her mind was already running through foster homes affiliated with her rescue, and if she was very lucky, Jill could take them, seventy-one and a retired vet tech who could quarantine and watch them twenty-four/seven. She also understood the sanitizing needed to keep the extremely contagious virus from spreading. It had to happen.

Lacey sent a quick text to Jill, pleading, then moved on to the next voice mail.

Next message . . . Her neighbor to the right, Sam Hershberger. "Have you seen that advertisement for land up county? I can forward you the listing. It would save us all a lot of trouble not to turn this into a confronta—"

Lacey sighed and hit delete. Sam would ramble on, and he would be polite in a veiled way, but his bottom line was the same as cranky Valerie's, her neighbor on the other side. They both wanted her and her rescue gone.

Next message. An automated reminder about the council meeting. Great. Even if she moved, someone else would have a complaint.

Even if she wanted to relocate, it would take weeks, months even, and that time lost would cost so many lives of animals she wouldn't be able to save. The Internet and e-mailed pictures of so many animals in need haunted her. She accepted that she couldn't save them all. Financially, emotionally or physically.

Too easily the line between rescuer and hoarder could be crossed by those who weren't able to recognize their own limitations. Her heart ached, too, for the shelter workers who didn't have the option of saying no because they were full. The shelters got demonized unfairly when the irresponsible pet owners were the ones to blame.

One battle at a time . . .

She took the next message, one from her vet. Not just his clinic, but him personally, Dr. Ramon Vega. She frowned. Something wrong with one of the fosters? She clicked through to the message.

A deep voice vibrated through with a clipped, "Lacey, call me."

Her stomach clenched. What could be so important? She owed him so much literally and figuratively. She had an unpaid bill that was already given at such cut-rate prices she knew he only covered office expenses with what he charged her, and given he was so fresh out of veterinary school, he must have massive college debt of his own. Had she pushed too hard? Asked for too much generosity and flexibility? If so, where else could she go with her rescues?

She thumbed redial. Two ringtones in . . .

"Lacey," he answered, "thanks for getting back to me so fast."

"Hey, what do you need?" She hugged her knees to her chest, phone on speaker.

"I've got a six-month-old German shepherd puppy here with a broken pelvis. She was dropped off by people who called our emergency line and said they 'found' her on the side of the road, but from the way their kid was crying and calling the dog by name . . . You can guess the real story."

The puppy was theirs, got hit by a car and they didn't want to pay an expensive vet bill. Still, she had to be sure. "No microchip to trace to them for Animal Control to at least record their abandonment?"

"Really? You have to ask?" He chuckled softly. "You know me better than that."

"Of course you've checked. No chip."

"Correct. The shelter is full, and their foster homes are full. They have to hold strays for five days regardless. The director and I talked through a deal. I'll do the surgery at a cut rate for them. They'll post the pup's photo on their lost and found, even though we all know nobody's coming for the dog. If on the off chance someone shows up and can prove the puppy is theirs, then I'll eat the surgery fee if they won't pay."

Sounded like a win-win. But there must be more if he was calling her. "And the catch is?"

"I've got nowhere here to stash her after the surgery for five days since I have so many super sick, freeloading boarders from a certain favorite rescue of mine."

She smiled at the phone, already knowing the answer. "At the end of the five days when no one claims the pup?"

"You'll have an incredibly adorable German shepherd puppy to adopt out." His office chair squeaked, and she could almost see him sitting upright again, boots off the desk as he went serious. "Hey, you know I wouldn't ask if I could figure any other way."

"You don't even have to ask. I'll make it work."

"Thanks, Lacey, you're the best." He paused without hanging up. "You're coming in with the Iraq dog tomorrow, right?"

"Of course. He needs a checkup and the neuter. No food or water after midnight. I know the drill," she said lightly, taking comfort in routine.

"You okay with him being there? This has to be . . . uh, pretty emotional."

The personal question caught her off guard coming from Ray. This was way out of their routine. She struggled for a way to answer that wouldn't have her bursting into tears.

The roar of a couple of four-wheelers approaching outside offered her a welcome distraction, even if the distraction happened to be the frustrating kind in the form of her cranky neighbors. "Doc, sorry to cut this short, but I need to run. Someone's, uh, at the door. I'll pick up the puppy when I bring Trooper tomorrow. Bye, now."

She pressed the off button, knowing she'd only traded one difficult situation for another. But leaving the question unanswered might make it go away.

And experience told her the duo outside wouldn't leave without direct confrontation.

AFTER A YEAR in the Middle East, Mike could sense confrontation crackling in the air, and from the second he'd seen Sierra go on alert at the approaching four-wheelers, he knew they were trouble.

The mother and son from next door. Mama looked pissed. And the son? His eyes raked over Sierra a second longer than normal.

Mike glanced at Nathan. The kid usually wore that disinterested slouch, but even he was bristling like an angry dog. Mike cleared his head—easier said than done since Sierra's kiss had knocked him on his ass. But something was wrong here. He vaguely remembered these folks from before, but they'd kept to themselves. Apparently not anymore. These neighbors were not on good terms by a long shot.

He couldn't pin the woman's age; her anger and sun-weathered skin shouted tough living. Her brightly died red hair didn't soften the image much, either. There was a "don't mess with me" edge to her that reminded him of his grandmother.

The son, on the other hand, was pretty-boy country. A little too slick and a little too old to still be living with mama.

Or maybe he was just being judgmental because he didn't want some other guy staring at Sierra that way when ten minutes ago she'd been his again, with a welcome home kiss to beat all others. Damn it, life shouldn't be this complicated, and damn it again, there he went thinking about Sierra instead of the menacing look on the woman's face.

The duo drove their four-wheelers at full speed right up to the second they stopped, leaving the grass pushed down and rutted as if to mark their arrival. He stepped between Sierra and the couple.

Sierra rested a hand on his arm and smiled tightly. "Mike,

you remember Valerie Hammond and her son, Kenneth. They're our neighbors to the left."

"Yes, of course. Hello, ma'am."

Valerie didn't smile back, just stayed perched on her vehicle. "You're the one who brought another dog to this place."

"Yes, ma'am. I did."

"A wild dog." Her lips pressed together in a thin line.

Nathan tossed a tennis ball in the air again and again. "Maybe we should teach them all to moo like cows since apparently farm animals to slaughter are cool by you but saving a life presents a problem."

Valerie leaned over the handlebars. "Are you one of those vegans now?"

Nathan kept right on tossing without missing a beat. "Are you some psycho stalker watching us with a telescope at night?"

"Nathan." Mike placed a hand on his shoulder. "I've got this."

Lacey McDaniel stepped out of the barn, tucking her cell phone into her jeans pocket. "Valerie," she called, "if you have a complaint, bring it to me, please."

"Why do you think I'm here? There's a hole in the fence and I don't want any more of your animals bringing God only knows what diseases into my yard. Now with that wild dog you've brought here—"

"Of course we'll make repairs right away, and Trooper is current on all vaccinations."

Sierra crossed her arms over her chest. "That wild dog is the one rolling around in the grass scratching his back."

Sure enough, Trooper was flopping around under a fat oak doing his best goofy-ass-dog act. Kinda strange since he was usually wary of threats. Maybe that meant this Valerie woman wasn't as menacing as she liked to put on.

Mike thought of all the times Trooper had saved their lives, warning them of approaching enemies. He'd never come close to biting anyone, but he could be damn intimidating. Thank God he seemed to somehow sense now wasn't a good time to scare off the trespassers.

"The fence?" Lacey pressed. "Kenneth, how about you show me the breach."

Finally, Valerie nodded to her son and he hopped down to join Lacey, walking alongside her to the fence. Mike exchanged a glance with Nathan, and without hesitation the teen followed them. Apparently the old Nathan was still in there alive and kicking. Good kid. Clementine loped along on three legs after them.

Valerie leaned toward Mike and whispered, "I know what you're trying to do here."

"By all means enlighten me. I'm still playing catch-up," he whispered right back with a grin. "I've been busy the past few months weaving a blanket of freedom for you to sleep under."

The woman jerked back, folding her arms over her chest. "No need to be smug with the whole war hero act."

Sierra hissed like Nathan's snake. "Last time I checked, the roadside bomb that killed my father and nearly killed Mike wasn't an act."

Valerie didn't even wince this time. "We've all lost someone around here, but you don't see me trotting out my problems. Lacey took in that wild dog to stir up a bunch of sympathy over being a war widow. You think the county council will feel sorry for you all rather than listen to reason and shut this place down."

Mike frowned, confused as hell. "County council?"

Sierra bristled, and until that moment he'd forgotten how damn fiery his Tinker Bell could get.

His?

Sierra stared down the battle-ax without flinching. "Only a crass, heartless human being would insinuate my mother is playing on the fact that my father was blown up in order to gain sympathy—or make money. Do you fully comprehend that? My father is dead."

She spit out the word so bitterly Mike fought the urge to haul her to him and comfort her. But Sierra was clearly having none of that. Her fists were clenched at her side as she said her piece.

"And my father didn't die in some gentle passing in his sleep. It was violent and ugly and he made that sacrifice so that even a horrible person like you would have that blanket of freedom to say whatever the hell rude thing you please in front of the county council."

Valerie shook her head. "Dear, I am very sorry about your father. But you're proving my point with making this emotional when it's a practical issue. This place and the disruption it causes are all facts. More facts? You have loud, dangerous animals living next door to me. Look at the place. It's not a ranch or even a farm, just a run-down eyesore full of smelly dogs."

Sierra's anger seemed to deflate in defeat. She sighed wearily. "You've made your point, Mrs. Hammond. We're fixing the fence. You can feel free to go home now, safe from our smelly dogs."

"My son's not back." Valerie shifted her attention to Mike. "Why are you still here anyway, hero boy? You've delivered the dog. Now you can go back to your blanket weaving."

"Leave? You've misunderstood. I'm not going anywhere." As soon as the words fell out of his mouth, he knew they were true. Nathan and Gramps might both be halfway off the rails, but even they could see this place needed help in more ways than one. And watching vibrant Sierra slump under the weight of this mean-ass woman's tirade stirred something in him.

Valerie's eyes narrowed. "I'm not sure I understand you. Are you two shacking up?"

Shacking up? Who still said stuff like that? Trooper flipped from his back and trotted over, stopping beside Mike. The woman's red dyed hair damn near stood up on end.

Mike's hand fell to rest on Trooper's head and scratched between the dog's ears.

"You have nothing to worry about, ma'am. No more broken fences or worries about wild dogs. The McDaniel family has a handyman moving into their loft apartment." He moved in closer, standing square in front of her four-wheeler with Trooper beside him step for step. "A war hero the whole town is sure to be impressed with."

"And who would that be?"

"Me, of course."

Before the woman could answer, Trooper lifted a leg and peed on her front tire.

I COULD SMELL victory, a lot like the magnificent scent of a sweaty sandal or a burned hot dog.

Or marking a bitch's tire.

Do you know one of the coolest things about being a dog? I can call someone a bitch and it's politically correct, since technically, a bitch is a female.

Although that demon woman on her beast mobile was scary. Her beta son liked to play as if he was all full of himself, but he was scared of her, too. I could smell the angry stink getting worse mighty fast. Trying to charm her by playing it low-key and cute rubbing my back on the grass hadn't worked. People usually lapped that stuff up. But this lady wasn't having any of it. I figured she was a cat person and left it at that. Hindsight, that was a mistake on my part.

But let's get back to the feeling of victory. Sorry to digress. I'm a dog. We're easily distracted. Squirrels. Hot dogs. Birds. Garbage trucks. You get the picture.

In spite of the cranky bitch on the monster machine, my primary mission was well on track. Mike was moving in with the McDaniel family. He'd finally gotten the message after I chased him down twice. That first trek to the motel was long with lots of sniffing to find him. My paws took a serious beating in the woods and then dodging cars.

Not that I had to worry about getting caught. These people were amateurs compared to threats I evaded in Iraq. We can talk about that more later. I hope you appreciate how hard I'm working to stay on topic here.

The last time I chased down Mike was easier. I just hopped in the back of his truck and whammo. They got the message. He was living with the McDaniel family. He was sticking around to help.

My mission should be complete. The Colonel would be happy his family was looked after. But things didn't feel settled yet. We dogs are all about sensing. You people would do well to trust your instincts more often and quit relying so much on things. Things were flawed. Breakable.

Instincts were natural. And my instincts were shouting at me loud and clear.

I didn't like that Mrs. Hammond much. She smelled like cabbage. I prefered the smell of hot dogs. But whatever. I knew in my gut that woman was out to cause trouble for Lacey.

There were so many people around here to figure out, it made me a little itchy at times, learning lots of new smells and routines and all the rules, rules, rules. These people lived by their clocks and rules. They were so uptight they couldn't appreciate the simple pleasures in life. Like rolling in the grass. Sleeping on a warm blanket. Sniffing a fragrant butt.

The people here were confusing. They really had me resisting the urge to chew my tail in frustration over all the conflicting signals. Gramps made me sad, but I knew what to do even when he lost his way or thoughts. Half the time he believed I was his old dog Trooper who had already gone to the Rainbow Bridge where critters wait for their people so they can walk together to meet the Big Master. The Colonel would go there in his mind sometimes and play fetch with the other Trooper. But I didn't think he would cross over the rest of the way until his family was okay.

And they were definitely not okay.

Sierra was sad and mad—and even if nobody else could smell it, I knew she was totally sexed up for Mike. I restrained myself from humping her leg, though, out of respect for the Colonel.

Lacey was tired and really needed a week at a spa, but instead she stayed busy so she wouldn't cry. I could smell the salt of those tears she held back, along with the scent of alcohol she managed to hide from everyone else. So far she'd kept her drinking to nighttime, but I was watching her. She needed a friend. I would work on that.

Nathan worried me most in those days. He smelled like death. The kind of smell when somebody had given up on life. I had more experience than most dogs in recognizing that stink from my time back home overseas. Soldiers got that smell right before they decided to eat a gun or step into the line of fire on purpose. When I was playing ball with Nathan and Mike, every time I picked up the ball after the kid threw it, I caught a whiff of him on it and I knew. The boy was in trouble.

One step at a time, though. I'd only been here a couple of days and I'd accomplished a lot. I would lie low, go slow and steady. I had my people all together. Life was chill for now, playing fetch, meeting new dogs that didn't fight me for food, and landing a clean, fluffy place to sleep.

There were even car rides. After the bitch and her beta boy left, Lacey told me we were going on a trip tomorrow. I figured that would be a good time to work on her friend problem.

All was on target. Except for a tiny language barrier I hadn't foreseen. When the guys overseas talked about vets, they meant military veterans. So I was completely unprepared for what awaited me when Lacey said we were taking a ride to see her pal Ray Vega—the vet.

PART 2

No one told me that coming to the United
Steaks of America meant I had to give up my
balls . . . and I don't mean the tennis kind.

—TROOPER, NEUTER DAY

Six

"SORRY I'M LATE, Mary Hannah." Sierra thrust her hands into her hair and dropped into a deep chair in the university writing lab by her best friend. "I had to drop off Trooper at the vet this morning. Mom had a crisis with a litter of bottle-fed puppies, so she couldn't take Trooper to get neutered. I don't know how many more balls my family can juggle—so to speak."

Mary Hannah Gallo hiccupped on a laugh, her sense of humor more rowdy than her buttoned-up appearance would indicate. She perched on the edge of her seat with an iPad in her lap, sweater set and pencil skirt coordinated with her green and blue paisley satchel—which also happened to match her iPad cover.

Mary Hannah was so organized it could be annoying, except for the fact she had one of the biggest hearts ever. She was getting her master's in Social Work, returning to college after her divorce from a man she only talked about if she had two glasses of wine, which seldom happened. "I'm sorry to hear about the puppies, hon. And about having the extra carpool duties, but that's nothing new around your house. What's got you so stressed today?" She passed a tin of breath mints. "Have one. They're stress mints. Completely homeopathic."

Sierra knew better than to argue and popped a "stress mint" into her mouth—which just tasted like peppermint to her, but whatever. She leaned in so none of the other grad assistants in the lab full of tables and computers would overhear. "In answer to your question, it's Mike again."

"Mike Kowalski?" Mary Hannah angled closer, her shoulder-length bobbed black hair gliding in silky sync. "As in your ex-boyfriend? The hottie soldier, Mike? Heartbreaker Mike? What's he done now? I'll kick his butt if he's hurt you again."

Kick his butt how? By pounding him over the head with her paisley binder? Sierra suppressed a smile. Then remembered the reason for her splitting headache. "He's moving into my apartment."

Mary Hannah frowned in confusion. "You two are moving in together? I knew there was still chemistry, but wow, that was fast."

A brief vision of unlimited sex with Mike flashed through her mind, a futile thought. "Not together. He's moving into my apartment and I'm staying in my house. I'm a twenty-three-year-old still living with my mother." She made an L with her pointer finger and thumb and thumped her forehead.

Mary Hannah pulled Sierra's arm down. "You're helping your mom," she said, using her oh-so-reasonable counselor voice. "She wouldn't be able to keep your grandfather at home without you."

"Intellectually, I know that's true . . ." Just some days selfish humanity interfered with her intellect.

"How did he end up taking your apartment?"

"Nathan blabbed about all the broken things in the house, and Gramps was, well, Gramps. So somehow Mike is staying in the barn's studio apartment helping us out for a while. It's really generous of him, actually." She shook off the self-pity and tried to push the conversation back on lighter ground. "I only wish I was half as organized as you are about life." She tugged the iPad from her pal. "How far into the future have you planned?"

"Say the word and you, too, can be set up with a matching organizer and lunch bag." Mary Hannah tipped her head to the side. "I'm thinking pink and purple floral would suit you best. If I toss in a matching lanyard, we can work in a mono-grammed saying. Maybe a Sigmund Freud quote like, 'Time spent with cats is never wasted.' Or if you're set on a literary approach, 'I dwell in possibility' would be appropriate." She winked.

Sierra laughed along with her. "Hmm . . . gotta appreciate the Emily Dickinson approach to life even if I'm not sure I'm dwelling anywhere near possibility these days." She shook her head. "I've missed talking to you."

"You need a girls' night out when you can find a breather from juggling all those balls. And speaking of balls again . . ." She crinkled her nose, tucking the stress mints back into her bag. "How's Mike, really?"

She choked on her answer. "Excuse me?"

"I was trying to lighten the mood before asking you something heavy. Guess my humor needs . . . fine-tuning."

"Oh, your meaning came across just fine. I was just surprised."

"Thank you. So, how's Mike handling the return from his deployment? You were really worried about him going again—before you two broke up."

So much for lighter conversation. "Mike's been helpful. He took care of cranky Mrs. Hammond, totally epic and so welcome."

But then there was that kiss . . . so good and so complicated. She still hadn't figured out how things had accelerated so fast. She wanted to blame her mess of tangled emotions, but she knew it was about more than that. That attraction wasn't going away.

Mary Hannah's perceptive eyes narrowed. "I saw the photos in the paper and all over the Internet of that home-coming. I saw the way you two looked at each other."

"Photos? What photos? I don't know what you mean." The media had taken a few group photos along with some close-ups of the dog.

"Seriously? You haven't been Googling yourself?" Mary Hannah snatched her iPad back and started tapping an Inter-net search.

"I barely have time to sleep and pee, much less Google myself. Hey wait, you Google yourself?"

"I'm OCD." Mary Hannah waved aside the question. "Of course I Google myself and my friends. And my enemies, for that matter, because you never know when—"

"You have too much time on your hands."

"I'm organized, and I never sleep. But you're not going to divert me." She tapped along the iPad. "The media was all over those deep, meaningful looks the two of you exchanged when he got home."

Mary Hannah held up an enlarged photo of Sierra with her hand in Mike's as he'd helped her to her feet after Trooper flattened her. No question, her heart was in her eyes. The steam between them all but smoked from the screen. With each image that Mary Hannah scrolled through—and there were a lot—the attraction crackled. The cameras had homed in on the connection between her and Mike, with romantic captions.

No question, it made for good news.

"The coverage is more extensive than I expected." She'd seen people whispering and pointing when she'd stepped on campus today, but she'd just chalked it up to media footage about the dog's arrival. "My father would be glad to know Trooper stirred up so much attention and support for other animals."

Mary Hannah smacked closed her iPad cover. "That's a nice speech."

Her OCD friend was far too perceptive.

"Don't you have papers to grade? Or patients to counsel?" Mary Hannah was a grad assistant, too, teaching intro to psychology classes as well as pulling time seeing clients in the counseling center.

"I have nothing more to do than talk to you." Her friend tucked her paisley-covered iPad into the matching bag.

"That's right. As the most organized human on the planet, you have plenty of spare time."

Her brown eyes sparkled with self-deprecating humor. "Life is better with a calendar app."

Sierra slouched in her seat, tugging the hem of her simple khaki skirt that she'd worn with a white button-down shirt. She tried to keep it simple for teaching, hair back, canvas slip-on shoes, minimal makeup and hard-hitting academics. She was younger than a quarter of her students but she knew her stuff. "My life doesn't respect calendars and schedules."

"Not into florals? Okay, I can deal with that. How about yoga? There's a hot yoga class in an hour at a place near campus. I'll loan you something to wear—"

"Hot yoga? Like I'm supposed to put on skimpy thong workout clothes?"

"No, my silly, overworked friend who's so living in a cave. You don't know about hot yoga? It's yoga done in a steaming hot and humid room to increase flexibility, made to simulate the conditions of yoga in India." She struck a pose and bowed. "We'll sweat out the stress."

Sierra would sweat and stretch plenty hosing out kennels and chasing down Gramps when he wandered off again. "Thanks. Sounds like . . . uh . . ." Hell? ". . . fun. But I need to finish this last batch of tests."

"Your mom can make do without you for a little while . . . unless there's another reason you're rushing home."

Sierra ignored the implication. "Trooper will need extra watching after his surgery today to make sure he doesn't run off again and injure himself."

"Put him in one of those cones."

The image had her grinning, but not for long. "This dog escapes our fence and hides in the back of trucks. I think he can beat an Elizabethan collar. My dad should have named him Havoc." She gathered up her papers and stuffed them into her canvas shoulder bag. "On second thought, I'll grade the papers while I'm hanging out with Trooper—aka Havoc."

Mary Hannah squeezed her wrist lightly. "I'm really so sorry about the apartment. I know you were looking forward to having that space for yourself."

She shrugged. No use ruminating over what she couldn't change. "The money will help out—Mike insists on paying even though he's helping with repairs until he moves."

"Whoa, whoa, sit back down." She tugged Sierra's wrist. "He's leaving soon? You left out that part. So if you need the money and help, why take in Mike when he will be leaving soon? Why not take in someone more long-term?"

"Trooper kept running away to be with him. We do have broken stuff all over everywhere that would break the bank if we had to call repairmen for each problem. And he gave up his apartment while he was deployed. But since he's already got an assignment to move, he would have been sleeping on a friend's sofa or in a motel—"

"Yada, yada, yada. Lots of talking and justifying usually covers something else. Please, Lord, don't say you're back together with him."

"I'm not," she said too fast.

"You still have a thing for him if those photos are anything to judge by. I would bet money you've already kissed him? More?" She tapped Sierra on the forehead. "Not smart."

"Not more." She swiped away her friend's hand. Best

friends were a blessing—and sometimes a curse since they knew you too well. "Why do you dislike him so much?"

"Why are you kissing him again after he stomped on your heart?"

"You are nosy and relentless. Quit using those counselor superpowers to peek into my psyche." Sierra caved. "It was just one kiss. That's it. Sort of a welcome home kind of kiss. He doesn't have anyone." And that still tugged at her emotions in spite of everything.

"I call bull, but whatever. I'm just worried that he's still in the military with no signs of plans to get out. That has to be tough for you, given what happened with your dad."

Sierra knew the concern was genuine, and that meant a lot. Friends were a gift. She wouldn't have made it through the past few months without someone to talk to, unload, not worry about being strong. She leaned in and hugged Mary Hannah hard and fast. "You know I love you, dear friend."

"Love you, too." Mary Hannah hugged her back, then stared at her with those super serious eyes behind black-rimmed glasses. "Just guard your heart around him this time, okay?"

"Of course," she promised, wishing she could feel as confident as she sounded of her ability to keep her head clear around Mike Kowalski.

LACEY SHIFTED THE old Suburban into park outside the Friendship Veterinary Clinic, right beside a truck in the spot with a sign declaring *Veterinarian Parking Only. Violators Will Be Checked for Worms.* Dr. Vega was fresh out of vet school, still full of frat boy humor and optimism that he could change the world. In time he would learn like the rest of them that they could barely make a dent in the endless flow of unwanted animals. But with that resignation came a fresh determination never to give up.

She hefted up the plastic dog carrier with the motherless

pit puppies inside. Three were healthy. For now. Two were struggling—Pinocchio and Thumbelina. She should have known better than to be so whimsical as to think that a fairy-tale name could somehow inoculate them. She just hoped Doc Vega would have something stronger to offer them.

Sunlight stung her gritty eyes. She'd barely managed to take a quick shower before pulling on jeans and one of her son's black concert T-shirts. All the more ironic since she could only find an old pair of red heels to wear. The stilettos click, click, clicked toward a simple brown-brick building wedged between a gas station and a thrift store. The sign out front blinked the slogan of the month: *Wednesdays, No Hump Day, 20% off Spay/Neuters*. She had other animals to check on. A neglected poodle that had seven teeth pulled, now groomed and on meds for a skin infection with a foster mom due to pick him up today. A Chihuahua and two cats being boarded until she could find foster families because her own house was packed to the gills. The German shep-herd puppy would be ready for a foster home tomorrow.

And of course, she had Trooper.

Her bill was skyrocketing even with the deep discounts. Saving lives had become an almost frenetic mission for her now in an effort to keep ghosts at bay. Self-awareness didn't always help change the behavior.

Heavy crate thumping against her leg, she pushed open the front door, chimes launching fresh waves of barks in the waiting area.

The new receptionist was all of twelve—okay, probably twenty-five, but sheesh, she was perky in every sense of the word from her scrubs with cartoon puppies and kittens on them to her golden-tipped pixie haircut. She had the slim kind of body that said she hadn't pushed out a baby yet.

And when had she started feeling petty?

Uhm, since looking at crow's-feet in the mirror this morn-ing and realizing that her underwear had seen far better days.

"Trooper's already in a room waiting for you," the new girl squeaked.

Lacey forced a smile on her face and thrust out her hand. "I'm Lacey from the Second Chance Ranch Rescue. I heard you were starting at the clinic this week, but we haven't met yet. We'll be seeing a lot of each other."

"That's what I hear. I'm Maisie."

"Glad to meet you, Maisie." She was trying. Truly. "Sorry to be running late." Perpetually.

"No problem, Mrs. McDaniel." Maisie said it as if Lacey was ready to apply for senior benefits. "The poor pup's still pretty much out of it. Here's Trooper's cone. He will need to wear it for at least a week to make sure he doesn't lick or chew his incision."

Lacey took the plastic cone, still flat for now. She would thread Trooper's collar through it later. She tucked the plastic under her arm. "I know the drill."

"Yes, ma'am, I hear you do."

"I really need to get these puppies seen if you could show me on into the room?"

"Sure thing, right. Just this way." She pushed open a door into an exam room. "I'll go tell Dr. Vega you're here."

Maisie's featherweight voice kicked up a notch higher when she mentioned the vet's name, her cheeks blushing pink like a freshman with a crush on the professor.

Lacey tried hard not to roll her eyes. Bad enough the attraction between Sierra and Mike announced itself every time they were in the same room together. Lacey did not need any more pheromones added to her day.

Grateful for the escape of the exam room, she found Trooper curled up in a dog bed in the corner, and he looked peacefully drugged. She let out a sigh of relief. She'd known he would be fine. But still. She knelt to trail a hand along his bristly fur before standing. She hefted up the carrier full of mewling puppies onto the gleaming silver exam table.

Senior vet tech Ghita walked inside and with a quick smile, reached into the carrier, pulling pups out one at a time.

Lacey liked Ghita, a farmwife who had a sense for the animals as good as any vet. She was all business, too, no wasting time, but there for the animals. She wore simple blue scrubs. The only hint to her outside life came from the occasional flash of tattoos, one featuring a prime-time vampire show hero and the other a family tree with her grandchildren's names. They didn't have to make small talk. They just got work done. Puppies weighed. Temperatures checked. Fecal samples taken. Updates given on other Second Chance patients.

The door opened again quickly and the vet stepped through. The newest vet, the one who worked with her most often. Dr. Vega had joined the practice eighteen months ago.

The two senior vets said their contribution was allowing their space to be used. Dr. Vega took charge of the actual care since he wasn't a partner in the practice—in spite of the fact that he wore a T-shirt that declared *Top Dog*. She could see the appeal for Maisie, even if the girl was too young for him in more than just years.

"Lacey, your poodle's already been picked up by the foster mama and you . . . look like you need a nap, lady."

And didn't that bring her back to reality? She shook her head. "Charming. Your bedside manner may work on the canines, but I'm seriously underwhelmed."

"Truthful. And concerned. Who's gonna keep me busy here if you collapse?"

"Like you need my deeply discounted business? Really." She tucked a straggly hair back up into the loose scrunchie, oddly self-conscious after seeing Maisie prance around in her pristine scrubs. "Speaking of my discounted customers . . ."

She needed to focus on the dogs now that she'd started this weird train of thought about the doc. It was not fair that after a day of work he looked like a young Sam Shepard with his craggy-faced appeal. In the winter, he wore a long black duster and an ebony felt cowboy hat. Although the coat was missing today due to the heat, he rested his hat on top of the medicine cabinet. And suddenly she realized she was drooling over him like . . . like a . . . Maisie. What the hell had gotten into her?

Maybe it was her raw emotions. Or seeing her daughter and Mike together with all that young chemistry crackling, reminding her of everything she'd lost. Her mind and body were in such a time warp. Her grief over losing her husband was only four months old. But he'd been gone for a year. Physically, she'd been alone for a year.

And even knowing all of that, she couldn't stop her eyes from lingering on the vet. He was too young for her. So why was she feeling cranky?

Perhaps because a couple of times she'd gotten the impression Dr. Vega was attracted to her—heaven only knew why since she usually looked like death warmed over and dragged through the mud when she came here. She wasn't in the market for a relationship, and she knew his interest was more of just the light flirting variety. Nothing that would survive the harsh lights on her naked body.

And since when had she gotten insecure about her body? Maybe more just used to knowing that when her husband saw her naked, she knew he envisioned the eighteen-year-old her. Or at least remembered.

She swallowed down those memories fast and focused on the present.

Dr. Vega knelt beside the dog bed, stroking the groggy dog before checking the incision. "Be good now, Trooper boy. You're a lucky dog. And famous, too."

"At least he's too loopy to slip away now." All the same, she clipped a leash on Trooper just in case he decided to make a mad dash for freedom again. At least now when the dog ran to Mike Kowalski, he would be running back to her house.

She felt guilty as hell over taking him up on the offer. Sierra had lost her loft. Mike had lost his vacation. She wasn't even sure what it meant for Sierra and Mike as a couple. Yet somehow she found herself falling in line with the idea. Mike would clear the to-fix list and have a place to stay for his month's leave. Things would be in good repair before the council meeting. The timing was perfect, and she had too many people and animals counting on her to fail. This was her only solution, a real godsend, actually.

She would make it up to her daughter somehow.

Dr. Vega glanced over at her. "Trooper's run away?"

"A couple of times, actually. He's a bit of an escape artist. I'm surprised Sierra didn't mention that this morning when she dropped him off. It seems surreal that he's finally here."

"You told me your husband always intended to bring him home."

"I wish he could have kept all his promises." She winced, tugging the long strap on her overfilled canvas bag. "I didn't mean to say that. I'm just tired."

"Not sleeping well or too busy?"

"Just busy. Bottle-feeding puppies is like having a baby again. Which reminds me." Her hand landed on the carrier. "I need you to check these little ones. Ghita took their stats. They don't have a fever, but something feels . . . off. I know that isn't scientific . . ."

"I've learned to trust your instincts." He stood, peering into the dog crate and pulling out the puppies, one at a time, in a big, calloused hand. He stared into their eyes, talking while he assessed them. "You're taking on too much. There are other volunteers, even other rescues who can help—"

"With five pit bull puppies? Maybe if I put little fuzzy coats on them so they look like poodles." She elbowed him. "Come on. Laugh. That's rescue humor."

"I'm genuinely concerned." His eyes searched hers. "For them and you. You're no good to anyone if you burn out."

She tried not to let it sway her to hear someone care about her needs. "Rest?" She made a weak attempt at a joke. "If you're trying to get rid of me just say so."

He clasped a hand on her shoulder. "Lacey, you know that's not true."

His warm, strong grip sent a tingle through her that had nothing to do with comfort. She stood still for a second, stunned at the unexpected—there was no other word for it—sizzle. She was not ready for this.

And she definitely couldn't handle the confusing mix of guilt and attraction that made her recall how long it had been since she'd been touched by a man.

Lacey stepped back carefully, needing distance from feelings she was completely ill prepared to face, not now, too soon. Too much. "Truly, Ray, have I overstayed my welcome? I can clear half the bill today and will settle the rest next week."

He eyed her for a lengthy moment before lifting out the next squirming puppy. "Another online auction of something from your home?" He put his stethoscope to the pup's chest. "I vow if you auction off the cuckoo clock, I'm going to start a protest march."

"No chance of that. Trooper may eat the clock first anyway. He's already tried to attack the bird twice."

Laughing, the doc shifted his focus to the stethoscope. She stayed quiet while he listened to Thumbelina's chest, and yes, that gave her a welcome moment to gather her scrambled thoughts. How had he remembered about the cuckoo clock in her house? Then she recalled how he'd come over late one night when someone let a horse loose in her yard and the mare was ready to drop a foal. She'd been at her wit's end, unable to transport the animal—aside from the fact she'd only ever taken in dogs and cats prior to that day. She hadn't even remembered Ray—Dr. Vega—coming into her house until now. She'd gotten him something to eat. He must have noticed the clock then.

Once he stopped listening to the puppy's chest and stomach, she continued, "We've taken in a boarder. I'll have more money to settle up my bill, and I'll have help around the house to lighten the load."

"A boarder?"

"A sergeant from the Army post, the one who brought Trooper to us."

"I thought Sierra was moving into the loft apartment."

A rogue thought blindsided her. Good Lord, was he interested in her daughter? That would make more sense. They were closer in age. Had she misread the signals earlier, thinking he was drawn to her when all along it was Sierra he had his eye on?

How mortifying that would have been if she'd let him know what she'd thought. "I feel bad about that for Sierra, but it's a temporary delay and she understands we're doing the best we can. What about the puppies?"

He draped his stethoscope around his neck. "Possibly the start of an upper respiratory infection. Their immune systems have taken a hit losing their mother and the antibodies from nursing. We'll start them on antibiotics now, just in case. I'll check the fecal samples Ghita took as well to see if they need a different dewormer." He glanced at her as he settled Thumbelina back into the crate and pulled out Pinocchio. The fawn-colored pup looked so tiny in his broad palm. "And don't worry about the cost. It'll just be for the meds. Nothing for the exam."

"That's not fair to you. I told you I have money coming in."

"I could scrap your bill altogether, write it off as a charitable deduction so you can save more animals."

"You already write it off as charity, and you've given us such a cut rate it's beyond unfair to you. But thanks."

His eyes locked on her—and held. She blinked fast and looked back wondering, waiting.

"Lacey, pay the bill if that's what it will take to make you more comfortable. I would give the same discount for any rescue with the same drive and integrity you have. The discount is about the animals. Our . . . friendship is separate from that."

Friendship?

His hesitation over the word hadn't been her imagination. Maybe she wasn't wrong in her feeling that he was attracted to her—this thirty-two-year-old, incredibly sexy, charismatic, smart man. Ten years younger than she was and eons younger in life's pain. But there was no mistaking the look of interest in his eyes right now.

Of course he wouldn't act on it. She was still newly widowed. She wasn't anywhere near over Allen's death or ready for a relationship. She couldn't stop herself from thumbing her wedding band around and around.

Yet deep in the pit of her exhausted, ulcer-filled belly a warmth flickered to life. For a selfish moment, she let herself bask in the tingly glow rather than push it aside out of guilt. She looked at him and *savored*.

His long hair curled up along the collar of his T-shirt. He was unconventional and the polar opposite of her military husband. Surely that's what made him attractive to her. He was safe, a no comparison, no competition kind of guy. She didn't have to question if she was filling a hole in her life with a substitute for Allen.

Could she possibly indulge her sex-starved body in one no-guilt night? She honestly didn't know. But she let herself imagine the possibility for a steamy, fantasy-filled moment where she wore his duster, his hat . . .

And nothing else.

Seven

RAMON VEGA HAD loved Lacey McDaniel since the first time she'd walked into his vet clinic eighteen months ago with a two-year-old chow mix she'd pulled from the local shelter. The dog had been a victim of owner neglect, and had been hit by a car and never received treatment for the crushed leg. Her regular vet had cried uncle once the rescue started picking up speed, so she'd come to his clinic after hearing about his help at the shelter . . .

There'd been no choice but to amputate the chow's leg. He'd performed the surgery while she stood at his side, never taking her eyes off the furry, matted beast she'd only just met but taken under her wing. This woman cared. Far more than the pet owner who'd had the animal for years. People like her were rare.

Ray struck a deal to help her with the special needs animals at her rescue.

He would have helped anyway. He already volunteered at the local shelter when he could. The fact he wanted to see Lacey again added extra incentive. He wasn't the kind of guy who chased married women—or even allowed himself to give them a second thought—but he hadn't seen a wedding ring that day. And he damn sure had checked.

Later, he discovered she'd had her rings off due to skin irritation from washing a litter of mangy puppies in a sulfur dip. By the time he'd learned she had a husband and two kids, it was too late for his heart. He loved her and couldn't have her. Didn't matter that she was older than he was—she was quite simply Lacey, sexy in a way that had nothing to do with years or cover model gloss. She would be every bit as mesmerizing when she turned eighty, no doubt still crusading for the animals.

He usually only let himself look at her when she was busied with something else. But right now, she was staring at him, really *seeing* him, so what the hell. He looked back. Her honey brown curls were the natural kind, not ones that came from hours in front of a mirror. She had wide green eyes, freckles and a crazy sense of style that slayed him. He'd always been a renegade, and he recognized the kindred spirit in her.

Finally, she twitched, her hand nervously tucking a sun-kissed curl back into her loose knot. "I guess I should go."

He hadn't meant to chase her away, damn it. He wanted more time with her. Just to be near her.

"I'll carry Trooper out to your car." He stroked a hand along the tan and brown mutt's chest.

Trooper growled softly, fangs showing.

"Easy, boy." He stroked again and again, watching the dog's respiration. Better not to make direct eye contact anyway with the possibly fractious canine.

Lacey shifted from one red heel to the other. "Guess he's still not pleased with you over the neuter surgery."

Ray smiled along at the joke. "More likely it's the aftereffects of the anesthesia."

Ray still wasn't a hundred percent sure he trusted this dog that had grown up feral, scavenging in the desert. Lacey had good instincts, but this animal had been thrust on her. She'd never been given a chance to evaluate him. And she certainly hadn't been given a choice, much like her whole adult life so far as he could see—bringing up two kids pretty much on her own and now taking care of her husband's father to boot.

Gently scruffing the skin along the back of Trooper's neck to calm him, Ray scooped him up, a warm weight with the smell of Betadine and dog funk. "Lead the way to your car."

"You really don't have to do this for me." She hefted the puppy carrier from the exam table. "I'm sure you've got other patients to check on . . ."

"Ghita," he called over his shoulder, "can you take care of filling the prescriptions for the puppies? I wrote everything down on the chart. We're carrying out the animals now."

"Can do, Doc Ray," Ghita's clipped Midwestern accent called back from the other room. "I'll bring the meds right out."

"No worries, Lacey, the rest of the vets have left for the day and I've only got one boarding patient left to check in on." A lie, but no need to worry her. "Ghita and Maisie are on their way out."

"If you're sure . . . Thanks." Lacey lugged the carrier and shouldered her way past Maisie half blocking the open door.

Good Lord, Ray thought, that girl hovered in doorways all the time. She was a lot like a gangly puppy, always underfoot. But she was the senior partner's niece and she made the customers smile.

Lacey walked alongside him through the lobby and out into the parking lot, the sinking sun warm, but not too much so thanks to a light breeze. She smelled like lavender soap and bleach. He'd dated a girl once who sold aromatherapy burners at home parties. She would have said lavender was a calming scent.

Hell, he didn't know except he liked it. He liked Lacey.

And there wasn't a damn thing he could do about it for now, if ever.

She opened the back of the Suburban, huffing a hank of hair off her forehead. "Thanks again. You can tuck him in the crate in back. I'll put the cone on him once we get home. He seems out for the count again now."

"Any complications, give me a call." He eased the sleeping dog inside, the weight of the woozy mutt weighing heavy on his conscience as well as his arms. Trooper was a living, breathing reminder of the man who should be here helping her. A man she'd married and loved for over two decades. A dead hero.

Jonesing over a fallen soldier's wife felt . . . low. Ray closed and locked the crate. Hell, his father the politician would have a coronary at the possibility of his son making a move on a war widow who'd lost her husband so recently. He never had figured out if his dad's code of ethics was born of honor or ambition.

Regardless, Ray had spent his elementary school years with his dad serving on the county council, encouraged to keep a low profile and pose for the campaign posters. Ray had flinched like hell over those haircuts and ground his teeth sitting through debates and fund-raisers. He wanted to be outside, or at least in his own clothes. By Ray's teen years, his dad was a U.S. senator and his mom pretended she still loved him, posing for those campaign photos in spite of the fact she had a weakness for pool boys.

For college then work, Ray had moved five states away and only had to make cursory appearances during the final days of an election cycle. But his father's code still tugged at him, especially when it came to Lacey, the best woman he'd ever met.

Then when her husband died—hell, he felt even worse, as if he'd somehow wished bad karma on the man. In fact, he had—to a degree—but more along the lines of wondering when Lacey would realize she deserved to have someone in her life take her welfare into account. She was so busy giving and caring for others. Who the hell took care of her?

He was so screwed. Not for the first time, he thought about the offer from a clinic out west, a college buddy who'd been lobbying to bring him on board. Practically speaking, the offer was enticing.

Yet, here he was. Still.

Ray slammed closed the back hatch of her SUV, his eyes drawn to her as she walked to the front. How the hell did she make a concert tee, jeans and red heels seem more high class than most of the women who frequented his dad's fund-raisers? Lacey's sloppy updo looked like the sort of thing his mother's friends paid big bucks for.

"Doc!" Ghita shouted as she half jogged out a side entrance with a bag of meds in her hand into the near empty parking lot. "I've got Mrs. McDaniel's meds."

Lacey stopped halfway in the vehicle. "I can't believe I almost drove off without them." She sprinted toward the vet tech with her hand outstretched for the bag. "Thank you, thank you."

Ghita rambled through all the medicating instructions—antibiotics for the puppies, plus pain meds and antibiotics for Trooper—even though Lacey had been through the drill more times than he could remember. Ghita had been around this place since it opened over twenty years ago. There were days he could swear she knew more than he did.

Lacey gave her a quick hug before bolting back into her vehicle. She shot an arm out the window to wave on her way out of the near empty parking lot, only employee cars left. Her bumper was covered in stickers, ranging from animal rescue logos to a simple gold star. A reminder that they belonged to the Gold Star Family network of people who'd lost a soldier in battle. A kick in the gut to him right now.

All those stickers and magnets on her SUV faded into rush-hour traffic, mostly cars leaving the nearby Army post.

Ray stuffed his hands in his lab coat to keep from doing something dumb-ass like waving back—waving her toward him.

He felt the weight of eyes on him, turned and found— "What, Ghita? Did we forget something?"

And what a sap he was for hoping they had so he would have an excuse to take it to her later.

The senior vet tech looked at him with eyes far too perceptive. "You gonna ask Lacey McDaniel out?"

Shit. He was that transparent? He scratched along the back of his neck just under his hair that, yes, was too long, but he was past the days of mandatory parental buzz cuts. "What makes you think I want to ask her out?"

"I'm psychic."

"Really?"

"No. I just have eyes."

He scrambled for something to say along the lines of a polite way to tell her to mind her own business . . . unless she had a suggestion. "What's so obvious you feel the need to initiate this awkward little conversation?"

"Relax. Nobody else would notice, except maybe Maisie, but she'll just crush on someone else next week." She sat on the back bumper of her truck, the kind with fat tires for farm work and four-wheeling. "I'm just older, wiser and less self-absorbed than most of the rest of the folks around here."

"You're also nosier."

"But I don't gossip."

True. Still . . . "I think it's time to end this conversation."

He started toward the clinic. Maybe he would give his friend at that clinic out west a call after all, just to explore his options.

"Does that mean you're *never* going to ask her out even though your eyes damn near catch her on fire when you look at her?"

Her words stopped him short. He turned on his boot heels

and faced her again. "She just lost her husband, Ghita. Maybe you recall accompanying the rest of us when we lined the streets holding flags when they brought his body back for the funeral."

The man was a hero. No question. His ghost loomed large.

"Allen McDaniel was a good soldier and he made the ultimate sacrifice for our country. That's beyond tragic and unfair." She paused, waiting until he moved a step closer. "But the Colonel was gone for a very long time again and again before he died."

Which didn't make him feel one damn bit better. Just so very sad for her. He dropped down to sit on the bumper beside Ghita. "Then Lacey has all the more reason to grieve, given there's more crap to sort through."

"Ah, so you *do* want to ask her out?"

He studied the steel tips of his boots. "You knew that before we started this conversation. But like I said. Now's not a good time."

Leaning back against the tailgate, she crossed her arms over her chest, exposing the fertile family tree tat on her upper arm. "When is the right time to hit on a widow?"

Now that was one helluva good question. "If I were to go out with Lacey McDaniel, I wouldn't want to be her rebound guy. I'm not gonna be the fling to move past her grief before she gets on with really living."

Ghita patted his arm slowly, with that mom sort of way he vaguely remembered from his own mother. "So you've got more than the hots for her. You've got *feelings* for her."

"Ghita." He avoided her green eyes that held a little too much pity for his comfort level. "Why is this so important for us to talk about?"

"Because it's not often a guy comes along who sees past a woman's age and whether or not she's got a tiny little ass from starving herself into clothes that could fit an eight-year-old." She nodded toward Maisie prancing across the far end of the parking lot to a Mustang given to her by Daddy on her twenty-first birthday. Ghita looked away, back at Ray with a grimacing smile. "I'm rootin' for you."

"That's not exactly a hopeful look on your face."

"Because I'm worried about you, too, boss man."

"Why's that?" He clapped a hand on his chest. "I'm not exactly Quasimodo."

"Quasi-what?"

"*Hunchback of Notre Dame*," he said offhandedly. "Why are you worried? You've all but said I'm a good guy that a woman would appreciate."

"Because just like you said, she's a widow with a whole lot of baggage. And even if she gets past that, women don't usually give younger men the time of day, not in a serious way." She held up both hands. "No offense, but younger men are too immature."

Her words sounded too logical. "That's a double standard, you know."

"No, sir." She patted his arm once more as she stood. "That's life."

And either way it turned out, he couldn't do a damn thing about it yet. Which put him in a holding pattern with a not-so-optimistic outcome. Waiting for time to pass until it would be "long enough" for him to make a move on Lacey McDaniel and pray like hell she was into younger guys.

Because while he might be confused about the timeline, he knew his feelings for her were one hundred percent clear. He wouldn't be making any phone calls to the clinic out west. Not today.

SIERRA LEANED AGAINST the wall inside the barn, by the stairs leading up to the converted loft apartment—Mike's apartment.

Wind blew through the open doors on either end of the barn, kennel runs open as well for the dogs to stretch their legs in the play yard before sunset. A couple of cats lounged in the rafters, and another sprawled on her mother's desk in her empty office. Lacey had taken the puppies to the house to feed and medicate while Mike moved in.

So far Mike and his buddy Calvin had carried in four boxes marked clothes, gear, kitchen and sports. Wrangling the mattress and leather recliner had come with ear-blistering curses only topped by the one currently floating down the stairwell as they wedged the wide-screen plasma television up, one step at a time.

She cradled an old tabby cat named Tom in her arms, a senior that had found its way into her softhearted mom's car on a trip to the shelter two months ago. Trooper stared at her from a crate, his eyelids at drunken half-mast, big plastic cone of shame in place. His eyes tracked all the movement as if half registering through his drugged-up haze. She'd put him there for safekeeping while Mike unloaded his stuff, then they'd decided the dog would do better staying with him. The last thing they needed was Trooper deciding to roughhouse with the other dogs—or make another escape attempt—while he was recovering.

Then it hit her—again. This was really happening. Mike was moving in. He was home and back in her life because of the drunken sailor of a dog across the barn. Her dad's dog.

What a mess.

Mike's buddy Calvin jogged down the stairs. "We're almost done. Easiest pony keg of beer I ever earned. Mike has virtually no crap, ya know." Calvin unrolled the sleeves on his pin-striped button down. "Nice reno job up there."

"Thanks." She struggled not to wince. Mary Hannah had gone with her to pick the color samples, then took a whole weekend helping her paint the space. She'd chosen the sooth-ing mellow greens and tans to create a *Secret Garden* effect.

Calvin looked around the barn from one open end to the other that offered a clearer view of the play yard. "Friend of mine's live-in love says they wanna get a puppy. I told her about this place."

"Thanks, my mom will appreciate it."

"Well, I gotta get the last box of shit—uh, stuff out of the truck. Sorry about the language. Takes a while to ditch deployment habits. In more ways than one." Calvin knelt by the crate and reached through the wire to scratch Trooper's haunches. "This fella brought us a lot of happy hours playing fetch and Frisbee. He gave us a chance to forget about where we were and pretend things were normal for a while."

She hadn't thought about how much Trooper meant to the others. To Mike. "I can tell Trooper knows and trusts you. Mom said he snarled at the vet today."

"That's strange. He never did that over there, not after the first month of socializing him. He only growled when . . ." He swallowed hard. "He only growled to alert us if the enemy was close."

"Sounds like Trooper picked his friends and stood by them."

"Friends are important." He gave Trooper a final scratch before standing. "Mike cares about you and your family enough to risk his career bringing this dog to you. I just thought you should know."

He shrugged and left before she could answer, sidestepping a pair of dachshunds trotting in from the play yard. Tom the cat jumped from her arms and bounded away into her mom's office.

Mike's career at risk? She'd known he was bending rules, but had he understated the risk? He was doing so much for her family in honor of her dad's memory.

She eyed the steps again. She'd thought a million times about climbing up them, moving in and settling her stuff. There was a moment she'd even considered moving in with Mike. She'd even thought for a while they might have something special—

Trooper barked once, a half-strangled effort of a drugged-up dog. Her heart squeezed. Concerned, she dropped to her knees on the soft earthen floor in front of the crate, opened the door and looked into his eyes. She ran her hands along his back. She didn't have her mother's instincts or skills with animals, but she'd picked up more than the average amount of animal knowledge just living with her. She reached inside to scratch his ears just as footsteps thundered down the stairs.

Ahhh . . . That was why Trooper had barked. His attachment to Mike. She didn't even have to look to recognize the sound of his walk, and wasn't that messed up?

He knelt on one knee beside her. "Is Trooper okay?"

"Probably just wanted some attention." If she leaned even a hint to the left, she could rest her head on Mike's broad shoulder.

"Fair enough. Tough day for the big guy." He scrubbed a hand over the dog's head, flopping both ears back and forth before his hand settled on top of Sierra's. He squeezed once.

She was tempted to hold tight and pull him to her for another kiss that would lead to more. And God, she wanted more. But not the hurt afterward . . .

Sierra squeezed his hand back but had to slip free. Better for thinking clearly. "I believe we need to set some house rules now that you've moved in."

"Rules?" He scratched the back of his neck. "I'm not so good at those."

"Well, it's time to learn." She sat back on the ground, hugging her knees to put space between them while she talked. "About that kiss."

He leaned an elbow on top of the crate. "Please don't be cliché and say it can't happen again."

"It won't happen again."

He grinned. "Sure."

She fought the urge to smile back and swatted his knee. "Just because you're living here doesn't mean you're allowed to sneak into my room after lights-out."

"Damn. I guess I'll have to return the ladder I bought."

"Please don't joke. I'm serious that we need to be careful about living this close together."

The smile faded from his eyes. "Is there someone else for you now?"

Surely he knew her better than that. "Would I have been kissing you that way if there was?"

"I sure as hell hope not."

"There's your answer, then. But it was impulsive. Now, I need to think this through, for both our sakes. I'm a mess. My mom's a mess. My brother . . . well . . . that goes without saying. I need peace. And for some crazy reason you feel the need to help us. I'm grateful for all you're doing, even if I want to kick you for putting your career in jeopardy to bring this dog home. I'm just not sure I understand why you're here."

"My career will be fine. And as for why I'm here? I wish I could say it's because I'm a nice guy, but I'm not some altruistic hero. I'm just a guy struggling to understand why I'm alive when others aren't."

"So you're feeling survivor's guilt. All the more reason we need to be careful." She tipped her head back to blink away tears. "I'm not saying never. I'm just saying . . ."

"You've been hurt enough." He reached to cup the back of her neck, caressing, comforting. "I hear you."

His touch gave her goose bumps and tested her resolve only seconds after she'd dug her heels in. It might be cowardly, but right now, her best option? Run.

She shot to her feet and made a beeline for the double barn doors, slamming into Calvin holding Mike's battered guitar case.

"'Scuse me," she mumbled before rushing out the back entrance to the play yard so there was no chance of running into them getting any last-minute items from Mike's truck.

Once outside, she slumped against the barn, gulping in air. The scent of fresh-mown hay from the next farm over tickled her nose and helped ease the urge to sprint into the barn again and bury her face in Mike's T-shirt.

Damn it. She squeezed her eyes closed and two tears leaked free. She scrubbed her wrists along her cheeks just as voices carried on that breeze, Mike's and Calvin's as they talked inside the barn. She should go . . . Should . . .

"Tazz, my friend, you don't have to stay here and get your heart ripped out for breakfast every morning. You know you're welcome on my sofa."

"Thanks for the offer," Mike's voice rumbled, "but I'm needed here."

"Are you two back together, then?"

Her fingers dug into the rough wood of the barn, splinters digging as she waited for Mike's answer.

"Are you writing a gossip column now?" Mike growled. "Check my Facebook status or something if you want to know. Find out this stuff the way the rest of the world does."

Calvin chuckled. "You're cranky, so you must not be getting any."

Sierra straightened, the locker-room turn of the conversation setting her teeth on edge.

"Cut it out." Mike's curt retort eased the tension coiling in her gut, and she sagged back against the outside barn wall.

"And your answer tells me even more. You've got it bad."

She held her breath as she waited for Mike's answer to that one. Silence lengthened, her heart pounding in her ears, her eyes locked on the family blue heeler—Gizmo—playing with a couple of black Lab puppies that had been found tied to the fence a month ago. Thank God no wild animals had attacked them in the night. Gramps had found them on one of his moonlight mowing adventures.

"Calvin, my friend," Mike said in that way of his that was unerringly patient, but she heard the undertone of frustration. "Want to help me set up the TV or are we gonna have to change your nickname from Pinstripe to Cupid?"

Footsteps echoed, heavy man steps going upward, as their voices grew fainter. "Your threats don't impress me. Although you should be at least a little concerned that the Sergeant Major's still not happy."

"I figured as much," Mike answered as Sierra slid down to sit, guilt weighing on her like cinder blocks on her shoulders. She rested her forehead on her drawn-up knees, too tired to even feel guilty about eavesdropping anymore. But she couldn't stop herself from listening to the two male voices floating out the open window in the loft apartment.

"Mike, it may seem you've lucked out with the publicity, but my guess is that the Sergeant Major will take his anger out on your hide some other way."

"I'm a big boy," Mike said. "Wanna pass me the box cutter?"

"You have a lot to lose here. Like your Special Forces slot."

And every animal lover blogger was filling the Internet writing about this with stories and stolen photos. She looked up sharply, searching the tree line suspiciously for cameras, then over to her four-wheeling neighbors riding the fence line, no doubt searching for more problems.

"Shit." Calvin's curse floated from an open window in the loft. "Where did that cat come from?"

"Really? We're in an animal rescue and you're surprised to see a cat?"

"Fair enough . . . All I'm saying, my friend, is maybe you'd be better off moving on. Protect your future."

"This isn't about me. It never was. Now, are you here to help me or harass me?"

She needed to leave. Listening to Mike was only torturing herself. Calvin had made her realize it wasn't just her decision as to whether or not she and Mike would be crazy enough to resume their old relationship. Mike had put her family first at a possible great risk to himself. This wasn't just about her.

It was about Mike's best interests as well.

Resigned, she shoved to her feet and walked back through the barn, toward the main entrance, double doors open to show Mike's truck and the winding driveway. Boot steps sounded overhead as the guys continued to work in the studio apartment.

Her feet slowed, her brain telling her something was off. She looked behind her into the barn again. Cats in the rafters stared down. The black Lab puppies had given up playing and curled up to sleep on a mesh dog cot. She turned to Trooper's crate—

Damn it. Empty. His cone and collar lay inside, ditched. The dog was a freaking Houdini.

Or wait, maybe Mike had taken him upstairs. She snatched up the cone, prepared to chew the man out for being such a softy and taking off the collar. She stomped up the steps and into her *Secret Garden* haven turned man cave.

Thrusting the cone against Mike's chest, she demanded, "Do not let him take this off."

Mike's eyes went wide. "Okay. I'll watch him." He took the cone. "Do you want me to carry him up the stairs?"

The blood went cold in her veins. "You don't have him?"

"I thought he was supposed to stay in his crate." Mike glanced at Calvin. "Do you have time to help us search?"

His buddy looked back at them, confused. "What do you mean? He went for a walk. See?"

Calvin pointed out the window to the lawn, the part of the yard Sierra wouldn't have seen while sitting outside or walking through the barn. The window in the A-frame eaves showcased the unmistakable image of Trooper walking drunkenly toward the gate. And he wasn't alone.

Gramps had a leash looped around Trooper's neck.

Eight

MIKE COULD RUN a four-and-a-half-minute mile. He could run a five-minute mile for five miles straight. But his heart was in his throat as he jogged down a simple flight of steps racing to stop a senile old man from slipping away with a newly neutered dog.

Damn it all, he should have thought to take Trooper upstairs with him. He'd come here to help, not cause more problems. He vaguely registered the sound of footsteps behind him, others running, too, but farther back. The sun was setting fast, an orange glow sinking into stretches of deep green fields. Who knew how lost Joshua McDaniel could have gotten? And the dog wasn't even supposed to be up and around for more than a pee break.

Then he spotted the General shuffling between trees. Mike closed the gap fast, then slowed at the last second so as not to startle the older man. Joshua hobble-walked with an arthritic gait, but those gym shoes of his made fast time. His arms pumped and he may as well have been wearing the Army T-shirt and sweat pants for a real workout.

Mike hitched his hands in his back jeans pockets. "Mind if I ask what you're doing, sir?"

"I'm just walking the dog, son. Like you should have," Joshua snapped, irritation crackling like lightning bugs in the early evening. "Guess I'll have to dock your allowance again."

"Well, I'm here now so you can go back to the house for supper." He tried to placate while Sierra and Calvin hung back, waiting.

Joshua shook his head sharply. "Trooper and I are already in a rhythm here." His shiny white New Balance shoes picked up speed, stomping in short and choppy bursts of anger. "You can go back."

This was escalating fast. He kept his voice calm, respectful. "Yes, sir, but it's getting dark. We should head home."

"I'm a grown man," Joshua snapped. "I can walk at night if I want."

There was no debating that stubborn tone. "Do you mind if I walk with you?"

Joshua stopped short and barked in Mike's face like a drill sergeant. "I don't need a damn babysitter."

Tendons stood out in the older man's neck, a pulse throbbing in his temple. Mike had seen enough combat to know when a person was about to lose it, and this man was seconds away from snapping.

Or throwing punches.

Sierra stepped up and touched the General's arm lightly. "Gramps . . ."

The General pushed her hand away, hard, knocking her back. Sierra stumbled for a couple of steps before regaining her balance. Mike stepped between them fast, fists clenched. The urge to protect surged. He just hadn't thought he would ever have to protect her from her own family.

"Sir—"

"Gramps?" Sierra repeated softly.

The General looked around confused, searching for . . .

a grandfather. He had no idea who Sierra was or who she was speaking to.

The pained expression on Sierra's face cut right through Mike. He exhaled hard, searching for the right words to defuse the tension. "We can take the dog on a walk or return to the house. Completely your choice, sir."

Joshua frowned, glancing down at Trooper, then back up at Mike. "Are you finished with your patrol duty, son?"

The Alzheimer's had him more disoriented than usual . . . Mike had Googled the disease, and this moment seemed to fit the term "sundowning," the tendency of a senile person to grow increasingly confused at the end of the day. There was an edge to that in the old man's behavior right now. A building rage. But then who wouldn't rage over being trapped inside a body with a diminishing mind? Agitating him would only make things worse. Reminding him of reality wouldn't accomplish anything. The man existed in this moment like a time traveler, trapped in another era.

"Yes, sir. Next duty shift has arrived."

"Good, that's good to know. Time to get back to the barracks, then." The old man clapped Mike on the shoulders. "Stay safe and keep your head low, soldier."

Joshua shuffle-walked back toward the house, his shoulders braced even when hunched with age, his grip steady on the leash, although Trooper slowed to match the man's pace.

Calvin cleared his throat. "Uh, I'll follow him to make sure he's safely inside, then I'm gonna hit the road."

Sierra shook her head. "You don't have to do that on my account—"

"Hey," Calvin interjected. "No worries. I really need to head out. You two look like you need a minute to decompress. See you soon, Mike."

"Roger that. I still owe you a pony keg." And a lot more. Calvin was a good friend. Strong bonds were forged serving in a combat zone together. "Thanks for your help today."

Calvin waved aside the gratitude as he jogged to catch up with the General. Mike swallowed hard, his hand clenching around the fence post as he watched silently while the older man walked all the way to the porch. Once they reached the door, Calvin waved again and Trooper looked back as if to say, *I've got this. He's safe.*

Sierra leaned against Mike's shoulder with a heavy sigh. "Trooper should really have his cone on."

Sliding an arm around her waist, he tucked her against his side. "Text your mother. Are you okay?"

"I'm fine." She pulled against his hold. "I'll just go back and tell her what happened."

"We don't need to go in yet. Give yourself a minute to breathe while we watch the sunset." He held firm and she relaxed against him. "Has your grandfather gotten that angry before?"

"Everything's under control."

"Really?" He looked down into her blue eyes that had aged far more than a year since he'd left for Iraq. "You looked upset by his behavior but not surprised."

She shrugged. "He has outbursts. The doctor put him on antidepressants. They helped some, but he's got good reason to be . . . agitated."

The weight of what she faced daily hit him fully for the first time. He rested his chin on top of her head, her silky hair catching on his late-day beard stubble. "Sierra—"

"I'll be all right."

"You don't have to say that. It's okay to lean on me. God, if my grandmother Ruby had just spent the past five minutes thinking we're soldiers in the middle of a war zone, I would be . . . unsettled."

"That's an understatement. Try crushed. Frustrated. Stressed."

"Words are your gig, Scrabble Gal." He scraped her hair behind her ear. "I'm trying to speak your language."

"And I appreciate it." She clasped his wrist. "Are you

really going to get in serious trouble with your Sergeant Major?"

"Let me worry about that. You have enough to think about with Gramps there and that council showdown coming up. And did I see some flyer in the barn about a big adoption event in the near future?"

"You did. A Doggie Palooza, an event for dogs lovers in the area. It's a great chance for positive press in advance of that council meeting."

"More pressure. Like I said. You have enough on you. Admit it."

"Life's definitely dog piling on us lately." She leaned into his touch, a smile twitching her lips. "Get it, dog pile. We're in an animal rescue."

"I got it." Smiling back, he cradled her face in his palm. The Tennessee sunset cast such a damn beautiful glow around her he could barely breathe. "How could I have forgotten how incredibly beautiful you are?"

Unable to resist, he kissed her, just his lips meeting hers and holding. But it felt like the right kind of reverent kiss for such a mystical sunset and incredible woman. She was so damn strong and brave, holding it together for her family when no one would have faulted her for moving on with her life.

Loyalty like that from relatives wasn't a given. He knew that all too well. He needed to give himself space to think this through. He owed her better than half measures.

In fact, he owed her father everything, including his life.

And with that sobering thought, he ended the kiss, allowing himself one stroke along her hair before he walked away.

BY FRIDAY, SIERRA was convinced Mike must have left all his T-shirts in Iraq, because he sure didn't bother wearing them while he worked.

She hosed off the outdoor part of a kennel run while the

dogs played in the yard with volunteers wearing out the pooches before other volunteers bathed them. Perfect time for Sierra to get some extra cleaning and sanitizing accomplished. Or maybe she was just looking for an excuse to be out here where Mike was working on a ceiling fan while shirtless.

She resisted the urge to hose herself off.

Her gaze returned to the V of his back as he reached overhead, his broad shoulders tapering down to narrow hips where the band of his boxers rode just above the low-slung waist of his jeans. Golden skin beaded with sweat. He twisted to adjust a wobbling blade on the fan, turning in a way that put a whole new set of ab muscles on display. Even better? They were right at mouth level since he stood on a stepladder. The urge to walk over there and skim her mouth along his hip was never far from her mind.

Except that he'd pulled away from her after that kiss they'd shared.

She almost wondered if he worked his ass off fixing things just to be sure he stayed at arm's length now. He'd added a basic security system to the barn, which had alerted them twice to the fact Gramps was wandering into the barn at night to take dogs out for a walk—which solved one mystery. They now knew who was prying open the kennels, even going so far as to break them to release his dog of choice for the night.

Mike had fixed the fences, repaired a leaky faucet, even changed lightbulbs. As an added bonus, they got to hear him play his guitar late into the night, a distant, tuneful strumming that carried on the breeze and helped her fall asleep imagining those nimble fingers playing over her body.

But no more kisses. He didn't need to. Just one look from him stirred up memories that fired through her. Tempting her.

Focus, damn it. Her mom needed all the help she could get today. The place was full to capacity after helping a shelter confiscate dogs from a hoarder that had started as a rescue, then got out of hand. Hopefully they would be able to find homes for some of them at the Doggie Palooza tomorrow.

Sierra had to commend her mother for setting rigid boundaries for herself in order to never cross that line of taking in too many rescues. Easier said than done some days when area shelters called with pleas for help with this or that animal. Like Lucky, who'd detoxed into a goofy and totally docile little fella, currently licking the inside of a German shepherd's ears.

Smiling, Sierra finished the last outdoor kennel run and shifted to hosing off the floor of the dog wash area. Dedicated volunteers Charlotte and Debbie were scrubbing a Great Pyrenees named Atlas, a gorgeous, huge dog—bought from a breeder as a puppy and dumped at a shelter once the owners grasped just how big the animal would get. Atlas gave teenage Charlotte a sloppy wet kiss in thanks.

Debbie scratched a lather along the dog's back, but was clearly distracted staring inside the barn. And Sierra had to say, she couldn't blame the woman. Mike on that ladder finishing up another fix-it project was a sight to behold. He stretched up, repairing a squeak and wobble in one of the fat-blade ceiling fans. Sexy didn't come close to describing how mouthwateringly hot he looked as sweat slicked his back, trickling down his spine, lower, lower.

She bit her bottom lip.

Not fair at all, especially when she resembled a drowned rat in purple rain boots. Smelling worse than the stalls before cleaning. Funny thing was, as much as she griped about this, she believed in her mother's mission. She believed in this animal rescue and the work they did, the lives they saved. But it was getting tougher and tougher to juggle the time here with the demands of her graduate assistantship teaching. What would happen when she went to work full-time after graduation? Would there be enough hours in the day to be a part of the beautiful mission here?

Even if her main contribution lately consisted of hosing out the stalls?

With that thought, she gave a final blast of water along the concrete walkway before closing off the spray of water mixed with a bleach-based cleaning solution. She felt eyes on her and followed the sensation until her gaze traveled back up again, to Mike. She hooked the hose onto the end of a kennel gate and stepped deeper into the barn. Her soggy boots squeaked at the same pitch of the volunteers' laughter as Atlas shook a monsoon of water and suds on them.

Mike's eyes stayed locked on her, and she could see him doing the same thing he'd done all week long. He was wrestling with the urge to come closer to her, holding himself back. The memory of their kiss was in his eyes even as he still kept his hands to himself.

"What?" She shifted from foot to foot, boots squeaking and squelching. "Did you need something? A wrench? A glass of iced tea?"

Or a shirt. Or her mouth kissing every inch of that sweat-slicked chest.

"I don't need anything . . ." A wicked gleam entered his eyes. "Just enjoying the view down your shirt."

She looked down fast, and sure enough, her soggy T-shirt was drooping in the front, not to mention plastered to her minimal curves. Of course he'd seen every inch of her before without clothes, so she shouldn't feel so self-conscious. But she did.

Not that she would let him know that.

"I hear there's a real market for pinups soaked in kennel water and wearing galoshes."

"You're even hotter when you talk." Winking, he gathered up his tools and started down the ladder. "Nice job cleaning, by the way. I'm amazed at how non-dog this place smells."

He referenced the scent of things a lot, good and bad. She hadn't noticed until now. She would have to ask him about that sometime.

"I'm just doing my part to get ready for the Doggie Palooza tomorrow. Since we'll be away most of Saturday, I need to double up on work today." She leaned a foot back against a kennel gate as he drew closer and closer. "We also get increased adoption traffic after an event like that. It's important to make a good impression, especially with the council meeting coming up. Your help couldn't have come at a better time."

He stepped off the ladder, muscles flexing in his jeans. Then that incredible chest of his came into close-up view. "What happens to all these animals if your mom's rescue shuts down?"

His question made her chest go tight. The sanctuary they ran offered shelter to precious lives that had nowhere else to go. This wasn't just a second chance. For them, the animals in their care, it was the last chance. She peeled off her gloves.

"I don't know exactly. Depends on how long we have to vacate them from the property. I guess first step, Mom stops taking in new animals and focuses on moving these as quickly as possible into forever homes." Except the litter of pit puppies weren't old enough for adoption, which meant they would have to find another rescue willing to take them when rescues were already full enough. And people weren't exactly lining up to adopt pit bulls.

Mike reached just past her to grip the kennel gate. "If she sells this spread and moves into a regular place, you would be able to go off to school."

"And my grandfather would end up in a nursing home." Her stomach lurched like that moment a roller coaster flipped upside down.

"Eventually, he will anyway," Mike said gently.

She scrunched her nose. "What are you? The reality police?"

His forehead scrunched. "Forget I said that. I'm still in combat mode."

She nodded simply, understanding too well. She'd seen her dad after deployments often enough to know it took a while for them to decompress. She should have remembered that for Mike. He'd been through . . . she didn't even know what since she hadn't bothered to ask about him. She'd been focused on her own loss. Her own grief. Maybe that was the explanation for his unpredictable behavior.

"How about you take a break, Mike? Go shower—" Put on a freaking shirt. "And I'll have some food ready for you over at the house. You must be starving."

"Correct you are," he conceded with a wink. "You're too good, you know that, right?"

"Puh-lease. The last thing I want or deserve is a Saint Sierra label."

"Fair enough."

They'd spent a week together, and for some reason he'd backed off after that last kiss. Sure, she'd been telling herself—and him—they couldn't pick up where they left off. Still, she couldn't stop fantasizing about taking that kiss further. Maybe they needed to talk about that if they were going to spend three more weeks living together—or rather, living next door to each other.

"Once we eat lunch, want to go with me to take Trooper for a walk? He's chomping at the bit to ditch that cone and run. I'd like to drain some energy from him before the event tomorrow. Even though he's not up for adoption, we're hoping all the press about him will bring people to our booth at the event."

"What if we end up in the woods on that walk? Alone is . . . dangerous. I might back you against a tree to kiss you. A real kiss this time."

There he went with those mixed messages again. Flirting but not touching.

"Do saints kiss?" she asked flippantly. "I'm honestly not sure . . ." Not sure now about the walk or what game they were playing. "This is strange."

"How so?"

To hell with waiting for the walk. She glanced over at the open doors to make sure Debbie and Charlotte were still occupied outside with rinsing off Atlas.

Sierra angled closer, lowering her voice. "You kiss me, then pretend for a week like nothing happened. Like the past year never happened. Even stranger, it's as if we're playacting that you were never gone. But you have been away and so much is different. We've both been scarred by this deployment."

His eyes shuttered. "You're the one who lost a dad. You're the one with cause to grieve."

"You went to war. I realize that leaves marks." She also knew better than to touch him right now or he would bolt before they had a chance to finish this conversation. "Even without what happened this year I can look at my grandfather and see that. The more he loses touch with the present, the more I see how his past in the military is so much more a part of him than his history as a father or husband."

"That has to be rough for you."

"It is, but that's not my point. This is about you, too, about things being rough for *you*."

"You're a strong woman," he said as if she hadn't even spoken, staying focused on her.

She ground her teeth. "I hate that word."

"Huh? That was a compliment."

"Strong. Like I spent the past year lifting weights? Strong because I do what's right like some martyr—or saint?" She shook her head. "I'm none of those things. I'm resentful and frustrated and tired. I want to scream over everything that's been taken from my family. I want to hug my father and punch him for choosing his duty to his uniform over his duty to his children. Hell, I don't know how my mother keeps from exploding. She's been shortchanged for so damn long. And yes, I'm also sad over everything I know you had to experience over there."

"You blame your dad for staying in the military?"

Still no acknowledgment of his pain or grief . . . What poem was it where Emily wrote, "Saying nothing sometimes says the most"? Maybe Mike was hinting at things in his own way. Asking how she felt about him leaving. Using this conversation as a shield to express his feelings without actually acknowledging he had them.

How like a man. He wasn't going to open up, not fully, and she wasn't sure how to sift through his hidden cues on top of the whole flirting/not touching dance they'd been doing. And what if she made the wrong step when he was still in his post-deployment recovery?

Forget taking a walk. She needed space of her own. More than anything she wanted to get advice from her mom, but that seemed cruel somehow.

"Mike, it's all a moot point now for my brother and me. We'll never have anything more from our father again." She edged to the side, away from him. "I think I'd better go clean up before lunch."

She spun away fast.

"Like I said," Mike's voice washed over her, "you're a strong woman."

Maybe so. But she was also confused as hell.

LACEY DROVE INTO the waterside lot along the Cumberland River, the barking in the back of her SUV reaching deafening levels. She had a dozen dogs in crates in the back for the Doggie Palooza. No cats today, since it was an outdoor event. Her family was supposed to be trailing her. Nathan was driving Gramps and Sierra's friend Mary Hannah. Nathan welcomed any chance to use his new permit, one of the few things that made him smile. Sierra was riding with Mike, who'd stored some puppy pens and a huge banner in the back of his truck. Traffic had sucked the whole way over, and she'd lost them in her rearview mirror long ago.

Hopefully one of them would show up soon to help her unload since she couldn't leave the dogs alone in the car. Foster parents would be bringing other dogs, for a total of around twenty-four adoptables at the event, but there were a lot of other shelters and rescues attending with equally cute critters in need of a family.

There were so many homeless animals the weight of it was overwhelming some days. Most days. She shifted the Suburban into park, wishing she'd managed to get here earlier so she could have parked closer.

Booths and tents were already set up and already packed with people displaying banners and tying balloons, anything to draw attention to their spot in the lineup. There were early birds for the festival hanging out at the dog park and joggers on the winding trail.

She tucked her face into the chilly air conditioner blast. Adoption events were always cause for excitement—and nerves. She had a stack of pre-submitted adoption applications. She'd called each applicant's veterinarian and sent volunteers out for home checks. The adopters understood everyone in the home and other dogs living in the home needed to meet with the new dog. But even so, people let her down. Worse yet, they let the animals down.

People misrepresented themselves. Sometimes they flat-out lied. Even as jaded as she'd become over time, she was still fooled on occasion. The stakes were so high if she made a mistake in misplacing her trust and handing over an animal into the care of the wrong person. That weighed on her mind along with the reality that she had to adopt out animals in order to pull more from overflowing shelters. Damn, she was talking herself into a freaking panic attack that had her longing for a halfway decent chardonnay in her Waterford wineglass.

A tap on the window startled her. She turned down the radio and looked over to find Ray Vega grinning at her, holding up two to-go cups of coffee.

Her craving for wine vanished. Her mouth watered for a million other reasons, not just caffeine or the fact a hot man held the cups. She was touched that someone had thought of her needs this morning. That was heady stuff for a woman who charged through life taking care of others.

Of course there was also that other feeling underneath it all. The one that had shocked the hell out of her at the clinic. She'd hoped it was a fluke then. But as her eyes tracked the lines on his face through the shadow cast by his black felt cowboy hat, she knew that it hadn't been a fluke. Something about this man drew her in a way that she wasn't ready to acknowledge.

She opened the door, weariness lifting as she breathed in the scent of java and aftershave. Yum.

"So, Doc, what brings you here this morning?" She pressed the button to open the back hatch and turned off the car. "Don't you have enough animals of your own?"

He passed her a cup of coffee, walking beside her to the back. "I thought you might need help unloading your crew, and I have about twenty minutes to spare before I head over to Animal Control's mobile vet unit."

"You're volunteering your time to help them again?" Animal Control's mobile clinic provided discount vaccinations and microchipping in conjunction with the services provided at their main shelter facilty. "Do you charge *any*one?"

"Let me worry about my finances. Suffice it to say, I make enough to cover my coffee habit. Now are we going to unload these dogs or not?"

Was it her imagination or was he standing a hint closer than casual? Her skin tingled and tightened like a building sunburn except it was only nine in the morning. How could she be so tangled up in grief over her husband's death and so attracted to this man all at once? She was likely being ridiculous, anyway. Ray spent so much time helping at Animal Control's main shelter, he probably had a thing for the director, who was more his age and certainly pretty, in an edgy way.

Mike's truck pulled up beside them, and Sierra jumped out of the passenger side. "Hey, Mom, where do you want us to set up the puppy playpens? Morning, Doc Vega."

Lacey stepped away, feeling a flush of guilt. "We're the fifth booth from the left. Sierra, do you mind staying by the car with the dogs until we get the last of them unloaded?"

Sierra nodded as Mike hefted the three stacked wire pens—folded flat—from the back of his truck. Nathan turned into the parking lot, driving the General's fifteen-year-old Cadillac they all called the Barge. She'd debated whether to leave Nathan at home with Joshua, but she felt better having him here in her sights; both of them, actually. Thank goodness Mary Hannah had been willing to ride along. The woman had empathy and organizational skills coming out her ears.

"Nathan," Lacey called, waving him to the empty spot near their cars.

He whipped the Barge into another nearby spot of his choosing, coming within a hair of scraping the side of a Mercedes. She bit back the urge to correct him in public. He was probably rebelling for her somehow emasculating him by waving him into a parking space while a cute female was in the car. Males could be so irritable about their egos at any age.

"Nathan—"

"Mom," he sighed, cutting her off before he could possibly know what she'd been about to say. Her sweet baby boy who'd turned into a remote, moody teen a month after Allen deployed again, then became outright surly after his father died, said, "I don't need any help. Come on, Gramps. Let's go sit by the water. You can warn me about hookers and condoms."

Joshua wheezed on a laugh, tugging a bag of old bread off the seat to feed the birds. "I like you, boy." He called to Lacey. "Give me Trooper. We'll let him lead the way."

"Right, sure." She clipped a leash onto Trooper, the only animal without an *Adopt Me* scarf.

Please Lord, she hoped the dog would behave. She passed him over to her father-in-law and gave her son a bowl to keep full of water for the dog. Her smile went unanswered, but at least she didn't get a surly comeback. Mary Hannah waved before walking over to help Sierra and Mike. So many people gave of their time to help her rescue. She owed them as well for their support.

A hand squeezed her shoulder and she looked back, straight into Ray's brown eyes, so dark they were almost black. "Lacey, Ghita's here, too. I'll have her check on them while you're working the event."

"Thank you."

"No trouble at all." His hand fell away and he reached inside to open a crate and snap a leash on a two-year-old Labrador and a five-year-old beagle mix.

A small crowd had gathered at a booth near hers. Normally a good thing. Then she realized the group was none other than Valerie Hammond and her posse, who'd somehow managed to land in the booth next to hers. They were offering free face painting for donations to go toward park beautification. The police officer next to them didn't reassure her in the least. He was the same cop sent to her door far too often on repeated noise complaints even when she had the whole place as peaceful as a library.

Lacey hitched a heavy bag of paperwork and flyers over her shoulder before heading to her booth. "Good morning, Officer Parker."

"Morning, ma'am," the cop answered with a Smoky Mountains twang coating every word.

She wondered if he'd ever stepped out of the state since he was born forty-some-odd years ago. "Is there a problem?"

"Not at all. Just logging some overtime." His eyes lingered in a way that sent an obvious message.

Had she been remotely ready to date, someone like

Officer Parker would at least make for a more logical choice. The cop was handsome in a forty-something way. The gray at his temples communicated "grown up," which God knows, a forty-something woman appreciated. He was fit, coolheaded even when dealing with the Hammonds of the world and took his job seriously. All of which she admired on an objective level.

But no matter what hot and flirty look he sent her way, Laccy didn't feel that scary mix of attraction and guilt Ray seemed to inspire.

She didn't have time to sort through the frustrating direction of her thoughts. Especially not while the Hammonds were busy looking totally innocent and angelic opening up paints and setting up brushes along with a sign promising cute little paw prints for children's cheeks.

She focused on the task at hand instead. Draping a banner along the front of the table. Setting out flyers and posters. Filling a basket with dog treats. Making a good impression at this event was important for her rescue. Let the animals tell the story, charm the people. They made a far better case for their cause than she ever could.

She directed Mike to set up the wire pens for the puppies and smaller dogs brought by foster moms. Charlotte and Debbie walked larger dogs wearing *Adopt Me* scarves.

Deep breaths. She wasn't alone. She had help from people who cared.

Even Nathan seemed almost happy today, sitting with his grandfather by the water, tossing bits of bread into the river for ducks. A loudspeaker squawked then launched into a local radio station broadcasting live.

She sipped her coffee and checked her watch. Setup complete with seven minutes to spare before the event officially began.

Ray passed the two dogs to Sierra and Mike. "Gotta head over to the rabies clinic. Good luck to you all."

Valerie Hammond painted a sample pink paw print on

one of her council cohort's cheeks. "Lacey, dear, I really wish you had a special adoption day to see these dogs so the owned animals wouldn't have to mingle with yours and catch some kind of shelter bug."

Lacey gritted her teeth and kept silent, setting down a donation box shaped like a doghouse. She tugged out a roll of doggie waste bags and placed them diplomatically on the corner.

Ray glanced over his shoulder. "If you have any problems today, Mrs. Hammond, be sure to come by to see me."

Valerie said under her breath, "Probably just trying to drum up business."

Lacey set her cup down carefully, away from the flyers. "Your problem is with me, Valerie, not him. So let's save the discussion for the county council meeting rather than tainting this beautiful event."

Officer Parker stepped between them like a muscle-bound barricade. "Now, now, ladies, I would really hate to land on the front page of the newspaper breaking up a cat-fight. That could really mess with my image as a badass lawman."

Sierra scuffed a heel in the grass and mumbled, "Like that wasn't already tarnished by your fear of a three-pound Chihuahua last time you stopped by on a nuisance call?"

"Now ladies," Officer Parker drawled, "that was one fierce Chihuahua girl. I've learned to listen to a lady, no matter the size."

Lacey did a double take. Had the cop just winked at her? The whole world was flipped upside down.

MIKE FIGURED HE could skip his daily run since he'd spent the last half hour jogging the energy out of the crazy Labrador he'd agree to escort today. Finally, the dog—Joker—had settled down enough for him to catch his breath.

Sierra and her mom were neck deep in showing off dogs

to potential adopters. If even half of those conversations paid off, quite a few of her rescue animals would have new homes.

God, Sierra was unstoppable. Damn near shimmering with energy even after hours in the heat. Her golden hair was twisted in some kind of ropy side ponytail with a few stray strands framing her face. She made jean shorts overalls and a tank top look runway sexy. Keeping his distance was tougher and tougher by the day, but leaving this family when they clearly needed help was out of the question as well.

He tore his eyes off her and checked on her brother on the same park bench where he'd been sitting with his grandpa since they arrived. Did Nathan ever go off and do kid stuff? Another concern when it came to this family.

Swiping the sweat off his forehead, Mike jogged slowly to their bench by the water. "Hey, Nathan? I'll stay with your grandfather and Trooper for a while. Want to go get everyone something to eat?"

"Uhm, yeah," Nathan said. "No-brainer."

Mike fished a couple of twenties out of his wallet. "Sodas and hot dogs for the whole family. That trolley cart with the balloons seems to have the best traffic. And don't forget your mom and sister."

Nathan shoved his earbuds in without bothering to answer.

Joshua held the empty bread bag in his hand, watching the ducks. "That boy's got an attitude problem."

That boy had a grieving problem, so it was tough to know how hard to push him on the attitude. "He's a teenager." Mike sat on the bench, letting Joker have the full length of the leash to go sniff at the water. "I'm sure my grandma said the same thing about me."

The old man shot him a quick sideways look with blue eyes the same color as Sierra's. "You've got that look to you. Be careful around my girl, you hear me?"

"Uh, yes, sir. I will."

Trooper ambled toward the Lab with loping-shouldered steps, sniffing in that wary "get to know you, here's my butt to sniff" way dogs did.

The General scrubbed the back of his neck. "I'm sorry for my ill behavior around you the other day when I was walking Trooper. You didn't deserve that."

He was getting so used to the General's bad days, a good day when the man's brain was clicking caught him off guard. "It's okay, sir. No harm, no foul."

Joker splashed at the water with both front paws, sending the ducks flapping away to a safer stretch of riverbank. Trooper inched forward to investigate.

"I like walking him." The General jiggled his end of the leash, and the curious mutt still came trotting back right away. "He always remembers the way home."

Joshua McDaniel's blue eyes went watery with unshed tears that made Mike's gut knot.

"He's a good dog, sir."

"The best." The General cleared his throat and looked away. "Getting much sleep, son?"

Mike had realized about three days ago that "son" didn't always mean the General was thinking of Allen. He just called all males that since he couldn't remember names. He'd also learned not to question the abrupt shifts in conversation with the guy. His brain traveled unpredictable paths.

"The studio apartment in the barn is quite comfortable, sir."

"That's not what I asked." Joshua glanced at him, wadding up the bag in his fist.

Not sure where this conversation was going, he said simply, "I don't need a lot of sleep."

"Coming back from overseas is tough."

Ah, now he saw the logic to the man's questions. The General was definitely all there today, and not in a way that was comfortable for Mike.

"Being here is better than staying over there," he said simply.

"Except this family of mine comes with a lot of extra baggage for you. You don't need all of that along with a cranky-ass old man shouting at you because he can't remember where the hell he's going."

"You have all been nice to me, really generous, too. I appreciate that."

"You're good at putting on the nice face, but you don't have to pretend around me. I know what it's like coming home, trying to flip that switch between being over there and being here, both places so . . . different."

Ironic that he had more in common with the senile old man than anyone else around him. Mike's hand fell to Trooper's head. "This fella here feels like a link, a bridge from everything that happened there to getting back here."

"Maybe that's why he kept chasing after you. To be the bridge."

Mike looked down at Trooper—currently licking his healed neuter incision. "You give the dog credit for thinking through quite a plan considering he currently has his head up his own butt."

"Maybe so." The General chuckled in agreement for an instant until his laughter drifted away out over the river. "I only know that when this guy is around, the world feels clearer to an old foggy mind like mine."

"Dogs can be quite a comfort, sir." Trooper had been a lifeline for a lot of them overseas.

"Becoming forgetful, well, it's embarrassing as hell. I'm an old soldier who survived." He waved his hand. "And this is my reward."

Understanding filled up the space between them in a way that went past years. For the moment they existed in a warrior's common ground of shared experiences even on different battlefields. Were the General's memories triggered by smells as well as sounds, too? The scent of munitions and blood filled Mike even as he struggled to draw in the fresh breeze off the river.

The past gripped him so hard—

Pop. Pop. Pop.

The sound out of nowhere had him ducking his head before his mind could register it was just balloons popping. Wincing in embarrassment, his heart damn near pounding out of his chest, he looked around to see if anyone noticed his shell-shocked reaction.

And found the General with his head ducked, too, staring right back at him.

"Shit." The General grimaced and grinned all at once. "Where's that boy with our lunch?"

Nine

SIERRA WAS DOG tired—before she finished the thought she rolled her eyes at the irony of shelter humor. She would have laughed. Except she was too weary to laugh at her own joke as she walked up the outdoor steps leading to the barn's studio apartment without tripping over the stairs in the dark.

The adoption event had been a success. They'd found homes for eleven dogs and had a half dozen people set up for meet and greets with cats. Some of the families already had pre-approved applications, which cleared open foster homes and spaces here as well.

As Sierra climbed the stairs, the low hum of a CD player in the kennels drifted through the walls. Classical tunes calmed the dogs. Her mom had a knack for bringing back the old ways of doing things, showing how they were still effective and sometimes less expensive. Like soothing music and aromatherapy. She sure could use some of those relaxing tunes for herself. If only she could walk up these steps just to hang out with Mike, sit and listen to him play his guitar. But she had a wily mutt to chase down.

Trooper wasn't in his crate in the family room where he normally slept, which had sent her into a tailspin initially. Then she stopped and thought. Their escape artist dog may have headed back to Mike again.

And yes, she'd jumped all over the excuse to see Mike.

Her mother had offered to check for Trooper, but Lacey looked wiped out and she still had to feed the puppies. At least they were well on their way to eating solid foods—a gruel mush. Thumbelina had a runny nose, and Lacey had been carrying the sick pup around in a baby sling.

Of course Nathan and Gramps were already in bed.

Outside the loft apartment door painted red with little brown paw prints, Sierra held her fist up, ready to knock. A television was on inside, some sports game, the noise meshing with the low music below. The world sounded . . . normal. Once she checked on Trooper, she also owed Mike a thank-you for his help today, and especially for sitting with her grandfather. She was here for that, just that . . . right?

God, she was a confused mess.

Before she lost her nerve, she knocked twice, fast.

The television silenced. Her stomach did a flip. The door opened and, holy hormone overload, that man knew how to fill a space. Even fully dressed in gym shorts and a T-shirt, he made her mouth water.

She forced her eyes off the dog tags resting on his hard, muscled chest and up to his eyes. "Is Trooper here with you? He's not in his crate and we can't find him, so I figured he must have slipped back over here to be with you like he did before."

"He's not here. But don't worry—" Mike stepped aside and waved her into the loft, remote control in his hand. "Hey, could you come in so we don't let the A/C out and the mosquitoes in?"

"Sure." She stepped into the sparsely filled loft apartment. *Her* apartment, with a man, a mattress and a wide-screen TV. Lord, that sounded like a country song. "Where is he then?"

The scent of soap and steam hung in the air from a recent shower. His hair was still damp at the tips.

"He's with your grandfather. The General said he wanted Trooper to sleep in his room."

Gramps? God, she hadn't even thought of that. Guilt tugged at her for not having considered her grandfather wanting the comfort of that companionship.

"Oh, I should have thought to check there. We did call for Trooper, but he must have chosen not to answer. Dogs can be so much smarter than we give them credit for sometimes." She inched deeper into the one-room studio. The door shut, sealing them inside together and making her all too aware of Mike and the scent of soap. "I'm just relieved Trooper's okay. Relieved . . . and feeling a little guilty. I should have thought to see if my grandfather wanted an animal in his room at night. Those alarms you put on the barn and the house take away worries of Gramps letting Trooper out . . ."

"You can't think of everything your grandfather needs. You're not a mind reader."

"I realize that, but still, I feel bad. We're running a rescue here, and I didn't think to ask my failing grandfather if he would like the comfort of an animal of his own."

"We?"

"What do you mean?"

"You said, 'We're running a rescue.' I thought it was your mother's."

The notion tripped her up short for a second before she continued, "Right. Mom's always working so hard to make sure no one feels inconvenienced—or rather more inconvenienced—by the animals." She sagged down to sit on the edge of his fat recliner chair. Better than sitting on the mattress. "I should have looked at the other side of this.

Like how Nathan enjoys his snake. Gramps can't articulate what he needs. But you saw it in only a week."

Mike tossed the remote from hand to hand. "You've got so much day-to-day caregiver stuff to consider for him. It's easy for someone on the outside like me to make one little suggestion. I just happened to notice at the park today how much the dog means to him."

She put herself in her grandfather's New Balance gym shoes—and wasn't that a metaphor for Gramps's life over-all?—and realized he'd lost so much more than his memory. He'd lost control of his life, even the most basic pleasures like driving, picking dinner, walking a dog . . . having friends. "Thank you for spending extra time with him today. It really helped free up Mom and me to process more adop-tions, and he seemed to enjoy talking with you. Most of all, thank you for listening to him."

"No trouble, and I enjoyed myself," he said, sounding sincere as he stood watching her with his sexy golden brown eyes of his. "A lazy day by the water, good company, grilled hot dogs . . . It's great being home. Joker and Trooper enjoyed their hot dogs while we hung out by the water."

Joker was adopted at the end of the day by a college athlete looking for a running buddy, a good match for the energetic Lab. Whatever family he had in the future would grow up with a great dog.

There was something special about the tug of a childhood pet. "Did you know my dad had a dog named Trooper when he was growing up? From the old family photos, the two dogs even kind of look alike." So much so, it freaked her out sometimes. "The original Trooper was a German shep-herd mix of some kind. I can see why my father was drawn to the dog over there."

"That could explain the connection your grandfather feels to him, too . . . the look and the name. Maybe if Trooper gets used to sleeping at the foot of the bed, he will quit running away to me before I leave for Fort Bragg."

Only three weeks until the council meeting. Not long after that and he would be leaving altogether. The reminder hung there between them, unsettling her. "Gramps seemed to have a really good day."

"He did. I enjoyed the chance to meet him, the man, unfiltered by the illness."

Tears choked her throat as she remembered visits with her grandfather. He'd taken her to military museums and battlegrounds. He'd shared war stories as they ate burgers at a museum cafeteria. She'd told her friends she had the smartest grandpa in the world.

Watching him fade away . . . hurt. While she was glad he'd enjoyed a good afternoon with Mike, she couldn't deny she was a little jealous she'd missed out on that fleeting moment. "I'm happy he had fun at the event. We really debated whether to take him or not." She added wryly, "Lately, we consider it a good outing if he doesn't try to take off his pants."

"He takes off his pants in public?" The remote control slipped from Mike's fingers and hit the rug with a thud.

She slid from the chair to pick up the remote, finding the metal still warm from his grasp. A spark snapped between them, a connection, like static crackling all over her body. "Only once."

As she stood slowly, he took the remote from her, his pupils widening in an answering awareness. "You should have warned me so I could be prepared to stop him if it happened again."

"I just did." She held on for a second, one of those loaded moments where they stood close, not quite touching but undeniably linked. She let go and walked past to the window overlooking the empty play yard that backed up to the woods, such a scenic view. "A blogger from a military e-zine stopped by my mom's booth today, took a bunch of photos of our animals, said the blogger's married to a guy in your platoon." She glanced over her shoulder at him. "You wouldn't happen to know anything about that, would you?"

"Glad she made it to the event," he said noncommittally, his eyes following her every movement.

"Come on." She turned around, her butt resting against the window ledge. "Did you arrange that?"

"I just let her know." He shrugged, still downplaying his part in bringing such good press their way. "It was no big deal."

"It's a freaking huge deal. Mom can use all the positive press she can get right now. Thank you for helping her."

"I did it for you, too." He joined her at the window, leaning one of those broad shoulders against the window frame. "Your heart is in this place, too. Don't deny it. So maybe I did it to score brownie points with you."

"Why can't you accept a thank-you or a compliment?" She tugged his dog tags lightly. "It's okay to be the hero."

"I made a phone call. BFD." He pulled his dog tags from her fingers and tucked them inside his gray Army T-shirt.

"It is a BFD." She pressed a hand over his chest, over the dog tags and his beating heart. "All you've done for us this week is a huge BFD. The grounds look better. Repairs on the house and the barn have never looked better. In what could be a tight vote on whether or not having a rescue here follows county codes, you've already won over some people to our side. Mom said she got two positive comments at the grocery store Thursday."

She wasn't sure if she left her hand on his chest to convince him or because she couldn't pull away. The warmth of his skin came right through his shirt. She wanted to lay her head right there and feel the beat of his heart against her temple

"Hey, I did it for me, too." He folded a hand over hers and held on, no phantom touch this time. This was the real deal. "The Sergeant Major will be hard-pressed to come after me now without making me look like a martyr. The blogger will start a fresh flood of stories to fill the Internet all over again. Did you see all the Tweeting and who knows what other kind of messaging going on as people snapped photos of Trooper at the event today?"

His fingers stroked her palm subtly. Softly.

"I did. But I don't care how much you say you did it for yourself, you didn't have to fix broken faucets and fences to impress your boss. You've done a lot out of the spotlight, too." No matter what else had happened between them, she couldn't deny the truth, that she'd been drawn by more than just his sexy body and handsome face. "Thank you for being a very good man."

"Perhaps I have other ulterior motives." His voice hit a lower pitch as he stepped closer.

Her body heated with desire, with memories, with the undeniable attraction between them, an attraction she couldn't seem to remember why she should deny. Suddenly, walking away tonight wasn't an option. She didn't want to think about tomorrow. She needed this moment. With Mike.

Decision made, she curled her fingers around his dog tags through the T-shirt. "What other motives do you have?"

His eyes went amber, more gold than brown, and he slid a hand up to cup her face. "Like getting you back into bed again."

ALL DAY AT the adoption festival, Mike had watched Sierra, mesmerized by the way she moved so confidently through whatever life tossed her way—from helping a child learn how to hold his new puppy to calmly explaining to an angry couple why the dog they wanted had already been adopted.

She was smart and funny and sexy.

And no matter how hard he tried, he couldn't stop wanting her.

His breath lodged somewhere in his chest as he waited for her reaction to his words. He searched her sky blue eyes as she stood a whisper away.

Finally, she blinked, chewing her lip. "Technically, you don't have a bed. Just a mattress."

That definitely wasn't a "no." His pulse revved. Temperature spiked.

"Technically, we didn't always wait to make it to a bed." Memories of three months of amazing sex filled his mind, and he saw it echo in her eyes. They'd known each other over a year, dated for months before taking their relationship to the next level. An unforgettable level. They'd had sex in his truck, on a blanket under the stars, even locked in a bathroom at a party when they couldn't wait . . .

Her throat moved in a slow swallow, her fingers twitched against his chest. Caressing. "You're right about our relationship being full of . . . impulsiveness."

"Suppose I was trying to win you back to my . . . mattress, not out of impulsiveness"—he paused, squeezing her hand—"but because we had something good. And even if there isn't a future for us, I can't seem to let go of the past. What would you say to that?"

He couldn't deny how important her answer was to him—too much so.

"I would say I'm swayed." She stepped closer, until her breasts pressed again him, her face tipped up toward his.

He slid an arm around her waist, and she didn't protest or pull away, so he continued, "What if I moved my hand down your back?"

Sierra slid her hand over his shoulder to cup the back of his neck. "I would sigh."

"You wouldn't pull away?" He stroked along her spine, up and down, going farther every time. Higher. Lower.

A soft moan of encouragement ratcheted up the heat.

She arched to skim her lips against his, her breasts beading into tight points he felt right through their clothes. "Find out."

His body throbbed in reaction. He stroked down her spine

with slow deliberation that pulled a sigh from her. He palmed her just above her bottom and brought her flush against him.

"What if I kissed you?"

"What if you stopped asking me questions and just started doing?"

"That's a very"—he skimmed his mouth along hers— "very good"—he kissed her lightly again—"question."

He sealed his mouth to hers.

The taste and warmth of her seared through him until he was hard and aching in an instant. Sierra, it was always about Sierra. He'd thought of her the whole time he was overseas. But he didn't want to think about those months now, or ever, actually.

He intended to live in the moment. And the moment was mighty damn amazing. His hands cupped her bottom, bringing her closer, fitting her curves to him in a way he remembered in vivid detail. Along with the taste of her mingling with the sweet tea she'd sipped at supper. He wanted to savor her after so long waiting and wondering if he would ever have this chance again.

But she pushed him toward the mattress. Not that she could budge him anywhere he didn't want to go. He didn't need much encouragement at all. The second the back of his legs bumped the bed, he allowed himself to fall, taking her with him. He hit the thick comforter, her body flush on top of his. A purr of approval breathed from her into him, igniting the heat to a frenzy.

The citrus scent of her was his drug of choice. He breathed deep, molding his hands to her curves and absorbing the feel of her. Hips. Waist. Unforgettable breasts. His mouth watered for a taste.

He tugged her layered tank tops over her head, and in the tangle of arms, she pulled at his T-shirt as well, pitching the wadded-up cotton aside. The sight of her creamy skin in a lacy yellow bra threatened to send him over the edge. Already, one strap drooped down her shoulder, the cup starting to fall away from the swell of her flesh. He arched up to take her in his mouth, tease and dampen the lace. She shuddered in response, so sensitive to the stroke of his tongue as he circled the taut peak. Her fingers fisted against his chest, her breath coming in soft pants while he teased and tasted.

Her head flung back and she urged him on, her hands roving him, stroking him, taking him in her hand and tempting, touch for touch. She tugged at his shorts and shimmied out of her jeans. With a growl, he rolled her onto her back, tucking her under him.

Her eyes were half open and dazed with a passion matched by the flush over her creamy skin. "Please say you have a condom."

"I do"—thank God—"since the day after we kissed that first time after I got back."

"You assumed a lot."

"I hoped. Really hoped." He levered off her and sprinted to the bathroom to get the box of condoms from under the sink. He couldn't get back to her fast enough. He stepped into the room again just as she dropped her bra to the floor.

His fist tightened around the package, crimping the cardboard box.

A seductive smile spread over her face as she inched her matching yellow lace panties down, down, down, revealing the Shakespeare quote tattooed on her hip. *Love is a smoke made with the fume of sighs.*

And God, how he loved to make her sigh.

He kicked aside his boxers on his way to cover her, throbbing, aching to lose himself inside her again. She took the box from him, tore into a packet and sheathed him with bold deliberation. He settled on top of her, nudging at her core, seconds away from being . . .

Inside her.

The warmth and clamp of her body around him drew him deeper, and he couldn't deny that this felt like the real homecoming. The one he'd been missing and dreaming about. She was . . . incredible. His.

A fierce hunger gripped him. Her legs wrapped around his waist, bringing him deeper still as she writhed her hips against him as he thrust. Need took hold, urging him to move faster, but then that could also be due to her voice in his ear, her hot breath on his neck.

He ducked his head to capture her mouth, hungry to connect on every level possible. Aching for her. Being with Sierra here tore down walls. Being with her narrowed the world to just the two of them, every nerve on fire to finish hard and fast. Other instincts shouted at him to make this last as long as possible, to draw out the pleasure and the connection because the thought of being without her again was damn near intolerable.

She scraped her fingernails down his back, the sheets rustling, tangling until he kicked aside the comforter. Restraint sent sweat dotting his brow as they moved, flesh against flesh. The ceiling fan overhead and air conditioner didn't stand a chance competing against the rising fire inside him.

Her heels dug in deeper, her body tensing and clenching around him as she cried out her release. She slid her mouth from his and nipped his shoulder, her body bowing up into him. As much as he wanted to hurtle right into that release with her, he kept his eyes open, taking in every nuance of her orgasm rippling through her. So beautiful.

Only once she sagged back into the pillow, sated, did he allow himself to thrust to his own completion, the power of the release tearing through him after so long without sex— without her.

And the thought of never being with her again had his arms shaking until he collapsed on top of her. He rolled to her side and hauled her close, his face inhaling the citrus fresh scent of her hair so he didn't have to look in her eyes.

So she wouldn't see the need for her in his own.

MAKING LOVE WITH Mike had been impulsive and probably not wise, but she refused to regret her decision.

They'd been moving toward this since he'd stepped off the plane just over a week ago. This welcome back moment was meant to be between them. Lounging in bed with him in post-sex bliss, while he played the guitar.

After this?

She didn't know and refused to think about it right now since odds were, deeper thought could wreck the moment. So she just let herself relax into the warm tones of his music. The sex between them had been every bit as combustible as she remembered—and yes, as she feared, because that would make it tougher to resist him.

And she definitely hadn't been resisting at all when they'd landed on the mattress. Or after when he'd made love to her again with his hands and mouth, bringing her toe-curling release over and over.

Like so many times in the past after they'd been together, Mike plucked out some melody on his guitar, humming softly. She lay on her stomach naked and listened, his voice stroking her senses as tangibly as his touch, even if there were no words. His tunes did all the communicating.

Some songs were familiar, fun hits. Other times he chose the more emotional, saying things in notes or lyrics that he would never talk about. But her favorites? When he made up silly songs if the mood needed lightening.

Right now, he was rhyming and rambling about crummy bachelor food in his refrigerator and how he was nothing but a nachos and bingo Romeo. All the more amusing since she knew he was an excellent cook, far better than her.

His voice stopped, even as his fingers continued in a riff. He narrowed his eyes. "What are you thinking?"

She shrugged, the sheet sliding along her skin. "Just reminiscing. I didn't expect we would ever be together again this way."

"Remind me why? Because right now all I can think of is doing it again." He grinned roguishly, then frowned. "You're not using this as an intro to leaving."

"I didn't say I was leaving . . ." She stroked her bare foot up his leg, the bristle of his manly thigh tickling her already tingling senses. In spite of her intentions to keep things low-key, she felt words itching to come out. God, why couldn't she simply enjoy the moment? Instead, she had to blurt, "I'm just not sure how long we can stay this way before the world and old problems intrude."

He shifted his hand from the guitar to her ankle, rubbing, then massaging. "Let's leave the world out there a while longer."

"How?" She sighed, flexing her foot. "And keep doing that. Please."

"More than happy to comply." He pressed his thumb along the arch of her foot. "In about twenty minutes I'll be up for the ultimate distraction, but for now, let's talk."

"About?" Although she would discuss anything if he kept rubbing her feet and she didn't have to face the outside world worries.

"Okay, you want to talk?" He looked around before meeting her eyes again. "Why did you paint this place the color of a John Deere tractor?"

She gasped, jerking her foot away as she sat up straight with the sheet clutched to her bare chest. "That's . . . That's just wrong. The walls are not the color of a tractor. That's bright green. This is light green, like a peaceful garden."

"Gardens are bright green . . ." His eyebrows pinched together as he tapped his temple. "They are *verdant*."

"Verdant?" She giggled, grateful for a light moment when there was so much dark baggage piled up on their doorstep. "Really?"

He tut-tut-tutted. "You wound me. I worked my ass off on vocabulary while we were dating." His hands went back to the guitar still in his lap and plucked, as he sang, "Crossword puzzles. Online Scrabble. Words with Friends . . ." Shaking his head, laughing, he propped his guitar against the wall. "I even went back and read some of the books I skipped in high school."

She hugged her knees to her chest, resting her chin on her crossed arms. "You did what?"

He reclined back on the stacked pillows, his shoulders broad and bronzed against white cotton bedding. "I brushed up on books I should have read in school. I had a habit of reading CliffsNotes and online summaries instead."

"That's an awesome endeavor, but what brought that on?"

"Making sure I understood your world, and yeah, maybe there was an ego issue over all your education and feeling your dad wanted more for you than a guy like me."

She sat—stunned. "Mike, I'm, uh, not even sure how to react. You're an intelligent man, successful in your career. Your strength is in computers, math and being a damn good soldier. My strength is a broad knowledge of some dead poets, which actually isn't that marketable and makes me question who's the smarter one right now."

"Just hedging my bets to make sure you kept feeling that way." He tugged her back against his chest. "Lime Jell-O green."

She glanced at his face and knew him well enough to see he was putting an end to serious talk. They were back to nacho Romeo land. Hard to fault him for that when they were alike in that way.

She hugged him harder under the pretense of cuddling closer, taking in the scent of his soap and a hint of sweat as she spent her first night in the apartment she'd thought would be hers. "I think it's the color of mint ice cream."

"Okay, I can see that." His voice vibrated against her ear. "Or if you want to go back to your garden theme, what about celery?"

She glanced up at him, thinking of him playing Words with Friends for her and him feeling her family didn't approve of him . . . She forced a smile. "Celery colored? Better, but blah, no taste."

His eyes lit with playful competitiveness. "Avocados? Pistachio pudding?"

"*Much* better." She angled up to nip his bottom lip, letting desire sweep away more complicated emotions. "You sound hungry."

"Ahhh . . . Then how about forbidden apples?" His hands roved up into her hair, his arousal stirring unmistakably against her thigh.

Her skin tingled in anticipation. "It hasn't been twenty minutes."

"Well, what do you know?" Mike tucked Sierra underneath him, his mouth hovering just over hers. "Time sure flies."

Ten

LACEY HAD STARTED drinking to help herself fall asleep after the sleep aids the doctor gave her didn't work.

She'd soon realized it didn't matter what she took or drank. Her insomnia wasn't going away even if she took double the dose of the medicine in her hand. So she kept busy into the wee hours of the morning until her body gave out and slept somewhere for a few hours out of pure exhaustion.

Now here she was, still awake with that damn cuckoo clock chiming two in the morning.

She'd worked her butt off at the adoption event, fed her family and taken a long shower. She should be totally wiped out. But all she could think about was that bed. That big, empty bed. Which reminded her of the empty spot for Allen's toothbrush. His missing shampoo. And the list went on endlessly.

She opened her closet, which wasn't empty. Allen's clothes still occupied half the large walk-in. He'd only taken his uniforms and workout clothes with him. His suits, jeans,

casual shirts and deck shoes all stayed. She hadn't gone
through his things, and she probably should figure out what
to save. What to give her father-in-law and her children as
keepsakes.

What to keep for herself.

Looking in the closet was never a good idea. Stepping
inside was even more dangerous. The first month after he'd
died, she'd closed herself in the space once a day, lights off,
and breathed in the lingering scent of him while she cried.

She shut the doors, staying firmly *out*side the closet. No
going backward. Forward was her only option, regardless
of how badly it sucked.

The clock was silent. So was her house. Sierra had texted
her about Trooper sleeping in the General's room. The fact
that Sierra had texted rather than finding her to speak was
telling. Her daughter hadn't announced she was staying in
the loft apartment with Mike tonight, but it was after two
and her daughter hadn't come back from talking to her old
boyfriend . . .

Lacey's head fell to rest on the closet door. She did not
need to think about sex. Not now.

She looked out of the corner of her eyes through the door
into her bedroom. Her queen-sized bed was perfectly made
with a green and yellow patchwork quilt, a gift from one of
her foster moms. The pillow shams were stacked, the most
orderly part of her house. Probably because she avoided
sleeping in her bed whenever possible, taking an afghan to
the sofa and telling her kids she fell asleep watching television. The fosters offered endless reasons to sleep by their
crate because they needed monitoring.

Actually, since the day she'd been told her husband died,
she hadn't slept under the covers at all. If she slept on her
bed, she stayed on top of the spread and used a blanket. So
far, no one appeared to have noticed. She kept promising
herself she would face that hurdle tomorrow, and tomorrow,
and tomorrow.

A cold knot lodged in her chest as she remembered sharing that space with Allen. Not just for sex, but also for those quieter married moments where they lay side by side, propped on pillows reading or with iPads out to surf news sites . . .

Tomorrow was definitely not coming today.

She pulled on yoga pants and a T-shirt before moving out of the bedroom and into the hall. She made it three steps and heard a scratching on a door—from inside the General's room. Must be Trooper wanting to go outside. He couldn't run off if she kept an eye on him. She cracked the door and let him out.

"Need to go potty, boy?" She scratched his ears, only managing one stroke before he sprinted toward the door.

She flipped off the alarm and opened the door to the fenced area. Trooper shot out and made a beeline for the fat oak tree in the middle of the play yard. He lifted a leg and . . . he must have drunk a gallon of water.

Finally, he stopped, kicking his back legs and sending grass flying. He ambled around the quiet yard, sniffing, exploring. She dropped to sit on the top step and let him stretch his legs. He stuck his nose under a bush, doggie butt way in the air as he inched his head farther under. Springing back, he came out with a green tennis ball in his mouth.

Allen had written to her about how he and the soldiers unwound by playing ball with Trooper. It made them all forget for a moment where they were by bringing a taste of normalcy to their lives. A piece of home.

It must have really felt like home for Allen given she always had a dozen or more dogs around.

Snorting on a teary laugh, she scrubbed her wrists under her eyes. "Trooper," she called, snapping her fingers, "come. Wanna play?"

He bounded toward her, dropping the ball at her feet and then sitting perfectly still, waiting.

"Good boy. Good boy. Fetch." She pitched the tennis ball across the yard. "Fetch."

He sprinted full out, retrieved and brought it back.

She tossed and counted stars.

He ran, picked it up, brought it back.

She lost track of how many times she threw the ball, lost track of the time altogether. She spent so much time caring for animals, she hadn't realized how rarely she got to play with them anymore. There was something soothing in this repetitive ritual, the easy give-and-take of it under a perfect Tennessee night sky.

Her first fostering experience had come about when Sierra was in second grade and she needed a service project for church. Their schedule had been so crazy with soccer practice and school, plus she'd just started teaching online. They'd decided to foster a puppy for the local shelter while he recovered from a skin condition. They'd fallen head over heels for that puppy as they'd watched and tended him, bathed him, loved him until his fur grew back and the light returned to his eyes. They'd almost adopted the pup, but when she'd seen the joy on the adopters' faces, she'd found a calling.

She'd fostered for years, helping shelters and rescues wherever her family moved during the crazy period of their lives when Allen had been transferred umpteen times. Fostering animals had been a grounding ritual for them, a way to feel at home each time they pulled up stakes. When they'd come here three years ago with the intent to retire and settle, she'd decided to act on her dream to open her own rescue. Since she finally had her forever home, she would share it with animals in need of shelter and love. She'd focused everything on making this rescue successful while keeping her job teaching online and bringing up her kids. Allen had been gone half the time, so the dogs were her family in his absence. She'd respected the fact that he'd been as married to his job as he'd been to her, and she'd tried to find work that gave her that same sense of duty and satisfaction.

For years, she and Allen had been on separate but parallel tracks, like dogs with their own kennel runs. She'd always thought there would be time for her and Allen, for their marriage, later. That one day, they'd be back on the same track again.

She'd launched her dream and she'd lost her husband. Lacey pitched the ball again only to realize Trooper had fallen asleep at her feet.

Lucky dog.

MORNING SUNLIGHT WAS only just pushing through, but once Mike got his internal clock set, he wasn't one to sleep late. He'd learned early to get up on his own for school if he wanted time to pour himself a bowl of cereal before he left.

So even though he'd made love to Sierra late into the night, he'd still woken at dawn, and slipped out of bed careful not to disturb her.

As she slept across the room, he moved quietly in the kitchen. In spite of his nacho Romeo tune, he could cook for himself, damn well, for that matter. He'd done so since he was a kid when cooking was a survival skill if he wanted to live off more than Ramen Noodles and school lunches. By eight years old, he'd figured out how to fry eggs, which made for a good breakfast sandwich. He'd graduated to pancakes—cheap and easy to find the ingredients in his grandmother's pantry.

His skills in the kitchen had come a long way since those days. And God, how he'd missed a good breakfast when he was overseas.

Today, he'd made French toast with roasted apples, and in a couple of minutes, he would have warm caramel to drizzle over the top. He stirred the wooden spoon in the simmering sauce. The moment was so damn *normal*. It had been so long since he'd experienced regular life, it was still surreal. Bleached clean sheets. Fresh food. Picnics in the park. Lounging in bed discussing wall colors after sex with a gorgeous woman.

A woman currently tugging on her panties, his T-shirt and nothing else.

Sierra walked across the studio apartment and leaned a hip on the island. "That smells *amazing.*"

"Your grandfather was a hundred percent right about missing real food during a deployment. I haven't finished working my way through meals I fantasized about." Speaking of fantasies . . . an image of painting Sierra with warm caramel then licking it off her almost made him burn the French toast.

He grabbed the spatula and flipped the toast.

Sierra toppled the pepper mill on the counter and spun it in lazy circles. "You've always been a better cook than me."

"Yes, ma'am, but that's okay. I like to cook." He lifted the wooden spoon and blew on the caramel. "And seeing pleasure on your face? All the better."

She leaned in to lick the spoon, her eyes closing as she swallowed with an appreciative hmmmmm.

His temperature spiked. Only the cooking food kept him from reclining her on the island and playing out that caramel fantasy. "You like it?"

"Very good. Thank you," she said as he returned to the stove. "You never told me how you learned. You always just said you picked it up out of necessity. So . . . ?"

"Watching television cooking shows." He winked at her. "I've always had a secret crush on Julia Child."

"You're kidding."

"Please don't take offense if I call out for Rachael Ray next time we're in bed together." Next time? Damn straight.

"You're wicked."

"I am."

"So seriously, no joking"—she hitched up onto a barstool

and leaned on the counter—"tell me about learning to cook. I want to know."

"My grandmother slept in mornings," from late nights at casinos. He saw the concern flickering across Sierra's face and found himself justifying before he could stop. "She was supposed to be a grandmother, not a parent, ya know? And honestly, I preferred my own food. When she cooked supper, her repertoire pretty much consisted of meat meets a can of soup."

"I thought men were happy with food. Period. But then . . . Wait. You said *when* she cooked." She frowned. "Your grandmother didn't feed you?"

He wasn't comfortable with her sympathy, but he was already neck deep in the conversation. "She kept stuff in the pantry—"

"Mike—"

"But I wanted to learn to cook the things I saw on TV, and I needed extra ingredients." The next part of his story was trickier to navigate. "Our budget was tight so I couldn't ask her for extra cash for my cooking experiments. I tried winning money at bingo like my grandmother, but that didn't work. Guess I don't have the family lucky touch with the daubers."

"What did you do?"

"One day I was walking home from school and I saw this guy in the subway playing his guitar with a jar for money." He slid the toast from the pan to two plates. "I didn't have the money for a guitar, but I signed up for the choir at school."

She grinned. "You were in the choir as a kid? I bet you were adorable."

"Adorable? Really?" He shuddered and leaned to kiss her nose. "Since there weren't many boys who actually volunteered—ones that could also sing on key—the chorus teacher made a point of helping me so I would stay. I took guitar lessons from her and she loaned me a guitar in exchange for recruiting more boys to join the chorus."

"She sounds like a good teacher."

She was. That guitar had changed his life by giving him something positive to do with his time—and a way to earn his own money. "By spring break I could play well enough to earn Easter dinner with my subway tips. By the summer, I made enough to feed us three square meals." A big deal once the school lunches stopped for three months.

Sierra frowned. "You worked in a subway? That doesn't sound very safe. What did your grandmother say about it?"

"She didn't know." Not because he was particularly sneaky, but because she wasn't that observant. But he left that part out. There were already enough barriers—differences between them.

"Where did she think you went?"

"A friend's house. The library." He'd lied so she wouldn't want a cut of his earnings. He figured she got plenty because she ate what he cooked. Strange how she never asked him how he got the food. Did she think he was shoplifting?

Hell, he couldn't imagine anyone getting away with that here at the McDaniel house. Even old Alzheimer's Gramps would have caught a glimmer, which likely would have led to another conversation on condoms.

Had the old man been more savvy about Mike and Sierra than it seemed?

Already this whole conversation was hitting a few too many nerves for his comfort level. "Breakfast. Eat up." He nudged a plate toward her. "And go easy on the caramel sauce. I have plans for the leftovers."

A HALF HOUR later, sated with French toast, Sierra leaned across the island to kiss Mike, savoring the taste of syrup and caramel on his tongue. "Breakfast was awesome, but can I take a rain check on the extended time with caramel sauce?"

Mike slid his hand into her hair, cupping the back of her head, kissing along her cheek to nip her ear. "Are you sure I can't entice you to stay longer?"

"I have to help Mom out." She picked up her plate and stood. "Later, though?"

He reached to take the dish from her. She held on for a second, tugging him closer until she leaned forward and kissed him. She wanted to stay but needed some space of her own to process all he'd told her. It wasn't so much what he'd said but the fact he'd never shared these things before. That made her question everything from their relationship before, and until she had that sorted out, she didn't know how to move forward. She ended the kiss, then kissed him once more. Briefly. Then she let go of the dish.

With a sliver of air between them, she said, "A lot happened here last night. I need space. I think you do, too. Having your help here has been a godsend, but it's also almost as if we're . . ."

"Living together." His forehead fell to rest on hers.

"If we're not careful, this could get messy fast at a time when we're both raw after what happened to my dad."

Mike flinched. There was no missing it. She felt that instinctive cringe all the way to her bruised heart.

"Later, okay?"

He just nodded, letting her go. Without another word, she finished dressing and slipped out the door. The fresh Tennessee air swept over her with the scent of farm fields and the first hint of a scorcher of a day to come. Her one day off since they'd worked all yesterday at the adoption event. Except there was no such thing as a day off here. She didn't have time for a "boyfriend"—especially when that relationship came with so much potential for an implosion.

She sagged against the closed door for a second before regaining her balance. She just needed to slip into the house and get a shower, return her life to normal and then figure out what to do next when she had a clear head. Away from the temptation of licking caramel sauce off each other's bodies.

Steeling her resolve, she raced down the steps, checking the yard carefully for her mom. At the sound of Sierra's footsteps, the dogs started barking even though feeding wasn't for another hour.

Her sandals slapped the grass, early morning dew squelching with each step closer to the house. The back porch fans were already churning, which could be an accident. Her family forgot to turn them off all the time.

Or someone could already be awake.

Not that it should matter. She was twenty-three, staying at home to help, not living at home. She paid her own bills and helped her mother out when the rescue made things financially tight.

So why did she feel like a teenager slipping in after hours?

Seeing her mom on the porch, Sierra considered bolting back to Mike's apartment—*her* apartment. Or making her way around to the front door so she could slip into her childhood room like a delinquent.

God, that sounded lame. And truth be told, she could use some advice. Or if nothing else, some sign of how to deal with what happened last night.

Shaking off the urge to run, she walked to the screened back porch where her mother sat in a wrought iron chair with a fat floral cushion. The fairy-tale-named pit puppies played in a pen in front of her. Watching them while they romped and rolled, Lacey tucked her legs to the side, still wearing her yoga pants and a loose T-shirt. She sipped a crystal flute of orange juice, a muffin on a plate beside her.

Her mom lifted her drink toward Sierra. "Would you like a mimosa? I actually have a matching flute. These didn't get broken in the moves like most of the other crystal."

"Thanks, but no thanks." Sierra sat in a wrought iron

porch chair next to her mother. They used to have wicker but the dogs chewed it. So Sierra went to rummage sales and found assorted pieces, and painted them all different bright colors. "Feels strange—you offering me a drink—especially at seven in the morning."

"You're over twenty-one. We've had wine with dinner before."

"Still seems . . . odd." Maybe because it was breakfast. She thought back to her mom's wineglass the night Trooper arrived. "Are you planning to go to church toasted?"

"One drink. Not toasted." She sipped, sticking a toe through the wire playpen to tease a puppy. "What about you?"

"Thanks, but I've already had breakfast." Memories of her and Mike feeding each other in between caramel kisses sent her sinking into the chair. "What kind of muffin are you having with the mimosa?"

"Apple nut. I guess I should eat it." She set aside her glass and pinched off a bite of muffin.

"I would agree. You skip too many meals, Mom." Sierra leaned into the pen and picked up a puppy . . . Rapunzel, a blond little girl who liked to snuggle.

"I'm having trouble scrounging up the energy to face the kitchen. I've cooked for over twenty years. I'm tired." She picked up her mimosa again, the bubbles rising to the top. "Nathan's still asleep, so I'm not a bad influence. Your grandfather is in the shower. And how's Mike?"

Well, there it finally was, out in the open. Sierra cuddled the puppy up under her chin, the warm little body curling against her with a sweet sigh. "Aren't you going to tell me I should be smart about seeing him?"

"You're an adult, completely capable of supporting yourself, only staying here because I can't manage life on my own." She spread her hands to include everything around her. "I don't think I'm in any position to lecture you on squat."

The cynicism in her mother's voice caught Sierra off guard. "Mom, are you okay?"

"Not even remotely." She tipped her head back blinking fast and gathering her tangled curls to shove them behind one shoulder. "But I'm working on it."

"I'm here if you need to talk."

"Honestly, I'm totally talked out . . ." She pulled a scrunchie off her wrist and secured her hair into a loose ponytail as if seeking to add some kind of order to her world. "You talk. Tell me about you, your love life, like a normal mother and daughter chat."

"Normal?" She lifted the puppy, rubbing noses. "Mom, you may not have noticed but we live in a zoo."

"Normal doesn't have to be boring." She tossed a squeaky toy into the puppy pen.

The four pups pounced on the toy while Rapunzel licked Sierra's nose.

"This family is at no risk of being called boring." Sierra placed the puppy back in the pen, on top of the toy.

"So." Lacey leaned back again, reaching for her drink. "Is he good?"

"What?" She couldn't be hearing what she thought. She'd wanted relationship advice. Not sex advice.

"Mike," Lacey clarified. "Is he good in bed?"

"Sheesh, Mom." She looked around to make sure no one was listening. "Do you really expect me to answer that?"

"I wouldn't have asked otherwise. I don't need details, just curious." She shrugged. "Chalk it up to my pathetic love life."

Sierra's heart squeezed with guilt. All her problems and grief were nothing compared to what her mother faced. And there was little she could do to make that better other than try to offer a lighter moment, a brief respite. "We were, uh, playing Scrabble."

"Scrabble?" Her mother laughed. "I've never heard it called that before."

She grinned sheepishly. "Really, really good Scrabble?"

"Ahhh, finally, you appease my curiosity."

Sierra scratched a tiny patch of rust on the iron chair, a purple one, her favorite of the hodgepodge colors. "I thought mothers didn't want to know these sorts of things."

"I just want to be sure you're being treated well. That you're appreciated." Something whimsical chased through Lacey's green eyes.

Happy or sad?

Sierra brought her thoughts back to the question at hand, trying to figure out how to answer. "Sometimes I think he appreciates me too much."

"And what is the problem with being placed on a pedestal?" Lacey picked up a magazine and fanned herself, the morning heating up past the power of the ceiling fans. "Clue me in. Because honestly, there are plenty of women who would appreciate a little more adoration from the man in her life."

"I'm not sure Mike sees me, the person. He keeps seeing differences between our upbringings." Barking in the distance reminded her the dogs needed feeding soon, kennels needed cleaning. This chance to talk uninterrupted was short. "It's setting us both up for failure again, even bigger this time when he finally sees me as a regular person, flaws and all."

"I'm still not understanding the problem here."

"I'm being serious about this, Mom." She clasped her mother's wrist. She wanted—needed—her mom's help in figuring this out. "He and I broke up before because he had this messed-up idea he couldn't give me the rich life. Now he's got a scorching case of survivor's guilt on top of everything else."

Her mom whistled softly, then downed the rest of her mimosa in one gulp. "Now that is problematic. What about you? How do you feel?"

The truth was scary and she wasn't even sure she should say it. She chewed her lip before confessing, "I'm afraid of living your life."

Lacey blinked slowly, exhaling hard as she slid both legs to the floor. "Well, hell, I didn't see that coming."

"I'm not trying to be mean, Mom." Already she regretted sharing. She should have kept her mouth shut. "You're an incredible person, and I admire all you manage here, keeping things together through Dad's constant absenteeism. Then to go through all of that and have him die? I don't know how you manage to keep your sanity."

Laughing weakly, Lacey pressed a hand to her chest. "Who says I'm sane?"

Sierra leaned forward, clasped her mom's hands in hers, tightly. "You are completely levelheaded and you know it. You've handled more than any one person should have to face, and I admire you for it." Even if she made it through all the long separations, she couldn't bear the thought of someday getting that knock on the door with the military notifying her that . . . She swallowed hard. "But honest to God, Mom, I don't want my tombstone to read, 'Here lies Sierra. She was *strong.*'"

Lacey sighed. "Sure you don't want a mimosa after all?"

Maybe. Probably. But first, she needed to explain—hell, figure it out as she spoke. "Since dating Mike, I see you with different eyes. Military life for a wife is strange in ways I didn't understand until I tried to envision myself in that role. You always made everything so normal for us, but I think that is because you were our normal."

Tears welled up in Lacey's eyes. Her hands trembled. Sierra half wished she could call the words back. Instead she slid from her chair and wrapped her mom in a tight hug. She couldn't hold back her own tears, the sting and the emotion building. She heard her mother sniffle once before Lacey pulled back with a brittle strength.

Sierra didn't bother to hide her tears. She just squeezed her mom's hand, but couldn't push any words past the knot in her throat.

Lacey laughed softly and squeezed back. "If I was normal, then heaven help you and Nathan both."

Eleven

LACEY GRIPPED THE steering wheel of her SUV, weaving in and out of Sunday lunchtime traffic on her way to the local Animal Control shelter to pull new additions to her rescue. Families filled the other cars. Young families. Multigenerational families. But it was seeing the senior couples that hurt the most. Each silver-haired man and woman reminded her of the future she'd lost.

After four months of grieving, she would have expected to shore up some defenses. But everything still made her think of Allen's death. Today images of their life together bombarded her, from memories of their first time making love to the day they'd bought the house here with plans of living out their golden years in Tennessee.

Maybe she was just particularly raw after seeing her daughter's face blushed with happiness and . . . well . . . the afterglow of good Scrabble.

Running on fumes after yesterday's event and a sleepless night, she still hadn't found her balance after her conversation with Sierra. She knew the military lifestyle growing up had left marks on her family. But she hadn't realized how deeply until she heard her daughter explaining exactly why she'd broken up with Mike initially. Lacey hadn't pried during the breakup, telling herself she was respecting her daughter's privacy.

Or maybe she'd used that as an excuse to keep from facing how messed up her own relationship was. She and Allen had loved each other. He had a funny, laid-back approach that offset her frenetic way of barreling through life. At least, they used to balance each other out before they spent so much time apart, working or parenting, which left little time to be a couple. What time they did spend together? Their marriage was a series of reunions. She would clean the house, cook his favorite foods and dress up. He brought gifts from around the world. He made sure to show up for major events whenever possible in party mode—first communion, graduations, special concerts. But they hadn't shared much in the way of day-to-day life, the routine chores and joys. They hadn't shared burdens. Conversations over the phone couldn't get too complicated or he would have a "bad connection."

She was independent because she had to be.

And to be fair, it was easier to do things herself than to try and integrate the man that came home. If she pushed too hard, her funny, easygoing husband turned moody. So she let him keep those superficial walls in place. It was simpler than pushing through, even though she'd grown damn weary with holding down the home front alone. So as years went by, she chose the easier route in her marriage and hoped they'd have time to work things out. Now, she would never have the chance to change that, to see if she and Allen could have waded through their problems to find what they'd once dreamed of having as they grew old together.

Had she robbed them both? Had he? There was plenty of blame to go around. Plenty of hurt to share that no doubt spilled over onto the kids. And still, she couldn't see a way they might have changed the choices they'd made. She was left with only this endless cycle of painful questions she would never be able to answer.

Nearing Animal Control's shelter, Lacey slowed as she drove down the river road. A raised levee with a rock wall lined the waterside on the way to the gray cement building a half mile ahead. She'd lived here so long she'd carved a niche. She'd built a life for herself. Allen had vowed this would be his last deployment, and if orders came to move, he would put in his papers. He would get out. They would start the second phase of their life.

Now she would never know if they could have made that work. The ache of that loss piled high on top of so many others already large enough the pain rivaled the Smoky Mountains.

Lacey accelerated through a yellow light, desperate to get to the shelter where she could lose herself in something besides thinking about the past. The shelter director was personally coming in to meet with her. In spite of Saturday's success for everyone, the county shelter was still packed to capacity. They were always full. And while Second Chance had adopted out more dogs than she'd expected, she remained stretched pretty thin these days.

Still, she didn't have nearly as many animals in her care as the county facility. And if her operation was shuttered, dozens of animals would have nowhere else to go . . . She couldn't give up. She had to win.

She couldn't lose anything more in her life.

Lacey turned into the parking lot, driving as close as possible to a side entrance with at least a half dozen cars parked. The shelter was closed to the public on Sundays, but the animals still needed feeding and tending. Even at a skeletal staff, the place hummed with activity.

One truck in particular caught her eye, one with a series of funny bumper stickers with paws. Her favorite? *My windows aren't dirty. That's dog nose art.*

Why was Ray here? And why did she care?

The side door opened, and shelter director Dahlia Taylor stood in the opening to wave her into the building. Pushing aside distracting thoughts, Lacey turned off her SUV and double-checked the blankets lining her seats, along with two wire crates in the back. It would be full and noisy soon enough.

She hitched her canvas sack full of paperwork, her wallet and her camera. "Thanks for meeting me on a day off."

Dahlia managed to pull off chic even up to her neck in floating animal dander. Her fitted pink dress, wide black belt and leather riding boots showed she hadn't taken time to change clothes before rushing over here after lunch. "We don't take days off in rescue."

"True, very true." Lacey angled past and inside to a din of barking, meowing, voices and a radio playing.

Usually she just walked back on her own to the kennel runs, familiar with the space and cleared by the staff, but Dahlia stayed with her today rather than ducking into her office to plow through paperwork. But then Dahlia had made a special point of being here, so she must have some special cases to point out.

And where was Ray? She found herself searching as she walked past through the waiting area.

Volunteers were snapping photos of animals for Internet and publicity campaigns. Two of them glanced through the doorway and caught sight of her. She smiled and waved, grateful they were here, but also knowing each volunteer and each worker would have a favorite they wanted her to rescue. There just wasn't room in her car or her budget. Still her heart squeezed. God, this work was not for the faint of heart. There were always more homeless animals than there were homes or spaces in shelters and rescues.

Kennel techs hosed down runs on the inside, while dogs stayed in the outside section of each run. Then they would reverse. The cleaning never ended, a constant battle to keep down airborne illnesses. Animals with suppressed immune systems due to anything from prior neglect to the stress of losing their homes were all the more vulnerable to germs.

Shelter work was thankless—but if people like Dahlia weren't here for the animals, they would be vulnerable to abusive owners or roaming busy highways . . . the list went on and on.

As the techs let dogs back inside, she walked down the kennel runs, knowing she should only pick four today, six if they were all healthy—which never happened. People who dumped their animals or let them wander off without bothering to look for them usually didn't take care of them. So the number she could afford today was four. She needed to be realistic and keep the upcoming council meeting in mind. Dahlia's boot heels clicked behind her, even though she stayed silent.

Cards hung on the kennel run gates. A yellow card meant the animal had finished the stray hold time and would be made adoption available. A red card meant the dog had been slated for euthanasia for some reason. It could have a dangerous temperament or a potentially fatal illness. Or it could be for the tragic reality of lack of space—the reason that broke her heart the most.

She saw a schnoodle with overgrown fur that had lapsed into doggie dreadlocks, and stepped into the kennel run to evaluate the temperament. The pooch needed a good dental, but seemed otherwise friendly, no food aggression, and the matted fur would be easily fixed with a trip to the groomer. She had a waiting list of people wanting a poodle-schnauzer mix reputed to be easier on allergy sufferers.

Lacey scratched the little guy's ears, reaching through the dreadlocks as best she could. She angled back to look at Dahlia. "I'll take Bob Marley here."

Dahlia tugged the kennel card from the gate, passing it over to a tech to pull the dog from the run and clear the paperwork. "Done and thank you." She started to turn away, then pivoted back, tapping her chin. "Oh, and did I mention we just got a mama Siamese with four kittens, three weeks old. We already called every cat rescue on the planet and they're all full."

Ah, the reason Dahlia had followed her. Cats were tougher to place lately, and a whole litter? "And the family doesn't want to keep mama after they wean?"

"Already tried asking," Dahlia said. "I even offered a free spay for mama cat and homes for the kitties later if they would just keep the little family until they weaned, but nope. They weren't interested," she said through tight lips. "The couple has a new baby, no time for pets."

Sighing, Lacey stepped into the next kennel run, her feet promptly trampled by a wirehaired Jack Russell, a beagle, and a . . . medium-sized brindle mystery breed. "I'll take the mama. Debbie's foster dog got adopted at the festival, and she's open to cats, too. We'll make it work."

"Sometimes I think we should just have a multiple choice form for the people who surrender their animals. Just a list of lame-ass excuses, one, two, or three. Check the box."

Lacey looked up, still stroking the three dogs so hungry for affection. "You're sounding weary and jaded today. Are you okay?"

"It's been a really rough few days." She smiled weakly. "Seeing you walk through the door is all that's getting me through right now. Have you heard about the new mama sheltie mix and her babies? Four beautiful puppies and all our foster homes are full. She'll get sick here. Her pups—"

Lacey held up her hand, already sold on taking them in. No wonder Dahlia had followed her. She had more than one plea to make today. And it just so happened Lacey had underestimated her personal rawness of emotions today after the talk with her daughter. She couldn't deny it. She was feeling an intense need to save animals as if to somehow do something right on a day she felt like a failure for letting her daughter down.

Her husband, too?

"I'll take them." And that put her way past her limit for keeping things low-key to survive this month's scrutiny—and she hadn't even walked the length of the kennel runs. "Do you mind getting them ready to go while I post some appeals to my foster family network on Facebook?"

"Already on it." Dahlia's heels clicked fast on her way across the sterilized floors back to the front of the building.

Sighing, Lacey looked toward her feet, at three pairs of eyes staring back up with such hope and joy over a simple scratch behind the ears. She couldn't take all three. She shouldn't even take one of them because there wouldn't be a foster home available. She would be adding to her "zoo" of a home.

She tried to be analytical, but God, it was all but impossible. Logic told her the beagle and wirehaired Jack Russell would be easier for her to adopt out . . . and the brindle mutt that looked like a mini Lab with tiger stripes, only eighteen months old at the most and still hyper, would almost certainly fade into the shadows. No one would pick her here.

Logic had many faces. Her heart was already ten damn steps ahead of her brain. She scooped up the brindle mutt, heavier than she looked, probably closer to forty pounds. The pup rested her head on Lacey's shoulder with a shudder-sigh.

"I'll take her, too," Lacey said before she could talk herself out of it. She would put in a call to a beagle rescue in Kentucky and beg for a driver to transport. It was so damn hard to walk away. She didn't know how Dahlia held on in a job where walking away wasn't even an option.

The mutt—already named Pixel, Pixie for short—glued herself to Lacey as she made her way back to find Dahlia. Her car was full and she had animals to vet . . . which she could conveniently take care of now.

Or was she just making excuses to see Ray? She wouldn't wish the dark numbness of her earliest grief on anyone, and yet the confusing punch of guilt she felt now made her consider running back to that desensitized blankness.

Go. Forward.

She tapped her foot against Dahlia's office door. "I saw Doc Vega's car out front."

Dahlia stepped around her desk, a kitten riding her shoulder. "He's in the quarantine room picking up a six-month-old Lab puppy that got hit by a car, will probably need surgery. Fund-raiser time." She waved jazz hands, rolling her eyes. "Thank you, by the way."

"We're both just doing our part."

Dahlia leaned her butt back against her desk, reaching up to stroke the gray tabby kitty. "I appreciate that you're real, beyond the damn politics about everything related to dog rescue. It isn't about winning or who gets the most kudos."

"We all love the animals." The bad guys were the ones beating a dog on the head or torturing a cat for some ritual. Even the ones dumping a family pet that peed on the carpet because no one trained the puppy. Speaking of puppies . . . "Did you say Ray's still here?"

Dahlia's eyes flickered with—something?—then she blinked and she was her chic, collected self all over again. "He's right down the hall, in the clinic. You know the way."

It wasn't wise.

Especially not on a day her emotions were so raw.

But she hefted up Pixie and walked to the clinic.

EVEN WITH HIS back to the door, Ray knew the moment Lacey walked into the small clinic area. He'd heard her talking when she arrived about a half hour ago, but now he could smell her lavender scent the second she entered the room. He just needed to get through the next fifteen minutes with his self-control intact.

He could have sworn something shifted between them

at the adoption event. Some flicker of life in her eyes when he'd brought her coffee that morning . . . but then again, he could be seeing things. He didn't have a plan for the way he felt about her, other than biding his time. So much could change in a few months. He would know when the timing was right and would make his move then.

For now, he had to be careful not to spook her.

He continued his assessment of the puppy that had been hit by a car. He would have to do a more thorough exam back at his vet clinic, but he'd stabilized the injured front leg. He had hopes the break would be repairable, no amputation needed. The recovery would depend on the pup's will. He studied the little guy's eyes, reading cues . . . He saw pain . . . and trust. He also saw hope and gratitude. That didn't pay his bills, but it sure kept him coming back.

He jotted notes on his patient's chart, even though he could see Lacey out of the corner of his eyes. "Hey, Lacey. Wanna come meet this guy and give him a name? He doesn't have one yet."

She'd clearly come straight from a family morning—church? Lunch out? She wore a flowing skirt with a vest top that had his fingers itching to open the buttons.

And her hair was down. Long and curly, light brown with golden highlights. Damn it. He swallowed hard.

"Sure." Lacey walked into the room and stopped beside him, a brindle dog in her arms, one of those mystery mutt breeds that seemed to snag Lacey's heart. "And you get me to name him so I'll bond with the stinker and take him, too."

"Ah, you've unearthed my devious ways."

She laughed low and husky. How crazy to be jealous of the homeless mutt with its face buried in her neck.

Ray breathed in the scent of lavender and bleach. "A name?"

"Opie. Let's name the dog Opie. And yes, I'll take him once you've finished treating him."

Of course she would.

She tempted the hell out of him on a regular day. But weekends, times when everyone else did family stuff and he just worked nonstop, he felt the loneliness of his life more heavily. "Don't you want to know how badly he's injured?"

"If it's minor, he will be easy to adopt. If it's bad, I can't leave him vulnerable in a shelter environment where he will get sick. So knowing the details doesn't matter to me at this point."

"That's my favorite rescuer." He winked.

"Ah, I bet you say that to all the rescuers who owe you a couple thousand dollars."

"Just fulfilling my oath to heal."

His job was important to him. He'd spent the past ten years working his ass off to get through veterinary school, every hour spent studying to prove to the world he deserved his spot and being the son of a prominent senator had nothing to do with his admission. He was past those days now. His own man. Even holding down a regular caseload and helping out homeless animals, his life still had these empty spots he didn't know how to fill.

Although right now, his mind was spinning with ideas. Scenarios that all involved a wild-haired woman with a crazy sense of style and a heart bigger than the state of Tennessee.

He went back to writing up details on the puppy that had been hit by the car. Even if Opie was not worst-case scenario, he would still need to be transferred to his clinic and prepped for surgery in the morning. The pup was currently curled in the back of an open crate, enjoying the haze of painkillers.

A much less stressful state than the thrashing, terrified animal that Ray had first found when he arrived. He'd narrowly missed being bitten by a dog with no vaccination records.

He skimmed a hand over the brindle dog in her arms, doing a quick mental assessment. "Who's this? And don't you ever take a day off, Lacey?"

"I could ask you the same and this is Pixie." She passed the brindle over to him and turned her attention to Opie.

Lacey soothed her fingers over the puppy, gaining Opie's trust while peeking in his ears and checking his teeth, touching his uninjured paws . . . all things to assess how well he dealt with strangers and being handled. "Why are you here doing pro bono work when there's an on-call vet?"

"I don't have a family at home waiting for me, and the on-call vet for the shelter will cost more than their budget can afford." And speaking of families . . . he needed to keep that family of *hers* in mind. Big-time. They were grieving, too, and even if Lacey wanted to launch into a relationship so soon after her husband's death, her relatives would likely have a coronary.

Thinking about families made him itchy with memories of his own. Not that he let them dictate his decisions. Still, even from across the country, his mom made a regular practice of sending clients his way—females who were connected to friends of friends. All the women were single and in their twenties.

Those new clients always guaranteed a follow-up call from his mom mentioning how much she wanted grandchildren. She was quick to remind him that his two border collies didn't count.

He pulled his attention back to Lacey's words rather than just watching the way her lips moved.

"Everyone at home is independent." She sighed, her head falling to the side, her hair swinging to brush his arm. "Well, other than my father-in-law, but there are plenty of people to watch over him. And my new boarder is a great cook. He's grilling burgers. Want to join us?"

She looked as stunned by her offer as he felt. She straightened, her hair sliding away. There were a thousand reasons he should say no. Starting with how his hand still felt the skim of her hair. And how he was too aware of the strand of her hair that clung to his lab coat. How he was afraid she'd recognized the undercurrent between them and only wanted a private place to tell him he had no right to feel that way about her.

The list went on and on.

Yet, all of those arguments were overridden by one compelling reason that trumped everything else. He wanted to be with her.

"Do you mind if I bring my dogs?"

She laughed. "You're kidding, right? Like I would even notice two more at my place."

"Okay then. Once I settle Opie at my clinic . . . a burger sounds great. I can even check Trooper's post-surgery recovery."

"I have to warn you." Her hand cupped Pixie's head. "My home is even more of a zoo than last time you were there."

"Then I'll be careful to guard my hamburger."

DID YOU KNOW that a male dog still has testosterone zinging through his system for days, sometimes even weeks after being neutered? Well, he does.

Or rather, *I* did during that first picnic at the McDaniel's place.

I might have looked all mellow and drugged up lounging under a tree while people burned meat on a fire, but the air was full of more than smoke. There were hormones in the air.

The mating kind.

Apparently these people had to be well fed first since they were grilling so much food. Although I still don't understand why humans take perfectly good meat and cook all the juices out of it. Seriously. Not that I could afford to be picky, especially then. I was all about keeping the peace since Lacey took me to get *the surgery*.

At least they weren't making me wear that stupid cone anymore.

But I could still smell sex in the air. And I could smell it everywhere. People were getting it or wanting it, and it was driving me crazy, because I still had that testosterone in me, urging me to *mate, mate, mate. Make lots of little puppies with the bitch in heat about three miles away.*

Yes, a dog can smell that far. Human males would be jealous if they knew about my superpower. Except I couldn't do much about it since I still wasn't feeling up to running a marathon. If you catch my meaning.

Don't feel sorry for me, though. There were serious perks to my new home. Major perks. Things that would make me want to stay with these people forever even if I didn't have a mission.

For starters, there was all that food, no more going hungry. And I got to sleep in Gramps's den. His bedroom, I mean. Sometimes the human words and dog words for things are a little different. Like how what you call a den, I would call a family room or a living room or a sofa room.

I learned fast about comfy sofas and how stingy humans could be about sharing them.

Anyway, in Gramps's room, I slept on the floor by his bed or under his bed. I wasn't feeling ready to jump yet, and it was high off the ground with four tall wooden posts. But I had my eyes on a corner of that mattress, near the end where there was a fat blanket folded at the bottom. It looked really soft and as tempting as a hamburger.

When I lived in Iraq, I slept on the ground or underneath whatever box or house I could find, curled up and hungry. Being out in the open was bad. Real bad. Downright dangerous. They didn't have shelters for stray dogs or abandoned animals in my old home country. If packs got too close to people or cities, police came out with big guns to pick us off one at a time until we either ran or died. Even when I stayed with the Colonel I almost got shot more than once when I barked to alert them those guns were coming for them. But it was worth the fear and the risk to help the man who'd saved me.

Here, it was safer to be a dog. It was a good thing I spent those months at the Army post getting used to people or I would have been too scared to appreciate how good I had it with my new family.

But I'm getting distracted again. That happens some-times, like when I see a bird or smell a hamburger.

I really like hamburgers, just as good as steaks but easier to chew. Even when they're burned.

Which brings me back to what I wanted to talk about. Even in my pained, recuperative state, I had enough testos-terone in me to know, the picnic was full of people on fire to have sex with each other.

PART 3

Chewing the crotch out of panties and blue jeans in the laundry is one of life's greatest pleasures. Almost as good as stealing a hamburger.
                    —TROOPER, AT A FAMILY PICNIC

Twelve

MIKE HADN'T EXPECTED to ever have Sierra in his bed again, and now all he could think of was getting her back there.

This Sunday picnic had been torture, and it wasn't showing signs of letting up as the sun set. All day, he'd been mesmerized by Sierra. God, she rocked those red cowboy boots with a loose cotton dress that brushed her curves when she walked past a couple of volunteers on a blanket finishing burgers. He'd been plagued by images of kissing every little flower on that pattern—and there were lots of flowers. Then sweeping the dress over her head and making love to her while she wore just the boots.

She stopped beside her grandpa, who was parked in an Adirondack chair, the horizon behind him turning purple in the wake of the disappearing sun. Sierra knelt in front of him, passing him a brownie and a glass of tea while they spoke.

Oh-kay. Sex thoughts seemed creepy now, like her

grandfather might sense it even through his Alzheimer's and come gunning for him.

Mike reined in his thoughts—again. Besides, much more boot fantasizing and he wouldn't be able to get up from the picnic table without embarrassing himself. He gave himself a moment to will away the erection by taking in the crowd, a larger group than they'd originally expected. When a handful of volunteers lingered to socialize after cleaning runs and exercising the dogs, Sierra had taken it in stride, just defrosting extra burgers and tossing out a couple of bags of chips. Then Lacey had shown up with the veterinarian. That had been a surprise. Mike hadn't given much thought to the fact that the guy hung out at their booth at the adoption event. But to see him here today, at the McDaniels' home? That was . . . surreal.

Surreal? Shit. He really had been working too many crossword puzzles to up his vocab game.

His eyes zeroed right back in on Sierra gathering up her grandfather's dinner plate while he ate the dessert. Nathan was technically on Gramps guard duty, lounging in a nearby hammock with a video game in his hands, one leg off the side, foot dragging the ground, then nudging again. The hammock swayed slowly, strung between two fat oaks. Trooper slept underneath in a mulch bed surrounded by solar lights that were just starting to pop on.

Sierra smiled at something her grandfather said, but strains of tension showed in the corners of her eyes. She patted him on the shoulder before tossing away the paper plate and walking back to Mike.

Sighing the whole way down, she sat next him on the picnic bench, her back against the table, her legs stretched out and those boots within taunting reach. "This was *not* a day of rest. I'm actually looking forward to escaping to my computer to do homework."

He forgot sometimes she held down a full load of classes as well as working a graduate assistantship teaching. Her dad had been so proud of her. The Colonel would be worried as hell if he saw his family now, overworked and over-stressed.

And what would the Colonel think of Lacey and Doc Vega? Lacey walked around the perimeter of the picnic, lighting a few old tiki torches that had been jammed into the ground, but the vet's eyes followed her. Mike wasn't passing judgment, but the expression on the guy's face spelled trouble any way you looked at it. Mike didn't envy the doc caring about someone who wasn't in a position to reciprocate. He understood what that felt like just a little too damn well.

Unfortunately, doing what was best for Sierra had proven impossible since he had zero chance of staying away from her.

He dipped his head to her ear, her citrus scent easing darker thoughts. "Are you all right?"

"Other than the fact that my grandfather just called me by my grandmother's name again? I'm good. A little preoc-cupied. It's been a long day." She touched his elbow lightly, careful not to be overt. No doubt she didn't want anyone to notice the shift in their relationship. "I'll be glad when we can both just slip away and be together."

Uh, yeah. He agreed ten thousand percent. The three people across the table from him got up to toss their trash and walked to the bonfire just beginning to crackle to life.

Leaving Mike and Sierra completely alone.

He said softly, careful not to be overheard, "Does your mom know what happened between us last night?"

She twisted her hands in her lap. "Why does that matter? We've already decided we're not announcing anything to the world. I'm fine with leaving things as they are for now."

Then why was she upset? "What's wrong?"

She nodded toward her mother walking out of the barn with Ray Vega at her side. "My mom brought a guy to din-ner, a much younger guy. It's . . . weird."

"She didn't bring a date to dinner. She brought the vet

who takes care of her animals to thank him for all the discounts." Another thought hit him. "Or maybe she brought a guy for you."

"For me? You're crazy. I've known Ray for over a year and there's never been the least spark between us. If Mom wanted to matchmake with him, she would have said something before now."

"Not necessarily. If she's worried about you ending up with me, she might be trying to steer you in a different direction." Maybe he'd just imagined the guy had been checking out Lacey. What did Mike know about stuff like that?

Besides, the idea of someone else thinking about Sierra that way took hold in his mind and . . . wouldn't let go. Especially not after he'd spent the whole day imagining bringing her back to his place. Possessiveness fired with a fierceness he hadn't anticipated.

"That doesn't make sense." She fidgeted with her side braid moving and tempting him to tug it—or unravel it. "She likes you. She invited you to move in here."

"That doesn't mean she wants her daughter marrying some Army grunt, especially after she recently lost her uniform-wearing husband." And just that fast the past started butting in again.

"My mother isn't trying to matchmake." Her chin went stubborn, and there was no budging her when that happened. "She's attracted to this guy and it's freaking me out."

So it wasn't the younger guy issue. It was *any* guy with her mom. Period. Right or wrong, at least Mike didn't need to worry about some other dude hitting on Sierra. He shook his head and hoped he could shake off the caveman feeling. Damn.

"She hasn't given any reason to indicate he's more than a friend. But someday she very well could bring a man here, date again. She's a young, attractive woman."

"Now *you* are creeping me out a little bit," she half joked, lifting an eyebrow.

"You know full well which McDaniel female has my full attention." He let his eyes linger on her mouth before continuing on a more somber note, "I promised your father I would look after you all, and I will."

"We shouldn't be your obligation." She fanned a bug away from her nose.

"You know you're far from that."

"Still, your sense of responsibility makes things very messy since we're having sex." She turned on him, her expression serious.

No games.

"I hear you. I understand." He might like their time together when they laughed and fooled around and he made up goofy lyrics for her. But he respected this side of her. "And I am staying, whether we continue to sleep together or not."

"Because you feel you owe my father?"

Why was she pushing this? He turned his plastic cup on the table, choosing his words carefully. "That's a part of it. I can't deny that. But honest to God, Sierra, I would really prefer not to talk about your dad while we're talking about sex. It's seriously outside of my comfort zone."

He drained his tea to wash away the lingering taste of smoke in the air.

Sierra tipped her head back, staring up at the sky, the first stars just starting to blink through. "Was he happy during his last days? I mean, as happy as anyone can be in a war zone." She glanced at him, the tail of her braid brushing along his arm in a silken touch. "Does that make sense?"

Memories of those months overseas churned in his mind like broken glass in a blender. How could he pick anything out of that mess to share? "We had our lighter moments."

"Please tell me one. Even though my dad's only been

dead for four months, it's been a year since I got to see him or hug him. Skype doesn't count, by the way."

She wanted lighter? That was definitely preferable if he couldn't avoid discussing Iraq altogether.

He searched his memory and settled on one moment that happened about a month before . . . before the end. "Your dad was proud of what you and your mom have built with this rescue—"

"You mean my mother built," she interrupted. "Not me. The Second Chance Ranch is hers."

"It may be hers, but it's obvious what a huge role you play in keeping this place—your whole family—afloat." He admired her for that. After the way he grew up, he knew full well how rare that was, seeing how unselfishly she pitched in for her whole family

"Even though I'm not sure I agree, thank you. Now tell me the happy story about my dad."

"This one time he was on Skype with you all, and connections were limited so he had to use a public area where there were multiple screens set up, rather than stay in his private room on his personal computer. So we all saw and shouted hellos."

A fleeting smile crossed her face. "I remember that call."

"Each of you took a turn talking to him while holding an animal, with other animals wandering around behind you. So many animals. Not just dogs and cats, but the goat and the snake. A couple of rabbits." The memory sucked him in deeper until he could smell the heavy cooking spices that had always hung in the air. "By the end of the chat, your dad's forehead was all furrowed. He just said, 'Well, when my Lacey takes something on, she's all in.' "

"He understood her well. That sounds like my mom." Sierra gestured to the yard full of people around a bonfire, dogs playing in the fenced-off area, the goat chomping around the hedges. "Thank you for reminding me of that time talking to him. I'd forgotten, and I don't want to lose even a memory more."

"That isn't all of the story." He tugged her braid that rested just on top of her breast, letting his knuckles graze her suggestively for a second before he pulled away. "All of us in the platoon made a bunch of origami animals. We worked on them for at least a week. Then while your dad was outside throwing the ball around with Trooper, we filled your old man's room with all those paper animals. Everywhere. On top of furniture, his bed, the window ledge. They were even ankle deep on the floor."

She smiled, leaning toward him as if to place herself more in that moment, closer to her father. "What did Dad do?"

"Laughed his ass off until he stumbled back against the door, then shouted, 'Honey, I'm home.' "

Sierra laughed along with him, such a beautiful melody that eventually trailed off along with her smile. "I guess that explains why he sent my mother an origami dog and cat." She looked down at her hands twisted so tightly in her lap her fingers had gone stark white. "The letter arrived the day after we buried him."

They'd lost so many comrades over there, and each one sucker punched them in the gut. But losing their commander, their leader, had left a hollowness in them all that nothing could fill.

Sierra looked back up at him, her eyes glistening with tears in the dusk of nightfall. "Do you mind if I share that story with my mom?"

God, she was breaking his heart here. To hell with keeping his distance or worrying if people realized they were . . . a couple? . . . together again for now. He angled nearer and slid a hand to cup the back of her neck. "Of course you can tell her."

He started to tug her toward him, to bring her face to rest against his chest—

A shout split the night. "Hey, somebody call the cops!" Nathan yelled. "Someone cut holes in half the kennel gates."

LACEY RACED TOWARD the barns. Vaguely she registered Ray shouting for her to stop and be careful, but all she could think about were her animals, helpless in the barn. Right under her nose, with her friends all around her and her defenses down, someone had invaded her home.

At just the time her newly installed security system was turned off.

An arm banded around her waist and lifted her off the ground. "Lacey. Stop," Ray said. "Think. You need to be careful. Let Mike check it out first. Look, a couple of the volunteers are already searching the woods for any loose dogs or whoever may have done this."

His words made sense, but her heart wasn't always logical. She resisted, but Ray held on to her, bringing her back flush against his chest. A muscular, warm chest. Before she could process that, Ray passed her over to the volunteer Debbie and her husband.

Lacey searched the picnic area, lit by porch lights and tiki torches. Mike Kowalski jogged toward the barn with Ray close on his heels. They stopped at the barn door, and Mike nudged Nathan aside carefully but deliberately. The barking inside was growing to a fever pitch.

The two men stood on either side and peered in carefully.

"Shit," Ray hissed softly, before looking over his shoulder at her. "Lacey, go get leashes and catch poles, anything you can find. All the dogs are out and they're fighting. It's bad."

Without another word, he and Mike slipped into the barn and out of sight. She sprinted to the mudroom to gather anything she could find to secure the dogs and the cats, oh God, the cats. "Sierra, everyone, get crates from the garage."

She worked so hard to keep these animals safe, temperament testing and carefully selecting playgroups that got along so they would all be more relaxed and happy. These animals had come to her for their second chance, truly their last chance.

And she'd somehow screwed up, lost her focus, missed a sign and let them down. She just prayed none of them would pay the ultimate price for her mistake.

SIERRA'S HEART STILL hadn't recovered from the shock that while they'd all partied, someone had vandalized half their kennel runs. Cutting through wire gating. Breaking water feeders off the wall. Slashing open bags of dog and cat food—which involved cutting the bolt on the supply closet.

Thank God Mike and the doc had gotten the dogfight under control in a hurry. Things could have been much, much worse.

She knelt with a small shovel, saving what food she could and storing it in a plastic container. Mike had a toolbox and a huge package of zip ties beside him as he made temporary fixes to gate after gate. Her mom was trying to settle down displaced animals while Doc Vega assessed and treated the injured—three dogs and a cat. Luckily, no injuries appeared lethal, but the vet would still be stitching for a long while.

Thank God, the vulnerable puppies had all been in a separate area. What if this had happened while Lucky was quarantined and detoxing? Thinking about how ugly it could have been was chilling.

The cops had come to investigate and take statements from everyone at the picnic. No one had been found in the woods, and the searchers running had ruined any chance of getting footprints. Considering that somebody at their party could have done this was beyond imagining. That kind of betrayal would destroy her mother. It had to be someone on the outside, like that creepy Kenneth guy next door who still lived with his mother.

Was he watching with binoculars—or night vision

goggles—while they struggled to repair the place enough to secure all the animals for the night? They couldn't bring them all into the house, and they couldn't leave even a few in the yard for fear they would wander off. There was also the danger of horrible people who trolled at night to steal animals.

A few volunteers had stuck around to help until around eleven, but people had lives of their own, jobs to go to in the morning.

Sierra shoveled and dumped, shoveled and dumped. They couldn't afford to lose all that food. Now and then, she had to sift out sticks and stones. Crickets and frogs sang in the otherwise silent night. Even the dogs were exhausted from the excitement.

Unable to take the wordless quiet anymore, she figured even small talk would be better than silence where she was left to wonder what he thought—and where they stood with each other. "Mike, thanks for helping—again." She didn't know what they would have done without him tonight. "I'm so sorry you're having to spend your time off doing crappy things like this for us. You should be partying with your friends, decompressing."

Her boot sank into a wet spot where their intruder had dumped a water container. The squishy earth clung to her footwear even as she tried to take a step. Yuck.

"This is definitely more productive than searching for different ways to overcome hangovers." Mike worked methodically, moving a work lamp down the line of fences with him as he patched holes with the never-ending zip tie supply.

"You don't have to spend all your time here." She watched him out of the corner of her eyes, taking in the flex of his biceps as he worked with his shirt off. As payoffs went for the overtime, seeing Mike half-dressed was a definite bonus. "My mom's not going to kick you out if you take time for yourself."

"Thanks. But I'm a big boy. I'm handling the whole decompression thing my own way. And I won't be able to enjoy jack shit if I'm worried about your family."

It occurred to her that he excelled at deflection, always turning the conversation back around to her. Or to anything that wasn't focused on him.

"What about *your* family?" She could only remember him discussing a father and a grandmother. But where had they been when he got back? "Don't you want to spend some of this time with them?"

"My grandmother passed away while I was overseas, and my dad . . ." he said tonelessly, shrugging, "I'll spend a weekend with him before I report in. A little bit of Dad time goes a long way."

"I'm sorry about your grandmother." She dropped the trowel and touched his arm, his warm sweat slicking her fingers and tingling her fingertips. "You lived with her for a while, right?"

He moved to the next kennel so her hand fell away, her arm dropping to her side. Was he deliberately shrugging off sympathy to hold back grief, or was he genuinely that over the loss already?

"She brought me up . . . but the relationship wasn't the same as the sort you have with your family."

"What do you mean?" she pushed, needing to understand him. She couldn't deny he was different than before, with new walls that hadn't totally fallen even after they slept together. He'd hinted that his grandmother hadn't always fed him and the woman had let him play his guitar in subways. How much more was Mike not telling her?

"My grandmother always found a way to pay the bills, and she sure as hell didn't let little things like—oh, the law—stand in her way." His work lamp flickered off and on like the bulb was shorting out.

"How do you mean?" She reached into the supply closet for a stack of clean bowls to replace two in each trashed kennel run. "Come on. You know everything about me, and I'm realizing I don't know much about you. I never even got to meet your grandmother when we were dating."

Had he always known they would break up?

"Granny hadn't planned on bringing up her grandson, but that's just the way it shook down once my mom cut out." He paused in his work to tighten the lightbulb in the work lamp before hanging it back on the fence. "Dad deployed often for the extra hazardous duty pay. There still wasn't really enough to go around. But Granny was . . . resourceful."

"How so?"

He used a pair of vise grips to bend a ragged chunk of fence to ensure there was no sharp edge that could cut an animal. "She ran short on the rent one month, so she shaved my hair and told the town I had cancer. There were collection buckets all over everywhere. I had a sunburned scalp that summer, but she pulled it off for three months before she got busted."

Sierra tried not to let her surprise show. No wonder he'd been closemouthed about his grandmother.

"How old were you?"

He bent another jagged bit of metal, overly intent on his task. "Six years old."

Six? She'd known his mother left, but somehow she'd always assumed he was older than that when it happened. "How was her . . . uh . . ."—scam?—". . . ruse discovered? Did you tell someone?"

"I knew to keep my mouth shut." He looked away altogether, weaving a zip tie through the jagged pieces he'd rounded off to close the gap. "She told me we would have to live in the station wagon if I talked."

Screw walls. They were more to each other than this. She knelt beside him. "Mike, that's horrible."

"Yes," he acknowledged, but without wincing. "My first grade teacher agreed when she figured it out. I didn't have medicines to take. And I was gaining weight fast. I looked too healthy to her, and she started asking questions."

"Gaining weight?" she said slowly, unable to believe what she was hearing.

"School lunches fed me more than I got at home."

Her hand went to her chest, to her heart. "Your grandmother was limiting what you ate in order to make you appear sick?"

"I didn't starve, but I sure as hell didn't get seconds or dessert." He laughed darkly, the joke falling flat. Damn flat. "We left town before she could get arrested. I'm not sure how long the statute of limitations is on that, but we never went back to that state."

How could she have not known this about him? How could they have dated for so long, been so intimate, and she had no idea how much of himself he'd kept from her—how much she'd let him keep back. "Why didn't you ever tell me any of this when we were together before?"

He set aside a fistful of zip ties and faced her full on for the first time since he'd started sharing the story. "Your family is so perfect . . . I just didn't feel like trotting out my dysfunctional childhood."

His golden brown eyes were narrow and defensive, his broad shoulders braced. But even with his badass warrior stance, she could only see those eyes in the face of a vulnerable, hungry little boy.

She wasn't backing down. "Why are you telling me now? What's changed?"

"Life. Life changed over there . . . this year." His voice went tight, his jaw flexing.

He leaned forward on one knee and hauled her to him for a kiss, not subtle and not painful, but definitely not gentle. His kiss was raw and full of a need to block out life's disappointments.

Without another thought she went into his arms. To hell

with tomorrow or how they would deal with origami animals or relatives who betrayed a defenseless child.

They were here. Now. And they needed each other. They'd done enough for the night with the kennels. Her mom would come to check on them and see she had a few more places set to settle dogs for the night. That was going to have to be enough until morning.

The ranch had distracted Sierra too many times from whatever was going on with Mike. He needed her, and she was going to be there for him. She stood. Or he stood. She wasn't sure which, because they moved at the same time. In sync with each other. Needing each other.

She looped her arms around his neck and held on tighter, holding him closer. Her breasts pressed against his chest, the hard muscle of him exciting a shiver of need that trembled all over. She wanted to erase all the things he'd told her, to burn them away with the force of what she felt for him. She let her fingers run wild down his back and up into his short hair, stroking everything within her reach.

He grasped behind her knees and lifted her legs to wrap around his waist, bringing the core of her flush against him. Then he walked outside to the staircase, each step creating delicious friction right where she craved him most. Thank God for the cover of night. She couldn't imagine how he saw where he was going because she never stopped kissing him. She didn't think she *could* stop if she wanted to, each step up to his loft building the heat inside her, flaming to life higher and hotter.

Not even winded, he shouldered open the door. His strength and power and passion sent a bolt of pleasure through her. He lowered her to the mattress with such gentle precision and control while she felt like a wildfire flaming in every conceivable direction. She scrambled for rational thought just long enough to pull his wallet from his back pocket, to find a condom.

He gripped her wrist, nuzzling her neck in a way that

sent ribbons of pleasure skimming over her flesh. "You're not going to need those just yet."

Sliding his palm up her wrist, he plucked the wallet from her hand and set it aside very deliberately. A shiver of anticipation went through her at the knowledge that she was about to benefit from his slow, methodical thoroughness.

Kiss by kiss, he made his way down her body, stroking and caressing. The barrier of clothes made little difference. Each touch, kiss, nip, lower and lower, igniting her every tingling nerve. His hot breath fanned along the neckline of her thin cotton dress, the proximity of his mouth making her breasts ache for more. His tongue dipped just below the fabric there, but then he was back to kissing her through her dress, working his way down her ribs. Slowing at her waist in a way that made his intentions delectably clear.

He caressed down to her legs, bunching the hem of her dress in his fists and inching it up until she felt the warm brush of his breath across her stomach. Restless and hyperaware, her fingers skimmed his short hair, raking over scalp. The rasp of his bristly chin on her skin as he teased her belly button ring with his teeth, then snapped the band of her bikini underwear.

She had to admire his efficiency.

One tug and air swept over her bared flesh. Her back arched, her whole body under the spell of his touch. He eased to one side of her, propped on an elbow to stare down at her in a way that said he wanted to take time and admire the view. He licked her thigh and then, as her skin cooled, he breathed warm air along her skin. Goose bumps tickled sensation up and down her legs while he stroked the lightest of touches behind her knee. Just inside her hip bone. Through the damp curls above her sex.

"Mike." She tried to fight the spasm of pure longing, but she did not have the patience of this man. "I'm going to take my sweet time paying your back," she warned him softly, more than ready to crawl out of her skin.

His slow smile gave her as much pleasure as anything he did to her body.

And then, yes . . . he shifted his gorgeous male body over her again and landed a kiss between her thighs that had her forgetting anything else. He nudged, nuzzled, teased her in the way of a man who knew her body well. He grasped her legs and hooked them over his shoulders, spreading her wider, arousing her faster. Her head dug back in the pillow, and she lost herself in pure sensation.

She hit the brink of an orgasm once and he pulled her back, slowing things down and making the pleasure last. Twisting beneath him, she closed her eyes tight, the vision of him kissing her almost too much for her overwrought senses. But then, as the tension built all over again, she cracked open an eyelid for just the tiniest peek.

His back bent to his task, his muscles taut and golden in the half-light from the moon steaming in a high window. His shoulders angled beneath her thighs, his hands securing her hips . . . it was all too much.

She flew apart with a shout she couldn't contain. Her heels dug in his shoulders, her fingers twisting in the pillowcase on either side of her head. And the waves of pleasure went on and on. He worked them with his tongue, nudging each one higher until she was utterly spent beneath him. He rested a cheek on her hip, his breath fanning along her stomach while the ceiling fan ticked overhead.

He didn't wait long, only allowing her to catch her breath until he ditched his jeans and his boxers. Stripped her dress over her head and off her limp body.

She knelt to help him, wriggling through the opening since they hadn't even unzipped it.

"Payback," she reminded him, trailing a hand up his hip toward his straining erection.

She'd missed this. Missed him.

But he caught her hand and held it as he knelt with her.

"Not this time, okay?" He was so rarely serious, especially in bed. "I need this."

Her heart squeezed tight for all of a second before he pushed her back on the bed.

"I'm all yours," she said simply. Because in spite of everything, it was true.

For now, with Mike, she could forget. She just hoped that, for a few hours at least, he could, too.

Thirteen

CAT IN HER lap, Lacey sat at the computer desk in the corner of her bedroom, her back to her pristinely made bed. She'd been playing catch-up with work all week after her crazy busy weekend with the adoption event and then the horrifying break-in during the picnic.

Thank heaven, there hadn't been any major injuries. The police said they were following up leads with some similar break-ins at shelters in neighboring counties. Some dogs had been stolen for fighting rings. The thought of one of her animals being taken like that made her physically ill.

The price of replacing and repairing the gates was near crippling to her already tight budget. She'd also had to face the reality of spending more money on additional security around the perimeter, such as an electric gate and cameras. She wouldn't be able to take in as many animals, and that hurt. She just had to keep it in perspective.

Hopefully this weekend would be easier and give her at least a brief reprieve. She almost managed to believe herself.

She read the last of the comments in the chat forum for her eleventh grade honors chemistry students in the online virtual school. She was lucky to have the job that allowed her to work from home—and she genuinely enjoyed it. She'd taught AP classes as well, and rumor had it she would be picked up by the local junior college to teach a couple of classes there. She could use the extra money and she'd wanted the job for years. If only she could figure out how to make more hours in the day.

Creaking back in her chair, she picked up the origami dog beside her computer screen. It was starting to get tattered along the edges, like the paper kitty also on her desk. Maybe she should have them laminated so she would always have this last gift from Allen, even if it was just a symbol. But somehow sealing the two origami animals off seemed like she would be turning a page, closing a chapter of her life. Like if she crawled under those covers into the bed alone. Or if she let herself acknowledge feelings of attraction for another man, for Ray . . .

Her mind filled with memories of the surprise awareness in his office, then the way he'd snatched her up to keep her from racing into the barn. He'd only held her for a moment, and it probably meant nothing to him, but her starved senses soaked up every detail.

Not happening. Not yet. Maybe never.

She put the dog back on her desk and finished tabulating grades. She had adopters coming to look at the Bob Marley schnoodle—all cleaned up and ready to adopt. As predicted, the pup had over two dozen applicants within a couple of days. She wished all the animals were as lucky.

Back to finishing work. Three quick discussion paragraphs later, she clicked save and exit. She yanked on a pair of pink Chucks and headed down the hall. She glanced in her father-in-law's bedroom door, which was cracked, the television blaring while he read a newspaper before supper. More times than not lately, he slept with it on all night. The cuckoo clock chimed six times, and thank goodness Trooper didn't go berserk over the sound this time. The General kept dog treats in his room, so maybe Trooper was finally feeling secure.

Finally, that was some piece of good news.

"Nathan," she called to her son on the sofa. When he didn't budge from playing his video game, she tugged one earbud out. "There's buffalo chicken in the Crock-Pot to shred up on buns. Salad is in the fridge. Just in case you get hungry before we're ready to sit down to eat."

She tucked her head to try to catch his eye. "Okay?"

"Chicken. Crock-Pot. Buns. Salad. Got it." He tucked the earbud back in.

She slid her hands in her pocket to keep from giving him a massive hug he would just reject. She missed her son, the little boy who ran toward her with a fistful of dandelions. There was something so sweet about those sweaty, chubby-cheeked hugs of a little boy who dug up worms to go fishing with his dad and grandpa.

Nathan and Allen had been at odds, though, in the year before her husband deployed. She knew their son was only trying to assert his own manhood in that timeless male coming-of-age ritual. Allen and Joshua were encouraging Nathan to look into Junior ROTC, which only made Nathan all the more determined to let his hair grow and wear scruffy, saggy clothes.

They would have made it through that rough patch given time. But time had been taken from them, leaving Nathan in a painful limbo she didn't know how to help him fix.

She was almost to the kitchen when the new gate alarm system chimed with a car asking for admittance at the top of the road. Peering through the blinds, she saw the minivan the adoptive family said they would be driving. She buzzed open the gate and let them in. She glanced around the yard, noting everything in place. Usually she handled adoptions at a park downtown, but she knew this couple. They'd adopted from her before, a young military family with a poodle. Their twin girls were preteens, and each wanted their own dog.

As she watched them drive down the dirt road leading to the play yard area, she couldn't help but think of when she and Allen had adopted Clementine. Their kids had been so excited. Clementine had still had four legs then. She'd lost one to a cancer a year ago. So much history and love wrapped up in making a family. She'd tried to do everything right, and still her children had suffered the harshest blow.

She hugged herself tight as the minivan stopped. The side door slid open and the girls hopped out, bubbling with excitement. It had been so long since she'd seen Nathan enthusiastic over anything. Shifting her attention to the husband and wife walking up arm in arm, their poodle on a leash, didn't make her feel much better.

To keep her heart from splitting in two over the family tableau, Lacey knelt down to greet the fuzzy white dog with pink bows on her ears. "Awww, it's very rewarding to see a former foster so healthy and loved." She smiled up at the couple, determined to hold it together. She had to put one foot in front of the other, no matter how much her heart ached. "Thank you, Allie and Sean. So happy to have you and the girls back. Come. Let's meet Marley."

RAY STOOD IN the mudroom doorway leading into Lacey's kitchen. She never asked him to make house calls. Ever.

So when she'd phoned him tonight, frantic about the sheltie puppies, he hadn't hesitated to drive over. He cautioned himself to take the call at face value and not read too much into her reaching out. Sure, there had been attraction crackling like a live wire between them at the picnic. And that moment when he'd held her back from going into the barn was seared in him until he could still feel the outline of her body.

He knew it couldn't go anywhere. Not now. He needed to keep himself and his feelings for her in check.

"Lacey," he called out.

"Come on in. I'm out on the patio." Her voice was shaky, to say the least.

His gut knotted. He stepped deeper into her home, past the utility sink and the row of galoshes, gym shoes and cowboy boots. Her kitchen sprawled out in a homey clutter he never would have found in his mom's immaculate house, but always envied when he went to hang out with friends. He walked through to her enclosed patio. A puppy pen surrounded a baby pool, empty of water but full of blankets and a mama sheltie with puppies.

Lacey stood by a table with a Rubbermaid container full of what looked like puppy gear and assorted dog care items. She wore yoga pants that showed off her legs to perfection. Her T-shirt was fitted, something she must have pulled from her son's drawer since it had a video game logo on the front. The whole outfit was so totally Lacey, her wavy light brown hair swinging down her back. But then the pink Chucks on her feet—well, those alone would have turned him inside out. He was once again slayed by everything about this unique, unpredictable woman.

He stepped down into the glass room, full of the scent of lavender and bleach. Signature Lacey. He smiled. "Congratulations on adopting out that poodle boy, Marley."

"Thank you. It's tough to remember to celebrate. Especially after what happened last weekend and knowing whoever did it is still out there somewhere. And then to be blindsided by more sick puppies and I'm blaming myself for missing the signs because there's so much going on."

"Where are the pit puppies?" Hopefully not exposed to the sick ones here.

"The pit puppies are thriving, fully weaned from the bottle and eating solid food, so I moved them to a regular foster home until they're old enough for adoption. These little ones needed me now."

He knew too well people didn't dump their animals at the shelter in perfect condition.

"I expected the mama and babies to be full of parasites, but I'm worried maybe it's worse than normal. They seem dehydrated and their gums are getting pale. I'm sorry to bother you but—"

"Don't apologize. That's definitely cause for concern." He knelt down beside the pen and lifted out one pup that looked particularly lethargic, a three-week-old fuzzy ball of white and black fur.

He pinched up the scruff of the neck and, sure enough, it didn't slide back into place as it should. He lifted the lip and checked the gums, pale pink, not great but at least not white. He looked into the pup's eyes cataloguing with a combination of training and instinct. "Any fever?"

She shook her head. "No nasal drainage either. They're just . . . not right."

And yes, yes, he'd noticed that while she'd always been careful she'd become particularly . . . jumpy. Fearful, even.

"Did I panic over nothing?"

"Don't apologize." He checked each of the puppies one by one, and they did need fluids, which she knew how to administer, even though most fosters wouldn't. Still, he was glad for the excuse to see her. "They could all use some subcutaneous fluids. Mama dog, too. I've got a bag with me and I see you've already got one ready." He pointed to the bag of clear fluids hanging from a chair. "We'll have them set in no time."

A sigh shuddered through her. "Maybe you should do them all."

"You're good. You know the drill. I'll holler if I see anything to worry about."

While he set up a second bag, she knelt beside the nursing

dog murmuring soothing words as she cradled a puppy. "It's okay, Mama. I'm just trying to help your babies."

"I'm glad to assist, but I'm wondering what's up with your sudden lack of confidence?" He dug in his vet bag for the smallest gauge needles.

She draped a clean towel over her lap and soothed the pup on her leg until it calmed, then reached for the needle attached to the line. "It's been a rough couple of weeks. Having Trooper here, well, I'm glad it worked, but—"

Understanding hit him. "But it's made losing your husband fresh again."

"Exactly. I'm not sure I even realized how much the stress was building until tonight when I tried to play catch-up only to realize I can't seem to find my footing."

He hated seeing her this rattled. So, even though he knew it was going to hurt, he had to at least try to get her to talk about it. Bracing himself, he asked, "How did you two meet?"

She injected the pup slowly, her hands steady even though her voice wasn't.

"I was a senior and this new guy came to school. His dad had just transferred to the local Army post, forcing him to move his senior year. I saw him in his Junior ROTC uniform and wow, call it love at first sight or lust at first sight, but I knew he was mine and I'd better act fast before the other girls moved in on him."

He could have done without the lust mention. Ray pinched up the scruff again, made a tent and positioned the needle, easing a flow of subcu fluids under the skin of another dehydrated pup. "Sounds like you both knew right away."

"He truly was a great guy, good grades and smart. He worked his butt off to make his father proud."

"Did he succeed?" God knows his own father hadn't been pleased with a hippie son who spent a fortune on vet school then didn't seem to care about raking in the big bucks back home so his father could trot out his successful son at election time.

"It's tough to tell with the General, and our window to find out is closing fast," she said sadly, withdrawing the needle from the pup and cuddling her close for comfort. "I think so. Allen made full bird. That's big. Would he have made general? I don't know. Allen wasn't as ruthlessly driven as Joshua—and I mean that in a good way."

"He sounds like the perfect guy." Great. When the time came, he had to compete with a saintly ghost. Not that he wanted her to be unhappy, but damn.

"He had his flaws."

"Such as?" He left the last two puppies for Lacey to hydrate while he stepped over a chew toy and checked on the mama dog.

"He put up with too much crap from me. Just look at our home." She held up a puppy. "He wasn't great at managing money, but since he was gone a lot I took over the bills. That helped."

He wasn't so comfortable talking about the married years, the successful man who genuinely seemed to cherish his wife's unique calling to save. "But back to high school when you met."

"Halfway through our senior year we learned Allen had gotten into West Point, but he turned down the appointment to marry me. He took an ROTC scholarship at a local college instead."

"What did your family say?" He put a fresh needle on the IV line and distracted mama dog with an ear scratch a second before he slid in the needle under her skin. She didn't even wince, poor, worn-out girl.

"They said that I should have encouraged him to take the amazing opportunity." She winced with guilt. "They were right. I pressured him for all the wrong reasons. I was scared he would outgrow me and find someone else . . . And then it was all a moot issue."

He stayed silent, finishing the fluids on the mama as Lacey set the last puppy back in to nurse.

"I got pregnant the summer before college. So he would have been kicked out of West Point for getting married or I would have had Sierra on my own." She glanced over at him. "West Point cadets can't be married during school."

"He seems to have had a successful Army career anyway."

"Did he? If he'd gone to West Point he might have been in a different place." She leaned against the puppy pen as if unsteady, her eyes glazed with unshed tears. "Or safer place."

Ah, now he understood the path of her life review, and it had to be hell. "You can drive yourself crazy with thoughts like that."

"I think I'm already there." She blinked and one tear slid free, tracking down her cheek.

To hell with restraint. He put his arms around her and hauled her to his chest. He cupped her head, his fingers tangled in the waves of her hair, every bit as soft as he'd dreamed about. This was okay, holding her when she was upset, and he'd waited so long to touch her he couldn't bring himself to cut this moment short. Even if he was a selfish ass for using her grief to take advantage of the chance to touch her.

A sigh shuddered through her. "I don't know what I would have done without your help this past week."

Hearing her say that led him to tell her the decision that had been weighing so heavily on him. "Lacey, I've gotten an offer from a practice back in my hometown out west, a big clinic with high-end clientele, which allows the vets a hefty budget to do charity work."

She glanced up at him, her smile tentative, her eyes glittering. "What a fantastic opportunity for you. Congratulations." Her throat moved with a slow swallow. "Are you going to take the offer?"

How could he tell her he wanted to stick around for her? How could he expect her to give him a sign there was a chance so soon after she'd lost her husband? "I don't know. I'm still weighing the options. I've grown really, uh, fond of the people I work with—"

A cleared throat in the doorway sent her lurching back. She scraped her wrists under her eyes.

He checked and found—shit. Her son, Nathan, stood stock-still and not happy, looking from one to the other of them with an accusatory glare that wouldn't have bothered him if it weren't for the pain he saw in those eyes that looked so much like Lacey's.

"Mom, the cops just called your cell phone, which you left in the kitchen and apparently were too *busy* to hear."

She stood up sharply, then stumbled, losing her balance for an instant. Ray palmed her back, taking his place beside her even as her son's eyes narrowed further. "Ray, I'm okay." She reached for her son. "Why are the police calling?"

"You forgot to turn the security system back on after Doctor Vega arrived and Gramps got out. He took the Barge and he's been in a wreck. You need to pick him up at the station." He turned away, then looked back with an attitude that some teenager should have patented a long time ago. "Oh, and Trooper's locked up at the pound."

YES, I UNDERSTAND when people talk even though I'm a dog, but that doesn't mean I always know certain phrases or labels. Like this "Animal Control" place Lacey talked about. It took a while for me to figure that one out. She would mention going to visit her friends at Animal Control, and the next thing I knew, there were more dogs or cats and one day even a bunny rabbit.

Those new pups on the block always smelled kinda different, but Lacey bathed them fast. God, these humans love baths. I like swimming fine, but baths? Get real. Soap gets in my eyes and I'm crammed in a tub. Then if I won't use the tub, it's time for a cold hose rinse off.

I get muddy. A lot. Sierra doesn't like it. She always sighs, "Not again, Trooper."

But I know. There will be an "again."

Anyhow, about this Animal Control thing. I understood that it was a place where animals lived, but not much beyond that. Until the night I went for a drive with the General.

The ride was fun at first, better than the late walks we snuck. I had my head out the window, breathing in a million scents coming at me all at once. All those smells were kinda like doggie crack, drugging my senses.

Gramps bought me a burger in a drive-through. I gobbled it right up, except I spit the pickles out the window. Made another driver really mad, but hey, I'm a dog. I thought it was highly advanced of me not to hide the pickles under the backseat.

The driver in the other car got pissed off. What's it called? Oh yeah, road rage. She drove faster, right up alongside us, blaring the horn again and again. Gramps started twitching that way he did when I could tell he was getting disoriented and having war flashbacks.

Humans have a fancy name for it. Post-traumatic stress disorder.

I understood, even without the fancy words. We dogs get the crap kicked out of us a lot. When I was a puppy, the local kids threw rocks at us to chase us away. Some of the dogs at the rescue have their own stories about war wounds from their previous lives.

It leaves marks. And there are triggers to those fears.

That honking horn triggered something in Gramps. He mashed the gas and lost control of the big car—the Barge. He swerved. Then bam. He popped up a curb and rammed a tree. We had a wreck.

Obviously I'm okay because I'm telling you about the accident now. I was flung from the car since the window

was down. I sprained my leg and it hurt. But I limped back
to the Barge against the tree. Steam rose from the hood.

Gramps didn't look good slumped over the wheel uncon-
scious, so I figured I should get help for the General. The
Colonel would want me to take care of his dad. Since it
didn't seem like I was able to do much for Lacey and the
kids except make more work with my baths, I was all in on
finding a cop. Someone like that Officer Parker we met at
the adoption event when he was sniffing around Lacey.

Cops equal help. Even a dog knows that.

Or so I thought.

The policeman I found that night wouldn't listen to me
no matter how loudly I barked. And man, he got mad when
I tugged his pants leg to show him where we needed to go
find Gramps. The dude acted like I was dangerous.

For real?

I wasn't a wild pup anymore. But apparently someone
forgot to give him the memo.

Prepare yourself for what he did, because it sure surprised the pee out of me.

He threw a blanket over me.

Not playing around, either. He wrapped me up tight,
making it tough to breathe and hurting my sprained leg. I
was not happy about that. I yelped and thrashed. Hard. He
adjusted his grip and he held me tighter, which didn't go
well for either of us. I knocked him down and we hit the
road. My leg felt like it was on fire it ached so bad, but not
badly enough to stop me. I bolted.

As I race-limped into the cluster of houses, I heard the
policeman on his radio shouting, "Need assistance from
Animal Control pronto. Wild dog on the loose."

And that's when I learned Animal Control is actually
doggie jail.

Fourteen

EARLY MORNING SUN steaming the dew off the parking lot, Sierra sat in her running car with the air conditioner blasting while she waited for the shelter to open so she could retrieve Trooper. The night had been beyond horrible, but they were lucky. Very lucky.

Her mother was home with her grandfather. He'd suffered a mild concussion from driving the Barge into a tree, totaling the car, but Lacey was terrified to let him out of her sight for even a minute. Mike had offered to feed all the animals so Sierra could get Trooper. How would they manage when Mike left?

What would *she* do?

As much as it hurt to think about, she was beginning to wonder if Gramps required a level of care beyond their scope at home. For his health and safety, was it time to consider some kind of assisted living facility?

Before she could even chase that thought any further, the front door to the shelter opened and the director poked her head out. "Come on in, hon. We're not open yet, but there's no need for you to sit out here waiting."

Please Lord, she prayed Trooper was really inside and okay. It had been a horribly long night without him barking his head off at that blasted cuckoo clock.

"Hope" is the thing with feathers, that perches in the soul . . . The words to a Dickinson poem flashed through her mind even as Sierra turned off the car and raced across the parking lot. "Thank you so much. He's here, right? We read your text message correctly?"

The Animal Control officer had scanned Trooper when he came in, plus he'd kept his collar on this time. They'd had to process him, but they'd sent Lacey a text message.

And sings the tune without the words, and never stops—at all . . . Damn but it was hard to be hopeful as that little bird, especially when life kept throwing one curveball after another.

"Yes," Dahlia reassured her, stepping aside for Sierra to enter. "Your boy is here. How's your grandfather?"

Relief flooded through her. Thank goodness. What was it about Trooper that made him so apt to run? And why had her last gift from her father been something that tested her at every turn? She took a deep breath.

"He's resting. Mom wakes him up every hour since he has a mild concussion, but we're lucky we only lost the car." Gramps was growing as escape prone as Trooper. She followed Dahlia back, the shelter humming with activity as staff fed the animals and cleaned, preparing to open for the public. "And Trooper's okay?"

"He's limping, and you'll want to check that out, but it doesn't appear to be more than a sprain. Thank God Trooper is microchipped and had his collar. I would have recognized him once I did my walk-through, but still, I'm so relieved for your family."

"I'm glad he's here. He lived on his own for so long, he

could have been missing, scavenging for who knows how long. Or worse." Hit by a car. Taken in by some stranger. Or picked up by one of those horrible dogfighting rings the cops suspected had broken into their barn.

As if it wasn't hard enough to keep watch over Gramps. There was just too much to remember in keeping him out of harm's way these days. Or was she allowing herself to be distracted by Mike? Guilt pinched as she admitted this was a distinct possibility.

Posters filled the wall with photos of adoptable pets, spay/neuter incentives and flea prevention reminders mixed with framed photos of the employees. Huge bulletin boards were packed with photos of adopted dogs with their families and letters of appreciation. A few notes written in crayon or scribbled marker pictures of stick figure dogs were the sweetest highlights.

She and her mom should do something like that at Second Chance Ranch. In all their spare time. She winced.

"Mom asked me to say thanks and to let you know we would love it if you joined us Sunday evening—any Sunday—for a picnic. They're becoming a bit of a Second Chance tradition."

Dahlia pushed open the heavy door leading to the section where they kept the strays. She stopped in front of the first kennel run with Trooper and a couple of skinny Labradors. "Thank you. I may well take you up on that."

Trooper lay curled up on a blue dog cot, low to the ground, his back pressed to the wall as he eyed everyone with fear and suspicion. Sierra stepped forward to reassure him, but Dahlia held up a hand, keeping her back for now. The director inched the door open, sliding her arm in and looping a leash around Trooper's neck with professional ease.

Given the shelter director wore leather knee boots and a sleek business suit, the image was . . . different. Sierra couldn't help but notice how the boss got Trooper herself rather than pull one of the kennel techs from their fast-paced morning routine.

Part of Sierra ached to walk down the length of runs and give each dog at least an extra hello or scratch on the nose, but the stray section was full of animals that hadn't been temperament tested yet. Dogs that were scared and abandoned. Some kennel runs held bold red signs warning *Quarantine Bite Case* or *Beware: Aggressive*. Even in the cleanest of shelters there was a scent of despair she didn't need a canine sense of smell to detect.

No wonder her mother came home with carloads full of animals half the time she visited this place. The conditions were clean, safe and caring, but with thousands of animals a year to process, the shelter couldn't possibly replicate the environment of a home-based rescue.

Dahlia passed over the leash and led them out of the stray area. Trooper limped alongside her, his head low, neck swiveling from side to side as he looked around warily. The soothing music hadn't come close to working its magic on him yet.

"Sierra, you can sign him out up front. I'm off to a breakfast meeting with the chamber of commerce. Tell your mom hello for me."

"We owe you."

"There are no tallies. If there were, I would be the one deeply in debt." Her hand trailed over Trooper's head so lightly a sigh rippled through the dog.

Then she left, efficient, always on the move with her cell phone in her hand as she texted.

The director's boots clicked on her way back out to the reception area. Dahlia passed the paperwork from the kennel across the desk before waving on her way out. Sierra realized she'd gotten the royal treatment thanks to her mom, and God, she was grateful.

She dropped to her knees and wrapped her arms around Trooper's neck, burying her face in his fur, which had gotten more than a little smelly from his night's adventure. What if she'd lost her father's dog? The dog that Mike had risked his career to bring to them?

What if something had happened to this whacky, quirky animal that was stealing her heart in spite of all the painful memories he brought with him?

"Hope" is the thing with feathers . . .

For the first time, she wondered if Emily Dickinson got it wrong. Because right now, it felt like Hope came with fur.

She kissed him on the nose. "You're a crazy lucky dog, do you know that? You have really got to stop running away."

Trooper plastered himself so tightly to her, Velcro dog style, she could almost swear she heard him promise.

A WEEK LATER, Mike scraped the grease off the grill, cleaning the racks as everyone finished up the last of their burgers and hot dogs, twice as many burgers as last Sunday. The weekend gathering was expanding. But he was grateful for the support today of all days.

Father's Day.

The McDaniel women continued on like it was any other day, but it had to be hell for them both. Helping those two fiercely independent females was easier said than done. At least Gramps had seemed to given up on escaping since his accident. The General might not remember the details, but something appeared to have resonated in him, a shift, a surrender of independence, necessary but so damn sad at the same time.

Sierra refilled the three-gallon cooler of tea, and another of lemonade. Her jean shorts and cowboy boots were driving him crazy to get her alone later. But it would likely be much later.

According to Sierra, it wasn't unusual for the rescue volunteers who came in on the weekend to gather around for a meal. In the past, they would order pizza or bring bagged lunches and sit around to talk.

Yet when Lacey had showed up with her vet buddy, the get-together grew more . . . official. More volunteers came, all bringing side dishes and sodas, while Lacey supplied burgers and hot dogs. He was surprised at the turnout today, though, given this was Father's Day. But then maybe these people—friends of Lacey and Sierra—were here for just that reason. They'd turned out to offer support because they knew this would be an especially difficult time for the McDaniel family.

His time to offer them support was coming to a close. Only a week left on his leave. Only a week left until the county made a decision on the rescue.

Only a week left with Sierra before he moved and he needed to figure out what the hell that meant for them.

Their relationship was . . . complicated. They weren't officially a couple—even though they'd had sex every day for the past two weeks, secretly, neither of them willing to face the implications of going back to the way things were before.

Her mother knew, though. That was obvious from the half smiles Lacey couldn't always hide, but Sierra didn't want to acknowledge anything, even in front of her mom.

Because her mom was recently widowed, or for some other reason? Like wanting to stay here and build a life rather than continue the military vagabond lifestyle for another twenty years?

Twenty years? Like marriage? Where the hell had that thought come from?

He slammed the grill lid and turned fast as if someone in the crowd might be a mind reader. Instead, he just found a row of dogs at the fence. A *very long* row lined up as the smoke of burning grease drifted toward them. Trooper, the other three McDaniel dogs, the vet's two border collies. And of course all the fosters, including a new brindle—Pixie? Cute mutt. He wondered if she might be staying.

His eyes slid back to Trooper. The dog cocked his head to the side as if listening, understanding. He was going to miss the mutt. They'd been together nearly seven months.

And the people? He would miss them, too.

What an—he dug for a Scrabble word—*eclectic* group of folks. Why couldn't the neighbors see this aspect of the Second Chance Ranch Rescue? The way Lacey and Sierra pulled the community together? This kind of camaraderie was rare. He would have given anything to be a part of a community like this growing up, relatives and friends.

The veterinarian had been here all three Sundays, the humanitarian who volunteered his services to a shelter fund-raiser. The kind of guy who would be perfect for Sierra. Not that Ray Vega made any overt romantic moves on any of the women.

Was Lacey matchmaking for her daughter?

The thought persisted over the weeks, no matter that Sierra had protested. And the idea stung. A lot. He shouldn't care what her mother thought, since neither he nor Sierra had committed to each other. In fact, she made it clear she didn't want a military life, and he could understand that her family had already made the ultimate sacrifice.

An acrid whiff from the grill stirred memories of that day. He swallowed down bile and turned fast to open the lid. Flames crackled. His nose twitched. He scraped more of the charred excess off, forcing himself to focus on the now, to be in the moment and stop worrying about a week from now, much less twenty years from now.

More than volunteers and the vet were joining in to offer support today. His buddy Calvin had come over as well— and was currently hitting on the shelter director, Dahlia. The echo of four-wheelers in the distance growled a warning that the neighbors were always watching, even from afar.

He didn't like the idea of anyone spying on Sierra. He couldn't deny the urge to protect her even though he had not acknowledged the right to do so beyond this week.

He turned off the grill as he watched Sierra by a tire swing that held a volunteer's kid. Sierra looked like the sort of woman in the kind of life he'd imagined having one day. So why the hell couldn't he just make that happen? A tic started in the corner of his eye.

Okay, to be honest, he wanted to take her out on dates, and instead they were sneaking around like teenagers forbidden to see each other. He wasn't sure why that rankled, because he didn't have a clue how to make things end differently this go-round.

His time out of the smoke was only temporary.

SIERRA SLIPPED HER hand into Mike's surreptitiously, under the cover of the darkness as everyone sat around the bonfire. Half the group had stayed on for the evening, and she was so grateful for her mom and for Nathan that this many people had cared enough to spend their Father's Day making her family's a little easier.

She'd made it through this day, one hour at a time for her mom and her brother. Now she wanted something for herself, a distraction, to think about anything other than grief, to feel something other than loss and regret.

To stop being *strong*.

No thoughts of the future. No dwelling on tomorrow. She squeezed Mike's hand as he sat on a blanket.

He glanced back over his shoulder at her. She held a finger to her lips and tugged him. His smile sent a thrill of anticipation up her spine.

Once they tucked around the barn away from the bonfire crowd, he ducked his head to whisper, "Where are we going?"

A welcome cool breeze ruffled through her hair, the night sky hung with a million stars.

"The supply room, in the barn."

His laugh rumbled softly. "To do inventory?"

"Of a sort." She ducked into the barn.

A cat jumped from the rafters, landing at her feet. She squealed and jumped back, slamming against Mike's rock-solid chest as the gray tabby streaked past to find another hiding spot. The past two weeks had been filled with sex, great sex, with a man who already knew her every want and need. She knew they couldn't go on like this forever, which made her want to savor every second all the more.

She turned into his arms and kissed him, fully, the darkness of the barn wrapping them in a blanket of privacy. She slipped her hands up under his polo shirt, the warmth and ridges of his hard muscled body a tactile pleasure she would never tire of exploring.

His hands tucked into the waist of her jean shorts, which conveniently brought her hips flush against his solid erection. She nipped his bottom lip. "Can we move to the inventory room a little faster, please?"

"Yes, ma'am, we most certainly can. Just making my way around another cat." He dodged a ball of fur curled up nearby as he kissed her neck in a delicious path up to her ear. "I'm just not as adept at maneuvering around the critters as you are."

Voices echoed outside, at least three. Volunteers, she suspected. But if they found them in here it would break the mood. "Then let me lead."

She fast-tracked around the corner and hauled him into the storage area stacked with bags and cans of food. The barn was climate controlled to keep everything fresh, and she felt the gust of cool air along her flesh—hot from the day in the sun, but more so from the man.

He pressed her against the closed door, sealing them in quiet privacy. He placed a palm on either side of her, focusing all his considerable concentration on a kiss that made her knees weak and her heart skip beats.

She slipped her fingers between them and worked open

his jeans, inching down the zipper and stroking inside, her hands much steadier than her ragged breaths.

Groaning, he broke the kiss and thunked his forehead against the door as he throbbed against her palm.

She tugged his wallet out of his back pocket and found a condom, grateful for the way he was always prepared. He rocked his hips against her, the hard weight of him against her feeling like exactly what she needed. Her fingers fumbled as she flipped the leather wallet onto the planked floor and tore into the foil packet. Growling in impatience, he took the condom from her and sheathed himself with quick efficiency.

He pushed inside her and she sighed in relief. She sagged back against the panel, her muscles going supple with sweet sensation. Her eyes flipped up to his to find him looking at her. Their gazes met. Held. She slid her boot up the back of his calf and wished they were skin to skin.

He surprised her when he cradled her face with infinite tenderness and kissed her all over again. Thoroughly. Sweetly. Her heart sort of folded in on itself, her knees weak with more than just sensual hunger. This man did things to her emotions that completely undid her.

She closed her eyes and lost herself in the moment and the man. She needed this. Needed him with a fierceness she couldn't question right now.

Soon, so soon, she felt release building inside her, from the urgency, the sweet forgetfulness she'd searched for in his arms.

Tingles spread through her, dissipating even as she tried to hold on to the escape she'd found here. She locked her arms around him and held on tight as he shuddered with his own release.

His heavy breaths caressed her neck, and she could feel the moment slipping away. He pressed a kiss to her temple and caressed her hair back from her face, all signs this interlude was nearing an end. Yet the look in his dark golden eyes just before wouldn't leave her thoughts. They would go back to the picnic bonfire and pretend to be friends, old lovers who'd moved on.

With her emotions a jumbled mess, she wasn't so sure she could pull that off anymore.

LACEY REACHED INTO the garage chest freezer to get two more bags of ice for a fresh container of lemonade to go with the s'mores being made over the bonfire. A cloud of cold air washed across her face, chilling the perspiration from hanging out by the flames. This huge show of support from her friends, helping get her and the kids through Father's Day, had her struggling not to cry all day.

Last year they'd celebrated Father's Day early, pretending to be happy and all the while aching at the impending separation. She'd been dreading the upcoming deployment, wishing he'd gotten out at the twenty-year retirement point rather than pushing on. He'd begged her to try just a little longer. That if the Army issued orders for him to move, he promised he would get out then. But for now, he owed his troops. They'd trained together. He couldn't bail on them. Intellectually, she'd understood. Her heart just shouted with a horrible sense of foreboding that had come true.

She clenched her teeth to hold back the flood of emotion and elbowed the freezer lid shut. Backing away a step, she bumped into a chest, a hard wall of chest. A definitely masculine chest. Doc Vega?

"Steady there, Lacey," a gravelly voice caressed her ear. *Not* Ray Vega's.

She turned fast and found—Police Officer Wyatt Parker—the two bags of ice in her grasp pressed between them. "Oh, hello. Uh, is there a problem?"

She shuffled back a step, hating the weird awkwardness that being single again had put into her brain. She always used to have easy relationships with guys, the social cue of being a "Mrs." a clear boundary that everyone understood. Now?

She freaking hated thinking about this.

"Kenneth Hammond from next door called with a noise complaint about the party, and yes, we all know Valerie put her son up to calling. I suspect she's pissed over that electric gate and cameras that keep her from sneaking onto your property. Amazing how suddenly the broken fences have stopped." His mouth went tight for a moment before he continued, "She's just trying to get more paperwork on the record in hopes of boosting her argument."

"And will it work?" Tension cranked across her shoulders and throbbed in her head.

"I don't see anything wrong here. Your gathering is well under control. The animals are contained properly."

"Thank God." She sagged against the freezer, the tension easing even if the throb of stress in her temples didn't go away.

When did it ever these days?

"You're making my job too easy."

"Let's hope it stays that way."

"Even with the added security, I figured given the problems you've had with vandals, it would be a good idea to drop by anyway on my way home. This is the last stop on my shift. In ten more seconds—" He stared at his watch, pausing . . . "I'll be off. Now. If you have any burgers left, I would be glad to make a donation to your rescue. Wouldn't want folks to think I was asking for free food."

"We have plenty of food left, and donations for the animals are always welcome. As is help." She thrust the bags of ice at him. "Would you mind carrying these?"

A wide grin creased his face that made him more approachable than the stern cop expression he wore more often. "My pleasure, ma'am."

His smile reached his eyes, and she thought of his wink

back at the adoption event. He really was flirting with her. A good-looking guy her age was making subtle and appropriate moves on her—well, aside from the fact that she was so recently widowed any move was a bit off.

An awful, awful notion hit her. That he might think she would be on the lookout for sex.

She flinched and slid away. "Let me show you where the food is."

"Lead the way," he said, without the least sign of disappointment or creepiness.

Damn him for being nice. That confused her all the more. She raced toward the door leading back into the house, only to find it blocked. Nathan stood with Doc Vega.

Nathan looked from his mom to the cop and blanched, looking downright pathetic, in spite of the fat snake draped over his shoulders. "Geez, Mom, two guys?"

"Nathan," she cautioned softly. "Don't go making assumptions. We'll talk later."

Her son shrugged. "Sure, whatever. Could you hurry up with ice?" he mumbled before sulking back into the house.

She touched Ray's arm lightly. "Would you mind showing Officer Parker where the food is? And where the ice goes? He's going to join us."

Ray searched her eyes with a hint of—anger? Jealousy? "Sure. Happy to. This way, Wyatt. We can talk about getting your cat caught up on his vaccinations on our way."

Confusion filtered through her like the fog that puffed from a freezer, chilling her to her toes in spite of the muggy night. Was she so messed up in the head over her husband's death she was misreading people's signals? If so, she could make a total fool of herself. Regardless, right now she had more important things to worry about.

Like making sure her son was okay. Her children and this rescue were all she had left. She didn't have the time or energy for anything—or anyone—else. Not in a serious way.

She just had to figure out what to do with all these crazy feelings blindsiding her when she was already such a mess.

LEANING AGAINST A tree away from the rest of the partiers, Sierra held Mike's hand in the dark. Such a simple pleasure, but nice in the afterglow of the impetuous sex they'd shared in the barn. Trooper and Clementine sprawled asleep in front of them, blocking the show of affection if anyone happened to look their way.

After making love, they'd fastened their clothes quickly and returned to the party before anyone could come looking for them. Hiding their relationship felt silly sometimes, and other times—like now—keeping this secret felt vitally important. Because if people knew, then they would start asking questions.

Are you two back together?

How do you feel about him moving?

Are you going to follow him?

Do you love him?

Mike slid his hand free from hers and leaned forward to Trooper and Clementine, giving both dogs equal time with ear scratches. The strong column of his neck called to her, and it took everything inside her not to lean forward and kiss him, just below his hairline, which had grown a little longer than usual during his time off.

These past weeks had reminded her of all the reasons they'd fallen for each other the first time, but now she had all the more reason for wariness and . . . Hell, it was too late to keep her distance. But she had to do her best to minimize the fallout when he left.

She squeezed her eyes closed tight for a second before blurting something, anything to keep from asking him to stay. "Do you ever wish you had a cat or dog of your own?"

He glanced sideways at her. "What?"

"Do you ever wish you had a pet?"

"Uhm, I . . ." He reclined back on both hands. "I travel too much for too long. The dog would be shuffled around too much. Why did you want to discuss this now?"

Feeling foolish, she swept back her hair. "Never mind. Silly question."

"Not silly at all." The moonlight overhead brought out the golden in his tiger eyes. "I don't have time for a pet, so that's not fair to the animal. I've also never had a pet. Ever. So I don't even know how to care for one—or rather, I didn't know until I stayed here."

"That's sad." She cradled his face, the stubble along his jaw a delicious abrasion. "I can't imagine my life without animals all around me. Nathan's pets are his only friends. I don't know how he would have gotten through these past months without them."

"You have a big heart like your mother. Like your father, too."

She swallowed hard over the mention of her dad, today of all days. She blinked fast to hold back the tears and blurted the first thing that came to mind. "Maybe you'll get a dog when you have a family of your own someday." She bit her lip. So much for keeping things uncomplicated during their remaining time together.

"A family?"

"Don't freak out. I'm not proposing to you." Her stomach lurched. "What we have right now is about . . . making peace with the past so we can move on to . . . build our own futures."

Maybe. She actually had no idea what they were doing anymore.

"So you're marrying me off to someone else right after we had amazing sex?" he teased lightly, tugging a strand of her hair. "I feel used."

Her lashes fluttered closed as she inhaled the scent of him, his hand so close to her face. "I didn't say that."

"Maybe Debbie would like to be my future bride?" he said, clearly joking.

Still, she couldn't help but snap, her eyes homing in on the vivacious volunteer dancing barefoot in the light of the bonfire with a local police officer. "She's ten years older than you are."

"She's hot."

"She's married." Not that it was slowing her down at the moment.

Mike kissed Sierra, whispering against her mouth, "Too bad for me then."

"Stop it." She tried to stand but he pulled her back to his lap in defiance of all their vows to keep others from knowing they were together. For now. "Forget I said anything about you having a dog or anything about the future." She needed a do-over button for her life. She'd have it worn out by the end of the day. Her eyes went to her mom on the far side of the bonfire, her face lit by the flames. "Maybe a ten-year age gap isn't really that much anyway."

"You're giving me your blessing to check out Debbie?"

She should be happy he was attempting to keep things light, but she couldn't deny what she was thinking and feeling right now. "Look at another woman and I'll cap you."

"Cap me?" He laughed.

"Okay, I'm not good at ferocious." She slumped against the tree again, watching the distant party with Doc Vega picking up empty plastic cups. "But I wasn't talking about Debbie with the ten-year thing. I think it was a Freudian slip. I get this feeling that Ray Vega is checking out my mom."

"The vet?" Mike asked, following her gaze. "I thought we decided there was nothing going on there. Sure, he's been coming around on the weekends and they spend a lot of time working rescue stuff, but I've never noticed anything more than a common focus on a cause."

"I hope you're right, because I don't think my mom's ready for anything more than that." Lacey had always been energetic and full of life, but lately she'd been moving through her world with a frenetic energy that worried Sierra. Beyond that, hell, she just wasn't ready to think of her mom moving on that way. "But he's here and he's watching her. Someday, she will probably return some guy's interest. I hadn't thought of that . . ."

"Grief comes in stages."

The simple truth crystallized so much of what she'd been thinking. Feeling.

His eyes glinted with an understanding and an echo of something resonating deep inside her. She knew Mike had lost family, friends, brothers in arms, and if she was in a better place, she would try to at least help him talk about it. But so much emotion charged the air between them at the moment it threatened to overwhelm her on an already emotional day. She couldn't do this. Not now.

She shot to her feet and held out her hand. "How about you play your guitar for everyone?"

He stared back for three heavy heartbeats before shoving to his feet and joining her. "Sure. I'll run up to the loft to get it, then meet you by the fire."

Fifteen

RAY TOOK THE last stack of used paper plates and tossed them into the bonfire, the cleanup almost complete. The recycling bin was already filled to the gills, so they used nature's power and let the bonfire finish off the rest of the mess.

He was finding himself drawn to this place more and more since Lacey's dog had arrived from overseas. If only he could shake the gut-deep jealousy over seeing Lacey with that cop. They were just standing there, nothing going on.

Except she'd jumped when he and Nathan saw her with the policeman. Ray kept replaying that moment in his head, and he could only think of two ways to interpret that guilty expression he'd seen in her eyes. Either she had something going on with the police dude and wasn't ready for people to know—more gut churning every time that crossed his mind—or, scenario two, maybe she returned Ray's feelings and didn't want him to get the wrong impression. While that was more definitely more encouraging, it also confirmed the fact that nothing was going to happen between them anytime soon. He understood he had no claim to Lacey, but he wanted a future for them. He was prepared to wait.

He just wasn't prepared for someone else to steal that future out from under him.

Which brought him back to the reality that he didn't want to be "that guy"—the one she had a fling with to get over her husband's death so she could transition to a more lasting relationship with someone else. Hell, he could be misreading the whole situation and she didn't want either of them. If he assumed too much, he would really mess up any chance he had with her.

He watched a stack of plates curl into ashes in the flame, a spot of ketchup in the middle sizzling before the rubbish poofed into dust. After a quick check of the animals with healing injuries, he would have no excuse to stick around.

Maisie and a friend of Sierra's . . . uh . . . Mary Hannah? . . . were walking to their cars. Maisie had a way of lingering too long, showing a social awkwardness he hadn't quite figured out how to handle without her bursting into tears. But Mary Hannah seemed to have her well in hand, steering her away with a quiet authority even he would be hard-pressed to ignore.

He heard footsteps crunching along the gravel path leading to the fire pit a second before Lacey reached his side. She held another paper bag full of trash to burn. "We had a lot of people here tonight. Thanks for all your help."

A lot? Definitely. But she deserved the support and distraction during what had to be a tough day for the family. Father's Day. Hell. He couldn't imagine. He didn't get along well with his old man, and they didn't talk often, but thinking about never speaking to him again? That hurt.

He searched for something to say to keep the evening and tone light for her. "I bet the dogs are starting to look forward to the Sunday picnic tradition. The leftover burgers are a big hit with the canine crowd."

A hint of a smile pulled at her cheek. "So true, especially Trooper. I could swear he has a doggie calendar tucked somewhere because he seemed to know first thing this morning that it was Sunday. He pawed at the freezer and the grill. He's a unique dog, to say the least."

They settled into a companionable silence for a few minutes, watching the flames eat the paper waste. A light blinked on inside the house on the second floor. Lacey's teenage son walked briefly into view before closing the blinds.

"How's Nathan? He seemed—" Ray searched for a diplomatic word to describe the kid, and yeah, to find out if anything had been going on in the garage between Lacey and Wyatt Parker. "He seemed off his game tonight there in the garage."

She studied a sticky paper plate in her hand, the fire casting her face in a golden glow that showcased too well the dark circles under her eyes. Finally, she pitched the plate into the blaze. "He's been quieter than usual since Trooper arrived."

Ah, so she wasn't going to address the garage at all. It was none of his business anyway. Not really. Not officially. "You're a good mother."

"I don't know about that. I'm just trying my best. Sierra was so much easier to understand as a teenager. Sure she had her moody moments, but they leaned more toward the teenage drama and tears. We could talk or I would just listen. But I knew what to do. With Nathan . . ." She shook her head. "The problems are so much bigger these days. I would give anything to spare him the hurt he's feeling—"

Her voice choked off with emotion.

To hell with keeping his distance and playing it cool. He squeezed her shoulder in comfort. "I'm so damn sorry, Lacey."

Her skin was soft and warm where the sleeveless shirt left her arm bare, and the heat he felt right now had nothing to do with the bonfire. Her eyes squeezed closed, and more than anything he wanted to pull her into his arms. She needed him, and it was killing him inside not to be able to help set her world right again.

Just as he started to draw her to him, she stepped away and thrust the whole bag into the fire. The greedy flames surged upward.

"Okay," she said with overplayed calm. "That's the last of it. Thank you again for your help."

Fair enough. She wanted him gone. This was a tough day and not the right time to push. "You can go on inside and I'll shovel sand on the fire to make sure it's out."

There were only a few people lingering on the grass, finishing up conversations or saying long good nights.

"Mike can take care of that," she said quickly.

"I know he can," Ray answered gently, stepping back from the leaping flames toward shadows, "but he doesn't have to and neither do you. I don't mind helping. I'm being a good guest. My mother would approve."

"Your mother, huh?" She crossed her arms over her chest and leaned back against a tree trunk, as if putting distance between them, but not leaving altogether. Interesting dichotomy. "Where do your parents live? Seems like we're always talking about my life or the rescue. What about the mysterious, altruistic Doctor Ramon Vega?"

Altruistic? Was that how she saw him? "My parents, hmmm, now I may need another beer for that one." He shouldn't have mentioned them in the first place. He shouldn't have crossed that line, but for some reason, he had. "My mother is married to a senator, my stepdad actually. My biological father died when I was six months old. I don't remember him."

"*You* grew up as a politician's son?"

"I know I don't look the button-up type, but what can I say? I'm a rebel." He picked up the shovel from beside the fire and started shifting sand onto the outer edges. The paper burned in a hurry, the blast of initial flames already quieting down.

"Me, too."

"What?"

"My parents were wealthy and elitist, all about being a part of the country club set. They had big plans to pair their only daughter up with one of their friend's offspring. To hear my mom talk, somehow I missed out on being a president's wife someday." She rolled her eyes, a smile lighting up her face for the first time in longer than he could remember. "But like I told you before, I got knocked up and married a soldier rather than marry a lawyer . . . or a doctor."

Her gaze zipped to him self-consciously. "I didn't mean . . . uhm, I wasn't hinting." She bit her lip then blurted, "Ah hell. Is it my imagination or are we attracted to each other? Because I really feel like I'm going crazy here sometimes wondering if I'm misunderstanding. And damned if I know what to do about it, because my life is such a mess—"

He dropped the shovel and grabbed her shoulders. "Lacey, you're not imagining anything."

His heart slammed against his ribs to have the truth out there. To have his hands on her again.

She swallowed hard, swaying toward him. "I'm not?"

He shook his head and prayed like hell for restraint. "But you're also correct about your life being in turmoil right now." The urge to kiss her pumped through him so intensely it took everything he had to hold back. Only his need for more from her kept him in check. "This is an especially bad day. I get that."

"Father's Day," she whispered softly, her eyes filling with tears, hovering on the edge until one fat droplet slid down her cheek.

He hurt for her even more than he hurt for himself. And with all the regret firing through him right now, that was saying a lot. He might never get another moment like this.

Ray thumbed away that moisture, her cheek softer than he'd even imagined as he captured her tear shed for another man. "You're always going to grieve for him. I understand. But when you're stepping into that last stage of grief, the acceptance part, I hope you remember that attraction we feel and find me."

Before the temptation could override his good intentions, he turned away. As much as it killed him to accept, someone else would have to put out the fire for her.

MIKE STRETCHED HIS arms over his head, working out the kinks in his back from shoveling sand into the bonfire pit. This place was so—Scrabble word search—*bucolic*? Sometimes he felt like an encroaching monster dark cloud invading a Norman Rockwell painting.

Sierra sat cross-legged in the hammock with her laptop, her face lit by the blue glow. Doing homework? Or lesson plans for the classes she taught as a graduate assistant? Her workload would stagger most people. He was so damn proud of her, but he couldn't deny there were times he felt her level of education put a distance between them. Their breakup before had been about different backgrounds and life experiences. And never had he felt that more acutely than as he'd told her a few stories about Granny at her finest.

He pinched the bridge of his nose right over the dull headache that had been throbbing ever since he left the barn. Hearing Nathan's video game blasting from a handheld system didn't help matters, either. Each explosion from whatever gaming creature the kid had destroyed sounded too realistic for Mike's peace of mind, especially with the smoldering bonfire throwing smoke his way. He thought Nathan had gone to bed for the night, when he'd disappeared into the house earlier, but maybe he'd just helped his grandpa get to bed. Nathan seemed to rattle around the place at all hours, as sleepless as Mike.

Except that Nathan was at an age where he still liked to blow up things. Another blast fired through the tinny sound system and wrenched the tension along Mike's shoulders. If he let himself, too easily he would be right back there in the haze of bad, bad memories. Shit that could pull him under until his only defense was to abandon sleep and play his guitar all night. The memories still hurt when he was awake. But at least they didn't distort and mutate the way they did in his dreams.

He started to turn away, just call the day quits altogether— until he heard a sniffle. He glanced back at Nathan, sitting on the step with just a video game and a snake for company. The teenager dragged his wrist under his nose and kept playing.

Could be nothing. Only the smoke or allergies.

Except Mike knew it was more than that. This was Father's Day and Nathan was feeling that. Hard. Had felt it radiating off the kid to a lesser degree every day, actually.

Something was up with the kid. Something . . . off. He'd sensed that same sort of vibe in guys he'd served with, that quiet despair. *Despair.* A darker Scrabble word he wished he'd never added to his vocabulary.

He stuffed the shovel into the dirt and walked to the porch steps where Nathan sat. "What's with wearing the snake all the time, kid?"

"I really don't like being called kid," he said without looking up.

The video game chimed with a new level reached, the screen flashing and a bomb exploding to show a new score. Mike winced again. War sucked ass. It wasn't a game.

"Roger that . . . my bad." He sat on the step next to him. "What's with the snake as an accessory, Nathan? I thought you were into lizards, or at least you were before."

"My iguana died right about the time Mom got a snake. I was grieving. Would you deny me the consolation of a new pet?"

Mike's mouth twitched at Nathan's humor. And it was the most the kid had ever said to him at a stretch, so he kept pushing. "Why not become friends with one of the dogs?"

"The snake looks more badass."

Fair enough. "Looking badass is important when you're in high school."

"How would you know?" Nathan looked at him sideways and snorted. "You've probably always been big and cool and fit in."

"I got into trouble a lot." There hadn't been much supervision from Granny in those days.

Nathan's thumbs flew along the controls, the snake watching from his perch draped around the teenager's neck. "Did you pick on people?"

Everything went still inside of Mike for a second, not liking the turn of this conversation at all. Concerned. Hell— worried. "No. I just . . . I don't know . . . liked to push boundaries. See how far I could go."

"How come?"

"Because I could."

"Bullshit," Nathan said, then looked at Mike defiantly as if daring him to call him on swearing. "Everyone has a reason for what they do."

This was supposed to be about Nathan, not him. But if it kept the kid talking, then he could play along. "To get my dad to notice or get back at him for leaving me with the craziest grandmother on the planet."

"Crazier than my mom?"

"Hey." Mike was quick to correct on that score. "Your mom's not crazy." The kid had clearly never spent a summer with Granny raising money for "cancer camp."

"She's weird." His fingers never paused on the keys, the clicking a constant dance. "This place is weird."

"Nah . . ." Strange how perceptions could be so different. He would have given anything for a home like this, a shelter from the storm of his messed-up childhood.

"We have a nanny goat and a pig. Seriously, dude."

"Okay," he conceded, "I'll agree that's a little . . . different. But then I like different. I'm guessing though that not everyone appreciates unique. So the snake keeps people from making fun of you because of your mom?"

Nathan's thumbs stilled, but he kept his eyes glued to the game, staring in that sightless way. "They make fun of me because I'm me."

The words cut right through Mike, sharper than any shrapnel. He sat with his hands between his knees, not knowing what to say or do to fix this day—this life—the kid was having. And no matter what Nathan said, he *was* still a kid, too young to be living with burdens this heavy.

Movement from the yard caught his attention, Sierra gathering her work off the hammock. For a moment he thought she was going to rescue him, but when her eyes met his, she shook her head. She nodded toward her mom, standing alone in the driveway as the vet's truck drove away.

Mike nodded back wordlessly, understanding. She wanted to be with her mother to help her through the day. Maybe to take some comfort for herself, too.

Sierra smiled and mouthed, *Thank you.*

This unspoken communication between them was a new thing, somehow more intimate than their quickie in the barn earlier.

Although he wasn't against quickies. Not by a long shot.

There just weren't going to be any more tonight.

He turned back to Nathan. He couldn't walk away from this kid, even if that meant facing a little time on the battlefield. "Hey, wanna move the video games inside so we can use two controllers?"

"Uh, sure," Nathan said, shoving to his feet, the fat boa's head lifting until it was nearly nose to nose with Mike.

"But could you put the snake away first? That thing scares the shit out of me."

Nathan snorted in disdain. "Some badass warrior you are."

ON HER WAY out to the front porch, Sierra pushed backward through the screen door, two glasses of wine in her hands and the corked bottle of chardonnay tucked precariously under her arm.

She stepped out onto the deep veranda that overlooked the driveway, letting the screen slam behind her. Looking up and down the long, planked space, she realized there wasn't an animal in sight. Unlike the glass-enclosed back patio where puppies stayed. Or the concrete slab picnic area where they kept an eye on the play yard or the barn. Not even in the house where various creatures in crates or cages may need tending.

Out here, all alone, her mom sat in one of the four white rockers.

Funny how she'd only just now realized that the front porch rockers were the only part of the house that wasn't devoted to the Second Chance Ranch's four-legged guests. Her mother and father used to chill out here at night and talk. She'd forgotten that.

Sierra held out the Waterford crystal wineglass she knew her mother treasured, the last left in her wedding set. "I thought you might like something to drink."

Smiling, her mother took the glass. "You thought right." Her head tipped to the side as she looked at Sierra's other hand. "Is that a Mason jar?"

Sierra grinned wickedly back at her mom. "Sure is. It holds more wine."

She dropped into the rocking chair next to her mom, all too aware that this used to be her father's seat. She set the bottle on the ground next to her, her arm chilled from holding it. Night sounds carried on the wind, crickets and frogs, a couple of barks. A hint of the soothing classical music from the kennel run area, although her grandfather's constant stream of television almost overrode it all. She smiled. Then there was also the occasional squawk and explosion from the video games inside. She appreciated Mike taking time to hang out with Nathan. He spent too much time alone these days.

She stifled a yawn, exhausted from the full day, physically and emotionally. Morning would come too soon.

As the moon rose higher, she found herself wondering, "Mom, do you ever sleep?"

"Not much. No." Lacey sipped her wine.

Sierra had meant the question lightly, but something in her mother's tone worried her. "Have you talked to your doctor about that? I thought right after Dad died, the doctor gave you some pills, just to get you through until things are . . . easier."

"They don't work." She took a larger swallow of the amber chardonnay, the moonlight filtering through the glass in a watery prism. "Besides, even if I medicate myself into oblivion, I still have to deal with this when I wake up. There's no escaping my life."

Okay, now she was getting seriously worried. This was about more than it being Father's Day. "There are balanced alternatives to the oblivion method."

"Thank you, Dr. McDaniel—" Her mom stopped short and looked at her quickly, apologetically. "Damn, I'm sorry, Sierra. I'm being bitchy and you're just trying to help. All the time. So much more than you should have to." She reached out and squeezed Sierra's hand. "I just want to get through this so my children can live their lives and be happy. You deserve more than this."

"What about you?" Sierra squeezed back. "Your life? What you deserve?"

"Go to bed, sweetie." Her hand slid away and went back to cradling the cut crystal glass. "Or go see Mike."

"Mom." Sierra set her Mason jar on the small table between them and crossed her arms. "I'm not going anywhere. I'm talking to you. We're both adults so I'm going to say it straight out. I don't think you should be alone tonight. Whether you're awake or asleep or drunk, you're stuck with me."

"I'm not drunk. Yet. But I would like to be." She took Sierra's jar and poured some into her own glass.

"Guess this means I have to stay for sure then since you shouldn't drink alone." Had her mother self-medicated more often than she realized? Had she missed this in the mad scramble to help her mom with the day-to-day chores, that Lacey was quietly falling apart alone at night?

"You staying here won't make me drink less. Not tonight," her mother warned.

There was a fierceness in her tone, but Sierra could almost hear the desperation underneath. God, she wished she didn't appreciate that set of emotions all too well.

She was scared to death she'd be right back here next week when Mike left.

"I understand." She took her jar before her mom stole all her wine. "And just so *you* understand when you're hungover and cranky tomorrow, I'll be too hungover and cranky myself to care."

Lacey cocked her head to the side. "There's logic in that somehow."

"For now, I'm all for the one day at a time approach." She would not borrow heartache when it would come her way all too soon. She sipped her wine. "Eventually, though, you need to start really sleeping. A full night's rest."

"I *am* sleeping some. Just not a lot," her mom admitted. "But I'll be okay. This is just a difficult time for all of us."

"Mom, it's Father's Day." Her mind crowded with images of construction paper cards and lopsided homemade cakes from celebrations in the past. "That makes this more than an everyday tough time. This is a really, really tough time. It's okay for you to be sad or mad or even just unreasonable."

Lacey kept rocking, but her chin started quivering, her hand trembling until the wine threatened to slosh. "I'm not ready to pull the cork out of those emotions yet."

What could she say to that? Hell. She sure could use some of her friend Mary Hannah's training in psychology and counseling right about now. Sadly, though, all she had was a bottle of wine and a line from *Macbeth*. " 'Give sorrow words; the grief that does not speak knits up the o-er wrought heart and bids it break.' "

Her mother shot a dry look at her. "Seriously, if you start bombarding me with the Emily Dickinson poems, I am out of here and I'm taking that bottle of wine with me."

Sierra snatched up the chardonnay and held it hostage. "I'm the official bartender tonight, but I promise to make it a quote-free evening if you'll let me stay here with you, however late that may be."

"You've got a deal." Lacey held out her Waterford glass, empty for the second time tonight. "Now fill her up so we can toast."

"Can do." Steeling herself for a long night, she hoped Mike would understand. She poured for her mom and then herself. "To girl time."

"To girl time," her mother echoed, scraping away a handful of honey brown curls from her face in a familiar gesture. "I don't even have to dress up or cook a fancy dinner. And no one expects a blow job."

Sierra spewed wine, then choked on a laugh. "Wow. You *are* drunk."

"Maybe a little." Her mother smiled, rocked, sipped some more. "Wanna hear something crazy? I think I got hit on twice tonight."

And wasn't that a hell of a mixed bag at a time like this? Sierra hitched up her feet and hugged her knees, her

Mason jar resting on top. "Okay. Definitely not a time to sleep. I want details."

IT'S TRUE WHAT they say about dogs having incredible hearing.

Even sleeping under the General's bed, with that television of his blaring war movies all night and Gramps snoring like a buzz saw, I could hear everything going on around the McDaniel house. I heard the creak of rocking chairs and the low voices of Sierra and Lacey laughing together. Mike and Nathan played stupid war games on the television, which was why I camped out under Gramps's high four-poster bed. It was like a bunker where I could be safe from those bombs.

My nose twitched with the memory of air raids. The soldiers put on weird suits and talked about possible chemical attacks. They didn't have a suit that fit me, though.

Smells are a big deal to me, too. I could get drunk off sniffing a glass of wine. I prefer the woody scents personally, but any will do. One of the benefits of my heightened senses. Give me a few sips and watch out, I'm cra-zy. Booze was bad for the McDaniel family, and I needed to figure out a way to get Lacey to give up that crutch.

The Colonel and I talked a lot in the desert about his family and alcohol. Okay, he talked, I listened, since I don't have many options for answering. A lick for howdy. Leaning closer for comfort. A few different kinds of barks and a whine. And yeah, I talk with my tail a little. I have nuances that other dogs understand, but people? Seriously, not much of a lexicon to work with.

So mostly I listened and leaned on the Colonel in those days, and he used me as his own personal counselor. Remember how I said there was something I had to share, but you needed to wait? That it was too much for me to take except in chunks?

Well, this is it, and even now, it's difficult to remember without wanting to shred something. Or hide.

This one night during an air raid, he was particularly chatty. We hunkered behind some sandbags to wait it out. Not much else we could do since there wasn't a ground assault.

"Mama was a drinker," the silver-haired Colonel said. "She spent a lot of days alone while Dad chased getting general's stars for his uniform. She held it together pretty well until my older sister died. Ruptured appendix. Can you believe that? Totally operable condition if they'd caught the symptoms in time. But we weren't big on complaining. My old man believed in staying tough. And my sister was the toughest. Dad called her his favorite son."

He smiled, but it was one of those darker smiles. Remember how I said dogs are better at reading people than people are at reading dogs?

"My sister was thirteen, old enough to stay on her own while Mom took me to an all-day soccer tournament. My sister's name was Sierra, too, and she told Mom she had homework. She knew if she told the truth, that she was sick, Mom would feel torn. Mom would have to stay with her, and I would ride with another family. So my sister took a couple of Tylenol and curled up in pain. By the time we got home, she was bad off. Her appendix ruptured on the way to the ER. The doctors tried . . . but the poison spread too fast and she didn't make it."

I leaned in closer so he could scratch my head. I could smell the pain in his sweat and the tears on his face along with the breakfast on his fingertips—eggs and pancakes.

Bombs reverberated, sounding a lot like the echo of Nathan's video games. Except over there, the ground shook and one of the sandbags slid off. The Colonel huddled closer to me, even shielding *me* while we waited out the attack, when I was supposed to be the one protecting *him*.

Talking to me seemed to make him feel better, so I listened rather than doing what I really wanted. Every bit of me trembled, desperate to dig a hole under the bags where I could hide even better. But the man who'd saved me, the man who taught me how to bond with a human, he needed me to hear what was weighing on his spirit.

"My mom started drinking after that, and Dad started chasing those stars harder." He held an origami cat in his hand, tweaking the folds. He carried those papers around in his pocket all the time now. "It was like they both found their way of numbing the pain. Except her drinking pushed him away, and his travels made her drink more."

I wanted to ask where Allen as a kid had fit into all that. I pawed his chest until he let me climb up in his lap. It was strange at first, being held that way. But then I realized I could hear his heart, and that sound, the heavy pounding, told me he was every bit as scared as I was. He wrapped me in a big bear hug and I could feel his pain radiating off him as that paper cat crackled, trapped between us.

"Yeah, it sucked for me. But you know what sucks most? I'm doing the same thing to my family. I'm hiding out here in the desert so I don't have to face feeling anything back home." He stopped for a ragged breath, his heart thumping louder against my ear.

"Trooper, my friend, this place has broken me." His words came slowly, as if dug up from deep inside where we animals keep things hidden so no one else can find them. It was about survival. I understood.

"I'm so hardwired to shut down and serve out here, going home feels . . . alien now. I want to be there. God knows, I want to go home." His fingers buried in my fur and scratched my spine as he spoke.

"But my throat closes up at the thought of being there. How damn stupid is that? I have a wife with a heart as big as the whole state of Tennessee who not only holds down the home front but takes care of my sick father."

The bombs grew closer, sending sand and rocks spewing over the bags. Once the noise eased and the dust settled, he continued, "I have a brilliant daughter and this great quirky son who I barely know anymore. And if I open myself up to experiencing all of that, then I have to let in all the feelings from the shit over here. When I'm here, I can compartmentalize."

He said that, but it didn't make sense to me, not since I could tell he was feeling all that pain inside even if he said he pushed it aside.

The next day, I heard the sirens go off again, but it was different. No airplanes were overheard and the Colonel had gone out on a mission. I saw the line of tanks racing back, coming home sooner than they should have. I never knew they could move that fast, so I started barking, louder than the sirens.

I knew something was wrong, something bad, and it pushed away a layer of the taming from the past months. I snarled when someone tried to restrain me with a rope—a rope that I quickly chewed through—and ran. I raced across the compound and wedged myself into a hiding place so small and tight, they would never find me.

From my hidey-hole, I watched as the medical people came out, running.

And then there was a stretcher. My eyes didn't tell me who was on the stretcher. They couldn't because I just saw blood. And I smelled the Colonel.

PART 4

I understand many human words in many lan-
guages, but it took me a long time to understand the word *death*. People death. Dog
death. And even worse, the death of the
spirit.   —TROOPER, THEN AND NOW

Sixteen

SIERRA HAD FELT like death warmed over at school all day, battling the hangover from hell.

Thank goodness her stomach had finally settled enough for supper. The smell of her grandfather's chili had called out to her growling stomach the moment she'd gotten home since she hadn't eaten more than a peanut butter sandwich during her break midway through the day.

A warm bowl full in her hand, she sat at the kitchen table in the last remaining spot, between Mike and Nathan. Which thankfully saved her from maneuvering to get closer to Mike. Or answering awkward questions from her family she wasn't yet ready to discuss since she didn't have the answers.

She grabbed a napkin from a basket in the middle of the table. "Sorry I'm late. I had a meeting with some of the other grad assistants."

There was something comforting about having them all around her after such a tumultuous weekend. Her ragged nerves soaked up the normalcy of the meal, her mom talking about one of her students making it to a state science fair

for virtual schools. Gramps reminded everyone—twice—
not to let him forget to watch that John Wayne marathon on
television. Trooper and Clementine curled up together in a
tight ball as if to disguise themselves while they waited for
a stray cracker to land on the floor.

And the press of Mike's warm thigh against hers made
the moment all the more perfect.

She could even manage to ignore the annoying sounds
of the Hammonds setting off fireworks next door. Kenneth
always did test out his Fourth of July stash early. Luckily,
the rescue didn't seem to have any fireworks freakers among
the current canine tenants, as the barking in the yard was
at a minimum and no howling so far.

Now if Mike and Gramps could remain half as steady
through the sounds. And if only Nathan would talk.

In between bites of chili she asked her brother, "How
long did the two of you stay up playing video games?"

"Late." Nathan gave his typical monosyllabic answer. At
least he'd left the snake in his room during tonight's meal
so no one had to contend with a surprise serpent head on
their shoulder.

Mike grasped the pottery pitcher and refilled his glass
with tea. "You don't want to know. After he whooped my
tail in Leagues of Something-Or-Another I unearthed one
of the music games so I would stand a chance at winning.
That stuff's addictive."

Lacey sipped her tea, her bowl already empty. "You're
all kids at heart. Nathan, could you pass the crackers?"

"Sure . . ." He shoved the pack across the table and stood
to leave, his bowl already empty.

Gramps cleared his throat. "You didn't ask to be excused."

Nathan kept walking.

Their grandfather stood up, scowling, fireworks outside
echoing the explosive air in the kitchen.

"Allen," his voice rose, "you did not ask to leave the table
and you did not take your dishes to the sink."

Sierra's stomach clenched. So much for peaceful normalcy. Mike's hand found hers under the table.

Lacey touched Gramps on the forearm. "Joshua, it's okay."

One of the doctors had advised them recently to all start calling him Joshua. His given name would be less confusing than Gramps and Dad; even his rank of General could be disorienting if he was thirty years in the past.

Gramps shook her hand off, his fist pounding the table until the dishes rattled. "No, it's not all right. The boy needs to learn some damn manners. This whole generation doesn't know how easy they have it."

By the time her granddad finished his rant, Nathan had already left. Sundowning sucked. Gramps looked around him, confusion stamped on his face as his fists unfurled.

He'd probably already forgotten why he was mad, only wondering why the feeling lingered. "It's after seven. Did I miss the start of that John Wayne marathon?"

Ironic that he could still tell time but couldn't remember his own family's names, another quirk of the disease.

Lacey took his elbow. "How about we go check?"

His old VCR player had a stack of John Wayne classics they popped in for a perpetual marathon.

Sierra reached for her mom as Lacey passed. "I've got the dishes."

Her mother mouthed, *Thank you*, on her way out.

Sierra sagged back in her chair. "Crisis averted. For now." She angled over to give Mike the kiss she'd been aching to plaster on him all day. The taste of him was spicy and sweet. Chili powder and sugar from the tea. She couldn't wait for more of him. Soon. "I missed you last night, but thank you for spending so much time with my little brother. He's pushed all his friends away since my dad died."

"It's a tough time for a kid to be without friends." Mike stood and stacked dirty bowls, Trooper and Clementine close on his heels looking for leftovers.

What would happen when Mike moved on? She'd been so busy thinking about how much that would hurt for her she hadn't thought about how much his absence would affect the rest of her family. Nathan especially.

She gathered the silverware, tucking it into empty glasses. "I wonder if maybe he should talk to some kind of grief counselor. I could ask my friend Mary Hannah what she thinks. Do you remember her?"

"From the picnics." He snuck both dogs a cracker before turning on the faucet to rinse dishes. "She's a grad assistant, too, right?"

"She's getting her master's in counseling." She set the glasses in the sink, then opened the dishwasher—hallelujah, someone had actually already emptied it.

"Sounds like a good idea. At the debriefs we get when we come back from a deployment, they're always stressing how having someone to talk to is important." He set a rinsed bowl in the other side of the double sink. "Did you and your mom have a good conversation last night?"

The shared hominess wrapped around her like a hug, drawing her back into hopes and dreams she'd had a year and a half ago of building a life with this man. "Depends on what you mean by good." She stacked one bowl at a time into the dishwasher, the window over the sink showcasing a splash of pyrotechnic stars from Kenneth Hammond's arsenal. "We had a productive talk, but I wouldn't call it a happy discussion by any stretch. Yesterday was particularly rough for everyone. Thank you again for being there for Nathan. He's so tough to reach these days."

"What about you?"

She glanced up, a fistful of spoons in her hand. "What do you mean?"

"You said it yourself—it was a rough day. You've talked about support for your mom and your brother." He turned off the water and grabbed a dish towel for his wet hands.

"But what about you? How are you handling what yesterday meant for your family?"

She avoided his too perceptive eyes. "I kept busy today." She looked up sheepishly. "And maybe I joined my mom in a drink or two while we were talking last night."

He grabbed her by the hips, pulling her toward him. "I missed a tipsy Sierra? Damn shame about that."

"Sober Sierra will be much more fun when I slip up to your room later. Trust me." She didn't even have to keep her voice down since the sound of John Wayne blaring in the other room drowned out everything except for the fireworks in the background.

"How much longer are we going to keep sneaking around? I feel like we're the worst kept secret on the planet."

She stroked his face, enjoying the bristle along his jaw. "We have some things to figure out first, don't you think? You're leaving soon. I have a year left of school and a family that needs me, so I'm not moving anywhere. Can we delay the serious stuff for a while longer? Things are already complicated enough around this house."

He winced against her touch. "Sure. Whatever."

"Hey, wait." She grabbed his wrist. "Say what you're thinking. If you disagree, I want to hear where you stand."

"It's not you. It's those damn fireworks next door. They've got me on edge." He scrubbed a hand over his face. "Fireworks, backfiring cars, hell, even popping balloons give me the . . . jitters. I just need a little more time to shake off the sand from being overseas."

He dropped a kiss on her lips before she could answer. "We'll talk later, okay? I'm going to walk Trooper and clear my head. Lucky for me, there are plenty of leashes around this place."

Sierra slumped back against the counter as the door slammed closed after him and Trooper. With all her worrying about her family and herself, she hadn't given a thought how yesterday might have weighed on Mike, too. No doubt he'd had to wrestle with the specter of her dad's memory all the stronger on Father's Day. Her dad had been important to Mike. They'd almost been related, and they'd served together for years. For that matter, her dad might have played the role of a father to Mike considering his strained family relationships.

Who did Mike talk to? Who took care of his grief?

Hell, who looked after Mike?

Her heart hurt just thinking about it and thinking about how much he'd held back his problems ever since she'd known him. She couldn't deny she wanted more from him, but hadn't she always? Who knew if he was even capable of giving her more when he was so reluctant to share his worries or his fears with her?

As she watched another firework sparkle the sky with a blend of red, white and blue, Sierra hoped that Mike was okay out there, facing his demons on his own. Damn, keeping things light and no commitment wasn't working out as easily for them as she'd expected when she'd climbed into bed with him again.

MIKE'S WALK WITH Trooper hadn't done much to ease the headache pounding behind his eyes. He didn't have a name for that tension. He simply knew he didn't want to go back to the way things were before between him and Sierra. That hadn't worked.

But he also wasn't ready to say good-bye to her, and the round and round in his brain trying to figure out how to resolve those issues was tying into a knot right between his eyes.

He unclipped the leash from Trooper's collar and hung it on a rack in the mudroom along with an assortment of other leashes, harnesses and collars. This place was starting to feel too much like home, and time was running out for him to get his head on straight about where he and Sierra were headed.

The kitchen was empty, the dishwasher humming its way through the load. The house appeared deserted, quiet other than the sounds of a John Wayne war classic echoing from upstairs. He climbed the stairway to the second floor, eyeing Sierra's room for an instant, then deciding he'd better settle Trooper for the night first.

He knocked on the door. "General? Er, uh, Joshua? Are you awake? Trooper's ready to come in for the night."

The television was so loud it was tough for him to hear an answer. He tipped his ear toward the door and . . . Was that a whimper? He hated to invade the man's privacy, but if he was in trouble and needed help, someone should check on him.

Decision made, he tapped on the door again as another firework popped in the distance. Stifling a wince, he creaked the door open.

"Sir, I have your dog."

Trooper slipped through the slight opening and shot into the room. Mike stepped in slowly, trying to give plenty of warning. The television blared, bombs exploding as a World War II battle scene played out.

Damn shame it wasn't a marathon of Westerns.

He looked around, but the room was empty. The bed was made and the recliner in the corner held nothing but a discarded lap quilt, trailing off onto the floor. Alarms sounded in his brain. Had the older man wandered away again? Or worse yet, driven? Biting off a curse, he turned back toward the door.

Another whimper stopped him short.

What the hell? He angled toward the sound, searching only to see Trooper bowing down by the bed. The dog scrambled underneath and barked. Shit. He didn't have time to deal with the dog's fear of fireworks. He squatted, snapping his fingers. "Come on, Trooper. It's okay, boy."

Then he noticed Trooper wasn't alone underneath the high four-poster bed. The General lay flat on his stomach, eyes narrowed.

"Soldier," the General hissed. "Come down here in the bunker quick before you get your damn fool head shot off."

Mike looked under the bed, then at the window where fireworks still lit up sky, and toward the television replaying a decades-old battle. The old warrior must be caught in some PTSD episode, somehow made worse by Alzheimer's placing him firmly in that moment for real, unable to pull himself out. The fireworks and the movie must have combined to create some kind of personal hell.

Mike turned off the television, hoping for a miraculous turnaround in Gramps's state of mind, but he stayed under the bed, gnarled fingers digging into the carpet. Trooper scooted around in a circle until just his nose poked out. Mike wrestled with everything he'd learned about dealing with the man and realized nothing he said or did could bring the General back to the present. There seemed to be nothing more to do than climb into that place in time with him and help him through.

Dropping to the floor, Mike commando crawled on his belly, carpet burning along his bare arms instead of sand, until he wedged under the bed, Trooper between him and the General.

"Good job, soldier, good job."

Soldier. The General avoided names when he was confused. He didn't even use a rank. Mike said, "My name's Sergeant Kowalski, sir."

He left it open-ended for an answer.

Gramps nodded, his face tight, not registering that he lay beside a gym shoe and a pile of dust bunnies. "I'm Captain McDaniel. Glad to meet you, Sergeant. Looks like we may be holed up here for a few hours till the firefight passes."

God, he hoped the Hammonds ran out of fireworks

sooner rather than later. Mike buried his hand in the dog's fur, rubbing the velvety ears. "Thanks for sharing the space with me."

"Is this your first tour of duty in a war zone?"

"No, sir. I've been overseas twice." He kept his answers generic, not sure exactly which war zone the "Captain" was currently in. Doing the math on where Joshua would have been at that time could be tricky if he picked the wrong place. And he'd noticed sometimes Joshua McDaniel moved from year to year in his past, blending memories and moments.

"Do you have a girl back home?"

Now wasn't that a loaded question? "Yes, sir." The shadows flickered under the bed, a quilt trailing over the side swaying from the ceiling fan circulating air. "There is a special woman in my life."

"Me, too. My wife, Millie. We have two little ones, a boy and a girl. They're what keeps me going on days like this."

A son and daughter. In the old man's mind, Allen was only a kid. And the daughter? Mike remembered Sierra telling him once that she'd been named for an aunt she never met, her father's sister who'd died young of a ruptured appendix.

A series of firecrackers snapped his every last nerve. Trooper rested his head on the General's arm, and Mike realized that even in his fear, the dog was seeking to comfort more than be comforted. So many times Trooper had done the same for them overseas.

The boom of the fireworks echoed again, mingling with the noise of the cuckoo clock piled on top, a strange blend of war and home. Another sound snaked through as a voice called out, "Sierra?" Lacey must be at the bottom of the stairs. "Sierra? Do you know if the dishes in the dishwasher are clean or dirty? And where did you hide Gramps's pills?"

The General blinked, confusion dulling his blue eyes to a murky shade in the darkness under the bed. "Sierra?" He turned his head toward the dog. "Trooper? Where's Millie? I'm not . . . I don't understand . . . Sergeant Kowalski?"

Ah hell. Sympathy for the man's confusion kicked through Mike. "Sir, would you like to, uh"—he searched for a generic phrase that would cover any time frame, any era, any possible mind-set for the General's confused state—"head down to the chow hall for a late-night snack?"

The shadows shifted in the old man's eyes like cataracts, then cleared. "I think I want to get out from under this damn bed before anyone sees us."

"Yes, sir. Agreed."

Mike commando crawled back out, sweeping the trailing blanket out of the way before he stood. Trooper scrambled free with the shoe in his mouth, then plunked on his butt, sitting, waiting. The General moved slower. Age stole agility as well as memories. Mike extended a hand and helped him to his feet.

Gramps reached to tuck in his T-shirt with Army stamped across the front in bold type, then stopped with a sigh. "Shit."

"Something wrong, sir?" Mike asked, then saw.

A wet stain splotched the front of the General's sweatpants. Whether from fear or incontinence, he'd urinated on himself while under the bed. It seemed age was a beast damned determined to steal dignity as well.

Mike turned his back and tugged open drawers until he found a change of clothes, not too tough since the drawer contained only underwear, sweatpants and tees. All alike. He passed a pair of gray sweats to the General without glancing back. "Here, sir. I'll just go now and check on . . . stuff."

He heard a rustling behind him as he walked to the half-open door. He started to slip out only to find Sierra standing with her back against the wall, face pale. How long had she been there?

Before he could open his mouth to explain or reach out to comfort her, Lacey's voice drifted down the hall again.

"Sierra?" Her voice grew closer, louder. "Where are you? I need to find Gramps's meds."

"Uh, Mom," Sierra shouted back, "hold on. I'll check in his room."

She started past. Mike reached out to stop her, trying to warn her, but his brain was still more than a little scrambled from the fireworks and witnessing the General's struggle.

Sierra pushed the door open and—thank God, her grandfather was dressed in dry clothes. Since he always wore the same thing, it was as if nothing had happened.

Except his pile of soiled clothes lay on the floor behind him.

Damn it. Mike launched forward, desperate for some distraction to preserve the old man's dignity a little longer, to shield Sierra from this one moment of pain in the middle of so much. Even if that meant "accidentally" tripping into her so she would stumble to the side. But at the last second, Trooper dropped the shoe and lifted his leg.

The dog aimed straight for pants on the floor. Bull's-eye. The yellow stream nailed the wet spot on the clothes dead-on.

Sierra gasped. "Trooper! What are you doing? You naughty dog." She charged into the room, grabbed him by the collar with one hand. With her other, she snatched up the clothes and pitched them into the laundry hamper by the closet. "No! Let's go outside, boy, and you sure owe Gramps an apology."

She angled past with the dog trotting alongside. "Mike, we can talk later. Okay?"

"Sure," he said softly, stroking a hand down her back only to realize more than giving comfort, he was taking comfort from touching her.

He watched her until she disappeared down the hall. Then he glanced back at the General. "We should head into the kitchen. Lacey said something about time for your meds."

Nodding, the General joined him, clapping him once on the back. "Thank you, son."

And in spite of the generic name, somehow Mike knew

that in this moment, those eyes were crystal clear, so much so, Mike could see straight into his own dark future.

SIERRA WAITED FOR Mike in his studio apartment, a space that would be empty and hers again all too soon. Her heart had been racing since she overheard him and her grandfather. When the television had turned off, she'd figured there must be something wrong. Gramps never turned off the TV.

She'd heard and seen enough through the crack in the partially open door to realize what was going on. Enough to break her heart in half seeing Mike there under the bed, doing his best to comfort her grandfather. She'd stood in the hall with her hand pressed to her mouth to hold back her sobs.

God, she couldn't ignore the truth any longer. Not with it staring her so firmly in the face. She was still in love with Mike. Her legs folded under her and she sat on the edge of the mattress. This love wasn't some beautiful sonnet. It was scary and tumultuous, full of an uncertain future. She didn't know if she could be the kind of woman he needed.

But she couldn't face the prospect of letting him go again.

Finally, she heard his footsteps climbing the outside stairway. Steady, sure-footed. How strange that he called himself a rebel, yet he was the most reliable man she'd ever known.

The door opened and Mike walked through, his features gaunt with a stress deeper than any she'd seen on his face before. She'd been so immersed in her family troubles, she hadn't thought about the fact this was supposed to be a decompression month for Mike for a reason.

He'd just come back from war, yet he'd walked right into all her family land mines, selflessly helping them when she should have offered him so much better.

She clenched her fists in the bedspread, unsure quite how to approach him. "How are you doing?"

"Fine." He walked to the refrigerator and pulled out a Gatorade.

"I appreciate what you did for my grandfather tonight."

"I didn't do anything except be there." He tipped back the bottle and drained the blue sports drink.

She wouldn't let him minimize what he'd gone through for her grandfather. "That's not as easy as it sounds when he's in another world, another time."

"I just went there with him."

Willingly, he'd returned to the hell of war for another person. Her heart was in her throat. "That couldn't have been easy for you, either."

He flipped his empty bottle into the recycling bin and cocked an eyebrow at her. "Are you about to recommend I go to counseling like your brother?"

He was putting up walls between them. No question. And she wouldn't let him. Not this time. She didn't know where they were going with their relationship or how to handle this love filling every corner of her heart. But she damn well wouldn't walk away from him while he was so clearly hurting. "I was going to offer to listen if you want to talk. If you don't, I thought I would . . . just be with you."

"For how long?" Tension showed in the flex of his jawline. The tic beneath one eye.

She hated that she contributed to that stress. That she hadn't been there for him enough. That she had no idea where their relationship was headed.

"What do you mean?" She hoped she'd misunderstood. But she wasn't passing up an opportunity to talk. Not now that she realized he'd gladly duck serious conversation wherever possible.

"How many times have you said you don't want to live your mother's life?" he pressed, diving right into her fears. "You know that's all I have to offer, and making a much lower salary than your dad."

"I've never cared about money." She was a bargain bin clothes shopper who preferred to spend her money on good books. "You know that about me."

"Well, thank God for that much." He half smiled, the humor never quite reaching his golden brown eyes. "What a relief to know you're not after me for my wide-screen television and beat-up truck."

Unable to stand watching him in pain a second longer, she stood, slowly unbuttoning the white cotton blouse she'd worn to the university today and offering the one distraction that always worked for them, even if only temporarily. "Right now, what I want most of all, is you. With your clothes off and your hands on me."

Seventeen

AFTER THE HELL he'd just gone through stepping into a mental war zone with the General, there was nothing Mike wanted more right now than to lose himself in what Sierra was offering, one sweet button at a time.

But he was teetering on the edge here, his head in a messed-up place, his emotions tied in knots thinking about losing her. He needed to lock all that down and make this a night she wouldn't forget. This was all-or-nothing time.

She reached for the clip in her hair and tugged it free with one hand, releasing a waterfall of silky blond hair down her shoulders. She was a fantasy come to life, his for the taking.

"Hold that thought." He scrambled for the handle on the refrigerator door. "Something sweet to top off dinner sounds about right."

"I've got dessert right here," she teased, walking her fingers up his bent spine while he dug in the fridge.

Sensation skittered over his flesh, landing in a whole lot of heat headed south. The rush of blood was damn near making him light-headed. He blinked and made a grab for the leftover caramel sauce he'd been looking for. Backing away, he slammed the door to the icebox.

Turning, he had to face Sierra before he could get to the microwave, but the sight of her in an undone blouse with her hair spilling down her shoulders and one tawny curl skimming the top of high, round breasts made him forget everything else. She took a step toward him and his thoughts went up in flames along with the rest of him.

The container of caramel sauce clunked to the counter behind her, his arms going around her. With a groan, he slid his hands around her waist and drew her to him, hip to hip.

Yeah.

He molded her to him, her breasts flattening against his chest, her slender arms sliding around his neck. She smelled good. Tasted better. He backed her into the kitchen counter next to the microwave and lifted her, setting her on the smooth butcher block top and making room for himself between her thighs.

Putting her lace-covered breasts right at eye level.

"The logistics of this could get complicated," Sierra whispered, shrugging off her unbuttoned blouse until it fell down her arms and landed in a pool of white cotton behind her, covering up the empty canisters for flour and sugar. "There's not a lot of room to work."

"You let me worry about that." He pressed a kiss to the full swell of one breast, breathing deep to draw in the scent of her. "I'm going to take great care of you."

Already, he worked the button on her khakis, sliding it free and tugging down the zipper, careful not to catch her skin while she edged closer to him on the counter. Her skin was so warm there, and she rolled her hips to help him free the fabric, her every throaty moan urging him on to get her naked.

She hooked her thumbs in the straps of her bra and tugged them off her shoulders until the white lace of her bra was hard taxed to cup her curves. Slowly, the delicate fabric gave up and rolled down to catch on the dusky tips tightening into delectable peaks.

He growled as he caught one between his teeth, nipping gently while she sighed and scratched her fingernails up his back. His erection throbbed impossibly hard. His pulse pounding with jackhammer speed right *there*.

He wanted her so badly he ached everywhere.

But this wasn't about him.

"I want to taste more of you." Straightening, he grabbed the caramel sauce off the counter and jammed it into the microwave. Pressed random buttons.

"I don't think I can wait," she warned, her fingers skimming his T-shirt up his back as she undressed him. "You might have to skip dessert."

"It's not me I'm thinking about right now." He slipped a hand beneath the cuff of her khakis and palmed her calf under the fabric. Finding the tender place behind her knee, he circled her skin lightly. "I'm going to make sure you feel very, very indulged."

The high, sweet moan she made was better music to his ears than anything his guitar had ever managed. Between that and the goose bumps along the back of her leg, he found enough will to break away from her. To slam the stop button on the microwave and ease her pants down her hips and off, taking her shoes with them.

"You need to be more naked," she warned, wriggling out of her bra and sending her breasts in a tantalizing sway.

"Tough to concentrate when my eyes are popping out of my head." He cupped the soft weight of her curves in his hands, lifting them to his mouth to kiss one and then the other.

Her fingers dug into his hair, holding him there while he laved and nipped and feasted. Caramel wasn't going to taste any better than pure, undiluted Sierra, but he had the feeling the warm play of the sauce on her skin was going to drive her wild.

"Put your arms around my neck, okay?" He lifted her

thighs and slid his hands down, down, to wrap her calves around his waist. She locked her ankles tight while he levered open the microwave and withdrew the heated container. "Hold on tight."

Scooping her off the counter, he carried her toward the mattress while she rained kisses down the side of his face in a way that made his chest squeeze tight. He needed her with a fierceness that had his feet moving fast across the open floor space. When he reached the bed, he hit his knees, taking the force of the drop himself and then easing her more gently to her back. She clung to him, though, not letting go. Her thighs tightened around his waist, her arms locking around his neck as she found his mouth with hers and nipped at his lower lip. She drew it between her teeth and nibbled. Sucked. Licked.

He throbbed so hard he'd have the outline of his zipper tattooed on his flesh.

Forcing himself to draw back, he yanked open the fastenings on his jeans and ditched the rest of his clothes while Sierra hooked her thumbs into the waistline of white lace panties and shimmied out of them. While she lifted her hips to get them off, he dove for the caramel sauce and cracked open the lid, lying beside her underneath the slow-turning ceiling fan.

Sierra's hand drifted up his thigh and along his hip, smoothing over his abs toward trouble. He had all he could do to maintain focus while he tested the temp of the sauce with one finger, stirring gently.

"Want the first taste?" He distracted her by waving a caramel-slick finger beneath her nose.

She didn't stop touching him, her hand splayed along his stomach as her nails lightly raked along his skin. But she opened her eyes at the sweet scent. She met his gaze while she took his finger in her mouth and swirled her tongue around it with deliberate erotic flair.

"Wicked girl," he whispered in her ear and slid his finger

from her mouth. "I can't remember my own name when you do that, let alone what I want to do next."

"You think too much," she accused, but there was no heat in the words, especially once the trail of caramel hit her hip from where it poured straight from the glass jar. "Oh!"

He set aside the container on the nightstand, watching the slow drizzle along her hip bone, down her belly into a tiny pool at her navel right next to the yellow rhinestone daisy that rested there. Gently, he rolled her to her back, ensuring the sauce remained right where he wanted.

Cupping her hips in both hands, he steadied her. When he traced the sweet path inward from her waist, Sierra's fingers knotted in the blankets on either side of her. She twisted against him, her thighs shifting restlessly beneath his chest as he pinned her to the bed and licked.

And licked.

He didn't want this night to end. He returned to the container to scoop out more, drawing a trail of sweetness between her breasts. Dotting each nipple. He savored every inch of her until she was clean again, the faint stickiness sealing their bodies together. Only when she was panting his name and whispering vague threats of sensual torment did he slide one finger inside her. Then two.

She came off the bed in a fast, hard orgasm. Her body spasmed around him, squeezing him. He worked her gently, coaxing every aftershock from her until she lay back on the bed, her whole body practically vibrating from it.

"You're amazing." He hadn't realized he said it aloud until she lifted her head to stare at him in the dim glow from the light over the range in the other room.

"I wanted to save it for when you were inside me." She swiped a lock of blond hair off her cheek, her face flushed from her release.

His heart fell in on itself, caving to this woman who'd had a hold on him for as long as he'd known her. She deserved so much better than him.

"We'll get you there," he said softly, his words warm against her cheek. He let go of her to find the condom box and sheathe himself before he came inside her. She watched him the whole time with glowing eyes full of emotions that slayed him.

For now, he could only offer this. One perfect night that he knew wouldn't be enough, but—then again . . .

He inched inside her slowly, her whole body shuddering. Sweat popped along his forehead from holding back for so long, but he'd come too far to get careless now. He watched her through half-lowered lids, trying like hell to keep a lock on all he was feeling.

"Mike." Her fingers cradled his face, forcing his full attention on her. "Kiss me."

The weight of her beautiful gaze was his breaking point. This amazing woman would do anything for the people in her life. Even if it meant following him, even if it meant following in Lacey's footsteps. The selfish part of him wanted to just take it. To take everything she had to offer and damn the consequences.

But it wouldn't be fair.

So his kiss was careful. Thorough. But in control. He cupped her breast while their tongues danced, his thumb circling the taut peak while he thrust deep inside her.

She met him thrust for thrust, her whole body straining closer. When he could feel the tension arch her spine, he reached between them to touch the tight center of nerves between her legs, the play over the slickness there. She stilled for a second before her thighs tightened around him, her release shuddering through her and squeezing him with soft, feminine warmth. This time, he let himself feel it fully, to savor the fact that he brought her there. To revel in the way she came apart for him.

That alone would have had him ready to lose it, but the sight of her head tossing and turning on his bed pushed him the rest of the way. He thrust once. Twice more. And just

like that, the surge of all his pent-up hunger roared through
him so hard it stole his breath.

Desire coursed through him like pure adrenaline, the
primal need to hold and possess as raw as anything he'd
ever felt before. Only for that moment did his control slip,
and she had to have heard it in the hoarse shout to the heavens when he came.

And came.

The force of it rode him so hard he had to roll off her at
the end, his breath gone while he gasped for a hint of air.

In the long, quiet moments afterward where neither of
them knew quite what to say, Mike couldn't escape the truth.
It wasn't just another night to make love and curl up in each
other's arms. The holes inside him had yawned wide open
today. Hell, he'd made them even more obvious by making
love to her like it was the flipping end of the world.

It felt like it to him. Even as he kissed her shoulder in the
moonlight slipping in through the curtains, he knew he was
going to lose Sierra again. He tugged up the blanket and
tried to fake like everything was normal. But these past
weeks at the McDaniel home had shown him all too clearly
what kind of future he had to offer a family. Getting out of
the military wasn't even an option for him for two more
years. He'd signed a contract. Breaking that was desertion
and would land him in jail.

And two years from now?

He would still be a soldier. The truth dropkicked him in
the solar plexus while Sierra curled up tight next to him. But
no matter how much he wanted her, he simply didn't know
how to be anything else. He wasn't trained for anything else,
and even if he took his G.I. Bill and went back to college,
he would still be a soldier.

What a time to realize he'd been fooling himself thinking
he'd chosen the military because it was his only path to
support himself. He'd joined up for the life, the fellowship,
the mission to protect.

He'd crawled under the bed because of the code, no one left behind. It didn't matter that the General had retired years ago. The muscle memory remembered to the end.

Once a soldier, always a soldier.

Even if he hung up the uniform, he would still be the wrong man for the only woman he'd ever loved.

SHOWER SPEWING OVER her, Sierra melted against the tile wall in the afterglow of another orgasm. After Mike had turned her insides as warm and fluid as the caramel they'd tasted on each other, he'd carried her to the shower where she'd taken great pleasure in lathering up every inch of him. They'd made love again, touching and sipping the clean running water off each other.

With her arms looped around his neck, she held on and just let the water sleet over them. The way Mike made love to her in the apartment and now the shower, she could sense an urgency in him. They couldn't dodge discussing their future forever. But not until she had her thoughts together on *how* to be in love with him. She didn't even know how to stop loving him, this dear and amazing man who'd been there for her grandfather with a sensitivity she couldn't have even imagined.

Thinking of her grandfather and how trapped he'd felt in that war moment took her mind to places she'd avoided, but pushed through now. She couldn't stop the question that had been burning at her since Mike came back.

"Tell me what happened when my father died." Her question echoed in the small shower stall. Maybe that's why she'd said it here, so they could walk away from the discussion when it was over. Leave the words and feelings they brought to swirl down the drain with the steaming water.

"Sierra, honey, you know what happened." He stroked her wet hair back from her face.

"I know what the authorized military spokesman and

chaplain told us the night they came to our house." That horrible night. They'd just finished supper when the official military vehicle pulled up. Their driveway was so long it had given them many endless seconds to dread what was coming as the car approached. "We even knew both of them, but they weren't there with my father. They were just telling me what they were allowed to say."

"Do you think they lied to you?"

"No, not really, at least I hope not, but I believe they gave us a scrubbed-clean version." She let the tears flow because with the shower, it's not like she had to hide them. "So all we have is that too brief conversation about my father's last minutes on earth and a folded flag we got at his funeral."

Mike looked down, and at first she thought he was trying to decide whether to tell her, but then she saw the distant look in his eyes and realized he was reliving that day. And she'd sent him there.

Guilt swept through her. "Never mind. Forget I asked. This isn't the right time or place—"

He pressed a finger to her mouth. "We'd been sent out to another FOB—forward operating base. I was assigned protective detail for your dad this deployment."

She moved his hand aside. "How did I not know that?"

"Maybe your father thought it would be awkward for you to realize how often he and I saw each other." He kissed the inside of her palm and pressed it to his chest. "We were briefing some local military leaders on training plans for their troops. It went smoothly. The sun was bright and it felt like a good day, which was strange because I usually had instincts for that shit."

She could almost feel the desert sun shining, hear the sand and grit in his words. The bittersweet image of him in his uniform walking with her father was too easy to envision.

"We were headed back to the convoy and . . . your father shouted an order for us all to stop. He just . . . knew. I'm not sure how, if he saw something or heard a click. Things happened so fast, probably in a matter of seconds, and yet I remember a million details that couldn't have all possibly happened in such a short span of time."

Horror for him clogged her throat as much as for what happened to her dad. Her hands clenched into tight fists as she absorbed his words like breathing in steam.

"But what stands out most to me is the expression in his eyes, exactly the same color as yours. He looked right at me and he held out a hand. Except it wasn't the come here sort of hand. It was stand back. I've got this. Good-bye. He knew."

She squeezed her eyes closed for a moment, the water stinging her skin like needles, every nerve on fire with the pain of loss again as she thought of that explosion ripping through her dad.

And then she remembered there was something more they had from her father's last minutes. A letter from Mike.

"You wrote to us that you were bringing Trooper here because my dad asked you to. I assumed that meant you spoke to him just before he . . . died."

Mike shook his head, his black hair sleek and saturated. "He asked me before that to make sure Trooper made it back to the States. More along the lines of, 'If anything happens to me . . .'"

"So he didn't say anything before he died? Nothing?" What was she looking for? Some last guidance from her father?

Mike's sigh heated over her. "He told me to reach into his vest pocket. He had one of those origami animals . . . a cat, I think. He made a joke about the zoo. He was trying to make me laugh."

"That sounds like my dad, wanting to see a smile." That single detail had given her so much more than any "official" report full of events. Her father hadn't been alone and in the end, he'd squeezed one last moment of joy from life. "He always asked us to send him off with smiles rather than tears."

Mike hauled her close and held on. She held just as firmly, her face tucked in the crook of his neck as they stood long enough for the water to begin to cool. Mike shut off the shower and the silence was deafening, but with her emotions still raw, she just wanted to curl up next to him and sleep in his arms.

Silently, he reached out for a towel and—

A scream split the night from outside. A horrible, gut-wrenching cry.

Gasping, Sierra grabbed the towel. "That's my mom."

Mike shot into action. He raced back into the main room, scooping up clothes. He tossed her khakis and shirt at her, then pulled on his jeans. She followed him, buttoning her pants and shirt, the fabric sticking to her damp body as she ran barefoot down the stairs after him. Her heart hammering in her ears, she sprinted to keep up with Mike, a tough proposition with his honed military body in full battle response mode.

Stones cut into her feet as she raced toward the house, security lights popping on left and right. Her mom was stumbling toward her SUV.

Carrying a dog.

Sierra frowned, slowing. Had someone broken in to hurt the animals again? But as she drew closer, she realized her mother was holding Trooper. The dog was twitching, foam bubbling from his mouth.

Her mother was trembling, crying and nearly babbling as she passed the dog over to Mike. "Somehow he got into my sleeping pills. He came to me holding the bottle, then this started . . . I don't know how he got them. I could have sworn I tucked them safely away in a zippered bag up high in my bathroom medicine cabinet, but I could be wrong. I've been so frazzled—"

"Mom." Sierra rushed to her mother. "It'll be okay. Mike

will drive you to the vet. I'll call Doctor Vega while you're on your way and I'll watch Gramps. It'll be okay."

It had to be. She looked at Mike's face, stark and set in the harsh glow of the security lights, and she saw the same fear echoed on his face.

The thought of losing this dog, their last link to her father, was beyond imagining for either of them.

RAY HAD TAKEN more than one emergency call from Lacey over the past eighteen months, and he'd always managed to maintain professional calm. But seeing her so shaken tonight rattled him. He knew she treasured each life in her care—as did he—but tonight he fully grasped how much this dog meant to her family.

Standing over the barely conscious animal, he couldn't afford to be anything other than completely focused as he took vitals and assessed his patient.

Lacey stood in the corner trembling by a row of dog and cat large canvas photos, her arms wrapped around her. "Don't send me out of the room."

He half smiled. "I wouldn't dream of it."

"Tell me what's going on." Her voice trembled. "I don't want to distract you, but please let me know what's happening. Talk to me while you work."

"Since you know what substance he took, that helps." Although hearing she needed sleeping pills unsettled him, but he would deal with that later. "Since he already vomited at your house and in the car, he's gotten rid of some of the toxin. That's a good thing."

"I never thought I would be happy to have a dog puke in my car." She laughed with a semi-hysterical edge.

He reached for a small plastic tube. "His heart rate is a little low, so I've given him some atropine and glycopyrrolate. Now you can help me by holding his head steady while I thread this tube down Trooper's throat. I'm using an activated charcoal treatment to absorb the toxins so his body absorbs as little as possible."

"Okay." She seemed to steady at having a task. Typical Lacey. "Then what happens?"

"We hope we got to him in time and protected his system, his kidneys and his liver." He carefully guided the tube down his throat, the dog's lethargy working in their favor. Lacey talked while he concentrated on the job at hand.

"I'm always walking around the yard and into the forest looking for mushrooms, afraid an animal will eat one and get poisoned. And plants. I read up on every plant. Chocolate is kept on the top shelf of the pantry inside a box. Medicines are in a zipper pouch, locked in a cabinet."

"Dogs are smart. If they want something badly enough, they'll chew through Fort Knox."

"He has to live."

"I hear you." This dog was her last link to her husband. He knew that well. Aside from his professional oath, on a personal level he'd be damned if he would be the one to break that link when she was so fragile.

Ray withdrew the tube and tossed it aside along with his gloves.

Lacey stroked her hands over Trooper's fur, smoothing his ears, grabbing a paper towel to dab a bit of charcoal stain off his chin from when the tube was removed. "What do we do now?"

"I'm going to give him some fluids to flush the toxins out of his system, but other than that, we wait."

He'd no more finished the sentence than Lacey had rolled the bag of IV fluids over to him. She knew the drill, down to the gauge needle he would need. She'd picked up a lot from her rescue work.

Once he taped the IV in place, he scooped Trooper into his arms, the loopy dog wriggling weakly in his grasp. "He has to stay here. But don't worry. I'll keep watch over him. I'm going to sleep in my office tonight so I can check on him. You're free to leave. Are you okay to drive home?"

Sierra had picked up Mike a half hour ago once her grandfather fell asleep, making sure Lacey still had her vehicle.

"I'm fine to drive, but I can't just leave him."

"Lacey." Pausing mid-step, he searched for the right words but couldn't bring himself to tell her the cold truth. "You should go home, rest. No offense, but you look exhausted."

There really wasn't anything more he could do for the dog, but if Trooper died, Ray didn't want it to happen at Lacey's house. He could protect her from that much at least by keeping the dog here through the danger time.

"I won't be able to sleep at home. The dog ate my pills, remember?" She was right on his heels every step to the kennels. "I'm not leaving."

"Is that a question?" He glanced over his shoulder.

"Oh, sorry. But I'm not thinking clearly. Yes, may I please spend the night with you?"

Now wasn't that a tempting offer? But definitely not the right timing. "Grab a blanket from the stack inside the top crate and spread it out in the bottom kennel for Trooper."

She moved with a frenzied efficiency, making up the bed for the dog then reaching to help settle him. She tucked an extra rolled towel under his head, adjusted his paw so the IV line wouldn't kink.

Ray closed the dog in, then knelt to look in Lacey's eyes. "Do you want some coffee?"

She pulled down a couple more towels and dropped them on the floor in front of the crate before sitting. She rested her head against the metal grate. "I just want to stay here and watch him breathe."

He wanted to offer her reassurance, but he couldn't B.S. her. She knew too much with her work in rescue. She'd taken on some of the shelter's sickest and most severely abused animals. Her passion for animal rescue was something to see.

With a long night ahead of them, he parked himself at his desk under the guise of work, all the while watching her watch her dog for . . . over an hour before he realized she truly wasn't going to fall asleep. And he'd run out of paperwork to catch up on. So, the next time he checked Trooper's vitals, he stayed and sat on the floor beside her.

"Is there any news on your neighbors' petition with the county council?" He could at least try distracting her to make the time pass more quickly.

She shook her head. "I've submitted all my 501(c)(3) paperwork for review and allowed them unfettered access to every corner of the place. I've followed the law. I've done nothing wrong."

"From where I'm sitting, you've done a helluva lot right."

"Sometimes being right isn't enough." The weary slump to her shoulders broke his damn heart. "Life simply isn't always fair. They may win. It happens to rescues all the time. So I'm focusing on placing the animals I have now. I can't take any new ones in until I figure out the whole cash flow problem of relocating in a crummy economy."

"You need to cut yourself some slack." He allowed himself to touch one of those slumping shoulders and wished he could do more. "Maybe you need a break. You've had a really bad year."

"I can't give up the Second Chance Ranch," she said, clearly holding on by a thread. "I've lost so much, Ray. I can't lose anything more."

Maybe it was her passion for her cause. Or maybe it was the tear streaking down one cheek.

Or maybe it was the way she said his name.

But he couldn't fight the urge any longer, and finally, after a year and a half of resisting, he kissed Lacey McDaniel.

Eighteen

SURPRISE HELD LACEY still as Ray's mouth settled on hers.

She hadn't been kissed in a year, not this way. Not in a man-woman sexual way. And there was no question that this was not just a comfort kiss. His hands clasped her shoulders, and the sensation of his fingertips just below her sleeves sent tingles showering through her.

A tiny sigh escaped from her mouth, and he gathered her closer, his tongue teasing along the part of her lips. Heat and longing surged. God help her, she couldn't resist. This might not be a kiss of comfort, but it felt so damn good. Wine hadn't come close to unwinding the kinks in her tense shoulders, but the awakening of simple hormones blanketed her whole body with languid pleasure.

She reached up, her hands fluttering uncertainly at his shoulders for a moment. She'd been feeling so lost, hurt, scared, alone . . . hell, she couldn't count the ways she needed this. And then she was all in. She kissed him back, fully, openly, her arms sliding around his neck.

She breathed in the scent of him, the faded hints of spicy aftershave mingling with the familiar smells of the clinic and dogs, both things that anchored her. His bristly jaw scraped her tender skin, not that he kissed her too hard, just that he grew facial hair fast and thick, the gentle abrasion a contrast to the warm, melting sweetness of the kiss.

He sipped her like fine wine, careful and reverent, as if he'd been waiting to savor her for a long time. Funny how she felt that in just a kiss, but she did. His hands slid into her curls, tilting her face for the best angle, his thumbs tracing her cheekbones and her temples. Most of all, the kiss made her feel like a desirable woman instead of . . . whatever she'd been for this last hellish year alone with too many responsibilities and worries.

Don't think. Don't think. She couldn't let anything intrude on just this one simple pleasure she was taking for herself. Soon, she would set this feeling aside and move forward. But tonight, with the world fracturing and falling apart in pieces so small she couldn't hold them, she would take Ray Vega's amazing tenderness and hug it close.

Behind her closed eyes, she let the sensations flow. Strong hands skimming down her back, her breasts grazing his powerful chest. Sheltered in the circle of his arms, Lacey soaked in the feeling of safety and caring, her skin coming alive with every shift of his hands on her.

More. Not questioning the need to be touched, something so very essential, she felt him everywhere. Her palms ran up his arms and curved around his shoulders finding more muscle as she went. The vitality of him recharged her, as if she could absorb all that heat and strength right into her.

He lowered her to the thick towels, following her down as he kissed her. His body stretched alongside her, one leg beside hers, one between hers, the unmistakable evidence of his desire lodged against her hip in a way that sent sparks through her nerve endings and upped the stakes in a hurry. An answering longing pooled between her thighs, and she couldn't suppress the small, needy moan that pulled from her throat.

Ray's lips left hers to kiss a path down her neck. Her pulse beat fast underneath the sweep of his tongue, desire building swiftly. His hand skimmed over her hip and slid beneath the hem of her blouse, covering her ribs just beneath her breast.

The cool air swept over her bare skin, bringing her back to reality of what she was about to do. What *they* were minutes away from doing. She couldn't tell herself "don't think" anymore.

Gathering up all her will, she clasped his wrist and carefully removed it from her blouse. Panting with barely restrained desire, she whispered against his lips, "I can't do this. I'm sorry . . ."

He went still over her, dragging in ragged breath after breath before he rolled off her, lying on the floor next to her, with his arm over his eyes.

Sitting up, she tried to blink away the pleasure still coursing through her and wondered how she could feel so certain and confused at the same time. Kissing Ray had been a surprise, not just because he did it, but how much she enjoyed it. But she couldn't escape the fact that she didn't feel ready. She hadn't even taken off her wedding band yet.

She couldn't escape the fact that she still felt married.

Lacey touched Ray's wrist lightly, only to have him flinch, so she pulled back. "Are you okay?"

Are *we* okay?

He'd been a good friend to her for over a year and a half, and she feared they'd just wrecked that because she was an emotional mess and she'd decided to shut down her brain for a few stolen moments.

He sat up, with his knees bent and his arms draped over them. "I'm the one who should be apologizing." His voice sounded strained. "I shouldn't have done that. I know you're not ready, and I shouldn't have put you in the awkward position of saying no."

"It's not that I don't want to. You're a sexy, fascinating man with a humanitarian streak a mile wide," and God, that made him sound like her altruistic soldier husband, which really freaked her out.

"You're not helping matters."

"I'm sorry."

"It's too soon. I get that. I've been doing everything in my power to keep my hands to myself, especially these last couple of weeks when I've known . . . hell, I don't know. I guess I've seen chances to touch you and I've done my damnedest not to every other time. But tonight . . ." He shook his head.

"This wasn't just an impulse?" Damn it, she shouldn't have asked that. She really wasn't helping matters. "Forget I said anything. I'm making a fool out of myself."

"Hey." He cupped her face, turning her toward him, and she could see how much that comforting touch cost him as his muscles twitched with restraint. "There is no possible way you could ever appear foolish."

"Really?" She laughed, but it choked off on a tear. "Have you seen my life? I'm living on the verge of bankruptcy because I spend too much trying to save every animal. The town thinks I'm loony and wants to shut me down."

"You have built an amazing life while facing unbelievable pressure," he said with unmistakable intensity. "You are an incredible woman."

His brown eyes burned with a fire she recognized because she'd felt it. For her husband. Ray Vega had feelings for her, deep feelings, and they'd crossed a line here tonight. Returning to a friendship wasn't going to work, and she couldn't consider anything more, not now.

A whimper from the crate gave her a convenient excuse to look away. Trooper shuffled and shifted until he sat up in the metal crate, watching her with those wide brown knowing eyes. He pawed the metal grate, still wobbly and uncoordinated. As her brain cleared, she thought back to the time one of her fosters had eaten a mushroom and underwent the charcoal treatment. And there was Lucky, who'd nearly overdosed on marijuana. Strange how all that objective knowledge about animal toxins had left her in the blind panic of the moment.

Now, she realized . . .

"Trooper doesn't really need to stay here tonight, does he? You've done everything you can for him."

"He needed the fluids and some monitoring . . ."

"Which you've done. But by keeping him overnight, you were just trying to protect me in case *everything* isn't enough."

"Is that so wrong of me?" He didn't even bother trying to deny her words.

"For the two of us, right now, yes, it's wrong for both of us." She held up a hand, wanting to touch him and knowing she couldn't, not even casually, not anymore. "You're a fascinating, smart man, and we have so much in common—"

"Stop letting me down easy." He pressed his palm to hers for a moment, his fingers curling to link with hers. "I get it. You're still in love with your husband."

"Ray, I'll always be in love with my husband. That's not going to change. The problem is, I'm still mourning him, and that's not something I can rush."

"You know that only makes you all the more special." He squeezed her hand once before letting go. "And no matter what you say to try and make this easier for me, knowing how amazing you are makes this . . . hurt."

She wanted to tell him that he was an equally special man. That he'd find someone else, especially being ten years younger than her . . . He had so much ahead of him. But she knew better than to minimize what he felt for her. She still couldn't quite believe it.

"I wish I was ready for this. Trust me, I do."

She would give anything to be able to sleep through the night. Not to hurt all the time. Not to question her choices every night as she lay awake. She gathered up her tattered nerves and accepted for the first time, she really was on her own. She couldn't keep depending on everyone around her—not just Ray, but Sierra and even Mike. She needed to take care of herself and her family.

Starting now.

"Ray, if there's really nothing more you can do for Trooper tonight, then let's load him up in my car. I should go home to my family."

His jaw flexed. His mouth was a flat line. "If that's what you really want."

"It is." And she did. For the first time in months, she didn't dread the day ahead of her. She knew it wouldn't be easy stepping up, taking charge. But it was time to move out of the frenzied limbo mode she'd been in these last few months and take charge of her life again.

"Okay then." He opened the crate and gave Trooper a once-over before lifting him out. He skillfully withdrew the IV line and bound the site to keep it from bleeding. "His pupils are normal, but watch and let me know if they dilate. The sleeping pills have made him groggy, but his pulse is steady, no more signs of bradycardia—uh, slow heart rate—and his breathing's normal. But—"

"I'll let you know if anything changes." She touched his hand lightly, tentatively. The ease she'd felt with him was gone now, still she owed him so very much, not just financially. They were going to have to work together, and sometime soon they would need to figure out how to handle that.

Stepping back, she retrieved her purse from the wooden bench where she'd tossed it eons ago when she'd raced in here, terrified of losing Trooper. She didn't have anything more to collect. Her shoes didn't even match. She'd yanked on one blue loafer and one brown loafer with her big toe poking through a hole in the canvas.

She really did need to get her life together.

Ray carried Trooper through the lobby and twisted the

locked front door while jostling the dog in his arms. The night air brought a cooler breeze, sweeping away the heat of the day and cooling her skin, still humming from a touch that left her feeling guilty.

Opening the front passenger door, she stepped back for him to settle Trooper beside her. She wanted him in sight at all times. She walked around to her side and sat behind the wheel, starting the ten-year-old family vehicle she and Allen had purchased for vacations.

Ray patted the dog on the chest once. "I'll call Sierra and let her know you're on your way home. It's late. Drive safely."

"Thank you, for your help tonight with Trooper."

She wanted to say more but sensed that would only make things worse.

He simply nodded and closed the door. More of that guilt piled on top of her. She'd hurt a good man because she'd let herself lean on him too much.

The drive home passed in a blur of Tennessee farm fields and trees, her body on auto pilot as the SUV ate up the miles. She and Allen had chosen this home because of the extra land, the space to call their own after so many years living as vagabonds. They'd even hoped to buy up some of the property bordering them.

She turned off the two-lane road into the entrance to her place, stopping at the security gate—where a visitor waited for her on a four-wheeler. She clicked her lights on high beam, nerves tingling. But it wasn't Kenneth. Valerie was the meaner of the two, but Lacey didn't physically fear the woman so she stopped. All the same, to be on the safe side, she stayed in her vehicle and just rolled down the window.

Personal safety. Yet another thing she needed to look more deeply into when taking charge of her life. She had a family to protect.

"Valerie, what are you doing here at this time of night?"

"Waiting for you to get home. I saw you peel out of here

with that young man hours ago." She sniffed disapprovingly, looking so damn ridiculous perched on the four-wheeler while wearing a floral muumuu.

What the hell? Was the woman spying on them? She knew the Hammonds wanted her gone, but how far were they willing to go? "I'm not the one running around at night in my pajamas, Valerie. Now please move out of the way so I can go home."

Her home. Her haven. Safe shelter for her and her family. And no one was going to take that away from her.

Valerie leaned forward on the handlebars, her face intense in the harsh beams of the headlights. "I'm giving you one last chance to handle this without a big confrontation. I don't want to see all those animals hauled off to a shelter. Place the ones you have and stop. You're driving down property values with those sick and mangy creatures. They're dangerous and untrained with heaven only knows what kind of history."

"We've been over this—" Lacey stopped. Screw trying to reason with this woman. Reason hadn't worked anyway. "Not tonight, Valerie. Okay? I'm not in the mood to politely pretend you aren't the worst neighbor and the most small-minded bitch on the planet. So if you don't want me to call Officer Parker to escort you off my property for trespassing, you will leave. Now."

Valerie's beady eyes narrowed. "You're going to be sorry. I have connections here and they owe me."

The vindictive woman revved her four-wheeler, and the vehicle lurched forward. The headlight streaked away into the night.

Good God, could this night suck the life out of her any further? She punched in the code for the gate and drove onto her land. Toward her home. A light was on in the kitchen, and she could see two people at the table. Mike and Sierra waiting up for her, no doubt. Her daughter was clearly in love with him again, and that was something else Lacey would need to address, listening to her daughter rather than letting her keep propping up this family.

That would be first on her agenda in the morning, along with figuring out how to reach Nathan. She parked the SUV by the mudroom door.

Lacey lifted Trooper carefully, and the dog nuzzled her hand gratefully. She walked through the mudroom, past the galoshes and leashes and other beautiful details that made up her life, things she needed to start appreciating. She entered the kitchen and sure enough, Mike and Sierra waited at the kitchen table for her.

Sierra looked at her hopefully. "Doc Vega called. Trooper's really going to be okay?"

"Appears so, but I'm going to keep him with me just to be safe." Lacey was just too exhausted to make small talk or pretend she didn't see the rekindled romance between them when her heart was especially tender with this new stage of widowhood. "I'm going to bed now and I'll just bring Trooper with me so I can watch him."

Mike shoved to his feet. "Let me carry him for you."

"I'm good." Which wasn't technically true. But she would be. She really didn't have a choice. "This is what I do. Right, Troop?"

Lacey started toward the enclosed patio, where she usually kept her sick animals while resting on a sofa. But something stopped her. She eyed the stairs leading up to her bedroom, that place she avoided.

No time like the present to start tackling her resolutions. With a bracing breath, she climbed the stairs, the weight of the dog a welcome distraction from going to her room alone. She nudged open the door to her bedroom. Hers and Allen's. She set Trooper down long enough to pull the quilt from her bed and make it into a nest on the floor for the sick dog. He hauled his groggy body over and curled up with a sleepy sigh.

She eyed her bed, steeled herself and whipped back

the sheet. For the first time since her husband had died, she pulled the covers over her and truly went to sleep in their bed.

MIKE HAD DREAMED of a lot of ways to help Sierra over the years. But in all of his fantasizing, he'd never imagined he would be cooking breakfast in the McDaniel kitchen.

Gramps sat quietly at the table, thumbing through a weekly newspaper, one of the few print papers left. But Sierra ordered it for him since teaching him to use an iPad was out of the question. The paper was just one of the endless ways this family reached out to be there for each other. That was a rare gift in life.

These people were growing more important to him by the day. Not just Sierra, but all the McDaniels. He'd never had anything like this, not even when they'd been dating. He'd been more concerned with downplaying the relationship, nervous about how the Colonel felt.

He liked being able to help them, the whole give-and-take that went on around here. The McDaniels had something special in the way they knew how to be there for each other. Sierra had slept on the sofa in case her mom needed her and to be sure her grandfather didn't slip out. Mike figured the least he could do was cook breakfast.

And yeah, he enjoyed the opportunity to flex his gourmet skills. Unable to sleep, he'd made fat butterscotch sticky buns from scratch, watching over Sierra in the next room on the sofa. The afghan draped on her rose and fell with each steady breath, her blond hair trailing down the side of the leather sofa.

The scent of the cooking pastries filled the kitchen until he could almost taste the cinnamon. He rifled through the refrigerator for fresh fruit as footsteps sounded on the stairway.

Lacey walked in with Trooper at her side, both of them

looking a little haggard but on their feet. He knew weary—
but victorious—warriors when he saw them.

"Good morning," he said. "I took the liberty of making
breakfast."

"Mom?" Sierra called from the sofa, sitting up sharply,
the afghan sliding to the floor. She shot to her feet, still
wearing the rumpled khaki pants and blouse from yesterday,
clothes they'd peeled from each other with such intense
pleasure last night—a lifetime ago.

Sierra walked up behind her mom and wrapped her in a
hug. "Good morning." She walked past, shoving her tousled
hair from her face and sending his pulse spiking just before
she knelt to scratch Trooper's ears. "You're looking good,
pup. You sure scared us, though."

No kidding. Scared? Understatement. And he still
couldn't figure out how it had happened. How had the dog
gotten those pills? Lacey had seemed so certain she'd
stashed them safely away in her bathroom.

Trooper pulled away from her and paced around the
kitchen restlessly.

Gramps glanced over. "Somebody take him out before
he pees in the house."

Sierra surged forward. "I've got him, Mom." She reached
for the dog's collar but he ducked away. "For a disoriented
dog, he sure is strong and walking a straight line."

Gramps folded his paper. "Looks like a bloodhound on
a scent to me."

Mike passed the pot holders to Sierra. "Let me get him.
He could be dodgy overseas sometimes, too. He's probably
still disoriented."

He squatted and extended a hand to Trooper, but the mutt
ducked away again, sidling to Sierra and grabbing hold of
her pants leg. What the hell? The pup dug in his paws and
tugged, hard, snarling.

"Trooper?" Sierra's eyes went wide.

Mike hadn't worried about the dog being dangerous since

those first few weeks, but had the drugs peeled away some layer of taming? The dog all but dragged Sierra to the stairs, then let go and sprinted up at lightning speed. There was nothing drugged or loopy about him. He knew exactly where he was going.

Mike charged after him. Trooper scratched at Nathan's door, pawing furiously until the knob spun and gave way. So much for teenage privacy. Trooper galloped inside and dove under the bed.

Mike sagged against the doorframe. "Really, dog?"

Had the time with Gramps under the bed in the mental war zone now become a canine game? Because if so, Mike had no intention of joining in. Real life combat was more than enough to handle.

Trooper barked again and again until finally Nathan peeked from under his pillow. "Will someone shut up that stupid mutt?"

Nathan's bleary eyes closed again, and he pulled the covers over his head. Trooper barked louder until Mike walked into the room, stepping over a pile of clothes, a pizza box and a couple of magazines.

He knelt by the bed. "Hey, Trooper. Let's go get breakfast." Shit, he'd left the sticky buns cooking. "I'm making bacon. Come on, boy."

Trooper scooted his nose along the tan carpet, pushing . . . carpet fuzz? Mike looked closer, and there was no denying what he was seeing.

"Sierra, there are two pills under Nathan's bed." He pinched each one up and put them in his palm. "Lacey? Nathan?"

The teenager sat up slowly, going pale, his groggy eyes suddenly making sense in the worst possible way.

Sierra's mother grabbed the doorframe for support. "Those are my sleeping pills." Her chin trembled for an instant before she said, "Nathan, what are my sleeping pills doing in your room?"

PART 5

Burying a bone is easy. Remembering where ya put it? Easy, too. But trusting others not to steal your treasure if you dig it up and expose it to the world? Now that's the tough part.

—TROOPER, CANINE PSYCHOLOGY 101

Nineteen

SAVING NATHAN'S LIFE was a tricky thing to pull off, but I did it.

The instant I saw Nathan sitting on his bed with the pill bottle in his hand and a glass of water beside him, I knew what he intended to do. That was the smell of death I'd sensed in the kid from day one.

So I waited until he pulled off the lid and then I leapt up onto the bed. He only got a couple down his throat before I ripped the bottle from his hand. I shook my head from side to side, spraying little pills all over the messy floor. I jumped down fast and gobbled those tiny tablets ASAP, hiding two under the bed just in case the humans needed an extra hint. Nathan tried to shush me but I barked and barked until he tossed me out of the room.

I wish I could claim credit for the idea, but I got the inspiration from a Second Chance Ranch Pomeranian named Lucky. He ate his owner's marijuana stash in order to alert the parents to the teenager's drug habit.

The pills hit my system faster than I could get the

attention of a human. I hadn't anticipated that. But I held on during the puking and the visit to the vet—I decided to forgive Doctor Vega for the tube down my throat and the needle in my paw since he didn't get busy with Lacey. It wasn't her time.

But back to Nathan. I had my mission to complete, to protect this family. The teenager sat on the edge of the bed, his face paler than sand as his family confronted him with the pills. He was groggy, too, probably from the couple he'd managed to swallow.

Finally, they understood how badly the Colonel's son needed help.

I curled up on his pile of dirty clothes, breathed in the sweet smell of people sweat on the armpits of shirts and watched the McDaniels put the pieces of their lives back together.

Lacey walked to her son, while Mike wrapped an arm around Sierra, tucking her to his side in the doorway.

Lacey sat on the edge of the bed with a careful calm. Nathan's jaw jutted defiantly. She zeroed in a laser-eyed look the Colonel had mentioned to me once or twice. It was the first time I'd seen it. A determined Lacey was a formidable force. "Nathan, why were these pills under your bed?"

He shrugged, his oversized T-shirt rippling on his bony frame. "Trooper must have brought the bottle in here."

Little liar. I didn't move, but I sent a growl-huff combo out there to make my opinion known.

Lacey wasn't buying it, either. She shook her head. "I can see you're not being honest with me. I've been trying to figure out the whole time how Trooper could have gotten the pill bottle from a zippered bag high in a cabinet. And the bottle wasn't even chewed."

"You must have forgotten leaving them somewhere else." He tried one last bluff. "Obviously."

"No," Lacey said firmly, "I haven't taken any since a couple of weeks after . . . after your father died."

"You haven't?" His eyes went wide, showing a vulner-
ability for the first time. Then the nice moment faded. "You
just drink instead."

"This isn't about me," she said with quiet authority.

"Maybe it should be."

"Nathan!" Sierra pulled away from Mike, starting toward
them.

Her mother held up a hand to stop her. "Son, I'll make a
deal with you. You talk honestly, then I will."

"Why do I have to go first?"

"Because I'm the mom and there aren't pills under
my bed."

"Fine. I took the pills from your cabinet because I wanted
to take them. All. Every one of them," he spit out with an
insolent teenage sneer, but the undertone of pain couldn't
be missed. Not even by a dog. "I opened the bottle and the
dumb dog ate them. I want out, Mom, I just want out."

His face crumbled and the tears started. Lacey pulled
him close and he didn't resist. I heard a sniffle from the
doorway, too, where Mike held Sierra. I tucked my head
deeper into the dirty clothes pile, letting the "dumb dog"
thing slide. I'd been called a whole lot worse.

Things weren't perfect. They still had the two crazy
people next door to deal with. However, I couldn't do anything about that beyond peeing on their monster machines
when they drove around to cause trouble.

But for the first time since I'd arrive at the Second Chance
Ranch, I had faith the family could take care of themselves
just fine.

SIERRA WAS RUNNING on fumes.

A month ago, she hadn't thought her world could be any
crazier. She'd been wrong. Her love life was on borrowed
time and her brother had just tried to kill himself.

She pulled the sticky buns out of the oven, over aware of

Mike's solid footsteps across the tile floor. "The ones in the middle didn't burn."

He opened the refrigerator. "I was planning to cut up a fruit salad and fry some bacon."

"Fine, but I'm going to eat my body weight in carbohydrates." She pulled a spatula from a crockery holder on the counter and dug out two sticky buns, nuts and butterscotch slathered on top. She didn't even bother with a plate and just started eating at the stove.

Mike tossed a cantaloupe, some grapes and bananas on the counter. "Are you okay?"

How could he be so calm? "Not even close."

His hands didn't even tremble as he sliced the fruit, but there was a comfort in knowing someone was operating on all cylinders right now. "I knew Nathan was having trouble, but I never guessed . . . Hell, I should have seen this. The military briefs us all the time on signs to look for."

"Signs?" She thumbed a drizzle of butterscotch from the corner of her mouth and couldn't stop the flood of memories from their caramel encounter the night before. "What do you mean?"

"Signs of suicidal tendencies."

Her stomach twisted and she set the roll back on the pan. "You get briefed on suicide prevention?"

"All the time—especially after deployments—to watch ourselves and keep track of our buddies. I should have listened closer to the part about watching for signs in our family."

"*Our* family?" Now her stomach really knotted, with nerves and hope, a scary emotion to entertain right now on such a dark morning.

"Slip of the tongue." He tossed chopped chunks of fruit into a serving bowl.

"Regardless, if anyone should blame themselves, it's me—"

"Hey, don't even go there." He dried his hands on a dish

towel and walked to her. "You already shoulder so much for your family."

"My dad would want me to help," she insisted, feeling more and more responsible by the second.

"Your father would want you to live your life."

"I guess you would know." She picked absently at the second sticky bun, her appetite drying up. "You spent more time with him than I did."

"I'm sorry—"

She held up a hand. "That came out wrong. I didn't mean to sound bitter." But she was. To be honest, today she was feeling bitter and angry, like life had stolen too much from her. "It's just . . . as if my mother didn't have enough grief in her life. Now this with my brother." Her chest went tight and she couldn't breathe, each word coming out between gasps. "My . . . baby . . . brother . . ."

Mike slid his arms around her and hauled her tight against his chest, her face tucked in his neck. He felt so good and solid, like forever. Except what if she lost him, too?

She was so damn tired of being strong. "Mike, I don't know if I can live this kind of life." She confessed between quiet tears. "But I also want to be with you, because no matter how hard I try not to, I still love you."

His body went still with shock, and she couldn't help but notice he wasn't turning cartwheels over her confession.

She angled back, her hands up between them. She needed distance because the warmth of his arms around her was too tempting. "Honest to God I do, but I can't be a military wife. The Army isn't about a thirty-year career. Or even a twenty-year career. It permeates the rest of our lives."

He didn't answer or deny it. He just stared back at her with a sadness in his eyes she felt all the way to her toes. And until that moment, she hadn't realized how much she wanted him to figure out a way around her fears. She'd hoped he would have an answer. That he would do for them what her father had been unable to manage.

The alarm from the front gate intercom sliced through the silence.

She grasped the distraction from this heart-wrenching conversation with both hands. She ran to the window and looked out to see . . . a police car? So much for happy distractions. What more could go wrong?

Her first instinct was to reach for Mike, but her pride stopped her. They'd never figure a way around this mess of their feelings if she didn't stop turning to him every time he came around. She keyed in the security code and let the car come through.

Mike frowned. "Any idea what's going on?"

"Not a clue." She brushed past on her way to the front door, stepping out onto the wide veranda, one of the rockers creaking slowly as a bird took flight.

She shaded her eyes while the police car drove closer, dirt puffing from behind the tires. The car stopped in front, the door opening and Officer Parker stepping out.

"Is your mother here?" He dropped his hat on his head.

"She's . . ." Tending a suicidal son? Bile rose in Sierra's throat.

Mike stepped up. "She's in the shower. Is there something we can help you with?"

"I just thought your mother should know." He sidestepped Clementine loping in lazy three-legged circles around him. "The Hammonds are on the warpath. They've used all their connections to call an emergency council meeting. They want a temporary injunction to close down your rescue pending a deeper investigation into the fights that broke out when the gates gave way."

Sierra grabbed the porch post, stung by the injustice. "The property was vandalized. That's not our fault. And I wouldn't be surprised if the Hammonds had something to do with it." Okay, maybe that wasn't fair, but damn it, life wasn't fair.

"Hey, I'm on your side," Officer Parker said. "That's why

I'm here giving you a heads-up. We know now that the vandals are tied to a dogfighting ring in the next county. But Valerie contends you didn't have the proper security in place and the public isn't safe. That this rescue draws in unsavory elements like that. I'm not saying she's right or that they're going to win."

Sierra swayed and would have fallen if Mike's hand hadn't palmed her shoulder for support. "But they could?"

How freaking messed up that they couldn't even have a moment to breathe in the good news that the people responsible for destroying the gates had been found. The Hammonds were going to use even that against them.

"I'm sorry," Officer Parker said. "Valerie Hammond has some powerful friends in town thanks to wealthy parents and her volunteer work. You need to be at that meeting and you need to be prepared for the worst. Just in case."

Mike squeezed her shoulder. "And when is this emergency meeting taking place?"

"Tomorrow evening."

Tomorrow? She looked from Mike to the policeman and saw no reprieve. They'd lost a whole week to prepare their case. And not only that, they were being ambushed by a legion of influential people in the community who might just stamp out her mother's dream after all.

CONVINCING THE MCDANIEL men to go for a walk with him hadn't been easy, but Mike had been given Nathan and Gramps duty while Sierra talked to her mother. And he wasn't going to let her down when she needed his help most. Sierra had called in sick to work and was helping her mother go over all the files and records for the Second Chance Ranch, making sure everything was in order and had been properly filed. Fortunately, he knew they kept meticulous records. Their home life might seem chaotic, but they'd taken no chances with the legalities of the ranch for the sake of the animals. Seeing them together, reviewing every possible detail, it occurred to Mike these two women could freaking rule the world.

But in less than twenty-four hours that world could be upended for them again. He wished he could give Sierra something more than babysitter patrol, but he wasn't any closer to finding the answers to their showdown in the kitchen.

She'd said she still loved him. He should be pumping his fist in victory. Except for the part about her not wanting any part of his life. There'd been no room for compromise on that point. She meant it. Which left them . . . where, exactly?

The lack of answers and futility of sitting around the farmhouse had been driving him out of his mind, which was why he'd organized his current trek with the McDaniel men.

Nathan trudged after him. "How much farther do I have to walk?"

"Not much farther." Mike hitched the golf bag over his shoulder. "General, are you still with us?"

"I'm doing fine, son. It's the boy here who's holding us back with all that attitude." Gramps's shuffling footsteps rustled along the beaten path. "Don't know why we have to march out here and get all sweaty. Why would anyone want to play golf in the heat? If you ask me, we need to find a good topless bar."

Shaking his head slowly, Mike stopped at the edge of a pasture that ran alongside the Hammonds' property. "Sir, I believe golf is a more age appropriate option for Nathan. I figured if the Hammonds are going to spy on us, we might as well give them something to look at while we're burning off energy." Slinging the bag from his shoulder, he gestured to Nathan. "Hey, buddy, come here."

"I'm not your buddy." But he walked over anyway.

"Fair enough." Mike pulled out a club, dusty as hell, but then it had likely been a long time since the General had used them. Hopefully he had some of that muscle memory left for the game. "You've got cause to be pissed off at the world."

Nathan took the golf club from Mike. "Did they send you out here to talk me into counseling?"

"Nah, I'll leave that up to your mom and your sister. But they're going to insist and you're going to say yes. You don't have a choice there." Mike slipped out another club and passed it to the General along with a three-pack of golf balls. "I was thinking more along the lines of an outlet for our frustrations today. Because sitting at home isn't solving jack, and like it or not, we've all three got shit weighing us down."

Nathan swung the club loosely back and forth. "What if I don't want to play golf?"

"Then we'll figure out something else to help you." Mike dropped a ball in front of the teenager, catching his eyes and holding, making sure he had the boy's full attention. "Because, Nathan, quitting is never an option."

"That's true, son," Gramps chimed in while he checked the height of the grass and lifted a finger to test the wind. "We don't quit."

Nathan stared at the ground, tap, tap, tapping the golf ball with the club lightly. "I'm gonna have to go to therapy."

That simple sentence coming from Nathan required courage. And for a flash, Mike saw a hint of the Colonel in him, even though the boy looked so much like Lacey.

Seeing such strength coming from a teen who'd taken some damn hard hits in life humbled him. How come the kid could man up and face facts with so much clear-eyed smarts while Mike was still chasing his tail going around and around with Sierra?

The moment was like a clap to his thick head, making Mike realize he'd been copping out. He'd told himself he was helping Sierra by staying away and denying the relationship so she wouldn't be subjected to her mother's life. Instead, he should have been putting her first, because damn it, she was first in his life and in his heart.

He was through running away from the promise of being happy with her. He understood exactly what needed to happen to show Sierra how much he loved her. And loving her meant he would be a part of this family, with an aging grandfather, a quirky mom and this confused teenager. Mike had been a rebel his whole life, with friends, but not family. He'd never had anyone to call family, not in the ways that mattered. But he was crazy about this one, and they'd taught him a thing or two about how families supported each other when times were tough. He'd watched the McDaniels enough to realize families just dug in and worked together.

He knew what to do to win Sierra and shut down this bogus council meeting.

"Nathan, I have an idea for how to save your mom's rescue"—and show Sierra how committed he was to building a life with her—"but I'm going to need your help."

Twenty

THE NEXT EVENING, Sierra rode in the SUV with her mom to the council meeting. Sunset cast a hazy, mellow glow over the sleepy little town, but she couldn't find the peace that should come at the end of the day. She felt like her grandfather, sundowning, disoriented and angry over the loss of control.

She could only imagine how her mother felt, with this showdown coming so close on the heels of the crisis with her brother. He had his first appointment with the psychiatrist tomorrow, a surprisingly easy victory to win.

Surprising her again tonight, Nathan had opted to ride with Mike ahead of time, something about grabbing a burger on the way, which sounded strange, but Mike had really taken her brother under his wing. And as long as her brother was safely watched, she didn't see the need to argue.

Not that she'd even had five seconds free to talk to Mike since they'd fought. Even if they did find a quiet minute alone, she wasn't sure what to say to make things right again.

To stop the ache in her heart that ran so much deeper than the last time they'd broken up.

Was this it? Were they truly over? Would he leave once the meeting wrapped up and he wouldn't have to feel obligated to help them anymore? As much as she dreaded the council meeting, she dreaded the aftermath more. Once this was done, she would find out where she stood with Mike.

Since Officer Parker had shared the news with them yesterday morning, Sierra and her mother had been in crisis management mode. They'd gone over every aspect of the rescue's paperwork, making sure they hadn't missed any legal loophole. Then, they'd put together a presentation with handouts and a PowerPoint.

They'd opted to leave Gramps at home with a sitter. Ghita's sister was an LPN at a local assisted living facility. Her mom had resisted at first, but at the last second acquiesced on that point after months of digging in her heels that she could handle everything. Hopefully, this would start a new era of care that would ease the strain on everyone, including Gramps. It was time to make that transition into the next level needed to keep her grandfather safe. The nurse had been full of information about activities and assistance that could offer Gramps a richer life beyond an endless stream of watching John Wayne movies.

A lot had changed in the past three weeks. For all of them. "Mom, it's going to be okay."

Her mother's knuckles went white on the steering wheel. "Sierra, I swear if you spew some morose, weighty Emily Dickinson quote, I'm going to make you walk the rest of the way."

"No Dickinson today." She searched her mind for something more appropriate, more uplifting for both of them. "I'm thinking a piece of wisdom from Helen Keller is appropriate. 'What we have once enjoyed we can never lose. All that we love deeply becomes a part of us.'"

Her mother's grip eased. "That's beautiful, Sierra, truly."

"You've sent a lot of love out there into the world with the animals you've saved and rehomed. I hope you never lose sight of that."

Lacey reached over to squeeze her hand. "Thank you. I don't know if I say that enough, but I don't know what I would have done without you these past few months."

"We're family. No thanks needed." She squeezed back. "Love you."

As they drew closer to the county building where the meeting would be held, Sierra noticed more and more cars parked on the side of the road, increasing until there wasn't a single space left all the way to the parking lot, also full.

Sierra grabbed the armrest, looking left and right at the rows of vehicles. Nerves kicked into high gear. "Did you know about this turnout?"

"I knew people were interested, but I had no idea Second Chance was on the radar of so many people. I just pray they're not all friends of Valerie Hammond."

The Hammonds were reputed to be related to half the county.

Could the rescue be lost simply because a large enough group of people held a personal grudge? Sierra couldn't imagine her mother without the Second Chance Ranch. It had become such a part of her. Biting her lip, she looked around, concentrating on one problem at a time. "Where are we going to park?"

Her mother started a three-point turn. "I guess we'll have to find a side street and walk. I really hope we're not late."

Two blocks away, they located a tiny space and somehow her mother wedged in the bulky family SUV. Sierra reached over the seat for her computer bag while her mother hefted out a fat box full of handouts. "Mom, we're not going to have enough for everyone."

"There's nothing we can do about that now." She grabbed her purse and hit the ground running. "We have the Power-Point and we have our voices."

She just wished she'd worn better running shoes for this rather than opting for businesslike attire. Computer bag bumping her hip, she jogged around the corner, her mother's feet drumming behind her. Louder. In sync with her hammering pulse and the barking dogs—

Barking dogs?

Sierra stumbled, looking at her mother. "Mom? Do you hear that?" Was she imagining the sound of dogs now even in the short time she was away from them? "What's going on?"

Lacey looked just as confused, jostling the box for a firmer grip. "I have no idea."

The closer they came to the town hall, the louder the noise grew. Not just barking, but the low murmur of voices. The sky grew darker, streetlights flickering to life one by one until a glowing dome showcased the crowd outside the building on the street. And as she looked closer, she began to recognize faces.

The young couple that adopted Bob Marley stood with their twin girls and both dogs. Lucky, the marijuana-eating Pomeranian, stood beside the senior citizen couple that had adopted him. One by one, Sierra recognized the faces of people who'd looked to Lacey and the Second Chance Ranch for their next companion pet. Each of those animals waited as well, glowing with health and love.

A cluster of people wearing the same T-shirt drew her eye and tugged her heart. Mary Hannah, other volunteers and foster families from the picnics held stacks of flyers. Ghita and her husband were there with their dogs on leashes beside them. Sierra couldn't help but notice the ditzy receptionist Maisie was nowhere in sight, but then she'd never been much of a fan of any animal other than the pedigree sort.

Mary Hannah, Debbie and Charlotte smiled and waved, each with a leash around her wrist attached to a current

Second Chance animal wearing an *Adopt Me* scarf. Sierra didn't question for an instant who was the organizational brain trust behind the color coordination. She smiled her thanks to her friend, but still wondered how so many of their allies could have heard about the emergency meeting. Mary Hannah wouldn't have had access to all the adopters' names or contact information. Lacey looked as stunned as she felt, mutely accepting hugs from people who'd turned out to help their cause.

Tears burned Sierra's eyes at the outpouring of support. Words of encouragement rippled from the crowd.

"We've got your back."

"You can do it."

"We're here for you all."

Dahlia and her staff started a round of applause, and the throng parted, revealing Doc Vega, Nathan . . . and Mike.

Sierra blinked to clear away the tears. Her heart tripped over itself. Her feet, too, as she stumbled to a stop. Mike met her eyes and held, his arms slowly raising as he held up a sign that read:

EVERYONE DESERVES
A SECOND CHANCE

A murmur of excitement rumbled through the gathering as others lifted their homemade signs as well with photos and slogans, all championing the McDaniel family.

Suddenly she realized exactly how all these people knew to be here tonight. Mike. Mike had made this happen for her and for her family. Beyond that, he'd involved Nathan as well, giving her brother a purpose, something positive to hang on to at the darkest time in his young life.

And Mike had done all of that for her in spite of how she'd wrecked things between them, shutting him down rather than talking things through. She knew better than that. Her mother and, yes, her dad, too, had taught her differently. But she'd acted out of fear, letting her doubts and insecurities push him away. How incredibly unfair to both of them, but to Mike especially. She wasn't just robbing him of their love, but of her whole family, a family he'd become a part of whether they ever swore vows to each other or not.

She'd said the words that she loved him but had been too frightened and selfish to act on those feelings. Love wasn't a noun. It was a verb.

And Mike had taken the leap and shown his feelings in action tonight. She owed him the same.

LACEY SAGGED INSIDE her SUV, soaking in the wash of relief—or at least reprieve. The council had been moved by the show of support from the community and adopters. They saw the positive ripple effect.

Although they'd surprised everyone by keeping the meeting closed while they reviewed the written data and statements. They'd listened to the Hammonds and the McDaniels, along with a handful of witnesses such as Officer Parker and Ray Vega.

Their ultimate ruling? Decide nothing fast. Take time to assess and evaluate Lacey's operation to make sure as the rescue grew, the safety and well-being of the animals stayed in the forefront.

The second she'd heard those words she knew all would be well. The council understood this was about saving the animals, not about personal grudges or self-glorification. The Second Chance Ranch was meeting standards now, but she would be closely scrutinized for a year.

She welcomed it. Her dream, her mission, was safe.

A tap on the passenger side window jolted her. Another supporter? She'd spent longer—hours, actually—speaking with people after the meeting than she had making her case

inside the town hall. Mike and Sierra had left earlier, taking
Nathan home. Lacey rolled down the window.

Ray leaned in. "Mind if we talk for a few minutes?"

She thumbed the unlock button. "Come in. The air conditioner's running."

He slid into the seat beside her, dropping his hat onto his
knee. "Congratulations on how things shook down. Mike
and Nathan really pulled off a coup with that gathering. Did
you see the news crews in the crowd? The blogger friend of
Mike's was there as well. I'll bet you get a slew of adoption
requests as a result of the added exposure."

"News crews?" She shook her head. "I must have missed
them. I was so scared tonight I could hardly think until after
I heard we got a reprieve. Everything before that was such
a blur."

He kept his hands on his hat. A couple of days ago, he would
have patted her shoulder. "You'd never know it from looking
at you. You appeared totally in control, poised . . . beautiful."

That final word hung between them for a few awkward
seconds.

"Thank you for all you said in there about the rescue's
work, testifying to the level of care we provide our animals."
She owed him so much. For his skilled help with the animals. For his support when she'd needed a friend most. And
for giving her space to pull her life together after she'd given
him incredibly mixed signals. Ray Vega was a good man.

"All true," he said simply.

"I mean it," she pressed. "Your professional opinion carried a lot of weight with the naysayers—and there were
plenty of them in attendance tonight."

Although not even half the size of the supporters Mike
and Nathan had brought together. She was so proud of her
son and . . . the man who already felt like a son to her no
matter what Sierra said about breaking up.

"I'm glad I could help." He spun the hat on his knee.

After all Ray had done for her, he still offered more. He deserved to have someone in his life who could give back.

"I wouldn't have blamed you if you had wanted to stay away after what happened between us the night Trooper ate those pills." She nibbled her bottom lip. "I never should have let that kiss get so out of control."

He gave her a half smile. "I'll chalk it up to my animal magnetism."

"That would be an accurate assumption."

He scruffed a hand through his overlong hair. "Maisie quit her job. She found your scarf in my office and she assumed the worst." He scratched behind his neck. "She was really unhinged about the whole thing."

"Truly? Your ego wasn't a little stroked by all that giggly attention?"

"Okay"—he grimaced—"maybe a little, but not to the extent of her reaction. Be careful of her. About the vandalism at your place . . . from a few things she let slip, I think she's friends with some of the people in the dogfighting ring Officer Parker's investigating."

Gasping, Lacey sat up straighter. "You really believe she would have steered them my way? That seems like a whole different level of cruelty." And she wouldn't rest until she found those responsible.

"I don't know what to think. But I passed along my suspicions to Officer Parker who already has the group under surveillance. He says one of the members is going to flip and give over evidence for a deal. I just wanted to make you aware of it."

"There haven't been any problems since I upped the security system that second time—not even with the General wandering or the Hammonds trespassing." She would be fund-raising like crazy to pay for it, but the safety of her family and animals had to be top priority. "Still, I will certainly keep both eyes open."

"Good, that's good." He nodded, his eyes falling. "Because I have something I need to tell you."

The ominous tone in his voice set her nerves on edge. "Is there a problem?"

"Do you remember my mentioning an offer to join that practice out west? I've been getting some pressure to make a decision soon," he started.

"And you're going to take the job," she said with a sinking heart, already understanding. Because of her, he was leaving, giving up the niche he'd built. She grieved for him as well as the animals here who needed a man like him.

"Actually, no. I didn't take the position." He looked out into the darkness. "The pressure made me think about what I wanted to do most. It pushed me to contact a missionary group that provides veterinary aid to animals in third-world countries."

That sounded like him. She told herself the stab of pain in her chest was for the animals here who would miss his warm manner and skilled treatment. But she also understood why it had to be this way.

"How long will you be gone?"

"About a year, give or take a month." He turned to her fully for the first time, sliding his hand to cup the back of her neck. "And when I return, we're going to dinner."

She cupped his face, her thumb stroking. "I would like that."

His throat moved in a hard swallow before he leaned in to kiss her forehead, holding for an instant. Then he pulled away sharply and left the vehicle—leaving her alone.

Completely alone.

For the past four months, she'd been filling every single moment with work and her family, hiding from her bedroom, terrified of being by herself. But right now as she sat in the silence of her car, the Helen Keller piece of wisdom whispered through her brain and seeped into her being.

What we have once enjoyed we can never lose. All that we love deeply becomes a part of us.

She wasn't alone at all.

MIKE SAT AT the foot of the steps waiting for Sierra to finish with her family. Soft country tunes seeped from the barn, soothing the animals to sleep with a twang rather than classical melodies tonight. His fingers drummed along the wooden step, mimicking the chords as he ghost-played along.

There hadn't been a chance for them to speak since the council meeting. By the time they'd gotten home, sent Gramps's nurse on her way and tended the animals, Lacey had arrived, which brought another rehash of the evening.

Along with a request from Lacey not to let Maisie from the vet clinic anywhere near her animals.

A strange request, but things were never run-of-the-mill around here. That was one of the many things he appreciated about this amazing family.

The screen door creaked and he stood straighter. Sierra stepped out, Trooper sliding through the door at the last second before it slammed closed. The porch light illuminated Sierra, bringing out the blond highlights in her braid. She'd changed into jean shorts and some airy pink blouse. Her flip-flops smacked the ground as she walked closer, her eyes full of love for him. She'd told him that she loved him, and finally, he let himself believe her.

Now he needed to let her know how very much he loved her. He held out an arm. "Wanna take a walk?"

She fit to his side, sliding her arm around him, tucking her fingers into his back pocket. "I would like that very much."

His arm draped over her shoulders, steering her toward the path into the woods. "I've been thinking about what you said, and I understand why you've already done your tour of duty with military life."

"Wait. I've been thinking, too, and—"

"Shhh, let me go first." He tucked her closer. He didn't want her making sacrifices for him she would later regret. "I've signed a military contract that lasts for two more years and I can't get out of that. But I talked to the Sergeant Major yesterday, and I have a couple of options."

"You did what?" She looked up sharply, her braid brushing his arm.

"I can withdraw my Special Forces packet right now." And he would do it in a heartbeat for this woman. He'd thought climbing the career mountain was his dream. He'd been wrong. Having Sierra in his life forever was the dream turned to reality. "If you say you want me out of the military two years from now, I can ride out the rest of my time here at Fort Campbell. I can't promise I won't deploy before then, but I'll have set a path to a new start for us."

"What would you do afterward?" She spoke carefully, almost as if the idea of them being together was so fragile it wouldn't stand up to scrutiny.

He needed to fix that. Starting now.

"I have the G.I. Bill to go back to college, and I'll have two years to figure out what to do with it."

He was a smart guy. Hell, he'd found a way to multiply nickels in a subway with his guitar as a kid. What might he accomplish now with a whole lot more brainpower and resourcefulness at his disposal?

"And the other option?" Her words were still soft, tentative. But he could almost hear the wheels turning in her smart mind.

"Defer my Special Forces assignment for a year. I would stay here for twelve months while you finish school, then we would move to Fort Bragg in North Carolina, together."

She stopped walking altogether and stepped in front of him. "You could really defer the slot for a year?"

"It's been done before."

"But it's not a guarantee the slot would still be there for

you." She rested her hands on his chest. "I can't let you give that up for me."

"I would do anything for you, Sierra." He could not lose her again.

She clenched her hands in his T-shirt. "What do *you* want to do?"

"I want to be with you." He cradled her face in both hands. "But I understand you have good reason not to want a military lifestyle. And then there's the rescue here. You've put so much of your heart into it."

"It's my mother's rescue. Not mine."

"Are you sure? Because from where I've been standing it seems you inherited your mother's sheltering spirit. So this is your call to make."

"It's not fair for me to choose your career path for you."

"Do you want to be with me? I love you, Sierra. Damn it, the words are getting tangled up here." He took a bracing breath. "I'm trying to propose. I want us to get married."

Her arms slid around his neck, the acceptance soft and immediate and so right it made his heart ache in the best way.

"Oh, Mike, I want that, too. I always have."

She'd never quoted better poetry than those words. He tucked them away to remember forever, because they had just turned his life around. More certain than ever, he kissed her forehead. Trooper darted out of the woods as if he sensed a happy moment and wanted to be a part of it. He barked and ran in a circle around them, tail whipping fast.

"Then we'll work out the rest."

"If you're comfortable waiting around here for me for a year, then I'm all in for North Carolina."

Which meant he got the green light for the military life he'd always envisioned for himself. A huge compromise for her.

"You don't have to decide tonight," he reminded her. "It's been a hell of a day."

"I'm sure." Her eyes were clear and . . . certain. She had more of her father in her than she knew.

"And the rescue?" He looked around at the Second Chance Ranch, a place she'd been a part of from the beginning.

"Animal rescue is a calling that won't go away just because I leave home." She bent to stroke Trooper's ear as the dog settled down from his evening romp. "There are shelters with animals everywhere in need of people to foster them. I'll carry what I've learned from Mom wherever we go."

"So we pack some of the Second Chance spirit to take with us wherever we move." He could picture Sierra loading up a few extra leashes.

"Exactly. We got our second chance here, too, you know. I'm too smart to let you get away from me again."

She leaned closer, her heart in her eyes.

Mike had to swallow the lump in his throat over the fact that she was going to make a place in her life for him. No, this incredible, beautiful, smart woman was going to build her life around him and with him.

"I love you, Sierra." He wanted to be very clear on that point. "Like crazy."

Slanting his mouth over hers, he kissed her with all the longing in his soul. He sucked at saying the right words, so he hoped she felt it in that kiss.

He wrapped her tight in his arms and lifted her off her feet, pressing her to him. When he broke away, he smiled down at her and set her back on the ground. Trooper's tail thumped the ground beside them.

"I found a poem for you." Mike had the feeling she wouldn't mind keeping things light for at least a little while tonight after the day she'd had.

"A poem?" She grinned, catching his mood and linking her arm through his as they walked under the stars, crickets and frogs buzzing from the undergrowth.

"Absolutely. I had to figure out a way to one-up my cross-word puzzle vocab games."

"But you know I enjoy your twist on Scrabble," she teased, matching her step to his.

"I believe it's time for us to take this to another level."

"Such as?"

"Poems. Poetry. I'm a musician but not much of a lyricist, so I figured I would use some of the ones you've studied. Maybe someday I'll pull out my guitar and sing them to you. But for now, 'How do I love thee? Let me count the ways . . .'"

Epilogue

I WAS BORN IN the land of Babylon.

But I'm an American dog now. I've belonged to an American family since I came here ten years ago. I've helped a lot of animals understand humans a little better. Most of all, I've helped one particular human hear me.

We're taking a trip today, so I'm a happy fella. I pretend I still don't like the leash much since the humans offer me great treats when I finally give in and walk nicely. It's a game we play.

I'm slower these days, and they slip carrots and peas into my food to make me think I'm full when I'm not. But they tell me my hips will hurt less if I don't get heavy. I remind myself of the days I had to scavenge for scraps and I eat the diet food they give me.

We walk down the corridor, one of those long tile kinds they bleach all the time to keep things sterile. It's not a hospital exactly, but I'm not sure of the correct word. I've been gone from Babylon so long sometimes the English words are just out of reach. Or maybe that's because I'm an old dog and they say my first six months were pretty rough. I've had it good since then thanks to my people. My family.

They're all here with me today and that's special, rare, too, since everybody grew up. I went with Mike and Sierra when they moved away for him to train to wear a green beret with his Army uniform. Sierra runs an online magazine about military life and she fosters for animal shelters wherever we move next. She's helped a lot of folks and makes good money with that magazine. Mike's gotten rows of medals from being a Special Forces guy—and he's a genuine family man now, with their little boy and a baby on the way. It's a girl and they're going to name her Millie. I can tell the gender even though they don't know. But don't say anything to them. Mike and Sierra say they want it to be a surprise when the baby's born.

Today, it's Gramps's birthday. Even if he doesn't remember, his family does, and they brought me along. The staff in this sorta-hospital is always nice about letting me visit the General.

I know the way to his room. We come here often when Sierra and Mike visit Tennessee. Nathan lifts me up onto the bed. My climbing days are over because of these creaky, achy hips. It's tough to keep the weight off when you can barely hobble across the yard to mark trees and poop beneath your favorite bush.

The mattress gives under me and I roll in closer to Gramps. He can tell it's me even if he can't talk anymore. He and I don't need words. We understand.

Sierra leans in. "Hi, Gramps. Happy Birthday." She presses a kiss to his forehead and whispers, "They say that in the Army the coffee's mighty fine . . ."

General Joshua McDaniel's mouth moves soundlessly, but I can hear the words in his head. Kinda like the way he could button his uniform even when he couldn't fasten jeans. The military man in him is deeply ingrained, one of the last parts to fade with the disease.

Sierra eases back to stand with Mike while he keeps their son occupied with a video game.

A hand falls to rest on my head, Joshua McDaniel's hand. The weight of it and scent of him remind me of that very first scratch from another McDaniel. The first time I experienced a human touch. I feel that connection now, father to son. The General feels it, too, in a way that goes beyond words or conscious thought. His mind doesn't understand where his son has gone, but in moments like these when he's scratching my head, Joshua's spirit understands about Allen. In these moments, I help him feel connected to his son.

My mission to heal this family takes on many forms and changes with the years. But I am here for them. Always.

I think I fell asleep for a while. I like naps more and more every year, but today that nap cut short my visit. All too soon Nathan lifts me off the bed again. The smell of him and his Coast Guard uniform is familiar, comforting. He smells like life these days. But then, that's his job as a Coastie helicopter pilot—rescuing people.

I get to see him when Mike and Sierra go to Lacey's for family reunions. She owns a lot of land for the Second Chance Ranch Rescue since she bought out the Hammonds. Lacey and her husband are standing in the doorway. They're happy, Lacey and . . . her man. It's not my place to tell you who she married. That's another animal's story to share.

And there are as many stories as there are animals. Because we are all meant to be with a person, to help them, to save them. They shelter our bodies and we shelter their hearts. It's what we were made for by the Big Master.

It's our mission.

And thanks to the Second Chance Ranch Rescue . . . so many more of us get the honor of knowing *mission complete*.

Read on for a sneak peek at the next

Second Chance Ranch novel from Catherine Mann

RESCUE ME

Available February 2015 from Berkley Sensation

FOR TWENTY-EIGHT YEARS I had three names—Bitch, Fat Mama and Dumbass.

I didn't dare ignore the voice that growled more fiercely than any animal. I didn't question if I deserved to have a single name of my own. My existence followed a pattern. Hungry, not hungry. Hurt, healed. Pregnant, nursing. And above all, obey or pay.

Looking back, the contrast from then to my life now is staggering. Some people have said they wonder how I survived so long in that cabin with limited human contact, only the drone of never ending game shows on television and the bubbling mix in the kitchen. How I kept my spirit intact. How I didn't turn into a mirror image of the voice that both fed me and hurt me. And I have to confess I came close to becoming like the soulless monsters that drifted in and out during those early years.

Until I was saved from crawling into the dark hole of hurt and misery forever. I was given a hint of hope beyond the rank four walls of my home.

I smelled honeysuckle.

Just a whiff of the perfume drifted through an open window one summer Tennessee day. At first, I thought I'd imagined it. I tipped my nose into that gentle breeze curling through the half-cracked pane, each puff parting the despair one ripple at a time. Overriding even the never-ending hum of the quiz shows.

And there it was again. Honeysuckle. Sweet. Soft. Light. Everything opposite of what I'd known from birth.

Desperate for more, I crawled to the window, slowly, praying no one would see me. Life was easier if I stayed hidden, because otherwise I feared I would one day have to fight back. Still I was willing to risk detection to breathe more of that flowery perfume.

I have a particularly keen sense of smell, so living in a filthy meth house for twenty-eight years took a toll on me. And just to clarify, twenty-eight human years equates to four dog years for me. As a dog, that explains why the stench hit me hard.

Did you know that canines can identify smells up to ten thousand times better than a human? Well, we can. Truly, aromatherapy is wasted on you people. My brain has forty percent more capacity devoted to smell than yours. Not that I mean to sound condescending or call you inferior. I learned that about sniffers on *Jeopardy*. Facts are facts. I have over two million olfactory sensors in my nose. You have opposable thumbs.

I like facts. The endless television programs offered that much at least, game show after game show. Back then, I embraced those quizzes, soaking up data, anything to prove I wasn't a dumbass at all. If I'd been a human and hadn't started having babies so early, I've often thought I would have become a professor with thick black glasses. I would have sequestered myself in an office lined with books, solitude. Peace.

But back to my sniffer.

And honeysuckle.

And how all that relates to the day I found freedom in a splintered door.

To be clear, I spent my life watching methamphetamine being cooked, smoked, shot, sold. The evil, rancid odor of the drug left me groggy. Sometimes it even made me snarl, though that's not my nature. The smell of it saturated the walls, peeling the paper down in strips I chewed in moments of frenzied boredom. It permeated the saggy sofa I never sat on. Even clung to the mattresses on the floor in both bedrooms where cranked-up junkies had sex. And worst of all, the toxic clouds hung in the kitchen, counters packed with everything from drain cleaner to funnels to my bowl full of scraps.

But that afternoon during my fourth summer, when I discovered honeysuckle, I considered that maybe, just maybe there was something better for me, if only I could wait long enough to escape farther than the chain in the yard allowed.

Easier said than done, because I was a moneymaker, just like that steaming meth cooker. My litters of boxer pups were worth a lot, so I ate well, periodically. And no one kicked me, periodically. Until my babies were taken away, always too early, so I could breed again.

You may already be thinking "puppy mill," but that's not one hundred percent accurate. The woman who owned me— I won't bother to distinguish her with a name—would be more appropriately labeled a backyard breeder who used me and other dogs to supplement her meth income. Up until that honeysuckle moment in my fourth summer, I thought my mission in life was to have babies for people to love even if I never got to experience that feeling myself, other than for the few brief weeks I was allowed to keep each litter, their warm tiny bodies snuggled up against me.

By the fourth winter, I wondered if I'd imagined a honeysuckle world just to survive. I began to lose hope, drawing in nothing but the fumes that made me mean.

Then, on the bitterest, coldest morning, my world changed on a larger scale with another beautiful scent. Peppermint. Yes, peppermint this time. Still my favorite perfume, even above honeysuckle. Because now I knew that two beautiful smells outnumbered the one evil stench of this cabin. There was more out there past my chain. So much more.

And I thank the Big Master who made us that the peppermint-scented lady understood I was not at my best the day she and the sad-eyed policeman broke down the meth house door to rescue me.

Taking a risk may be all that saves you . . .

PROTECTOR

A DARK OPS NOVEL

FROM
CATHERINE MANN

Assigned to the investigation of a mob boss whose luxury cruise ship is reportedly a hub for terrorist activity, Captain Chuck Tanaka is going undercover. His target: Jolynn Taylor, the mob boss's daughter.

Ever since she saw her beloved uncle murdered, Jolynn has stayed far away from her father's crooked empire. But after her father falls ill, she finds herself on the run, one step ahead of unknown enemies. Only Tanaka stands between her and certain death . . . but can she trust him?

PRAISE FOR CATHERINE MANN

"An exciting storyteller, Catherine Mann weaves deep emotion with intense suspense for an all-night read."
—Sherrilyn Kenyon, #1 *New York Times* bestselling author

"Exhilarating romantic suspense."
—*The Best Reviews*

penguin.com
facebook.com/CatherineMannAuthor
facebook.com/LoveAlwaysBooks
catherinemann.com

M1089T0412

Reckless passion is right on target . . .

FROM
CATHERINE MANN

RENEGADE

A DARK OPS NOVEL

Tech Sergeant Mason "Smooth" Randolph lives to push boundaries. But he never anticipated how far outside the box he would land when an in-flight accident sends him parachuting into Nevada's notorious Area 51—and into the handcuffs of sexy security cop Jill Walczak.

PRAISE FOR CATHERINE MANN

"Riveting action, relentless suspense, heroes to die for—
Catherine Mann delivers!"
—Suzanne Brockmann, *New York Times* bestselling author

"One of the hottest rising stars around!"
—Lori Foster, *New York Times* bestselling author

penguin.com
facebook.com/CatherineMannAuthor
facebook.com/LoveAlwaysBooks
catherinemann.com

M1090T041